# GIRL OF VENGEANCE

## VENGEANCE

A Novel
by
**Charles Sheehan-Miles**

# RACHEL'S
# PERIL

# Books by Charles Sheehan-Miles

**Thompson Sisters**
A Song for Julia
Falling Stars
Just Remember to Breathe
The Last Hour

**Rachel's Peril**
Girl of Lies
Girl of Rage
Girl of Vengeance

**America's Future**
Republic
Insurgent

Nocturne (with Andrea Randall)

Prayer at Rumayla
A Novel of the Gulf War

Saving the World on Thirty Dollars a Day: An Activist's Guide
to Starting, Organizing and Running a Non-Profit Organization

# GIRL OF VENGEANCE

If you enjoyed this book, please share it with a friend, write a review online, or send feedback to the author!

www.sheehanmiles.com

ISBN-13: 978-1-63202-094-9

Printed in the United States of America
Cincinnatus Press
PO Box 814
South Hadley, MA 01075

www.cincinnatuspress.com

v091314

# Dedication

*for Amirah*

*My Girl of Courage*

# Acknowledgements

**T**his book took a lot of help along the way to complete. I'll probably forget some people but I especially want to thank Lori Sabin for your editing, and Sally Bouley for your extensive assistance reading through the book. Thanks to my beta readers: Emma Corcoran, Kathy Baker, Dimitra Fleissner, Laura Wilson, Bryan James, Michelle Kannan, Sarah Griffin, Amy Burt, Jennifer Mirabelli, Stacey Grice, Kirsten Papi, Beth Suit, Rita Jenkins Post and Kelly Moorhouse. You guys looked at a lot of first draft material and have my everlasting gratitude.

As always, to Andrea Randall: thank you for everything along the way. You listen to my fears and frustrations and deal with my crazy insecurities even as we wind our personal and professional lives together. I thank God every day for having you in my life.

# Cast of Characters

## The Thompson Family

Richard Thompson

Adelina Thompson

Julia Wilson (Thompson)

— Crank Wilson

Carrie Thompson-Sherman

— Ray Sherman

— Rachel Sherman

Alexandra Paris (Thompson)

— Dylan Paris

Sarah Thompson

Jessica Thompson

Andrea Thompson

## The Wakhan File

Roshan al Saud

Leslie Collins

Mitch Filner

Vasily Karatygin

Senator Chuck Rainsley

## The British

George-Phillip Patrick Nicholas, Duke of Kent

Duncan Howard, Prime Minister

Oswald O'Leary

Stephen Easton, Ambassador to the United States

## Diplomatic Security

John "Bear" Wyden

Leah Simpson

Scott Kelly

## The Washington Post

Anthony Walker

## The Investigation

Rory Armitage, Special Prosecutor

Wolfram Schmidt, Internal Revenue Service

Emma Smith, Internal Revenue Service

# Prologue

In the silence of the room, the knock on the door startled Carrie and Sarah. Carrie jerked in her seat and looked up, just as a youngish looking doctor with slightly too long hair stuck his head in the room. Doctor Willis was older than he looked, and Carrie had as much confidence in him as she had in any doctor, which wasn't much. Willis wore a white lab coat with a pocket protector, pens in several different colors poking out of the pocket.

"Mrs. Sherman? May I come in?"

The question was rhetorical, of course. She wasn't going to stop him. A nurse or physician's assistant accompanied him—Carrie didn't know which. The nurse was in her thirties with severely cut blonde hair.

Carrie gave him a weak smile and shifted in her seat. Her left hand rested beside Rachel in her baby carrier. Her right instinctively reached out and took Sarah's hand. Sarah gave her an almost imperceptible squeeze.

"We're ready to begin prepping baby Rachel for the transfusion. But before we start, we need to take a moment to go over the procedure again."

Carrie nodded. She'd been over the procedure a thousand times in her dreams. She'd talked about it with the nurses and doctors, and gotten a second opinion, and when that one confirmed the bad news, she got a third opinion. The results were unequivocal—her daughter suffered from Thalassemia Major and would need regular blood transfusions for the rest of her life, which would be cut short unless she could find a bone marrow donor. Now, at six weeks old, they couldn't delay her first transfusion any longer. Rachel was listless and pale; her eyes and skin had a slight yellow tinge.

"Okay, in a few minutes the nurse-team will prepare her. You'll be able to stay with her the whole time, of course."

"What about Sarah?" Carrie asked.

"Of course she can stay. Now, we need to go over the risks again."

"I'm familiar with the risks," Carrie said.

"I know, but it's the rules."

Carrie sighed and nodded. She'd spent far too much time in hospitals. She knew the drill. "Go ahead."

"Okay … so generally transfusions are one of the safest possible procedures. But there are some risks. First, of course, is the risk of infection. That's substantially reduced by the fact that Sarah donated the blood."

Carrie squeezed her sister's hand again. Sarah's hands were soft, except the tips of her fingers. Those had heavy callouses from her many hours of guitar playing.

"Our second risk is a hemolytic reaction, or allergic reaction. Transfusion reactions are rare in newborns, and Sarah's blood is a good match, so it's unlikely. But it is possible. We'll introduce the blood slowly, so we can monitor her for side effects."

Carrie swallowed. "Okay."

"Those are the main short-term risks. And, as you know, we've gone over the long-term risks. Monthly transfusions will cause an iron buildup in her system. She'll have to begin regular chelation therapy at a year to eighteen months old or risk organ failure."

"Right. Unless we can find a bone marrow donor."

The doctor nodded. "Which we'll keep searching for." He rested a hand on her shoulder. "Listen, Carrie, you've had a hell of a time. I promise you we'll do everything we can for Rachel. Okay?"

Against her will, Carrie's eyes watered. She *hated* not having control of her emotions, but ever since Ray's death she'd been on the verge of tears half the time. Her stomach wrenched at the thought. Sometimes the ache of loss was just too much. She needed Ray here with her. She *needed* him. She rolled her eyes up to the ceiling and nodded, trying to keep control of her face and the watering of her eyes, but that didn't work so she squeezed them shut.

"It's going to be okay." A whisper. And for just a second she felt a hand on the side of her face, brushing along her jawbone. Her eyes jerked open, but the doctor was halfway across the room, and Sarah was answering a text message.

She shook her head, confused and brushing off the disturbing feeling. Dr. Willis held out a clipboard.

"Okay, Carrie, if you can sign here. This just acknowledges that I've walked you through the risks of the procedure. Nurse Reynolds?"

The nurse said, "I'm to sign as a witness. Do you understand what the doctor just told you about the risks?"

Carrie was irrationally irritated. She knew she had to sign. She knew the medical procedures. After all, she'd had to sign the papers allowing them to let her husband die. Shuddering, she took the papers and pen that Doctor Willis held out. She scrawled her signature on the document and said, "Yes. I understand."

"All right," he said. "The nursing team will be in, in just a moment." He took the clipboard back from her and walked out of the room.

Fifteen very long seconds passed by, then Sarah said, "You all right? You looked like you saw a ghost."

Carrie sniffed, then reached over and unbuckled the straps holding her baby in the carrier. She lifted Rachel to her and snuggled her daughter. It was comforting. She didn't have Ray, but she had a piece of him, the little girl he'd left behind. The little girl who Carrie would do anything for. She took a long shuddering breath then changed the subject. For right now, talking about Ray or Rachel was just too raw.

"What's going on?" she asked, nodding toward Sarah's phone.

"Alex just texted me and said turn on the news."

Carrie arched an eyebrow. They didn't have a television in the exam room in the hospital. Sarah's face was a little pale.

"What is it?"

Sarah handed her the phone. She was shaking.

Carrie had to reread the headline three times before it made any sense.

## WIFE OF U.S. SECRETARY OF DEFENSE RE-QUESTS POLITICAL ASYLUM IN CANADA
### Cross-border shootout ends in hospital-ization of 18-year-old daughter

"Oh, my God," Carrie said. "Political asylum? What?"

"I have to go there," Sarah said.

"To Canada?" Carrie demanded.

Sarah nodded. "If Jessica's hurt, I've got to go to her."

Carrie sighed. "Of course." She paused a second, scanning through the article. It described how their mother had dragged Sarah's unconscious twin across the international border even as a shooter was trying to kill them both. The shooter—the paper read 'the *alleged* shooter'—had been captured by the Border Patrol two miles south of the incident following a high-speed chase. Jessica's injuries weren't described in the article.

Unconsciously, she pulled her daughter a little closer to her.

A single knock was followed by the door opening. Two people stepped into the room—nurses or physicians' assistants. The first,

a copper-haired woman, said, "Hello, and how is baby Rachel doing today?"

She walked toward Carrie and reached to take the baby. Carrie
pulled Rachel closer.

The woman stopped and said, "Sorry—I'm Melissa, the NICU
charge nurse. I'll be supervising the procedure today. May I take
the baby?"

Carrie was uncomfortable and tense, but she nodded and held
Rachel up an inch.

Melissa, the nurse, took Rachel expertly from her hands and
laid her in the plastic bassinet. Rachel's arms and legs contracted
and she let out a cry.

"Oh, you're such a sweetie," the nurse said in a sing-song voice,
scrunching up her nose. Rachel cooed. "I bet your mom and dad
are so proud of you! I bet they are!"

Rachel smiled up at the nurse, even as Carrie flinched.

A second nurse entered the room. Expertly, the two of them
began moving around Rachel, laying out towels and other equipment. The second nurse positioned a catheter next to a tiny needle,
still in a sealed plastic wrap.

Melissa said, "Get a 25 gauge, please." She began to swaddle
the baby, leaving her right arm out.

The second nurse nodded. Melissa said, "This is Jodi. She's one
of our NICU nurses."

Jodi smiled and took out a needle, slightly smaller than the one
she'd previously placed on the table. A set of tubes stretched across
the room, and various kinds of equipment were lined up. Both
women wore gloves.

"Mom, we're connecting monitors to watch her pulse and respi-
ration and other vitals right now. Then we'll start the lines. She's
going to cry a little bit at first, I don't want you to panic."

Carrie nodded and squeezed Sarah's hand again. She was breathing too quickly and closed her eyes for a second, trying to force calm.

It wasn't working. The second nurse, Jodi, held a pacifier with some liquid, and Rachel happily sucked on it as Melissa taped a board to Rachel's arm and attached the various monitors and sensors. Then she wiped a brown fluid on Rachel's upper arm.

In a low voice, concentrating, Melissa said, "Start the line."

Jodi ripped open the plastic packaging on the smaller needle. Carefully, her face pinched in concentration, she pushed the needle into Rachel's arm.

Rachel let out a choked cry, then a full-throated scream. Carrie flinched as the baby began to struggle inside the swaddling as her face turned bright red. The screaming got louder and Jodi shook her head, just once, negatively.

"Try again," Melissa said, her voice quiet.

Jodi nodded and pulled the needle back. *Oh, God. She missed.* Rachel's mouth was wide open, screaming as loud as Carrie had ever heard her. She sniffed and squeezed Sarah's hand tighter. But she refused to close her eyes or look away from her daughter. She was stronger than that. She'd watched helplessly as her husband drifted away into death. She could be there for her daughter.

After preparing a new needle, Jodi pushed it in again as Melissa held Rachel down with one hand and dripped fluid from the pacifier with the other.

"Got it," she whispered. She expertly inserted the plastic catheter. Rachel screamed louder, and Carrie's vision blurred as tears rolled down her face.

Carrie struggled to hold back a sob.

Jodi attached a tube to the catheter.

"Ativan," Melissa said. She looked up at Carrie. "Mom, that's the pain killer. It will help pretty quickly."

Jodi inserted a hypodermic into the line. Rachel continued to cry, her tiny mouth and eyes wide open. Tears rolled down Carrie's face, mirroring the one on her daughter's.

*Damn it, why couldn't you be here, Ray?* For the millionth time, she cried out inside, *Why?*

# CHAPTER ONE
## His Highness The Prince

Dylan. May 4.

**D**ylan Paris still felt a little woozy, a sharp pain stabbing his forehead as he walked between two Royal Marines. They wore sharp uniforms—form fitting navy blue suits with white belts, rank insignia on the shoulder just like U.S. Marines (though upside down to Dylan's eyes), and white leather-brimmed officer's caps with a red band. Unfamiliar insignia graced the collars and belts, and they wore medals on their chest rather than ribbons. Despite the finery, they wore serviceable sidearms, mean-looking Glock 17 pistols with a dull black finish. These guys were for real. And they were pissed.

At Dylan.

It was all right. He was alive, and by the fact that he was now being escorted into the Embassy for an interview with Prince George-Phillip, he guessed he'd successfully distracted the Marines long enough for Andrea to make it over the wall. His hands were zip-tied behind his back, and his head hurt, but he was pretty sure she'd made it.

Mission accomplished.

The Marines didn't take him toward the main Embassy building, a modern three-story glass and brick structure which dominated the grounds. Instead, he followed them (or rather, was frogmarched in between them) toward the three-story brick building he recognized from the satellite photos as the VIP residence. His heart was pounding. What if Andrea was hurt?

At the sound of a roaring engine, Dylan glanced over his shoulder. The fluorescent green Oldsmobile he'd bought from Mendoza now had a Royal Marine behind the wheel. It was moving into the Embassy compound. He turned back to their destination.

The temperature dropped rapidly when they stepped into a large, dimly lit foyer inside the building. Dylan's eyes scanned the room, noting the three other exits and the broad staircase, which circled around the left side of the room. The floors were highly polished and sported a twenty-foot wide Persian carpet, which probably cost more than Dylan's lifetime income.

The first Marine said, "Stay here," and the second grabbed Dylan's arm. The first then walked away, his heels clicking on the marble floor.

That was the first chink in their armor. Real soldiers didn't click their heels; they wore combat boots. Dylan continued to scan the room, noting escape routes along with more prosaic details like the crown molding. A moment later Clicking Heels came back down the hall and announced in stentorian tones, "His Highness The Prince will see you now." The guards then took him by both arms and guided him down the hall to a scene that looked nothing like he expected.

Prince George-Phillip he recognized instantly. For the one thing, the family resemblance was startling. He was at least six feet six inches—Ray Sherman's height. Tall and lanky, with thick eyebrows and a hawk nose, but otherwise with facial features similar to both Carrie and Andrea. His eyes, deep blue-green, were watering slightly.

"This is your accomplice, then?"

Andrea, who stood several feet away, nodded. Beside her, a girl—maybe six or seven years old—stood holding Andrea's hand. The girl looked just like Andrea. Then she spoke in a wary voice. "Yes."

"Remove the restraints, please," the Prince said to the guards. "Please have Gertrude set up coffee and drinks and lunch. In the sunroom. Jane will be joining us—"

One of the Marines spoke rapidly. "Your Highness, I must insist—"

"You'll insist on nothing. I realize their entry was unconventional, but here they are." Without another word, Prince George-Phillip dismissed the Royal Marines and approached Dylan. "I'm George-Phillip. And you are?"

"Dylan Paris, um … sir. I'm Andrea's brother-in-law."

The heel clicker produced a pair of scissors and cut the zip tie. Dylan immediately brought his hands in front of him and rubbed his wrists. Then he shook the hand Prince George-Phillip extended.

Andrea spoke immediately. "You acknowledge you're my father, and you expect us to be able to just sit down for a cozy lunch?" Her voice was a high tension wire, ready to break at any moment.

"No, Andrea. But I'd like a chance to get to know you and for you to get to know me."

Her expression remained blank, guarded. She nodded once. Dylan breathed a sigh of relief. He guessed he understood her hesitation. After sixteen years of being rejected by the person she *thought* was her father, it was no wonder she was gun shy about opening up to this remote man she'd never heard of until yesterday.

"Dylan," Andrea said. Her eyes were wide and her jaw was clenched as she spoke the words, and her vocal inflection strange.

She was on the verge of hysteria. "Did you know I have another sister? Who I've never met? Jane, meet my friend Dylan."

Her eyes watered, and mouth closed, she released a low rumbling growl in the back of her throat in an effort to suppress her tears. George-Phillip looked at her aghast, as if he'd never seen a woman cry before and had no idea what to do.

Maybe he didn't. Dylan looked at him, met George-Phillip's eyes, and then jerked his head toward Andrea, trying to mentally send the command, *Hug her, damn it.*

Dylan didn't know if George-Phillip got the message from his bad miming, or if his human instincts had suddenly clicked in, but regardless of the cause, the Prince moved toward Andrea with his arms out and a sympathetic expression on his face.

"There, there," George-Phillip said. He rested his hands on Andrea's shoulders. "There's no need to cry. This is one of the happiest moments of my life. I want it to be the same for you."

Andrea began to shake, violently, and she sobbed, unable to contain the tears. George-Phillip pulled her to him and put his arms around her. Andrea stayed still, arms at her sides, but she couldn't contain her crying. She sobbed, loudly, the pent up terrible grief of a lifetime of hurt. George-Phillip murmured some meaningless sounds, and Jane put her arms around Andrea's right leg.

"Why are you sad?" Jane asked.

That just caused Andrea to sob more. Finally, she managed to compose a meaningful sound, a single word that rang out in the room with far more weight than he would have guessed possible.

*"Why?"*

After she said the word, she pushed back against the Prince's chest, forcing him to release her. Fiercely, she wiped her face with the sleeve of the George Mason University sweatshirt they had bought—what ... two days ago? Dylan couldn't keep track any more.

"Andrea ... my daughter." As he said the word *daughter*, Prince George-Phillips eyebrows seemed to do a solo dance, rising high up on his forehead. Hard to imagine, Dylan thought, that a man with no poker face at all could survive as the Chief of Intelligence of a large country.

George-Phillip continued. "Are you asking why I'm your father? Or why you never knew about it?"

"All of it," Andrea demanded. "I want to know everything. I want to know why I was dumped off in another country and never knew either of my parents. I want to know why ... why..."

She paused, trying to compose her face, then said, "I want to know why I was left to believe I wasn't worth loving."

George-Phillip looked somber. Dylan was usually a pretty good judge of people. There was no question in his mind that the Prince was sincere. Men didn't get that close to crying unless they were devastated.

"I'm so very sorry, Andrea. It breaks my heart that you didn't grow up feeling loved."

"You already broke mine," she responded.

George-Phillip sagged. "Indeed. And Carrie's, I suppose."

"My mother would never have been..." She whispered, "...beaten and raped if she hadn't gotten pregnant with Carrie. It was *your* fault."

"That happened first nine months before Julia was born," he replied in a sad voice.

Andrea closed her eyes. "They met in Spain. When she was eighteen. You're telling me he forced her then?"

George-Phillip sighed and said, "I'm deeply sorry to be telling you this, Andrea. It happened when she was sixteen. And her father died a few weeks later."

"I don't ... why did she marry him?"

"She was forced, Andrea. By her priest and her mother. Those days, things were different, especially in Spain."

Andrea shook her head forcefully. "No. *Abuelita*? Not possible. She would never force her daughter to marry a rapist." She hissed the next word. "*Never.*"

Dylan hoped Andrea wouldn't piss off Prince George-Phillip to the point where they were forced to leave. He didn't know what kind of legal limbo they were in—would they be arrested the moment they left the Embassy? For that matter, the police probably didn't know where they were.

He didn't think George-Phillip would do that. But neither of them really knew him, did they? And he *was* the head of the British intelligence agency. You didn't get to that kind of high-level position without the ability to make some cold-hearted decisions.

Prince George-Phillip remained patient. He said, "I know there is much you don't know, Andrea, and much that you have every right to be angry about. I'd like to tell you as much as possible, if you'll let me."

With a quick, firm nod, she said, "Yes. Fine. And I am hungry. Wrestling with your guards is a lot of work."

"Come, then. Both of you. Jane, go wash your hands, and you may join us in the sunroom."

Prince George-Phillip showed them where they could clean up—the *water-closet*, he called it—and a few minutes later Andrea, George-Phillip, Dylan and Jane were sitting at a cozy table in a room dominated by large windows on three sides. Surrounding the sunroom was grass, leading off to the trees and the row of houses on the other side of the fence.

With a wry smile, George-Phillip said, "We'll have to do an audit of security here," he said. "If you'd been an assassin I would have been done for."

Dylan thought the Prince was right, of course. Even though Dylan had distracted the Marines, a sixteen-year-old should never have made it into the building.

A woman wearing a knee-length double-breasted tunic poured tea for all of them. There was no sugar in sight, unfortunately.

"Summer sausage rolls, Your Highness, with mini sandwiches and custard kisses."

Jane's face lit up at the last and she reached for the pastry.

George-Phillip blocked her hand with his. "Have a sandwich or two first, Jane."

The little girl pouted, but obeyed. Andrea watched with misty eyes, and Dylan—whose childhood had been a mess of alcoholics and abuse—understood exactly why. It's what he had always wanted too—a simple, domestic existence, with parents who cared.

Andrea said nothing—simply watching, her eyes moving back and forth between the father and daughter.

"You should know," George-Phillip said conversationally, "I've come to the conclusion that my career is interfering with me spending time with Jane, here. Regardless of what happens with the current scandal, I intend to resign my position as Chief. I've no right to ask this, Andrea—but I'd like you to consider coming to London with me. When you have the opportunity. I'd like for us to get to know each other."

Andrea didn't reply. An awkward silence fell over the table, and Dylan leaned forward. He cleared his throat, covering it with his closed fist—*should he have used his napkin?* Then he spoke. "Do I call you … Highness? Or sir? Or…"

"In public, Highness or Your Grace is generally my title, but here, please call me George-Phillip. Do I have it correct that I have you to thank for my daughter still being alive?"

Dylan gave a wry smile. Not in a million years was he going to call a royal prince by his first name. "Sir, Andrea did that all on her own. She's just about the most courageous person I've ever met."

Prince George-Phillip gave his daughter a warm look. "Would that you hadn't had to deal with those situations. But I'm proud and amazed at how you handled them."

"I was just trying to survive," Andrea said, shifting in her seat. Dylan tried to parse out George-Phillip's sentence, but it still didn't make sense. Would that ... what?

Without preamble, George-Phillip said, "I think you should both stay here for the time being. You've been on the run and in hiding, and this is the safest place for you. Not to mention that until things are sorted out with the American investigation, both of you are wanted by the police here."

Dylan met Andrea's eyes. She was impassive. He nodded to her, as imperceptible of a motion that he could make.

She nodded back, then her eyes cut back to George-Phillip. She pursed her lips for a moment then spoke. "Yes, we'll stay. I have a thousand questions for you."

"I'll tell you everything I know," George-Phillip said in a soothing tone. "You can ask anything. Within the bounds of the confidentiality required by my position, I'm an open book to you, daughter."

"You say that my—the person I *thought* was my father—" she whispered the next words, her eyes darting to Jane, "raped my mother. And that she was forced to marry him?"

George-Phillip nodded. "She was seventeen when they actually married. Your eldest sister Julia was born a few months later."

"When did you meet my mother?"

"In the winter of 1984. We met in February, at a dinner party here in Washington. I was new in the city, and so was she. Richard

Thompson was traveling much of that spring, back and forth to Central Asia. Your mother and I fell in love."

In the back of Dylan's mind, the worst ran through his head. *Why the hell didn't you protect her, then?* He didn't say the words out loud. It wasn't his place. But he hoped Andrea would ask.

"And so Carrie was conceived," Andrea said.

"Yes."

"And what happened after that?"

"I didn't know about Carrie for many years after that. I ... in May of that year ... I'd just returned from a trip to London. She broke it off with me ... with no explanation. I didn't see her again for twelve years."

Andrea gave him a pained look. "Did she tell you later?"

"Yes, when we encountered each other in China. We were both a little older and wiser then. But Adelina ... it was tragic. He'd destroyed her spirit. The bright, courageous woman I'd known had become a mouse in public, never contradicting anything her husband said. She told me that the reason ... the reason..."

George-Phillip's face twisted in pain.

"Da?" Jane said. "What hurts?"

George-Phillip placed his left hand on Jane's shoulder. And his right hand on his chest. "My heart hurts, Jane. My heart."

*Jesus*, Dylan thought.

George-Phillip said, "Jane, I think it's time for you to go see Adriana."

Jane's eyes watered. "I want to be with my new sister."

"I promise you can later. Right now, we need to have some adult talk."

She climbed down from her seat, as always looking precarious—as if she might any instant go flying in one direction while the chair went in the other—then walked around to his chair the long way around the table, passing Andrea and Dylan along the way. She stood on her tiptoes and gave the sitting George-Phillip a kiss.

"Play with me later?" she asked.

He nodded and said, "Yes, of course."

"Will you play with me too, sister?" she asked Andrea.

Andrea might be distrustful of George-Phillip, but it was clear she held no reservations about her six-year-old half sister. Her eyes went glassy, and she nodded and said, "Yes, I'd love that."

A few minutes later, after the little girl had left the room, George-Phillip continued. "While I was out of town, out of the country, Adelina had realized she was pregnant. And she believed that Richard would kill her, or Julia, or possibly her brother Luis, if he found out she was pregnant. She believed he was a complete sociopath. I don't know if that's the case or not, but she provoked him into attacking her. So that she could convincingly make him believe that Carrie was his."

Andrea winced. Seemingly without volition, she reached out and grabbed Dylan's hand.

"I tried to persuade her to leave him. I did. I'd have gladly given up my career and taken her hand in marriage. I wanted that more than anything else in the world."

"But you didn't," Andrea said.

George-Phillip gave her a sad smile. "I didn't. When we met again in Beijing ... many years had passed. Your mother and I ... resumed our affair. But with very strict rules that *she* set. You see, a great deal had happened in the years we didn't see each other. Richard began to suspect that Carrie wasn't his child, because she was so incredibly tall. He took her to a lab and had them both tested. And when he found the results, he beat Adelina almost to death."

Andrea winced. She didn't say anything, just listened. She hadn't touched the food.

"Later, she told me what those years were like. Your family moved a lot—based in San Francisco, then Belgium for three years, then China. Your father had the perfect deep cover—he was Central Intelligence Agency, but as far as the world was concerned, he was a diplomat. That gave him license to operate anywhere. As the years went by, he kept her off balance. Randomly he would terrorize her—keeping her anxious and confused. That just got worse as the years went by."

Andrea gritted her teeth. "She was crazy," she said.

"What do you mean?" George-Phillip asked.

"You describe a victim who was terrorized by Richard Thompson, but what I remember is that she was crazy. She'd break down at the slightest provocation. She was completely unpredictable—the same behavior that one day resulted in a mild scolding would, the next day, provoke screaming rage. She cut us to pieces with her words."

Dylan sighed. He knew what that was like—his father had been a complete bastard and a drunk. For the first time, he felt real sympathy for his mother-in-law. Adelina Thompson had been the terror of all of her daughters. He'd never imagined she'd undergone that sort of trauma.

George-Phillip's eyes watered at Andrea's words.

## George-Phillip. May 4.

*She cut us to pieces with her words.*

*Oh, Adelina, why didn't you leave him when I asked? When I begged?*

He tried to imagine the Adelina he'd known being abusive. He couldn't. She had been kind and honest and terrified. She'd been anxious often. She'd told him how she'd struggled to separate her daughters from the emotional devastation of their father.

He remembered sitting with Adelina in the Maryland suburbs of Washington at an anonymous restaurant, sometime in April 1984.

*It's not Julia's fault that he's her father,* Adelina had said. *She deserves all of me, but sometimes I flinch back.*

George-Phillip had sighed, slightly squeezing his hands at his temples. *Please leave him, Adelina. I'm begging you. You deserve so much better.*

Adelina had smiled, a wide, false smile that didn't hide her glassy eyes. *Do you know what he sent me the other day, George-Phillip? He's in Pakistan or some place, but he stopped in Spain long enough to take a picture of my brother. It was a threat.*

George-Phillip had shuddered. A few weeks later she broke it off with him.

He shook his head, coming back to the present. Right now, Adelina wasn't his problem. Convincing his daughter—*his daughter!*—that she could trust him—that was the task at hand. He looked Andrea in the eyes and said, "I'm so sorry. I didn't know that it had gotten so bad."

Andrea shook her head, her mouth turning up on one side, her expression of skepticism breaking his heart. "Of course you didn't know," she said. "You weren't there."

He was shaken, and covered it by taking a drink of his tea, giving him a few seconds to compose himself. Finally, he said, "Of course, you are correct. I *wasn't* there. And regardless of the reasons—which there were many—there's no real excuse."

Andrea looked at the floor. Then she said, "But you came to Spain. The first time I went there with Carrie."

George-Phillip smiled. "I did. And other times. I was at your concert two years ago. You have a beautiful singing voice."

Andrea blushed. "You were there?"

"Of course. I couldn't make it often, you see, without revealing something. But when there were opportunities to not be observed—I tried to take them."

Every summer in Calella, on Friday nights in the old town, there was a series of live performances. When he'd learned that she would be performing in one, he had discreetly traveled to Spain. He remembered standing in the back of the crowd that milled around the square, and Andrea's nervousness when she walked out on the stage. She'd hesitated at first and looked at a woman he now realized must be her *Abuelita*, or grandmother. Then she smiled, a beautiful smile, and began singing *a cappella*.

He didn't understand the words—George-Phillip spoke fluent French, but no Spanish—but her expression, her vocal intonation made it clear she'd inherited her mother's gift for music. His eyes began to mist again.

"Forgive me," he said. "I'm afraid I haven't a firm grip on my emotions today. I'm wondering—have you heard from her? Do you have any idea where she might be? Your mother?"

Dylan and Andrea looked at each other before speaking, a look that was heavy with meaning.

Dylan leaned forward and said, "Sir ... I spoke with her very briefly. On April 30th. It was right before the shooting started."

George-Phillip sighed. "That was the last time I spoke with her as well."

Dylan tilted his head to the right, raising an eyebrow. "I thought you guys weren't talking."

"We weren't," George-Phillip said. "But I was tracking the family as closely as possible when I got word Andrea was going back to the United States. There are some people with powerful secrets who want them kept. I think they thought that if it came out in public that Richard had raped his wife, his whole career might come under fire. Which would risk exposing Wakhan."

Dylan flinched. "Wakhan? In Badakhshan Province?"

"You're familiar with it?"

Dylan grimaced. "I served in Badakhshan Province during my time in Afghanistan. We didn't get out to the Wakhan Corridor though. Too remote—not even the Taliban is interested in that place. What is it they're trying to keep secret? And what does Richard Thompson have to do with it?"

George-Phillip sighed. Then he said, "What I'm about to tell you is highly classified. But *The Guardian* actually broke the story today, so that secrecy is of dubious value. In 1983, a group of Afghan militia dropped nerve gas on a village in Wakhan, killing everyone in the village. Two CIA officers and a Saudi intelligence officer procured the nerve gas from Russian stocks. Richard Thompson was one of them."

"Holy shit," Dylan said. Then he flushed, an uncomfortable red running down his cheeks and neck. "Excuse me, uh, Highness ... uh ... sir."

George-Phillip chuckled. "Really, man, I served in the Royal Marines. I've heard salty language once or twice. In any event, I was already on high alert after Andrea's kidnapping." He turned and looked at his daughter, musing for just a moment on how incredibly courageous she'd been. "You really are something," he said. "Any man would be proud to call you his daughter, you know."

She just looked down at the table. She didn't trust him yet, of course. That would take time. He just hoped he would get the time.

"In any event," he said, "we were monitoring the communications of certain people who were known to associate with Tariq Koury."

"Hairy Chest," Andrea said.

George-Phillip raised his eyebrows.

She responded, "That's what I mentally called him. The entire flight over he sat next to me, with his shirt unbuttoned halfway down. It was disgusting."

"I see," George-Phillip said. "You understand Koury was an intelligence operative with nearly twenty years of experience. He started out with the Saudi *mukhabarat,* but went on to freelance. He was very dangerous. You're a very resourceful young lady to escape him."

"I didn't kill him," she said. Her eyes were watering as she said the words.

George-Phillip tilted his head.

She went on. "The police killed him and his partner. I just— struggled to survive. The newspapers keep saying I somehow killed those two men with my bare hands. It's not true."

"Unfortunately, the newspapers often write things which are untrue," George-Phillip said.

Dylan frowned and muttered, "Ain't that the sad truth."

The guesthouse butler appeared at the door. "Your Highness, the Ambassador wishes to see you."

On a Sunday? It had to be about the disturbance. He stood, wiping his mouth with the linen napkin, and said, "Excuse me a moment, Andrea. Dylan."

He walked to the door, glancing back once. Andrea and Dylan were huddled together, talking already. He walked out the door.

Stephen Easton was a younger version of the doddering old fool who had been Ambassador to China when George-Phillip was stationed there in the mid-nineties. Much like his older brother Ronald, Easton had traded on his good family name and wealth to get ahead in the diplomatic service. Neither of the brothers had ever really accomplished anything, though Ronald's son Harry—

currently an attaché on the staff here at the Embassy—did go from scandal to scandal throughout his formative years.

Easton leaned on his cane as George-Phillip approached. He was approaching seventy years old and looked every second of it, thanks to a lifetime of heavy foods, sitting behind desks, and drinking plenty of port.

"Your Highness," Easton said.

"Ambassador."

"Your Highness, I must protest. I'm given to understand that a pair of intruders invaded the grounds of the Embassy, and instead of turning them over to the proper authorities, you have taken them in and given them lunch? What has gotten into you, sir?"

Easton's face was already turning red. George-Phillip promised himself that he wouldn't antagonize Easton too much—the old blowhard was likely to pop off with a heart attack at any moment.

"Ambassador, one of the two intruders is my long-lost daughter."

Easton's eyes widened. "Dear God, it's true?"

"It is, Ambassador. She's had a dreadful week. People are trying to kill her, and it is my intention to keep her here, safe and protected. This is not negotiable."

Easton shook his head, waving a hand vaguely in the air. "Surely, a hotel nearby with proper security..."

George-Phillip raised his eyebrows. "That is not an option."

"Is it true that both of them are fugitives from American law enforcement? Do you realize the sort of international incident you might be precipitating?"

"There will be no international incident if the Americans don't know they're here. Will there?" George-Phillip raised his eyebrows and leaned close, restraining his urge to verbally flatten the old man. *She's my daughter.*

"Your Highness, they mustn't be here more than a few days. I won't allow it."

George-Phillip sighed. A lot could happen in a few days, and there was little he could do to prevent it. He still didn't know where Adelina was, nor had he spoken with Carrie. Not to mention that terrible article in *The Guardian*.

"Fine, then, Ambassador. I should be able to make other arrangements in a few days."

Stephen Easton started to turn away, but then turned his head back toward George-Phillip, his myopic eyes huge in the thick lenses he wore. "Your Highness ... how much of this has to do with the article in the Guardian?"

George-Phillip sighed and said, "It's tied closer than I'd like. But I assure you that the accusations against me are false, and I shall prove it in due course."

Easton raised his eyebrows and minutely shook his head. The old man was skeptical. "Well, then," he said and turned away.

George-Phillip turned to go back into the sunroom, but saw his assistant for thirty years, Oswald O'Leary. O'Leary was Irish, short, with the face of a pug. Foul-mouthed, unconventional, and brilliant, he'd served George-Phillip tirelessly for decades, and he was the only person who had George-Phillip's full confidence. Now he stood at the door looking grim.

"What is it, O'Leary?"

"He's right, you know, Highness. No good can come from you harboring them here."

"Someone is trying to harm my daughter," George-Phillip said.

"She should be turned over to the American authorities. She'll be safer there anyway."

George-Phillip muttered an internal curse then said, "I thank you for your advice. But she's staying here. What do you have for me, O'Leary?"

"Highness, Adelina Thompson turned up."

"Dear God, where? Mexico?"

"No, sir. Canada, actually. She and her daughter crossed the border on foot. It seems there's not even a fence on the Canadian border. They ran across as someone was shooting at them."

"She's still with her daughter?"

"Yes, sir. Jessica Thompson is in the hospital, sir."

Alarmed, George-Phillip said, "Was she shot? Is Adelina all right?"

O'Leary shook his head. "Not shot, sir. I don't know all the details yet—only what's been reported in the news. We don't have anyone on the ground yet. But the Canadian media is reporting that Adelina Thompson is demanding political asylum."

George-Phillip gave O'Leary a grim smile. "It's about time," he said. "I must get back—thank you for the update, O'Leary."

George-Phillip stepped past O'Leary, reaching for the door, when O'Leary touched his arm.

"Highness? Remember that Adelina Thompson is not the nineteen-year-old girl you once fell in love with. She's..."

"She's what, O'Leary? Old? As are we both."

"No, Highness, that's not what I meant. She's ... not healthy. Mentally."

Anger flooded through George-Phillip. "Well, maybe it's time she was given the opportunity to heal." He pushed past O'Leary.

# CHAPTER TWO
## He won't stop until I'm dead.

Adelina. May 4.

"**M**rs. Thompson? I'm Liam Tremblay, with Citizenship and Immigration. I've been assigned to your asylum case."

Adelina came to her feet. Tremblay was an unprepossessing man, roughly thirty years old. He had a crooked and mashed nose, which looked as if it might have been broken in a fistfight, but he wore a respectable looking suit.

"I understand your daughter is undergoing some serious medical issues, so I won't bother you today if you don't have time to talk."

Adelina shrugged helplessly. "My daughter is in treatment right now, I've got nothing but time."

"I hope her prognosis is good..." He raised the pitch of his voice slightly at the end of the sentence, as if he were asking a question.

Adelina looked at the floor. How was she supposed to answer that? Her daughter had become addicted to crystal meth. She'd done irreparable harm to her body and her brain. She might survive the stroke, but it was equally likely there would be more.

"All we can do is pray," Adelina said. Which was bitter. She'd prayed for a lifetime, to no avail.

Tremblay sighed. "I see," he said in a soft voice. "I'm sorry."

"Please, Mr. Tremblay. What can I do for you?"

"Well, Mrs. Thompson, I'm the preliminary immigration officer. What I'm empowered to do is to reject your request for asylum out of hand, if I determine there's no merit to it, or I can forward it on to the tribunal which will make a ruling after a hearing."

She nodded. "My claim is valid," she said, her voice confident.

"Be that as may, the process must be followed."

"How long does it take?" She needed *time*. If Canada wouldn't take them in, maybe the United Kingdom would. *Somewhere*. She needed time to find out why Richard was sending assassins after her and Jessica.

"Well, ma'am, if we go forward with your case, then your hearing will be within sixty days."

"And how long does it take to make your decision?"

He smiled at her. "That I can do with a simple interview, here and now."

She breathed a sigh of relief.

"Please. Please, go ahead."

"All right, then. I'm going to ask you a few questions. I want to make it clear right up front, as a matter of normal rulings, we don't accept asylum cases for people who crossed the border from the United States."

Anxiety shot through her. "Why not?"

He gave her a gentle smile and held a hand palm up. "Normally," he said. "The fact that someone was shooting at you when you came across the border changes things. Typically, the reason is because the U.S. and Canada have an agreement that if a refugee reaches our borders, then they must apply in the first country reached."

She nodded. "Okay. I understand. That makes sense. But I'm a refugee *from* the United States."

"That may be a first, ma'am. So I'd like to take you through some questions to determine the validity of your case. I'm going to ask you some basic questions. Please answer them briefly and truthfully."

He took out a notebook and a pen, then perched a pair of reading glasses on the end of his mashed up nose. The reading glasses hung a little crookedly.

"Mrs. Thompson, first of all, where were you born?"

"Spain."

"Do you hold Spanish citizenship?"

She shook her head. Another pang of loss. "No. I renounced my Spanish citizenship at the time I obtained United States citizenship. That was in 1987."

"I see. Why did you not keep dual citizenship?"

"My husband was an American diplomat."

"When and where did you marry?"

"In Calella, Spain. April, 1981."

"Why did it take so long to get your U.S. Citizenship?"

Adelina stared at the man. Wondering if she was making a mistake. She'd kept Richard's secrets for thirty years, to protect her children, to protect her brother. But then she remembered. Richard had hired killers to kidnap their daughter Andrea. He'd sent killers after her and Jessica. He'd finally gone insane. There was no more keeping secrets.

In a flat, toneless voice, she replied, "Because Richard didn't want anyone to know he'd raped a child. So we waited until I was significantly older than eighteen."

Tremblay coughed, his eyes slightly bugging. "Please clarify."

"I was sixteen when Richard Thompson raped me. He was a serving diplomat in Spain at the time. He then murdered my father a few weeks later, when my father became suspicious. My mother and priest forced me to marry him when they realized I was pregnant."

"Dear Lord," Tremblay said. "Yet, you've stayed with him more than thirty years."

"It's not that simple that I could just walk away. I had to stay to protect my children and my brother," she said. "They're worth a lifetime of torture."

"Why did you flee now?"

"My youngest daughter, Andrea, is not his. When he learned she was coming back to the United States, he sent assassins after her. And me."

"Andrea Thompson," he mused. "I saw a great deal in the news about her. And you believe that if you go back to the United States, you'll face risk of further attacks?"

Bitterly, she said, "He won't stop until I'm dead."

Tremblay closed his notebook then took a sheaf of paper out of his briefcase. "Wait just a moment, please. I'm going to approve your case to go forward, which is going to raise a stink since you're from the United States. You'll likely be facing some media attention. Sorry about that."

Adelina gasped. He dialed his phone, and a moment later was speaking with someone. "Yes. Yes. I need a date. Okay..."

Tremblay hung up the phone and scribbled a date into a blank at the top of the stack of forms.

"Your hearing date will be June 26th. In the meantime, you'll need to fill these forms out completely. You have fifteen days to complete them and return them to me. I'm issuing you and your daughter two-month visas. Welcome to Canada."

Adelina burst into tears. Tremblay looked helpless, so he continued to awkwardly fill out paperwork and look away while she tried to collect herself.

"I'll need to see your passports, ma'am. Do you have your daughter's?"

"I do," she said. She fumbled in her purse and passed over their personal passports. Tremblay scanned them with his phone then took pictures of the photo pages. A moment later he stamped both.

"Thank you," she whispered.

"My pleasure, ma'am. Do you have a place to stay while you are here?"

"Not yet, but I have money to rent a couple of rooms. For now I'll stay at the hospital until Jessica is recovered."

He smiled and passed her a business card. "Here is my number in case you need to reach me. I'm based out of the border station in Abbotsford—the one you sneaked by when you crossed that field. I hope you'll allow me to help if you need anything at all."

She gave him a smile, and he left. Her heart was pounding, hard, a feeling that was all too familiar. A full-blown panic attack was on the way. She closed her eyes and began to pray. Once they started she couldn't stop them. Every time. Her heart rate would increase, then chest pain, and unbearable fear in her body.

She didn't have to have a reason. She'd begun having them in Belgium more than twenty years ago, when Richard cruelly tormented her with words and threats, leaving her unbalanced and terrified.

*You know,* he said once, *it's only a twelve-hour drive to Calella. And I've never met young Luis. What is he, thirteen now?*

*You leave him alone!*

*Then you behave,* he had snarled back.

The random cruelty he'd begun to visit on her had begun after he'd learned Carrie wasn't his daughter. He didn't need to make threats. He'd thoroughly cowed her with the hideous assault in February '90, which had impregnated her with Alex and left her with lifelong scars.

She stared at the door, beyond which the doctors were treating Jessica. She hated herself for not leaving him thirty years before. He'd threatened all along that he would hurt their children, that he would hurt her, that he would kill Luis. If she "misbehaved." But now he'd done it anyway, and Jessica was in the hospital, and she had no one but herself and Richard to blame for it.

The pain in her chest was worsening. It always did. The first time it happened, in 1991, she'd been rushed to the hospital, thinking she was having a heart attack. *No*, the doctors informed her. Nothing physically wrong with her at all. They suggested Paxil, a powerful antidepressant.

She tried it, but it made her feel like bugs were moving under her skin. For the next twenty years she went through a series of different anti-anxiety and antidepressant medications. Her doctors were baffled.

But she did remember, one day not long after Julia went off to college, Doctor Thornton spoke with her. *No amount of medication will stop anxiety that's well-founded in something in your life, Adelina. Is there something I need to know about?*

She behaved. She denied it, changed doctors and stayed terrified.

She clutched her fist against her chest and whimpered. The pain was severe.

"Mrs. Thompson—are you all right?"

She looked up, tears in her eyes. It was a nurse. "Panic attack," she whispered. "I've had them before. I normally take Ativan when I have one, but I don't have any."

"Let's take you down to an exam room," the nurse said.

"No! I need to stay near Jessica."

The nurse smiled. "Jessica's going to be just fine. The doctor is actually on her way to see you now."

Hope suddenly flooded through her. "What? Really?" She shook so hard her teeth rattled against each other, and it seemed like an hour before the doctor appeared.

"Mrs. Thompson? I'm Linda Gates, the chief of neurosurgery."

*Neurosurgery.* That's what Carrie's husband Ray had ... before he died. She looked up. A tall woman with long blonde hair tied in a bun stood in front of her. She wore a white coat with blood stains on it. Adelina continued to shake.

The surgeon continued. "So ... first of all, your daughter is in recovery. She had a hemorrhagic stroke, not an obstructive one. That means blood was pouring into her brain when you arrived at the hospital. Once we clearly identified that, she went immediately into surgery. I was right down the hall at the time she was brought in. We cleared out most of the blood and repaired the damaged vessel."

"She'll fully recover?" Adelina asked.

"It's too soon to tell, Mrs. Thompson. Your daughter had a life-threatening stroke. I understand she was a regular crystal meth user?"

Adelina nodded. Ashamed. "Yes."

"I'm so sorry," Doctor Gates said. "That's heartbreaking." She reached out and touched Adelina's shoulder. "Panic attack?" she asked.

Adelina nodded, quickly. Tears rolled down her face.

"She said she's had them before," the nurse said. "And she takes Ativan."

"Well. You don't have any here with you? Is there anyone at home who can bring it to you?"

Adelina shook her head. "We're ... refugees, I guess. She had the stroke when we were attacked just before crossing the border from the United States. I've asked for asylum."

"Oh, dear. Well ... I'll write you a prescription for Ativan then. Good luck with your application."

Adelina sank back into her chair. Three people in a row had been incredibly kind to her. She thought about how isolated she always was. It had been since the 1980s when she last had friends. Richard had put a stop to that, insisting that she never go alone anywhere except church or school events.

*I don't want you hanging out with the Rainsleys any more. Charles always has his eyes all over you, and Brianna does too.*

*They're friends*, she'd replied.

*You don't get friends, Adelina. You raise your daughters and go to church and you behave. Understand?*

As the years went by, she'd hated Richard Thompson more and more.

## Bear. May 5.

"Scott Kelly speaking," said the rough voice on the line.

"It's Bear."

"Bear! When are you coming back?"

"Heh, that's a funny joke. I'm suspended, asshole."

"Yeah?"

"You got time to meet? I got some questions for you. It's about your sisters." Kelly didn't have any sisters, and Bear knew it.

"Sisters? Yeah, sure. Where?"

Bear thought for a moment. Huh. He knew a good place with a loud fountain. The International Monetary Fund had a large building at 19th and Pennsylvania, which wasn't a bad walk from State or from Bear's apartment.

"Meet me at 19th and L. Coffee shop in the lobby of the IMF building."

"I'll be there in twenty minutes," Kelly said. "You're buying."

"I'm unemployed, motherfucker."

Kelly laughed and hung up the phone.

Eighteen minutes later, John "Bear" Wyden walked into the ground floor of the tan stone and glass headquarters of the International Monetary Fund. Outside, like all government and quasi-governmental buildings in Washington, the building was surrounded by concrete bollards and plants, which looked decorative but were designed to protect against car bombers coming into contact with the building.

Inside, only a small area was open to the public, a coffee shop on the ground floor and a cafeteria on the second floor, accessible via escalator. Otherwise the building had fairly tight security, with armed guards checking credentials and running people through metal detectors.

Bear walked toward the coffee shop and muttered a curse. Kelly had beaten him there. Which meant Bear was buying.

Kelly joined him in line. In a conversational tone, he said, "You won't believe who I talked with for the first time ever this morning."

"Yeah? Who's that?"

"A certain Vietnam vet turned Senator turned Cabinet Secretary. He called me up to tell me that I'm officially in charge of the State Department side of the investigation—that you've been suspended indefinitely. He also told me that *informally*, I'm to cooperate with you. Which I would have done anyway."

Bear chuckled. "I bet that caught your attention."

"What is going on, Bear? The IRS and Justice Department just crawled up my ass. They're all over this investigation, Diplomatic Security is just peons now. I'm making copies of documents for the independent counsel."

They had reached the front of the line. Bear ordered a thick mocha with whipped cream and a chocolate croissant, one of his several vices. Kelly snorted when Bear placed the order, and said, "Give me coffee and a donut."

Two minutes later they were sitting next to the loud, glistening marble fountain in the ten-story atrium. "All right, so who is actually running the show now?"

"Guy named Rory Armitage. Independent counsel, he was contracted out by the Justice Department and handed a whole bunch of investigators and a near unlimited budget."

"You'd have to have that to go after the Secretary of Defense."

"Yeah, well, he doesn't have a chance in hell of being confirmed as Secretary now. His hearings start tomorrow, and I'm guessing the President will pull the plug before then."

"All right. So who else?"

"The other biggie is some guy from the IRS ... Smith ... no ... crazy name ... Schmidt. Wolfram Schmidt. From *Texas* if you can believe that. The Justice Department guys are working with DEA to try to track down drug connections because of the stuff they found in the sisters' condo. IRS is following the money. They've found a bunch of accounts in the Caymans registered to Thompson. Lot of money there, a lot of recent large transfers."

"That's crazy," Bear said. "What else?"

"You heard Adelina Thompson and her daughter Jessica turned up? They ran across the border of Canada on foot while some asshole was shooting at them with a rifle. The daughter's in the hospital now. And get this: Adelina Thompson—the wife of the Secretary of Defense—asked *Canada* for political asylum from the United States, because she claims her husband hired assassins to kill her."

"Whoa," Bear said. "What happened to the shooter?"

"He tried to get away, but the Bellingham Police got him. And now they've got a big jurisdictional dispute going on, because the shooter was arrested in Bellingham, but the Justice Department and Customs and Border Protection want him."

"Huh," Bear said. "What's his name?"

"Nick Larsden. He's a ... a grifter. Small time bounty hunter from LA, he makes his living tracking down bail jumpers. He makes a big deal about having been a veteran, but he was a personnel clerk in Germany when he was in the Army. Failed as a private investigator, then migrated into bounty work."

"That's a big help, Kelly. It's huge. Larsden's the guy I want to talk to."

"Good luck. Everybody wants a piece of him. What's your angle? Why are you working this on your own?"

"Let's just say something about the official story stinks. Richard Thompson may be a scumbag, but I don't buy that his daughters were his couriers and enforcers and shit. That's crazy."

Kelly shrugged. "I've seen crazier."

"Yeah, well, I'm operating on the assumption that there's a different angle. For one thing, from what I understand, Thompson's daughters found files related to the Wakhan Massacre in his office, right before the house was destroyed. Then a few days later, the Sunday *Guardian* runs a special report implicating Thompson in the massacre. I want to know what the links are, and who else was involved."

Bear's mind ran back to the photograph in Thompson's personnel file. The photo which was stolen from his apartment, along with the rest of the documents. He remembered who was in the photo. "Here's who I'm interested in ... Prince Roshan of Saudi Arabia. Leslie Collins. Richard Thompson. Prince George-Phillip of England."

Kelly's eyes widened. "You don't think small."

"That's why they call me Bear."

"Bullshit. They call you that because you're so hairy."

"Seriously. I need to know everything I can about those four."

"You want everything. Files on the chiefs of intelligence of three countries, including ours. Access to a criminal who the feds are fighting over."

"Yeah. Can you make it happen?"

Kelly stared at him. Then he said, "I'll do what I can."

"I'll be headed west then, on the cheapest flight."

"Yeah? You going on vacation?"

"I was thinking Washington State."

"Nice. Catch you later, Bear."

Bear stood up and stretched. He walked out of the building, thinking hard. How the hell could he get at Larsden? And who hired him? Richard Thompson? That didn't make sense, unless he had a massive vendetta against his wife. Which was possible. He'd never seen two people less suited for each other.

He needed more information, and he didn't have any resources. As he walked up 19th Street, headed back to DuPont Circle, his mind circled around and around. Then he landed on a neat solution. He knew somebody with access to high-level officials, lots of staff and information, and who had no trouble flying all over the place chasing information. It went against every instinct he had, which meant it might be an awful idea—or a brilliant one.

His brow furrowed. Then he took the phone out and dialed 411.

"*The Washington Post*, please. Editorial offices, not subscriptions."

He was connected sixty seconds later. It took a couple of minutes to get through receptionists, but then he landed directly in Anthony Walker's voicemail.

"Yeah—Walker. This is Bear Wyden. Call me." He gave the number and hung up.

He sighed as he walked. He felt better rested today than he had since Andrea Thompson had arrived in the United States on April 28th, one week before. Leah was stabilizing, and she was awake and crabby as ever. The kids had to be told they couldn't climb all over her due to holes in her body. Teenagers—just like toddlers.

*Leah*, he thought. *Time to move on, Bear. She's remarried.*

Yeah, he knew.

His cell phone rang. It was a 202 area code—Washington, DC. He answered.

"Mister Wyden? It's Anthony Walker."

"Call me Bear, please."

"All right. Call me Anthony. What can I do for you?"

"I think you and I have some things in common right now. Want to get together?"

"Sure. I'm at the Thompson condo right now. The FBI forensics team turned the condo back over to Carrie."

"I'll head up the red line then, and meet you there. I need to talk to them, too."

"See you shortly, then."

# CHAPTER THREE
## The road to hell

Andrea. May 5.

**A**ndrea leaned back in her seat, luxuriating in the rare feeling of relaxation. The morning sunlight shone through the glass of the sunroom, and for the first time since her departure from Spain a week before, she'd slept the night through.

She still didn't trust Prince George-Phillip. She might never. But at least, for once, she felt safe.

Just outside the glass door of the sunroom, Dylan sat on a bench. He had a cigarette in his right hand, and a pen in the other, writing furiously in a small notebook Andrea hadn't seen before. She didn't know what he was writing about, but his expression was pained, sometimes furious. Dylan had barely been civilized when he first woke up, and immediately poured the coffee and went outside, leaving Andrea to Prince George-Phillip—*her father.*

"Your friend has a real storm on his brow," George-Phillip observed.

Andrea shrugged. "He served in Afghanistan. And Ray Sherman was his best friend."

George-Phillip's face softened. "Carrie's husband."

"Yes," Andrea replied.

"I want to reach out to her." As he said the words, his eyebrows moved furiously. Andrea tried to interpret their dance, but she couldn't.

"Why?" she asked.

George-Phillip blinked. "What do you mean, why? She's my daughter, just as you are."

Andrea sat up, studying him. Then she said, "Don't do us any favors."

"I truly wish I hadn't hurt you so terribly." He sighed as he said the words.

*"El camino al infierno esta empedrado de buenas intenciones,"* Andrea muttered. *The road to hell is paved with good intentions.*

George-Phillip raised an eyebrow.

"Don't worry about it," she said. "Just ... this is all a shock. I just wish I could trust it."

George-Phillip sighed. "I do too. It will take some time, but I promise you, I will prove it to you, and to your sister Carrie."

"So what's next?" she asked.

"I have a meeting with your President this morning, and several other meetings in the afternoon with the Ambassador and others. This evening I would like to have you and Dylan for dinner. And—I'd also like to invite your sisters. Carrie, at least, and the others if they wish to come."

"I think Alexandra will come," Andrea said. "Dylan's wife."

"Yes. I'll have an invitation sent. Is she likely to be at the condo?"

"I have no idea. Last time I was there, someone was trying to kill us."

"Indeed. I'll find out where they are. Is there anything you need in the meantime?"

"I need to call my uncle and grandmother in Spain."

"Of course. Feel free to use the phone in the parlor, just through that door."

He stood, and so did she. She felt awkward. She didn't even know what to call him. "Um ... um ... Your Highness?"

George-Phillip's eyebrows twitched uncontrollably. It was almost funny. His words were sobering, however. "I'd be grateful if one day you would consider calling me *Father*. But in the meantime, George-Phillip will do. Please, no titles. Not between us."

Andrea swallowed. Then she said, "George-Phillip, then ... I ... I know I must seem ungrateful or ... I don't know." She wanted to stomp her foot in frustration. Andrea didn't get tongue-tied. She rolled her eyes up to the ceiling, because she felt a sudden welling in them. Then she said, "I've always wanted a father who loved me. Who cared about me. And I never understood why *he* didn't. I never understood why they sent me away. So forgive me if you seem to be too good to be true." Then she held her breath and blinked her eyes, willing herself *not* to cry.

He looked at her with a loving expression and said, "Take as long as you need, Andrea. I understand that I'll have to earn your trust."

Then he was gone. She considered storming outside where Dylan was. Yelling. Throwing something. She didn't know what to think, how to react, how to behave. She didn't know what to believe. There was no doubt what he said was true. He *was* her father.

But the rest of it. Could she possibly believe him that her mother had told him to stay away? That she'd *begged* him to stay away. That he'd wanted to reach out to her, that he'd wanted to meet her all along, that somehow he'd watched her and paid attention and showed up at the festival when she sang.

*Why had Abuelita never told her?*

## Adelina. July 5, 1994.

"All right," Bear Wyden said. "You're cleared to go, but I want you to check in with me when you cross into France and again into

Spain. You understand? I know Washington says the threat to you guys is over, but I just want to be sure."

"Thank you, Bear," Adelina said. "You can't know how much this means to me."

"I got a pretty good idea," he muttered, tugging at the straps on top of the Fiat Tempra station wagon, a vehicle that Adelina hated. The suitcases were just as secure as they'd been for the last fifteen tries.

"Girls, get in the car, please," she said. "Julia!" she called. Julia was clear across the garage, sitting on the hood of a highly polished classic Fiat. Normally she would have been horrified to see one of her daughters behaving that way, but Adelina had a special place in her heart for Corporal Barry Lewis, the strapping young Marine who had been assigned as Julia's guard. Twelve-year-old Julia had a massive crush on her bodyguard—whenever he was around, her face would flush red and she would stammer and stutter. Lewis took it all in good humor and spent a lot of time with her even when he was off duty. In some ways he'd become a surrogate father for Julia. A father she needed, given the emotional absence of her real father.

"Julia! Come!"

"Go on, princess," Lewis said. "I'll see you in a few days."

Julia blushed bright red at the word *Princess*. Then she jumped off the hood of the car and ran across the garage. Carrie was already buckling in. Adelina winced a little as she lifted almost-four-year-old Alexandra into her car seat and began buckling the straps. She'd infuriated Richard again, this time by not remembering the correct military rank of the Danish military attaché. He only rarely used physical violence with her anymore, preferring to keep her in continuous low-grade terror.

Whatever his current state, he'd agreed to her driving to Spain with their daughters for a week-long visit with her family. It would be the first time she'd been home since her wedding.

Adelina got into the driver's seat. Julia was buckling in next to her, and her lower lip was pouting out. As Adelina started the car and put it into gear, she said, "What's wrong, Julia?"

A moment later she was driving out of the Embassy compound and onto the streets of Brussels, Belgium. Of the cities she'd lived in so far, Brussels was probably her least favorite after Washington. In San Francisco, she'd mostly felt a sense of freedom—at least until the night Richard almost killed her (*the night Alexandra was conceived, whispered her unconscious—she shoved the thought down*). Washington had mostly been terror. Belgium was unstable. One day he was incredibly kind, the next cruel and erratic. She lived in a constant state of tension and fear, and the panic attacks continued to grow worse all the time.

As she drove into the traffic, she considered turning around. What if she had a panic attack on the road?

She looked over at Julia again. Tears were running down the girl's face, smearing her mascara. *Her mascara?* When did she start wearing makeup?  She thanked God Lewis was an honorable man and looked at Julia as a daughter, because the girl had no sense at all when it came to him.

"Why the tears, Julia?"

"I don't want to go to stupid Spain. I want to stay with Daddy."

Bitterness swept over Adelina again, but she swallowed it. "We'll be back in a week, dear. Your father has important meetings this week"—*with prostitutes and his secretary, undoubtedly*—"he won't be around to look after you."

Julia shook her head and looked out the window. She muttered something under her breath.

"What did you say?" Adelina asked.

"I said, that's nothing new. No one looks after me except Corporal Lewis." Her tone was sullen.

Adelina looked in the rearview mirror. Carrie was already wrapped up in a book. *Steel Beach* by John Varley. She didn't understand Carrie or the strange things she read. Science fiction mostly, but also a fair amount of romance. The girl was smart beyond her age and had abandoned young-adult books by the time she was nine.

She looked so much like George-Phillip sometimes it broke Adelina's heart. It broke her heart that she would never see him again, and it broke her heart that he didn't know his daughter. She often wished she'd acceded to his demands—that she'd run away, that she'd given in.

But when she thought that way, her mind always returned to Richard's threats. The most recent had been crude. She'd walked into her bedroom and found a photograph on her pillow. Black and white, it depicted a young man—fifteen or sixteen years old, with a crude crosshair drawn over his face in black Sharpie.

It was her younger brother, Luis.

She was stunned, really, that Richard had allowed her to make this drive. But he'd been distracted, preparing for the upcoming NATO summit, and for a moment the leash loosened. She took immediate advantage.

On the dashboard, she had taped the map, which Corporal Lewis had painstakingly highlighted in red. Beside it, directions were handwritten and also taped to the dashboard. Lewis and Bear had been fanatically protective of Adelina and her daughters, as if they sensed something was seriously wrong in her family but didn't quite know what it was.

Julia had slipped on a headset and put a cassette in her Sony Walkman. It had been one of her Christmas gifts, and she listened to it constantly. She never wanted to do her piano practice, but there was no question she loved music. Although Adelina had doubts about some of the "music" Julia listened to. Right now it sounded like the croaking of frogs was leaking out of her headphones.

"Julia," she said. "Turn that down."

Instead of turning it down, she turned it up. It *did* sound like frogs croaking, with a haunting violin in the background.

"Julia," she said again.

No answer.

"Julia!" she said sharply.

Julia glared at her, then said, "Leave me alone," and whipped her face away from Adelina, her brown hair flying everywhere. She curled up, leaning against the window and staring out.

## Andrea. May 5.

*Why had Abuelita never told her?*

The phone George-Phillip had indicated was visible through the doorway. It was an oddity, an antique, a rotary phone with an ivory handle and gold inlay. It was highly polished, and she was almost afraid to touch it. The phone sat on a fine looking table with a marble top and mahogany legs. Two luxurious high-backed chairs upholstered in sapphire brocade flanked the table.

She'd never used a rotary phone before, but she understood the principal of the thing. She sank into one of the chairs, much more comfortable than it looked, and awkwardly picked the handset up out of the cradle. She reached out and began dialing.

*011* … The first number took forever, the dial cranked around all the way, then circling back, odd clicking sounds coming from the headset as the dial turned. It was difficult to imagine how people could have used these things regularly without wanting to smash their head into the phone. As she watched it turn, she felt her anxiety increase, her stomach tensing.

*34* ... The country code for Spain. She'd known how to make a direct dial international call since she was ten years old. She wasn't sure that was knowledge any ten-year-old needed.

*937* ... She continued dialing the nine digits of her grandmother's phone number. And as she did so her jaw hardened, her hand squeezing the grip of the phone hard enough her knuckles were white.

As she finished dialing, she heard silence for a moment, then a series of clicks and hisses. She didn't use landlines generally, and certainly not antique phones. But a moment later the phone at the other end began ringing, a shrill burst of two tones, pause, two tones, pause.

"*Diga.*" *Speak.* It was Abuelita's voice.

Andrea couldn't breathe for a moment. She sniffed, horrified at herself, then said, "*Abuelita,* it's Andrea."

"*¡Gracias a Dios!* Thank God you called, I've been so worried about you!" Her grandmother paused for a moment—as Andrea knew she would—then launched into a tirade. "Why have you not called me? It's been a week, and all I see is headlines that you've been attacked and kidnapped and running for your life. Have you lost your mind? Andrea, I want you on a plane home today! Today, do you hear me?"

Andrea heard the phone thump, and then her grandmother shouted, "Luis! Luis! Come here now! Andrea is on the phone, tell her she must come home *now.*"

Luis was there? It was Monday morning; he should be working in Barcelona.

"Luis!" her grandmother screamed.

"*¡Abuelita!*" Andrea shouted into the phone. Unconsciously she stood up and began pacing, forgetting that the phone was *wired to the wall*. The pretty gold telephone base fell off the table, stretched out the cord and tugged Andrea toward the floor. Awkwardly, she fell to her knees and grabbed at the base with her free hand, trying to keep it from landing on the cradle and hanging up the phone. Her grandmother was still shouting in the background, so Andrea had an opportunity to right the phone and get it back on the table, then sit on the edge of the chair again.

A moment later, a harried sounding Luis came on the line. "*¡Muñequita!* I'm so glad you're okay, we were terrified."

"Thank you, tío," she replied. "I need to speak with *Abuelita*."

"What? You don't even ask how your poor uncle is doing?"

"I'll ask in a minute," Andrea said, her voice cold. "I have *other* questions to ask right now."

"I don't like the sound of your voice, *Muñequita*. Tell me what is going on. *Madre* has a weak heart."

"I *must* speak with her, Luis."

"Fine. Fine! And if your poor old grandmother has a heart attack, you will feel guilty the rest of your life. Yes? Is that what you want?"

"Luis, I'm *begging* you." Her voice was ragged as she said the last words.

He didn't say anything else. A moment later, her grandmother came back on the line.

"Andrea, it's time for this nonsense to end. I didn't raise you to be disobedient, I expect you to—"

Andrea interrupted. "Why did you never tell me my mother was raped? And that my father is *not* Richard Thompson?"

Her grandmother said, "Is your mother telling those lies again? I am so disappointed in her. She was not *raped*. Her father, *he* let that man touch her—"

"*Stop!*" Andrea whispered. Hot tears ran down her face, a sudden pang of disappointment gouging a hole in her heart. "Did you force her to marry him? Did you?"

"Of course not. I would never do such a thing. She threw herself after that man."

"You *lie*," Andrea cried out. The tears were running freely now. "He raped her, Abuelita. He did."

"It's not true! Your mother lies to you! You *know* you cannot trust her."

"*She* didn't tell me," Andrea whispered. "*She* didn't. My father did. My real father. And the police report. He did it again. After they were married. More than once."

Her grandmother gasped. "Where do you get these crazy ideas? Your *real* father? I don't know what—"

"Did you know he was coming? When he showed up at Miguel's wedding? And on the beach? At my concert?"

*Abuelita* didn't answer. On the other end of the line, her breathing was hoarse. "Andrea..." she finally whispered.

"*Why?*" Andrea said.

"She was *lying*." Her grandmother repeated the words again, and again, as if saying the words repeatedly just might make them true. As if saying those words was a talisman that would protect her from what she'd done to her own daughter. "She was *lying*."

"No, Grandmother," Andrea said. "She wasn't. And that changed everything. It ruined her life, and it twisted all of her daughters' lives."

"No," her grandmother whispered. Andrea heard the phone thump against the table a continent away. She waited, thinking

Luis would pick it up. She waited, but no one ever picked up the line. After five minutes, the knife-edge tone of the off-hook signal sliced through the silence into her chest, cutting her loose from the only family she'd ever trusted.

## Adelina. July 5, 1994.

It was nearing midnight when Adelina drove the last few blocks to her mother's flat in Calella. Even though she hadn't been here for more than a decade, the blocks surrounding the flat were familiar. She had few good memories here.

Adelina had come to live with her mother after her father, Juan Ramos, had been murdered, most likely by her now husband. She'd spent those weeks in terrible pain and grief, occasionally walking or sitting for hours along the beach. She could still taste the bitterness of her tears in those months. It took her years to reach any internal peace about her mother's role in her marriage. If she had any at all. Whatever peace she once had was shredded by driving down these streets.

All three girls were asleep. Julia was still curled up against the window, her tape long since ended. Carrie was halfway sprawled across the back seat, and Alexandra was asleep in her car seat, pacifier in her mouth. Adelina brought the car to a stop half a block from her mother's flat, and with tired eyes she stared up at the windows, which were undoubtedly open this time of year to let a breeze through. The windows were dark—everyone had gone to sleep, she supposed, even though they knew when Adelina would be arriving.

That was a bitter thought. She hadn't seen her mother or brother in a dozen years. The least they could do was stay up past dinner time. But then she saw a shadow pass in front of the window, and a flickering light. They were home and awake after all, but the lights on this side of the flat weren't on.

She still didn't want to go up. What would she say? She was regretting having made this trip. The conversation with her mother two days ago was difficult, to say the least. They had little in common, little to say to each other. Adelina asked about Miguel and Luis, and her mother asked about Richard, which merely put a sour taste in Adelina's mouth. But she couldn't pass up the opportunity to get out from under Richard for an entire week, and the girls did deserve to know their grandmother.

She didn't know if their grandmother deserved to know them.

She sighed and pulled the car to a stop in the tiny parking lot behind the apartment building. She didn't know which spot was her mother's. She would find out soon enough—she pulled into the only empty spot then turned off the car. Despite the late hour, loud music poured into the streets from a bar nearby, and she could hear people talking and laughing. It was July in a resort town on the Mediterranean—the night sounds would continue until two or three in the morning. Even so, she could hear the crash of the surf against the beach, and the sound instantly took her back to Ocean Beach, where she often walked in the mornings during her too brief time in San Francisco.

Julia stirred in her seat. Adelina leaned in and touched her on the shoulder. "Julia, wake up, we're here. Carrie, you too."

Both girls grumbled, but she got them moving. Alexandra began to whine as Adelina woke her to get her out of her seat, but settled in Adelina's arms as she walked out of the parking lot and around to the sidewalk and the front of the building. A man stumbled toward them, partially shadowed from the streetlamp, and Adelina instinctively gathered her daughters around her. And that's when it hit her.

Adelina had been sixteen when Richard raped her. Now her *daughter* was almost that age.

Without volition, her heart suddenly began racing, her pulse pumping loudly in her ears, a sharp pain in her chest, terror closing her throat and mind. She staggered, clutching at her chest, and Julia cried out, "Momma?"

Unbidden tears began to run down Adelina's face as her chest tightened in even more pain. "*Madre de dios,*" she whispered, not realizing she'd fallen to her knees with Alexandra still calmed in her arms. "*Help me.*"

"Momma!" the girls screeched, terrified. *Momma!*

\*\*\*

*Dreams.*

Adelina was floating, and it was peaceful. She was sitting on the edge of North Beach, the sun shining down on her like the love of God.

But she knew Richard was coming home soon. The sky was getting darker, heavy with dark clouds. She felt a raindrop, thick like oil, one, then another, the fat drops crashing against the ocean, drumming, pounding, crashing, aching, like hammers against a metal roof, and she was in the flower shop again, but not with her father. *Richard* was there and she was just a girl bound for the National Youth Orchestra and he took it all away.

She screamed.

\*\*\*

"She's waking up."

Her eyes slid open, vision blurred. She looked up. Her mother was sitting there next to Luis. Luis was a big strapping sixteen-year-old with a huge grin.

"Hey, big sister," he said. Adelina's eyes were getting heavy again.

Adelina's eyes bored into her mother's. "Why did you make me marry my rapist?" she demanded, her voice heavy.

"I didn't *make* you marry anyone, Adelina. What are you talking about? How dare you?"

"Get out. You've made my life a *living hell!*" Adelina screamed. "Get *out!*"

She screamed long after they were gone, until her throat was raw, and the cool medication ran through her veins and took her back into a deep sleep.

\*\*\*

"Mr. Ambassador, we recommend against taking her now. Your wife has been through a terrible shock and needs medication and treatment."

"She'll get treated in a hospital with American doctors. She wouldn't have had these problems in the first place if she hadn't come to Spain. None of them are coming back to this place. *Ever.*"

# CHAPTER FOUR
## What hearing?

Leslie Collins. May 5.

**M**onday morning was never pleasant for Leslie Collins, but after the longest week of his career, *this* Monday was the worst he could imagine. As always, he'd gotten out of bed at 4 am, beginning his day drinking coffee as he reviewed the intelligence summaries of the day. It was more of the same. Violence spreading in the Ukraine as nationalist and pro-Russian forces came into conflict. The German newspaper *Bild am Sonntag* had somehow gotten wind of the fact that the US had sent specialists from FBI and CIA to advise the Ukrainian government on how to stop the rebellion in Kiev. Leslie made a note to have someone follow up and find out the source of the leak. Iraq had just finished its bloodiest month in a year, with more than 750 Iraqis killed in April, most of them civilians. As always, Leslie bristled at the implication that the Agency should be doing more there. If Congress and the President would give him the resources, he could do something. As it was, the President had crippled the Agency.

At least he wasn't heading up the NSA. Edward Snowden's revelations of NSA spying had diverted a lot of attention from CIA in recent months, and while technically they were all on the same side, Leslie wasn't above a little interagency competition. Collins had come to believe that his career was going to mirror that of his predecessor George H. W. Bush, who had moved from the Director of Central Intelligence to Vice President and finally to President. He had the ability. He had the ambition. One day he would be at the helm, and he would destroy al-Qaeda and ensure his country's safety.

Review of his official files completed, he turned to his less official reports. And he froze.

*Adelina Thompson* had been shot at crossing the border into Canada? And she had asked for political asylum? Asylum was the craziest thing he'd ever heard, first of all, but he'd been very clear with Danny McMillan that there was to be no more violence directed at the Thompsons. He had more than enough paper trails established to ensure that Thompson was destroyed, and more violence would only serve to raise suspicions. What he needed right now was for the independent prosecutor and the grand jury to indict Richard Thompson. Smear his name until nothing he said was believable, before he went public about Wakhan and somehow tried to blame Collins for it.

*Christ*, he thought. If his role in Wakhan—or Andrea Thompson's kidnapping, for that matter—ever came to light, he could forget about his ambitions. Was Danny trying to sabotage him? Danny had to know he was replaceable—after all, he'd taken care of Mitch Filner, who had *once* served as Collins' chief confidential aide.

He picked up the phone and started dialing, never mind that it was 4:30 in the morning.

The phone rang—once, twice, three times. Then a groggy voice answered. "Hello."

"McMillan. It's Collins."

At the other end of the line, was a muttered curse and fumbling. Then the sluggish voice said, "Do you know what time it is?"

"I don't care what time it is. What the hell happened on the border yesterday?"

"The border with where?"

"With Canada, you idiot. Why did you send someone to attack Adelina Thompson? I thought I made it clear I didn't want any more violence."

Silence for just a second, then McMillan said, "Collins, I don't know what the hell you're talking about. I didn't send anybody after her. We've been watching, and that's it. I didn't even have a bead on her. She turned up?"

"She turned up at the border crossing with a former soldier in pursuit, then demanded political asylum. Which she's not likely to get; it's Canada, after all. But I guarantee you it's going to make a lot of news."

"I don't know what that's about, Collins."

Leslie thought furiously. If McMillan's people hadn't shot at Thompson's wife, then who did? And why? It didn't make any sense.

## Richard Thompson. May 5.

*I understand, Richard. I really do. But the political liability at this point is massive. And we can't have the Secretary of Defense wrapped up in a scandal on the eve of his confirmation hearing.*

Richard Thompson gritted his teeth in rage as he sat in the back of the car and rode back toward the base at Fort Myers. As always, traffic in and out of Washington was snarled. At least he didn't have far to go, Fort Myers was right across the river. He presumed that he would have some days to clear his personal property out of the house there. The bigger sting was the President just dropping him. As if he had no confidence that Richard would survive this storm.

Survive he would. But first he had to make it through the next few days. And those would be difficult enough.

The last week had consisted of nothing but wave after wave of shocks. First, the news that Adelina's daughter, Andrea, was coming to the United States, after he'd expressly ordered Adelina to keep her away. It was bad enough that Carrie's height continually reminded him that Senator Chuck Rainsley had been with Adelina—*Senator Chuck Rainsley, of all people*—but to have a second daughter by him. It made Richard queasy to think of it.

In truth, he'd tried to be a good father to both of them. But he just couldn't stomach it when it came to the youngest girl. He supposed it was because he knew from the first that she wasn't his. Carrie he'd had as a baby, and it stayed that way until she'd had her blood typed at six years old. With Andrea, he knew from the beginning—he knew in the surest way possible that he was not her father, because he hadn't touched that hag since the night he'd, in a drunken stupor, forced himself on Adelina and conceived the twins.

Richard Thompson no longer drank to excess.

His phone rang. Richard almost pressed the ignore button, because he recognized the number. It was Joseph Bergmann, the senior staffer of the Senate Armed Services Committee. Bergmann had been a thorn in his side for weeks as he'd prepared for his confirmation hearings—hearings that had been scheduled to proceed in the morning, but were now pointless. But the fact was, this scandal wouldn't last. He'd be cleared soon enough, and then hopefully he'd be able to move on with minimal damage to his career.

"Richard Thompson speaking," he said, answering the phone.

"Ambassador Thompson, this is Joseph Bergmann."

*Ambassador* Thompson, not *Secretary* Thompson. Clearly Bergmann had gotten the word already.

"I suppose you've heard the President is rescinding the nomination?" Richard asked.

"I have, I'm sorry to hear that, Ambassador. Please allow me to offer my condolences. I'm sure when all this is sorted out you'll be back on top again."

"Thank you, Joseph," Richard replied in a dismissive tone. He didn't need sympathy from a mere Senate staffer. "If there's nothing more, I'll—"

"Actually, Ambassador, I was just calling to verify that you'd gotten word the hearing is being moved to the Central Hearing Facility in the Hart building because of the increased interest from the public and media."

"Excuse me?" Richard said. "*What* hearing? Why would you hold confirmation hearings when my nomination has been withdrawn? Get it together, man."

Bergmann's tone went cold. "There's no need to be rude, Ambassador. In fact, Senator Rainsley insisted on going forward with hearings into your conduct at the Central Intelligence Agency, and specifically events in Badakhshan, Afghanistan in 1983."

For the first time in years, Richard was rendered speechless. He sat in the seat, phone at his ear, unable to speak, unable to think of what to say. *Your conduct at the Central Intelligence Agency?* He'd never been officially associated with the Agency except in the very early 1970s. Some people in the government were aware of his role at the Agency and the State Department, but they were few indeed.

Chuck Rainsley, the bastard who had seduced his wife, was one of those people.

Bile flooded through Richard Thompson. He wanted to hurt someone very badly. *No one* took what belonged to him. And Chuck Rainsley had been undermining Richard's marriage and his career for more than thirty years.

"Ambassador? Are you still there?"

Richard shook his head, suddenly aware that Bergmann was still on the line. "Of course I'm here. And I have no intention of showing up for your fishing expedition. As it stands, I'm no longer a part of this government."

"Ambassador, I wouldn't recommend that. When you get back to Fort Myers, you'll find a subpoena waiting. Senator Rainsley is in a rare mood, and I suspect if you fail to appear you'll be cited with contempt of Congress."

Richard closed his eyes. He responded in as calm a demeanor as possible. "Fine, then, I'll see you in the morning."

Bergmann hung up without further comment. Richard thought through the appalling events of the last few days. Andrea kidnapped—most likely by thugs working for Leslie Collins. That inept son of a bitch was doing everything he could to undermine Richard and prevent him from becoming Secretary of Defense. But he wasn't the worst of it. His wife—his *stupid bitch of a wife*—had made an international laughing stock of him. *No one* asked for political asylum *from* the United States. People came here to be free. They didn't run away. Yet that whore had dragged their daughter across the border and asked for *political asylum.*

It was all over the networks. The Secretary of Defense's wife flees, claiming he's trying to murder her. The Monday morning *Washington Post* had his and Adelina's photo on the front page. The headline read, "Embattled Secretary of Defense nominee's wife flees country claiming abuse."

He wanted to put his hands around her neck and watch her slowly turn blue. He wanted to watch her eyes bulge. He wanted to feel her terror. He *hadn't* been trying to kill her, but that said absolutely nothing for her future. And her stupid brother Luis should start counting his days. He'd *warned her.* For thirty years he'd warned her.

And not just her. Chuck Rainsley. He remembered how he'd shown up at their condo back in 1984, self-absorbed and fancy in his Marine Corps uniform, all smiles and loud exhortations of his own heroism. As if getting all your men killed made you a hero.

He knew what to do. He took his phone back out and dialed. Moments later, the phone was answered.

"Richard!" The cultured, rich voice of Prince Roshan al Saud was friendly.

"Roshan, how are you? I understand you are in the United States?"

"Only for a few more days. I intended to ask you to dinner, but I know you've had a great number of challenges in the last few days."

Richard waved a hand. "It's quite all right. However, I'd like to meet for a bit if you have time."

"Are you free this morning? I'm just leaving a meeting at the Embassy, I'll be back home in twenty minutes."

"That's perfect."

He leaned forward and said, "Driver, change of plans. We're going to Langley, Virginia."

Twenty minutes later, the car pulled into Prince Roshan's palatial Virginia home. He waited for the driver to come around and open the door, then got out of the car, carrying his briefcase.

Roshan met him at the door. He wore a conservative looking grey suit and red tie, with a pin representing the Saudi flag pinned to his lapel. It bizarrely reflected the de rigueur Washington uniform since September 11th, 2001, which required men in any government role to wear an American flag, as if that somehow proved their loyalty. Roshan's greying hair and beard served to highlight his dark skin. His fat, puffy body, with rounded cheeks and a prodigious belly, was a caricature of his former self.

Richard weighed no more than he had when the two men met in 1983, and he took Roshan's weight gain as a lack of self-discipline.

Of course, that wasn't the only sign of a lack of discipline. The endless parade of call girls was another, as was Roshan's DUI two years ago. Roshan had been behind the wheel, careening through downtown drunk when he drove his Maserati through the front windows of an old townhouse on 16th Street. The State Department had to go to considerable effort and expense to cover the incident up, and to bribe both the appropriate officials and the elderly widow who owned the house.

However, right now, Roshan looked fine, besides the bloodshot eyes. "How are you, Richard?"

"Good, good!" The two shook hands, then Roshan took his shoulders and grinned. "Come in, please."

Moments later, Roshan served Richard a gin and tonic without asking what he preferred, pouring the gin from a bottle of Hendricks. Richard sipped. Roshan had made the drink stiff.

"I hear things are rough for you, my friend," Roshan said in a sober voice.

Richard nodded. "A little, but not as bad as it appears. May I be frank?"

Roshan nodded.

"Leslie Collins is behind much of it. The financial stuff, the accounts in the Caymans? That's all his work. No one else it could possibly be."

Roshan leaned forward and said, "We have several mutual problems. Collins is one, I agree. He's a loose cannon. But that's not all. You saw the report in *The Guardian?* It's everywhere now. And you've been named in it, along with Prince George-Phillip.

You understand how wrong this could go. I'd expect your Congress to announce an investigation within a week."

Richard grimaced. "Already happened. And I bet you can guess who is behind it."

Roshan rested an index finger against his cheek. "Rainsley?"

Richard nodded. "He wasn't satisfied with fucking my wife. Now he wants to destroy me. But I'm not going to let that happen."

"What will you do to prevent it?"

Richard took a sip of his drink. He loved Hendricks gin. In a dry voice, he alluded to his thoughts. "Roshan, you and I both know that we did everything we could to keep Collins under control in Afghanistan. I was as appalled as anybody that he would commit the crimes he did there."

"Yes, Richard," Roshan said in as unnatural a tone as Richard had ever heard. "We both felt that way. But how can we prove it?"

"Believe it or not, Collins received an official reprimand. It was classified, of course. But it's not beyond belief that it would be leaked now, given the circumstances. Possibly to the special prosecutor, which might divert them from me."

Roshan chuckled. "I'm not surprised you kept some insurance around Collins, Richard. It makes me wonder what you have on me."

Richard smiled. "I *trust* you, Roshan."

Roshan nodded. Richard knew Roshan didn't believe his polite lie.

"All right, Richard. I will help take care of our mutual friend. You concern yourself with Rainsley and make sure that document gets leaked to the right people."

## Marky Lovecchio. May 5.

The death metal blasting out of the speakers of Marky Lovec-chio's 2014 Dodge Challenger was loud enough that the rearview mirror vibrated with every thump of the bass drum. He liked the music. It drove out the ugly thoughts, and Marky had plenty of ugly thoughts, whether it was memories of his first enlistment (Somalia) or his last (the Sunni triangle), whether it was his failed marriage or the accountant who had seduced his wife while he was in Iraq. Sometimes his ugly thoughts were of prison, where he'd ended up after he beat said accountant within an inch of his life, then threatened to shoot his wife in the face. It had been ugly there for a few minutes, the standoff with the police, but he finally dropped his weapon. Suicide by cop wasn't his style.

Three years later he'd gotten out. He couldn't go back in the military, not with a felony conviction, but that didn't stop a career with a private military contractor, which paid better anyway. Lately he'd been taking on jobs for the mysterious Oz, an Irish gentleman (possibly) who had been keeping Marky busy for more than a year with jobs big and small, some interesting and some not so much.

The latest job was a problem. He'd been ordered to track down a woman and her daughter. It should have been simple. The woman's house in San Francisco was bombed (he didn't know by who) and it turned out she was pretty smart, disappearing off the face of the earth. Lovecchio had drifted south out of San Francisco, showing pictures everywhere he could, until this morning, when he saw the woman's picture on the front page of the paper. She'd gotten away, making it across the border into Canada.

That was a problem, but not as big as the next problem. When they ran across the border, Nick Larsden had been in pursuit, and fired shots across the border after them, which was a big no-no as far as cops on both sides of the international border were concerned. Then Nick had the bad grace to get caught.

He and Nick had gone through basic training together, way back in 1994, and when Nick had told Marky he was looking for work, Marky hooked him up with Oz.

Big mistake. Now Marky was waiting for a phone call, and he had a pretty good idea what that call was going to involve.

For now, he sat in his car along an overlook, watching the ocean far below. He loved the Pacific Ocean. But not as much as he loved getting into the shit. Somewhere along the way in Iraq, he'd gotten the taste for it. He felt invincible—he'd been through five combat tours in three theaters of war. Lesser men all around him had fallen to bombs and bullets, disease and suicide. Marky just kept going.

Sometimes he thought he was immune. He had to be. In October 1993 he and his squad had been separated from the main body of Bravo Company, 75th Rangers in Mogadishu and fought their way through half a dozen city blocks surrounded by literally *thousands* of pissed off Somalis. 18 Americans dead, 80 wounded, somewhere upward of 3,000 Somali casualties, and Marky had walked through it without a scratch. Twelve years later, as a senior sergeant in Special Operations, he'd been briefly captured in Fallujah in the Sunni triangle, only to have a squad of Marines come in fast and dumb into the building he was being tortured in. The result, fortuitously, was four dead Hajjis and one free Marky.

Lately though, he'd been starting to wonder. Like, maybe there was something more to life than all this bullshit. He didn't like running around shooting at people, and that's what the jobs for Oz had consisted of, at least in the last couple of weeks. That was bullshit.

But he also knew that once you were on the hook, Oz didn't take no for an answer. Which was why he was sitting here in the car, waiting for the phone to ring.

Waiting. Waiting.

The volume on the music was so loud that he jumped when the music suddenly cut off, replaced by the ringing of his phone through the car speakers. He quickly turned the volume down then answered.

"Lovecchio."

"Mister Lovecchio, this is Oz." Oz—or whatever his name was—did not sound happy. As always, his voice was gravelly, the Irish accent a quarry full of age and aggravation.

"Hello, sir."

"We have a problem, Lovecchio."

"Yes, sir. Nick Larsden?"

"That's right. First, he had the woman in his sights and let her cross the border. Second, he let himself get captured. If he's in custody, then he can talk."

"Yes, sir."

"You're going to correct that situation. Do I make myself clear?"

Marky nodded slowly, even though he knew Oz couldn't see him. He'd had the feeling it would come to this. Marky owed some level of loyalty to Larsden—after all, they'd both served in the Army at the same time, though Larsden was nothing but a paper pusher. But he didn't owe him *that* much. Larsden had screwed up and he couldn't be allowed to keep screwing things up.

Worst of all, Larsden knew Marky's name.

"I'll take care of him, sir."

"Good. Let me know when it's done. It needs to be quick, before he tells the American police anything. Am I clear?"

"Yeah. He's in the Bellingham jail. I know how to take care of that."

"Then the woman and her daughter."

"Yeah?" Marky asked.

"Yes. They're in a hospital in Abbotsford. Once you've taken care of Larsden, then I'll get you more details."

"I'm on it, sir."

Oz hung up without another word. Seconds later, the Bluetooth switched back over and the death metal came back on the radio, once again causing the rearview mirror to pulse. Marky started the car and backed out of his parking space. It was a four-hour drive to Bellingham.

# CHAPTER FIVE
## He's not my father.

**When** Bear stepped off the elevator on the 20th floor, he immediately saw two armed and uniformed security guards standing in the hall. A third was at the opposite end. All three wore tactical vests and carried both pistols and rifles.

The occupants of the other three penthouses must be overjoyed.

Bear walked down the hallway toward Carrie Sherman's condo and one of the guards immediately approached him. The other stood back, hand on his hip, while the first said, "You're here to see Mrs. Sherman? Identification, please?"

He took out his Diplomatic Security Services identification and badge and showed it to the guard. He approved of their thoroughness. The guards wore the logo of Pinkerton Security Services, a firm that had been doing security and private investigation since before the Civil War. Julia Wilson, who was undoubtedly paying for this, didn't kid around.

A moment later they cleared him to head into the condo.

Bear's first impression was utter chaos. He'd last been here on Friday night, a few hours after the attack. The forensic team had been through over the weekend, searching the entire condominium, and they'd left behind a tremendous mess. They hadn't made any attempt to clean up the fan of blood stains on the wall near the front door, where Dylan Paris had cut off the hand of one attacker with a meat cleaver, then stabbed the other in the back during a short and extremely violent melee.

He continued inside.

Carrie Sherman was standing in the middle of the chaos. Papers everywhere. The coffee table turned over. Bookshelves emptied, the books scattered in a pile on the floor. Knick-knacks taken from the mantle and left—somewhere? Carrie's face was strained, angry.

Across the room from her, Anthony Walker was gathering up a pile of papers and stacking items. He could hear the others—Sarah and Alexandra, he supposed—talking in another room.

When Carrie spied him, she said, "Was it your people who did this?"

Bear shook his head. "FBI forensics. Normally they straighten up after themselves. This was—excessive."

"Well, you can help straighten up."

Bear grunted. "Sure. I need to ask you guys some questions, and have a talk with Walker here. What brought you out here anyway?"

Anthony shrugged. "I had questions too, but when I walked in the door, Carrie put me to work."

Bear chuckled.

Carrie was staring at the mantle. She muttered, "The god-damned head is missing."

"The *what*?"

"My father brought back this stupid head from Indonesia or someplace. It's been on this mantle for thirty years or more. It's gone."

"The forensics team should give you a list of anything they removed from the apartment," Bear said.

Carrie muttered something under her breath and walked out of the room.

"She's cranky," Bear said.

"Wouldn't you be?" Anthony replied.

Bear surveyed the ruin of the room again and frowned. "Yeah."

Anthony stood and faced Bear. "So what's this about?"

Bear said, "First, what I'm about to tell you isn't official."

"All right," Anthony said.

"I've been temporarily suspended by the Secretary." He made air quotes as he said the word *suspended*. "DSS is officially off the investigation."

"Gotcha. But you're doing some looking on your own?"

"Exactly. Something stinks in this investigation. I'm trying to find out what."

"So what do you want from me?"

Bear shrugged. "I'll help you, you help me."

Anthony nodded. "Information."

"That's right," Bear said.

"Agreed."

"What do you say we sit down? I want to go over what we know. What you know, what I know. Who did what, and when."

"Let's move into the dining room," Anthony said. "I want to lay this out."

The formal dining room was twenty-five feet long and had a table capable of seating sixteen. Highly polished wide plank flooring and extensive crown molding gave an impression of luxury and wealth.

Bear said, "I've seen a picture of this room. The Thompsons used to host dinners here. There's one in particular I keep getting stuck on."

Anthony raised an eyebrow.

Bear said, "The guests were Prince George Phillip. Prince Roshan al Saud. Leslie Collins. Chuck Rainsley."

"Are you serious? When was this?"

"February of '84."

Carrie, walking by in the hallway, stopped and stood in the door. Beside her, Julia touched her arm. Both of them were listening.

Anthony said, "February '84 was not quite three months after the Wakhan massacre."

"What does that have to do with us, though?" Julia said, interrupting. "Why did Dad have pictures and files about that?"

Bear stared at her, stunned. "He had pictures? Of Wakhan?"

"Yeah," Anthony said, his voice grim. "It was unmistakable."

Bear said, "Before Thompson's personnel file was stolen, I read through it. It looks pretty clear that Thompson was stationed in Afghanistan in '83. So was Leslie Collins. And—Prince Roshan was also in Afghanistan at the time."

Anthony said, "I want to suggest an idea here."

"Go," Bear said.

"Okay, so ... Richard Thompson goes to Afghanistan. Let's say, just for speculation—that it wasn't the Russians who gassed that village. We'll speculate that *The Guardian* is correct, and it was Afghan militia, backed by Thompson. And not just him, but that Collins and Roshan were involved."

"Okay? But what does that have to do with now?"

"I'm getting there," Anthony said. "First—again, according to *The Guardian*, and also some of my co-workers at the *Post*, Prince George-Phillip was responsible for the British investigation. Second—he is Andrea and Carrie's father."

Bear shook his head and said, "That's confirmed now?"

Carrie nodded. "Andrea and Dylan turned up last night after Andrea jumped the wall into the British Embassy."

Bear chuckled. "That girl has more balls than a basketball team."

"I've received an invitation from the Prince to come to dinner this evening."

"All right. So—he's your father. Which means he and your mother had an affair—what—when?"

"Spring of 1984."

Bear nodded. "Then at some point later on, they got back together. When? Where?"

Julia said, "In China. 1996."

Bear said. "What I don't get is this: who tried to kidnap Andrea? Why?"

Anthony said, "To ... keep the affair secret? Who would want to do that? I assume George-Phillip."

"Maybe. The Guardian says he suppressed the findings of the investigation. Why? Something to do with her? With Richard Thompson? Was someone else involved?"

"Maybe he was threatened somehow?" Julia said.

"Or *she* was," Carrie replied.

"We know that he had *some* reason to suppress the findings," Bear said. "We know your mother had a long-standing affair with Prince George-Phillip. And, based on the police report, your mother and father didn't have much love lost between them."

Carrie said, "He's *not* my father."

Julia closed her eyes and sighed. "He is mine. But the more I learn about him, the more disturbed I am. I've seen the police report you're talking about. It raises a lot of questions. So does her diary."

Bear said, "Her diary?"

Julia nodded. "Yes. It's—in Spanish—difficult to read handwriting. But she makes it clear that she felt like she was a prisoner."

Bear sat down in one of the embroidered dining chairs. "I don't get it," he said. "There's something we're missing. All right ... who are our suspects?"

Anthony's eyes darted to Carrie and Julia. Then he said, "I don't think we can rule out Richard Thompson."

Bear felt his stomach tense. "Yeah. Yeah, I don't think we can either. Especially if he knew Carrie and Andrea weren't his kids."

Carrie sighed and sat down at the table. Julia walked up behind her, resting her hands on Carrie's shoulders.

Carrie said, "He knew. He told me Chuck Rainsley was my father. But Rainsley said no, and now ... well, you know."

"Okay, so Thompson is one possibility. What's his motive?"

"Revenge?" Anthony said. "He's still pissed his wife had an affair. He was fine until Andrea came into the country."

"Okay. Who else?" Bear asked.

"Leslie Collins," Anthony said.

"Okay," Carrie interjected. "Who is this Collins guy?"

"He's Director of Operations at the CIA," said Julia. "He's basically the second-in-command. I remember him, sort of. He used to come over and meet with Dad. Mom always got weird when he was around."

Carrie raised her eyebrows. "How long ago?"

Julia shrugged. "When I was in high school. Sometimes he'd come over and he and Dad would lock themselves in the office for hours. Mom and Dad had Collins and his wife over for dinner a few times. Can't remember her name. Mary? Meredith? I think I may have met him before that, when I was really little. I'm not sure."

Bear grunted. "Okay. So Richard Thompson and Leslie Collins are both suspects. Who else? Who would need to keep your parentage a secret?"

"Mom?" Julia asked.

Carrie shook her head. "No ... but what about my father? My *real* father?"

Anthony nodded. "It would make for a ferocious scandal. George-Phillip isn't that close to the throne, but he is a royal Prince. Plus, the head of the SIS. He's got good reason to keep your parentage under wraps, Carrie. I'd be careful. Especially if you're going to the Embassy for dinner."

Carrie looked at Anthony thoughtfully. Then she nodded, once, slowly. "I will. My daughter needs me. I'll be careful."

Bear looked back and forth between Carrie and Anthony. She was still grieving, of course, though it had been close to a year since Ray Sherman died. But one day she would heal. And Anthony Walker could do a lot worse than Carrie Sherman. He kept looking at her kind of like a sad puppy dog. She was indifferent, or at least still too bludgeoned by pain to respond to any stimulus other than protecting her daughter. But something in Bear wanted to protect both of them.

Right now, though, he had more important things to think about. Like finding the son of a bitch who had shot his ex-wife.

"All right, all right. So we have three suspects. Anyone else? What about the attack on Friday night? Not to mention whoever shot at your mother on the border yesterday."

Anthony said, "I think Richard Thompson could be a suspect in all three. If he wanted Andrea out of the way. But Carrie has the same father ... and apparently he knows it."

"Plus," Bear said, "the drugs and money were planted by somebody. And they've been used by the special prosecutor as ammunition in his campaign against Thompson. Don't forget the grand jury will be meeting soon."

Anthony nodded. "So the drugs and money were planted by someone else. To smear Thompson?"

Carrie looked back and forth. "What if it was this Leslie Collins? He and Dad ... I mean ... whatever we call him ... he and *Richard Thompson* were involved in the incident in Afghanistan. Now he wants to shut my dad up, smear him, whatever. So he sets up a scheme to discredit him."

Julia nodded, rapidly. "That would explain the mysterious accounts in the Caymans I keep hearing about. Maybe."

"So how do we figure out who it is?" Anthony asked.

Bear answered. "Well, we've got two prisoners. Joe Paretsky is in Federal lockup—he was one of the shooters in Bethesda last Tuesday, when you guys were going over to dinner. The one Dylan Paris took down. We've identified him, but not who he's working for, and he's not talking."

"And the other prisoner?" Anthony asked.

"Nick Larsden. He's in the Bellingham City Jail, and the feds are fighting for jurisdiction. They've got him for at least one murder in California, the owner of a campsite just out of Redwood City. He's the guy who was shooting at Mrs. Thompson and Jessica when they tried to cross the border yesterday."

Anthony's eyebrows ran together. "I think that's our guy. Plus, I know a guy in the Bellingham PD."

"Yeah?" Bear said.

Anthony nodded. "Yeah—you know I went embedded as a reporter in Iraq. One of the guys in the platoon I went in with, he works for the corrections department there. Or he did."

"Call him. I think I see a trip to the West Coast in my future."

# CHAPTER SIX
## It's your mother

Carrie. May 5.

**A**s it often was, traffic along Embassy Row headed toward downtown Washington, DC was snarled. Carrie normally needed to feel in control—and preferred to drive herself for that reason—but today she was grateful that one of the Pinkerton security guards was behind the wheel of the black Suburban. She sat in the back seat with Alexandra, fidgeting and nervous.

Another black SUV—the guard had referred to it as a *chase car*—drove closely behind them. Carrie kept looking down at the invitation. Cream paper with gold and black lettering.

*You and your guest are invited to dine with*
*His Highness, Prince George-Phillip*
*at the Embassy of the United Kingdom,*
*4 pm on the Fifth of May, 2014.*

*His Highness*, Prince George-Phillip, was apparently her father. And this invitation felt all too formal to her. Too distant. On the other hand, what else could he have done? Called her up and said, "Hey, this is your birth father. Want to get together?"

Obviously that made no sense. And even though part of her wanted to meet George-Phillip and learn just what had happened between him and her mother—another part just wanted to turn her back. She had nothing to lose by walking away—right now she didn't have a father at all. Not meeting George-Phillip wouldn't change that.

On the other hand, meeting him—that held another kind of risk. A risk of getting hurt again. She'd lost her husband and her father. She didn't want to lose anything else.

But then her eyes fell on her sister. Alexandra. The middle child. She'd never been sure of herself, never had the confidence that Carrie and Julia had, never had that spark of brilliance that Sarah and Jessica had. But one thing she had was strength and loyalty. She wouldn't shy away from any risk. She'd *chosen* that risk, she'd chosen to love a man who was broken by war and trauma. And despite the pain that came with that, she was richer for it.

Carrie closed her eyes. She'd also chosen. Ray had been dead now longer than she'd even known him. Nine short months from the day they met to the day he died. They were the hardest, most difficult and yet the best months of her life. She wouldn't go back and change them. She wouldn't give back *one ounce* of grief and loss if it meant losing even the slightest memory of Ray.

Ray—ever courageous, ever honorable, would have chuckled and pushed her to go on.

So, instead of panicking, or withdrawing into herself, Carrie did the only thing she could, the thing she was fated to do, the thing that defined who she was. She reached out and took Alexandra's hand and squeezed it gently, reassuringly. "Dylan's going to be fine," Carrie said.

"Thanks," Alexandra whispered. "I know. I know he will."

Carrie sat back in her seat and stared into space. Everything was upside down and confused. She thought of the phone call earlier, as she'd been trying to make some order out of the chaos of the condominium. It was the house phone that rang, and she'd rushed to it, not recognizing the 604 area code.

"Hello?" she'd said.

"Carrie, it's your mother."

"Mom?" she had nearly screeched. "What's happening? I saw the news—you're in Canada? Is Jessica okay? What happened to her?"

"Slow down, Carrie," her mother had said, even as the other sisters crowded around Carrie. Then Mother began to speak, but Carrie missed the first few words, because something was *different* about her mother. She sounded—not strained, or panicked. She didn't know what she sounded like.

"... so for now we're just outside of Vancouver, and I think we'll be here for some time. Jessica's in intensive care."

"What happened? Did she get shot? I heard there was some kind of shootout?"

Her mother had sighed. "No. Your sister is very sick, Carrie. She—she got into using meth somehow. She's addicted."

Carrie winced and almost doubled over, involuntarily clutching her stomach with one hand. Julia, alarmed, put her hand on Carrie's shoulder. Carrie waved Julia off, then said, "Mother, how—when— I don't understand."

"It happened this winter, when your father was locked up in his office."

Carrie had gone cold. "He's not my father."

Silence for a moment. Carrie's sisters, Julia, Alexandra, and Sarah, blanched. They all expected the same thing Carrie did—a hysterical rage response.

Instead, her mother had simply said, "No, he's not. Your father is Prince George-Phillip."

Carrie had put her hand to her mouth and sobbed. Then she had whispered, "Why did you lie to us?"

Her mother gave the strangest answer, an answer that made no sense, an answer that she couldn't understand. Her mother had answered, "To save your lives."

Now, hours later, she still didn't understand. And she didn't know if she ever would.

Carrie unconsciously slid down into her seat a little when she saw the two news vans parked in front of the British Embassy, and the crowd of reporters and cameras arrayed along the sidewalk. She knew they couldn't see into the SUV—the tinted windows were so dark you had to press your nose into the glass in order to make out anything. But all the same, the sight of cameras, of reporters—it took her right back.

The driver swung the car into the driveway of the Embassy, making no concessions to the reporters who had to scramble out of the way.

"Jesus Christ," Alexandra muttered, unconsciously echoing Dylan.

The clamor outside the car was crazy. The guard cracked the window, rolling it down just a few inches. He spoke with the Royal Marine who guarded the gate, then a moment later, the gate opened. The SUV and chase car entered the Embassy compound, pulling to a stop in front of a three-story red brick building. Half a dozen Royal Marines in uniform were at the front of the building. Two of them approached the car, one opening the door almost immediately as it came to a stop.

"Doctor Sherman? Mrs. Paris? Come this way, please. Quickly, we're still in sight of the reporters."

Alexandra got out on her side, and Carrie slid across and followed her out. Quickly, they followed the Marine up the steps. Almost one hundred feet behind them, at the fence, she could hear shouting. The reporters called her name.

She hustled inside, entering a well-appointed, air-conditioned room. The anteroom had highly polished marble floors, the center covered with a beautiful Persian carpet. Across the room from her stood Prince George-Phillip, holding the hand of a precociously tall six or eight-year-old with raven hair and blue green eyes. An older version of that girl—Carrie's sister Andrea—stood a few feet away.

Alexandra didn't wait for introductions. She launched herself at Dylan, who gasped as he touched her, his face the expression of a drowning man who'd just gripped a life preserver.

"I missed you," Alexandra sobbed. "God, I missed you."

At the same time, Andrea ran to Carrie and the two women embraced. Carrie gripped Andrea tightly, as if she could somehow know by touch whether or not Andrea was well.

George-Phillip gave Alexandra and Dylan a brief, kind smile. Immediately Carrie liked him better. Then he looked back at Carrie.

"Carrie," he said, tentatively. "I'm George-Phillip."

Carrie's eyes darted to the little girl, then to Andrea.

"You're my father," Carrie said.

He nodded slowly. "I am. I'm so sorry I couldn't tell you before."

She walked closer, as if to study him. "We shook hands the day of my graduation from Columbia."

"We did," he said. "It was one of the proudest days of my life."

Carrie felt as if she were swimming in uncontrollable currents. She'd once thought she was closer to her father than her mother. But so many things made no sense. His remote behavior. His long absences, both traveling and locked up in his office.

She remembered discussing Ray's trial with her mother, and her father saying, *Perhaps we can find a more suitable topic for dis-*

*cussion. I find this entire subject distressful on the day my daughter got married.* She remembered when she found out her father had hired detectives to run background checks on Dylan and his mother. So much never made sense.

Abruptly she said, "I don't know if I'm prepared for any more terrible revelations. It's been a tough week."

He held out a hand. "I understand, Carrie, and I'd like to—I don't even know where to begin."

Carrie took his hand. His hand was warm, and dotted with age spots. His eyes were tired, but they were her eyes. She smiled at him, trying to reassure, and said, "Why don't we start with a drink, then, and we can talk."

Gratitude flashed openly in his eyes. She glanced over her shoulder at Alexandra and Dylan. They'd sunk into a couch, whispering to each other, oblivious to everyone else in the room. Carrie turned back to Andrea and pulled her sister into another embrace.

"I'm so glad you're safe," she whispered. "We were so afraid for you."

Andrea shook in her arms.

After a moment, they broke apart, and she said, "And who is this?"

She knelt down in front of the little girl.

"I'm Jane," the little girl said. She wore a blue dress and patent leather shoes, too formal for a child this young.

*Jane,* Carrie repeated in her mind.

"I like your dress, Jane. I'm Carrie."

"Daddy says we're sisters. You and me and Andea." She stumbled over Andrea's name. "I never had a sister before."

"Well," Carrie said, suddenly stifling a sob. She couldn't force her eyes to stop watering though. She tried. Every time she cried, she thought she'd run out of tears. But there were always more.

"Now you've got a lot of sisters. Now and forever, if—if our father says it's okay."

"I want nothing more in this world," George-Phillip said, his voice low.

"Can I pick you up?" Carrie asked Jane.

Jane nodded, and Carrie stood. She reached out and lifted Jane up and slid her onto her hip. She said, "I've got a little girl too. Though she's a *lot* smaller than you are."

"Smaller? I like that. I'm always the smallest," she said, her voice sounding sad. "What's her name?"

"Rachel," Carrie answered.

George-Phillip smiled and led them into a sunroom. As they walked in, he said to Dylan, "We'll be in here, whenever you two want to join us."

Dylan looked up and said, "Thank you, sir." His voice was rough.

Jane asked, "Is Rachel a sister?"

Carrie smiled and sat down on a wicker couch, keeping the little girl in her lap. "No, she doesn't have any sisters yet. I'm her mommy."

Jane said, "My mommy's in heaven now."

George-Phillip looked stricken, his eyes bleak. He whispered, "Pancreatic cancer."

"I'm so sorry," Carrie said. She looked back at Jane and whispered, "Sometimes sisters can be like mommies too."

Andrea slid in next to her and said to Jane, "It's true. Sometimes they can take you to the zoo. Or give you Band-Aids when you're hurt. Or get you ice cream, and give you hugs, and take care of you when you cry. Sometimes big sisters do things like that."

Andrea gave her a meaningful look, as if to say, *I remember.* Then she said, "Carrie was like that for me when I was little, just like you."

*Goddamn it,* Carrie thought, stifling more tears.

"You know, I never thought I would see you—the three of you—in the same room. If only your mother were here," he said.

Carrie looked up at George-Phillip. "Can you tell me about her?"

George-Phillip tilted his head. "What do you mean?"

Carrie took Andrea's hand in hers without even thinking. "What I mean is ... what we know is a mother who was ... erratic. Mentally ill. Sometimes the rage got so bad she would completely lose it. She'd scream at us, and ... rarely ... would hit us. I want to know why. Why did you fall in love with her? Who was she before ... before all that happened?"

George-Phillip's face took on the bleakest expression she'd ever seen on a man's face. Jane stirred in Carrie's lap and said, "Da, may I go play?"

"Of course, Jane. Let's go find Miss Adriana." He stood, and said, "Excuse me just a moment."

As he walked out of the room, Andrea said, "I'm not sure I care what she was like."

Carrie sighed. "I'm not sure what I want anymore. Except the truth. I want to know the truth. All of it."

"Do you think he'll tell us?"

Carrie shrugged. "As much as anyone else in the world will." Her eyes shifted to the glass and the grounds outside. "So ... please tell me ... how you ended up here anyway."

Andrea shrugged. "Alexandra told Dylan to Google George-Phillip. We did—and so we drove over here. Dylan crashed his car into the gate to distract the guards and I climbed over the back wall."

"It's a good thing you weren't an assassin," Carrie said.

Andrea said, "They caught me before I got to him. But I screamed loud enough he came looking for me."

The door opened, and George-Phillip walked back in. He smiled and said, "Young Dylan and his wife are still sitting on the couch. They love each other very much, don't they?"

Carrie smiled. "They do."

He sat and said, "She reminds me a little bit of her mother too. Though Alexandra does have a look of her father about her."

Carrie glanced at Andrea, then back at George-Phillip. "He raped her, you know. When he found out I wasn't his daughter. He beat her nearly to death, and raped her."

George-Phillip flinched. "I'd have done anything to prevent it," he said. "I didn't know until much later. She named her Alexandra as kind of a poke in the eye. Your mother's a courageous woman, but she's also been trapped in a prison for many years. I tried to persuade her to leave, but she was always convinced Richard would harm one of you, or her brother."

"Luis?" Andrea said.

George-Phillip nodded. "I don't know if it was a real fear or not. But it was enough to keep her entrapped."

"You understand," Carrie said, "how difficult this is? Everything we've ever believed is upside down."

He nodded. "I'll try to give you everything I possibly can. I can't even imagine the difficulty you face."

"When did you meet her?"

He smiled. "We met in February of 1984, just a few weeks after your mother arrived in Washington, DC. I was on assignment here at the Embassy then. Though I didn't live in such luxurious quarters." He said the last with a wry smile. "My office was next to the boiler in the basement back then."

He smiled. "Your mother hosted a dinner party—that's when we met. For a nineteen-year-old, she was incredibly poised. Everyone believed she was older, of course. I remember she captured the attention of everyone there. I thought Colonel Rainsley was going to embarrass himself, to be honest."

"Rainsley was there? Senator Rainsley?"

He nodded. "That's right. Your mother ended up being good friends with Brianna, though I don't think she ever confided the nature of her marriage. But they had music in common."

"And why did you end up involved with a married woman?" Carrie asked.

He sighed. "Of course, that was my downfall. I could see even at that party that something was broken between the two of them. He was so much older than she was, and she was terrified of him. But I had no idea how serious it was. Remember that back then, she was not much older than Andrea."

Fascinated at this view of a mother she'd never really understood, Carrie leaned forward and said, "What ... what was she like?"

George-Phillip smiled, his eyes twinkling. "She was fierce. Passionate. Your mother loved music ... did you know she'd played for the National Youth Orchestra? She smiled, even when she was falling apart inside. She was fiercely protective of you girls. When we first met it was just Julia, of course. What a little rascal. Two years old and full of fire. I think your mother would have gone to hell and back to protect her. Adelina was the strongest woman I've ever known."

Carrie shook her head. "I find that difficult to believe. All of it."

"Can you imagine any other reason she stayed with him all those years? Other than to protect you?"

"Tell me more." Carrie's words were a demand. She felt an urgency to ferret out this woman who she'd never known.

George-Phillip shrugged. "We weren't together very long then. A few short months. Richard spent much of the spring going back and forth from Afghanistan and Pakistan, trying to bury any backlash from the Wakhan massacre before it destroyed him. We took advantage of that. Whenever we were in public—not often—Julia acted as chaperone. I finally rented a studio apartment in Chevy Chase, not far from your condominium. We could meet discreetly there. She was terrified Richard would find out and harm her brother, or harm Julia."

He closed his eyes. His voice shook unevenly as he said the next words, "I married, many years later, but I've never loved anyone the way I loved her. I've regretted it my entire life that I did not just—take her. That I didn't fight hard enough, or strong enough to pull her away from him. When I think about how much he hurt her, how changed she was when I met her again in China, so many years later..."

He shook his head, bringing his hand to his mouth. "I would do anything. *Anything*. To take it back. To protect her."

"Why did you leave? Was it because you found out she was pregnant?" Carrie didn't voice the words, *with me*. But they fell in the room anyway.

George-Phillip shook his head. "No ... Carrie. Adelina broke it off with me without explanation in late April '84. I swear to you, I didn't know you existed until 1996."

"Tell me. When did you see her again?" Carrie's demand was sharp.

George Phillip. May 1996.

By the time Prince George-Phillip got off the airplane in China—commercial, of course—and cleared customs, he'd been en route for more than seventeen hours, thanks to an unnecessary layover in Paris. He was hot and tired and desperately needed a good night's sleep.

That, unfortunately, was not to be. A young woman, perhaps twenty-five, waited for him at the end of the terminal with a cardboard sign discreetly labeled "GP." He'd been told to expect her. Wendy Li was a British citizen, born in Cambridge, but her parents were native Chinese. She spoke fluent Mandarin. Purportedly a protocol officer for the Embassy—she was, in fact, the deputy chief of station for MI6. She was exceptionally young for that role, but the combination of an internal shakeup and her own expertise had catapulted her career forward.

"Hello, Your Highness," she said. "Is this all your baggage?" She directed an assistant to collect the bags. "Come this way."

"Thank you. Miss Li, is it?"

"Yes, sir."

George-Phillip was thirty-three years old, and his actual job in China was to be the chief of station for the MI6 in China—the most senior position he'd held to date. His "official" position was Senior Attaché with diplomatic service, a job with so few specifics that he could do virtually anything he needed. Like Wendy—and anyone else who works for the secretive intelligence organization—he required an official, diplomatic cover for his job, which was, of course, to spy on the Chinese.

It wasn't the glamorous job people would expect. Spying typically involved finding people in sensitive positions, determining their weaknesses, and exploiting them. Sometimes the weaknesses were simple—greed, sexual peccadilloes and other means of turning people against their country. Sometimes they were more complex: people who sold out their country believing they were patriots. The most useful asset MI6 had in the Chinese government was secretly a Christian convert who worked in the Chinese Foreign Ministry. The Chinese government, of course, suppressed Christianity along with all other religions. That oppression gave spies a wedge.

As they got into the chauffeured car, she said, "Forgive me, Highness, we do have one issue. Are you fully up to date on the tensions between China and the US?"

"Yes, unless something happened while I was in the air." She was referring, of course, to the spying scandal erupting in the United States, which was severely straining relations in Beijing. Chinese intelligence operatives had stolen significant nuclear secrets from the United States, and as of yet no one knew the extent of the damage.

"Nothing new, sir. Except the American Ambassador had an extremely ... tense ... meeting with the Chinese premier today. There's some concern that the Chinese may retaliate in some way, so most of the NATO allies and Australia will be attending a large reception this evening at the US Embassy. As a show of solidarity, sir. I'm aware how long you've been in the air—but the Ambassador would like you to attend."

He frowned then said, "All right. I'll need to shower and shave, and someone to press one of my suits. They're certain to be rumpled. And perhaps some coffee." George-Phillip didn't typically drink coffee. But he'd been awake so long now it was necessary.

"Of course, sir."

"Who is the US Ambassador anyway? Isn't there a new one?"

"Richard Thompson, sir. Previously he was the US Ambassador to NATO."

George-Phillip felt a chill. He didn't answer, just murmured, "Hmmmmm."

"Sir? You know him?"

*Damn.* His expression had betrayed him. "I do. But it's been many years. What's your impression?" George-Phillip asked the question just to get her talking so he didn't have to.

"Honestly, sir, something about him ... bothers me. I'm usually a pretty good judge of people. But I can't make him out. He's stone cold."

"Is he married?" George-Phillip didn't breathe after he asked the question.

"Yes, Your Highness. Younger woman, her name is Adelina. They have five children."

"Five? That's quite a lot, isn't it?" *Five? She'd had four more children with him? What the hell?*

"I believe the last two were twins, they were born this April. Confidentially, sir ... I think she's afraid of him."

"His wife?" he asked. He arched an eyebrow, trying to look surprised.

Wendy didn't look fooled. She raised a skeptical eyebrow right back. "Yes. His wife. I think she's afraid of him. You know her too, don't you, sir?"

George-Phillip frowned. "You don't miss very much, do you, Miss Li?"

She shook her head. "Very little. Is there something there we should be worried about?"

George-Phillip grunted. On the one hand, it wasn't an appropriate question for a subordinate to be asking. On the other—she had a point. "No. There might have been, many years ago. But that's long since over."

The look of concern didn't leave Wendy's face. But she wisely chose to steer the conversation away from Adelina. "Thompson has been the Ambassador since last October. It's been a difficult time—with the spying revelations, relations with China and the US are souring rapidly."

"Indeed," George-Phillip said. "Spying is one thing. Nuclear secrets are another. It's difficult to blame the Americans for their response."

"Yes, sir."

Ninety minutes later, George-Phillip and Wendy Li arrived at the US Embassy compound and were cleared through the gate. He felt somewhat refreshed after the shower, but nothing would completely do it other than a lot of sleep. Which he was unlikely to get in the next couple of days. So be it. He had a job to do, and sleep wasn't in the job description.

George-Phillip and Wendy were late, but not too much so. It never hurt to be close to the last to arrive anyway. As he walked into the ballroom in the Embassy, his eyes scanned the room and the sixty or more guests who were crowded in various circles and groupings.

He immediately recognized some faces. Rick Smith, the Australian Ambassador to China, and of course Ambassador Ronald Easton, who stood next to his American counterpart—Richard Thompson. Thompson stood in profile to George-Phillip. His expression was grave as he and Easton spoke. Richard had aged, his hair gone grey in the dozen years since they'd encountered each other. He must be in his mid-forties.

Adelina wasn't standing with Thompson, which was a good thing. After a moment, George-Phillip found her. She was standing near the back wall of the ballroom, talking with a young girl. Adelina's back was to George-Phillip. She looked much the same, her back still well toned, exposed in a backless dress. After five children, her body had changed, of course—broader hips and larger breasts. She was lovely. He froze, unable to focus clearly as he looked at the young woman.

*Fourteen*, he guessed. Curly brown hair, large pretty eyes. Julia. She wouldn't remember him, of course—she'd been a mere toddler when he last saw her. She'd turned into a beautiful young woman.

For a moment he gave into a fantasy that she was *his* daughter, that he and Adelina could have had children. But of course, that was impossible. *Five* children. He wondered if she'd finally been emotionally seduced by her husband.

For the last decade and more his mother had constantly harped at him. Get married. Have a child. But he'd kept a false hope, all along, that one day she would leave him, that a miracle would happen and he would be with the woman he loved. But at the moment he saw her again for the first time, he didn't feel that longing, he didn't feel that love. What he felt was *anger* and *hurt* and *grief* he hadn't imagined he was capable of.

"Your Highness! Welcome to Beijing."

Startled, George-Phillip averted his eyes from Adelina and Julia, only to come face to face with Ronald Easton, the US Ambassador, and Richard Thompson.

Automatically, a smile lit across George-Phillip's face, though it was no more sincere than the friendly face Thompson showed.

"Ambassador Easton! Ambassador Thompson! A pleasure to see both of you again!"

Easton smiled. "Prince George-Phillip, I'm pleased to have you here. So you know Richard?"

Forcing his thoughts away from Adelina, he replied. "Indeed. Ambassador Thompson once hosted me for a *very* interesting dinner at his condominium in Washington, DC."

Julia was walking away from Adelina now. Likely leaving, she was young to attend a diplomatic ball of this nature. Adelina turned around and her eyes locked on his. The shock was obvious. Her eyes widened and watered, and a hand involuntarily covered her mouth. Almost instantly, however, a mask descended on her face, her hand dropped to her side, and she looked away.

"Perhaps, then, you can settle a friendly wager for us," Easton said. He stank of whiskey. "Richard here maintains that it was the advances of John Hawkins on ship building that allowed for English settlement of the Americas. But I have the correct answer—that it was the defeat of the Spanish Armada in 1588. What do you say?"

Easton was a boor. But he was the Ambassador. "Both answers are equally true, Ambassador—the defeat of the Armada would not have taken place had it not been for the improvement in ship building."

"Spoken like a true diplomat, Your Highness," Thompson said. His eyes were cold and his voice low. "You used a lot of words and avoided the question entirely. Bravo."

Thompson was decidedly unfriendly. Did he suspect George-Phillip's affair with his wife? Or was it something else entirely? Had he somehow guessed George-Phillip's involvement in the investigation of the massacre at Wakhan? Whatever it was, even Easton noticed, his face sobering as he heard Thompson's tone.

The three men engaged in small talk, maddening small talk, as George-Phillip kept his eyes everywhere *except* on Richard Thompson's wife, who moved from group to group like a good hostess: entertaining, friendly but not too friendly, a smile always on her face.

Finally, George-Phillip managed to offer his excuses and step away from the two Ambassadors. Unable to face any more meaningless conversations, he stepped into the hallway, needing to have a few moments of solitude. His eyes scanned the hallway looking for the water closet.

He was almost at the end of the hallway when he heard her voice behind him.

"George-Phillip."

He froze, his spine rigid. He couldn't show his face. He *couldn't*. He closed his eyes and took a deep breath. "Adelina."

He heard her footsteps, heels clicking on the marble floor, as she approached. He slowly turned around.

"I ... I..." her voice trailed off.

"You miss me?" he asked. "You're sorry for breaking it off with no explanation? You're sorry you broke my heart? What is it?"

Her eyes filled with tears. "I'm sorry," she whispered.

His shoulders sagged. "What am I to say?"

"Just ... tell me you're well."

George-Phillip felt his eyebrows twitch, and he narrowed one eye, trying to hold in the wave of emotion that flooded him. He looked up at the ceiling, unable to control his grief. "I must go, Adelina. Please ... just..."

"I didn't have any choice." The pain in her voice was palpable.

George-Phillip gritted his teeth with an anger he didn't know he contained. "You didn't have a choice? I would have protected you, Adelina. I would have protected your daughter."

He turned and nearly staggered down the hall. She ran after him, calling his name. *There*. A door labeled *Men*. He pushed it open, stepped inside, and leaned against the wall.

# CHAPTER SEVEN
## Don't patronize me.

Carrie. May 5.

**L**ooking back, Carrie vaguely remembered the night George-Phillip referred to. She'd only attended two or three diplomatic functions in her eleventh year. But she had been a poised eleven-year-old, and her mother had given her permission to accompany Julia for the first hour of the reception. She must have missed him by minutes.

Did she remember seeing George-Phillip? She couldn't recall. The room had mostly been filled with adults, almost all of them shorter than she'd been, and she had stayed close to the wall at the side of the room, Julia at her side, until their mother sent her away. They'd been in Beijing for months by that time, but that was the first time she'd been accompanied by armed guards.

"I remember the reception you're talking about," she said. "The twins were born a month or two before that, and Mom had been—especially difficult. It's not that she doesn't love the twins—but I don't think she'd planned on them. I don't think she'd planned on *any* children really."

George-Phillip nodded. "No. But she still looked on all of you as gifts from God."

"She didn't act like it," Andrea said. Her tone was bitter.

"No. But I don't think you realize how much it cost her."

"How could I?" she riposted. "I don't know her. She never talked to me. She sent me away."

George-Phillip closed his eyes. "Of course you don't. I'm sorry."

"*Tell me,*" Andrea said. "She couldn't. So you have to."

He nodded and began speaking again. "I didn't see her again for several weeks. The diplomatic community is small, of course, but not so small that you see people routinely unless they are friends. And Richard Thompson and I were never friends."

"I can imagine," Carrie said.

His lips turned up in a wry smile. "Anyway. It was ... four or so weeks later, at the end of May, and the United States Embassy was holding a service for Memorial Day." He paused a moment. "That's not a holiday we have in the United Kingdom, but our Remembrance Day in November is similar. In any event, it's fairly common for allied Embassies to attend such functions, especially in a country like China where the diplomatic community is so isolated. So I made arrangements to represent the United Kingdom."

He leaned back, his face thoughtful, and said, "I knew, of course, that your mother would likely be at the ceremony. And I knew I needed to stay away. But I couldn't. As soon as I arrived, I ran into Richard and Adelina. It was a bad day for her. I'd never seen her so lost, her eyes searching everywhere, her hands twitching."

Carrie spoke in a soft, urgent voice. "It was awful. I remember that day. Julia had somehow gotten spots of bleach on her dress, and Mother screamed at her. It was garbled and confusing and ... frightening, really. Then when our father came into the apartment, she went suddenly silent. Whispering at Julia in an urgent tone to change her dress, to get into something more appropriate, to *hurry.*"

George-Phillip shook his head. "She was terrified," he murmured.

"I think so," Carrie said. "But *we* experienced it as crazy."

Carrie could almost feel the pain and regret radiating from George-Phillip as he closed his eyes, not responding to her words. After all, pain and regret were the emotions she was most familiar with. It was easy to recognize a kindred spirit in pain. She continued. "Anyway, she calmed down a little once Julia was dressed and we were on our way. But ... you know what I remember?"

Oh *Christ*, she thought. She started to shake a little.

"What is it?" George-Phillip asked.

"He kept leaning over in the car. As he was driving. And he'd whisper. I thought it was romantic whispers, you know? She kept ... shivering, and jerking away from him. She had goose bumps on the back of her neck. All I could think of was how angry I was because she'd treated Julia like dirt and here she was..." Carrie closed her eyes. She remembered what she'd thought. The words had come unbidden to her mind, *I hate her. I hate her. I hate her.*

"You couldn't have known," George-Phillip said. "You were a child."

She sighed. "I know. But I still wish I'd understood. I wish I could take back how much we all hated her. She didn't deserve it. Tell me what else happened."

George-Phillip nodded. His eyes were a thousand miles away. "I ended up seated next to your family—Adelina in between me and Richard. You were on the other side of him."

Carrie thought back, trying to remember if she'd known George-Phillip then. She vaguely remembered a man sitting next to her mother, but it was maddening really, to know her father had been *right there* and she hadn't realized. Of course the adults hadn't deigned to actually introduce the children to anyone. The ceremony had gone on forever—she remembered feeling tired and frustrated, and whispering to Julia, "Will this *never end?*" Of course she would never have said those words to her mother or father—*damn it!* She kept doing that. Richard Thompson *wasn't* her father and she didn't have a clue what to call him. She missed George-Phillip's next few words, but brought herself back to the present as quickly as she could.

"...I could tell something was very seriously wrong. But I couldn't *do* anything. So we sat there for the first forty-five minutes of what seemed like an excruciatingly long ceremony. Finally, Richard was called up to speak."

Carrie nodded. She remembered that. It had been blisteringly hot. By the time Richard went up to speak, her dress was sticking to her back, and even with the broad floppy hat she wore, her skin was starting to feel distinctly hot.

"While he was up there—it was no more than twenty minutes—I was able to talk with her very briefly. Even though I'd only just found out about you, Carrie, I still loved her. And I was worried. Deeply worried."

"Why?"

"She didn't sound like herself. The woman I fell in love with was—vivacious. Energetic. Even in the midst of her awful marriage, she was still inherently an optimistic, cheerful and spiritual person. But when I talked with her at the Embassy, and again that Memorial Day, it was clear she was profoundly damaged. Her voice and inflection were slower. Tired. Sad." His voice dropped to a whisper. "I hated seeing her like that. She was such a kind and caring soul, to see her abused in such a way as to break her spirit ... I wanted to kill Richard Thompson."

Carrie closed her eyes. It was too much. Too much to imagine the kind of life her mother had. Carrie had undergone the most excruciating pain she could imagine in the last nine months with the loss of her husband. But at least Carrie still had her sisters. She still had Ray's memory. She had his best friend.

But Adelina Thompson had lost *everything*. And not for nine months. Not for nine years. She'd been forced to marry Richard Thompson *thirty-three years* ago.

Carrie felt a tear run down her cheek. She whispered, "I've hated her all my life. I've always believed my father was the sane one. I've always believed she was *hateful*, but it wasn't that at all. She was *tortured*."

Andrea stood up and began pacing.

Memories kept washing over Carrie. Julia shouting, "I want *Daddy!*" Her mother collapsing on the sidewalk in Calella, and their terror until the ambulance came. Her mother breaking down after Maria Clawson had begun writing about the family, week after week, posting vicious blogs about Julia and both of her parents, derailing her father's posting to Russia. She remembered her mother lying on the couch, her face red and puffy, on Valentine's of 1990. Carrie stifled a sob. She'd thrown a *tantrum* because her mother wouldn't take her to the church Valentine's party.

She knew about the harm her mother had done. The freak outs and the pain and the screaming and the horrible things she'd said. But she also remembered her mother rushing to her defense when Ray's mom had gone off into crazy town after the accident. She remembered finding herself back at the condo after Ray's death, unable to understand how she'd even gotten there, and her mother lying down beside her and holding her as she cried for what seemed like days.

"If I never do anything else in my life," she said, "I'll make it up to her. I will." She looked up at Andrea. Andrea nodded in agreement.

Andrea. May 5.

"What happens with us?" Andrea asked. As she asked the question, she waved her hand in the general direction of George-Phillip.

"What do you mean?" Carrie responded.

George-Phillip leaned forward in his seat and said, "Perhaps I could…"

Carrie nodded in response. Andrea waited to hear what he would say.

"Obviously I've been … no father to you at all. Either one of you. And I know there's nothing I can do to go back and change that. All the same though … I would like to get to know you both. I would like to … try … somehow … to make amends to you both. It is my intention to retire from my position once the current unpleasantness is over. Perhaps you'll consider coming to London?"

Carrie slowly nodded. "It's possible. I have work commitments, of course, so timing might be challenging."

Andrea shrugged, not knowing how to answer. "I don't know. I'd have to speak with my grandmother about it." Her response was automatic, but a stab of concern and worry hit her. She didn't know where her relationship with *Abuelita* stood. Her grandmother had lied to her. And not about something small. "I don't know what to think anymore," she continued. "No one—not my mother, my grandmother, not you—no one has ever told me the truth. About who I was, or why I wasn't wanted. Why should I believe you now? And what does all this have to do with why someone tried to kill me?"

George-Phillip nodded. "That's a very good question."

Irritated, Andrea said, "Don't patronize me."

He shook his head in response. "I don't mean to. It doesn't all make sense."

"Tell us what you know. Or what you guess."

"All right. First, I believe your kidnapping was originally planned by Leslie Collins, the Director of Operations of the Central Intelligence Agency. Not an official operation, you understand. But on his own."

"Why?" Andrea asked.

"I think he believed that your presence in the country, and specifically the blood tests, would lead to questions which would ultimately reveal what happened in Wakhan."

"That makes no sense it all."

"It does if you know—as he does—that I was responsible for the original investigation conducted by the British government. You see, Collins and Richard Thompson, along with the current Saudi intelligence minister, were the three prime movers in delivering chemical weapons to the Afghan militia. The three of them have been trading favors and boosting each other's careers ever since. But their cooperation depended on secrecy."

Carrie sat forward. "And you've known about it? All this time? Wait ... since when?"

"1984."

Carrie slumped back in her seat. "Why did ... if you knew he was responsible for it, why didn't you report it then?"

"I did. My official report directly addressed that, and recommended that the issue be brought up with the United Nations Security Council. I was overruled."

"I don't understand why."

"Carrie, it was the Cold War. The Soviets had invaded Afghanistan, and their occupation was brutal. At the time, the United States and the United Kingdom used Wakhan as a tremendous propaganda tool against the Soviets."

Andrea didn't get it. "Okay … so after I escaped the kidnapping … that brought media attention to the family. It seems like it would make it more likely all of it would come out."

"Exactly," George-Phillip said. "Once you escaped, it threw a huge wrench in the works. We intercepted some phone calls last Friday. As far as I can tell, Collins decided the only move left to make was to completely discredit Thompson. He had an agent planted in your Diplomatic Security Service, who placed the drugs and money in the condo and launched the attack against you. As you may know, someone fired shots at my home at nearly the exact same time. At me, rather."

Andrea sat back, shocked. "I didn't know that."

"Right. Now the question is, what is their next move? Thompson's role in Wakhan is public now, thanks to *The Guardian*. But whoever planted the story adjusted just enough of the truth to also tarnish me. The way *The Guardian* reports it, I was part of the cover-up. I believe Collins was likely responsible for that as well. Again, because it attacks the credibility of anyone who can go after him."

Carrie said, "I don't see how he could possibly have done all this in just a few days."

George-Phillip responded, "It isn't possible. I suspect he began planning it and putting it together the moment your father was raised as a replacement for Secretary of Defense."

"But that was only three weeks ago."

"No, Carrie, it was many months ago. The President knew the former Secretary was very ill. Your father was approached about the job in December of 2013."

"Six months ago." Carrie's face was grim as she said the words.

Andrea said, "Then who tried to kill our mother? Someone chased her to the border and shot at her there. Collins? Why?"

George-Phillip leaned his head in his hands. "I'm not sure. The news media is speculating there's some kind of drug war connection. Perhaps Collins thought he could reinforce that narrative? The shooter was captured, by the way."

Carrie said, "Right. Nick Larsden. Bear and Anthony were discussing that earlier, they want to go out to Washington to see if they can question him."

"Bear and Anthony?"

"Bear Wyden—he's with Diplomatic Security. And Anthony Walker is a reporter with *The Washington Post*." As Carrie said the words, her face flushed a little. Just a tiny bit. But enough it caught Andrea's attention. George-Phillip did not appear to notice, and Andrea thought it best to not say anything.

"I know Walker," George-Phillip said. "He interviewed me a couple of years ago. I rather liked him."

Andrea said, "Okay, so this Collins guy tried to have me and my mother killed. And you. He wants to burn the house down before anyone gets wind he was involved in this massacre. So how do we get ahead of him?"

George-Phillip's brow furrowed. "I think we need to prove, publicly, that he was involved."

"Won't that look like it's just defensive?" Andrea asked. "That you or ... Richard Thompson ... are trying to muddy the waters?"

"It might," George-Phillip said. "But the report I wrote was unequivocal, and the evidence implicating Collins was fairly clear."

"That report needs to be publicized."

"I'm afraid it's highly classified. I would need to consult with the Prime Minister before releasing it."

"Can you do that?" Carrie asked.

"Yes," George-Phillip responded. "But first, I believe dinner should be ready. Why don't we gather your sister and brother-in-law, and we'll dine."

Andrea nodded. She was famished and needed to rest a little. She still didn't understand all of what was happening. But tendrils of trust were beginning to grow. George-Phillip seemed sincere. And the truth was, she *wanted* to believe him. She was tired of being hurt. She was tired of carrying around the knowledge that her supposed *father* never wanted her.

A few minutes later, Alexandra and Dylan joined them in the large dining room around a large table. As they took their seats, Dylan's eyes darted back and forth between George-Phillip and his daughters.

"Wait a minute, I just thought of something. If he's your dad," Dylan said, waving a hand in George-Phillip's direction. He grinned. "Wouldn't that make the two of you ... Princesses?"

"Dylan," Carrie said. "That's ... ridiculous."

"It's not really," George-Phillip said. "I'm styled Prince because my grandfather was George VI. But I'm extremely far outside of the line of succession. Jane is not considered a *Princess*, but she will inherit the title of Duchess. I'm truly not certain where the two of you will fall. To some extent that will be up to Her Majesty to decide when we make your parentage public. You'll certainly want to come to London."

Andrea slowly shook her head. "Neither of us are citizens of the United Kingdom."

George-Phillip smiled. "I promise you, we will sort that out. I'm not sure the time is right to make it public, however."

"Why not?" Dylan asked.

"I want to ensure that you are all safe first. Andrea and Dylan, I believe you should both remain here for the time being, at least until we can sort out whether or not you'll be charged in relation to the attack on the condominium."

Andrea nodded. That made sense.

"Carrie—my understanding is that you've lost your Diplomatic Security protection?"

She nodded.

"Quietly then, for now, I intend to inform the President that the two of you are my children. And I'm going to request that you be provided official protection until all of this is resolved. I may be able to obtain assistance from the Special Escort Group as well, but they'll need clearance."

"Thank you," Carrie responded.

The remainder of the evening seemed to Andrea to be almost ... normal. Whatever that was. For the first time since leaving Spain, Andrea found herself laughing and enjoying herself. After dinner, they moved to the parlor, where Jane snuggled in Carrie's lap as they all talked. George-Phillip told them about his late wife Anne, and Carrie told him about Ray. For a little while, Andrea found herself feeling the warmth of a real family, no matter how odd it was.

George-Phillip sent Jane off to bed at eight. A few minutes later, Carrie said, "I'll need to get going too. It's not really fair leaving Rachel with Julia this long. But I wonder ... George-Phillip ... perhaps Alexandra can stay here with Dylan?"

Alexandra flashed a grateful smile at her, and George-Phillip assented. Soon after, the party broke up, and Andrea returned to her room on the second floor, overlooking the grass she'd run across to break into this building just a day ago.

She rummaged in her bag, pulling out one of the throwaway cell phones she and Dylan had purchased a few days before. She turned out the light and got into bed, then sent text messages to Luis and then Sarah.

A response from Sarah came almost immediately.

**Hey, what r u up to? Are you at the Embassy?**

Andrea responded, **Tired. Still here. Safe. Carrie is on her way back to the condo.**

**Sarah: I'm not there. Snuck by the guards, I'm at Eddie's.**

Andrea smiled. Eddie was Sarah's boyfriend, a muscular emergency medical technician who was working his way through med school at George Washington University.

**Andrea: Good! Have you heard from Mother? Or Jessica?**

**Sarah: Jessica's awake and recovering. Mom's weird.**

**Andrea: How?**

**Sarah: She's nice. I don't get it. I don't get her.**

**Andrea: We've learned a lot from GP. I think he still loves her.**

**Sarah: Details?**

Andrea filled in some of the details George-Phillip had related. As she was typing out the story on the tiny cell phone keys, she was concentrating so hard she didn't notice the lock turning behind her.

**Andrea: So, GP thinks it's Collins who sent the attackers. And that we might still**

Andrea barely had a second to move when she sensed, rather than saw, the door open behind her. She jumped up, tangled in the blankets, but she was too late. Her vision went black, spotted with stars, when a heavy fist hit the back of her neck. She fell forward on the mattress then suddenly felt her own pillow shoved against the back of her head. A knee pressed into the small of her back, the weight of a heavy man on top of her. She struggled to throw him off, pushing to the left, then the right.

Then, a voice. Near her left ear, muffled by the pillow, the voice said in a contorted tone, "This is a gift from your *father*."

A crushing pain in her back as the man kneed her in the spine. She tried to scream, but the mattress was pressed against her mouth, the pillow crushing her head. She struggled, her hands grasping for something, anything.

Her hand closed on something. It was metal, cylindrical. A *pen?*

She closed her fist around it and swung downward, as forcefully as she could.

The man howled as the pen connected, gouging into his skin. She pulled back and hit him again, then saw stars when he pummeled her.

"Run away," he said. "Run fast, or you'll die."

Then he was gone, the door shutting behind him. She heard footsteps receding down the hall, and she curled up, gasping for air, her heartbeat racing, the pulse whooshing in her ears.

Whoever it was had a key. Had George-Phillip sent them? Was it all a lie, and he just wanted to lull her into trusting him? Was there something else?

She became aware of a repeated buzzing. Vibrating.

The *phone*. It was silenced, but vibrating. She grabbed for it, pulling up the messages.

**Sarah: You still there? Details?**

**Sarah: Andrea? Are you okay?**

**Sarah: Andrea! Call me!**

The phone showed two missed calls from Sarah's number. She dialed without thinking.

"Hello? Andrea? Are you okay?"

"No," she gasped. "Someone attacked me. In the room."

"Holy shit," Sarah said.

Her mind racing, Andrea knew she had to leave. Right now. "I've got to wake up Dylan—wait..."

She stopped. Dylan was still wanted by the feds because of the attack on the condo. One of the attackers had been a federal agent after all. He was safe here, with Alexandra.

"No ... he'll be safe here. Can you ... can you get a car? Can you come get me? I need to find a place to hide."

"Where? I'm on my way."

"There's a park across the street from the Embassy. Let me know when you're close. I'm going to have to sneak out somehow."

"Be there soon, sis. I love you. Stay safe."

"I will," Andrea said.

Just to be on the safe side, she pushed and pulled, blocking the doorway with the heavy bed. Then she began to gather her bag, with the cash, spare phones, fake ID and Visa gift cards. She began to get dressed. It was time to go back into hiding.

Then she waited. One minute turned into five, and five into twenty. Thirty-three minutes after she'd called Sarah, her phone vibrated again.

Text message.

**Sarah: Five minutes away.**

That was it. Andrea came to her feet and threw on the backpack. She unlatched the window and opened it up. A few feet from the window, a long metal gutter ran to the ground. Leaning out the window, she grasped the gutter, then let her body swing onto it. Slowly she slid to the ground.

There would still be guards out here. It was about seventy feet to the fence, which stood in the shadow of a line of trees. But the darkness wouldn't do her any good—she was certain the Royal Marines guarding the place had night vision equipment. She'd just have to run.

She took a deep breath then sprinted for the line of trees. The good news was they weren't expecting anyone to try to *escape*.

She was halfway there when she heard a dog barking, then another. Fifteen more feet and she was under the trees, then fifteen more before she reached the tree closest to the fence. She took a running leap and grabbed a branch and pulled herself up. She slid up the trunk, reaching for another branch.

Shouting, and footfalls. A dog, and a man, running toward the fence. A shout. "Who goes there!"

She pulled herself up another branch, then another. She was above the top of the fence now. As quickly as she could, she stood on a branch that leaned toward the fence, and grabbed another one above her head. She worked her way out the branch.

"Stop!" A shout from below. A guard. Two of them, and more coming.

She didn't have time. She leapt, grabbing the top of the fence and flipping over, then slid down the fence, coming to rest on the outside, facing the two Marines.

"Tell the Prince I'm sorry," she said. "But it's not safe." Then she ran.

She ran through the brush, headed toward Massachusetts Avenue as quickly as she could. She could see heavy traffic moving up and down the street. It was close to midnight, she thought. Finally she reached the street. A gap in traffic—she ran through it, stopping on the double yellow line. Horns blasted at her as drivers crossed by her in both directions, then another gap, and she was across. She heard shouts across the street, and a siren in the distance.

Then she heard Sarah's voice. "Andrea! Over here!"

She turned that way. Twenty yards away, the park was dominated by a memorial, a stone wall with an oddly disembodied head attached to it. She saw the name *Khalil Gibran* as she ran toward Sarah, who was comically straddling a huge Harley Davidson motorcycle. Her tiny legs barely reached the gearshift, and the helmet she wore seemed badly oversized.

"Are you kidding me?" Andrea shrieked. "How did you even drive that thing?"

"Can you drive one?"

"Yeah. Slide back!"

Sarah handed her another helmet off the back. "It's Eddie's," she said. "He kinda doesn't know I took his bike. I left him a note. Let's go! I hear sirens!"

Andrea got the helmet fastened and straddled the bike. She cranked it, the machine roaring to life underneath her.

"Ready?" Andrea asked. At Sarah's nod, Andrea eased the bike into the traffic, headed north away from the Embassy.

"Where are we going?" Sarah shouted.

Andrea paused for just a second. Then she said, "Want to come with me to see Mom and Jessica? I've got questions I need answered."

Sarah thought for just a second. Then she shouted. "Hell, yes!"

Andrea nodded. "Let's go!"

# CHAPTER EIGHT
# Rogue

Anthony. May 6.

"**I think** you should let me do the talking," Bear said, his voice low. "I'm a cop. I know these guys, even if I don't know them personally."

Anthony shook his head as he eased the rental car into the parking station of the Whatcom County Sheriff's Department. "Listen—you may know cops, but I know Sergeant Coyle."

"How?" Bear asked.

"81st Brigade Combat Team. Coyle was National Guard, gunner on a Bradley Fighting Vehicle. I was embedded with his unit. It was my first overseas assignment."

"Yeah? What year?"

"2004. They lost a lot of guys during their tour there. I spent three months humping around Iraq with Coyle's company."

"Gotcha. Okay, you do the talking."

Anthony nodded, reaching to turn the key to the off position. He pulled the key out and stuck it in his pocket. "I've kept in touch with those guys over the years. Coyle went back again in 2009."

Anthony got out of the car. It was chilly out, and the sun wasn't up yet. Their flight had arrived at Bellingham International Airport at 6 am after a flight featuring vomit-worthy turbulence, and then Bear had insisted on a search for a newspaper stand. He still didn't feel completely steady as he locked the car and crossed the street, Bear beside him.

At the front, Anthony opened the door for Bear, who walked in and immediately flashed a badge at the cop at the entrance. "Bear Wyden. US Diplomatic Security Service. This is my partner, Anthony Walker. We're here to see Sergeant Coyle."

The cop at the desk, who looked not a day older than 18, appeared rattled when Bear mentioned DSS. *Good move*, Anthony thought. The young cop picked up the phone on his desk and dialed.

Five minutes later a door opened to the rear of the lobby, and a large man, completely bald, walked out. He wore the brown uniform of a sheriff's deputy.

"Walker!" he shouted. He walked over and grabbed Anthony in a bear hug. Anthony returned the hug, slapping Coyle on the back. "Get in here!" Coyle said. The kid at the desk looked bewildered.

Two minutes later, Coyle had ushered the two men to his desk and put two cups of coffee in front of them without asking. He leaned close enough to Anthony that he could smell the pungent tang of Coyle's chewing tobacco.

"First things first," Anthony said. "How's Rogue?"

Coyle shook his head. "Shit. He's not good. He was in the VA hospital for a couple months earlier this year. He got in a fistfight with a cop."

Anthony shook his head. During the tour in 2004, Rogue—his actual name was Manfred, of all things—had been the youngest member of the unit, at seventeen years old. His mother had to give him written permission to join the National Guard. Six months into the deployment, he'd been riding in the back of a hummer when it hit an IED—an *improvised explosive device*. The incident had earned Anthony the trust of the soldiers in the platoon. While they fanned out in a protective circle around the Humvee to fend off attacking insurgents, Anthony dropped his camera in the dirt, bandaged Rogue, then held his hand keeping him calm while the insurgents were shooting at them. He'd never forget the moment Sergeant Mumsford walked up to him, balled a fist and tapped him on the chest. "You may be a reporter but ... that was okay, man."

Unfortunately, Rogue's extensive injuries required immediate massive painkillers. Morphine, and later valium in the hospital, Oxycontin on his return to the states, and when the Army cut that off, he moved on to illegally purchased drugs. When he got caught, the Army threw him out with a bad conduct discharge, which made him ineligible for veterans' benefits.

Mumsford—by then retired—and Coyle contacted Anthony, which resulted in a front page profile of Rogue and how he'd been screwed by the Army. His veterans' benefits were restored, but his psychological health was still a disaster.

"Oh, man," Anthony responded. "How'd he stay out of jail?"

Coyle shook his head and jerked a thumb toward his face. "I know the guy. We talked it out, no charges pressed, but we drove him down to the VA and checked him in. He'd said several times he wanted to kill himself."

"Jesus," Anthony said. He wished there was something he could do for the poor kid.

"All right. So what's the scoop about this guy Larsden? Why do you need to see him? Why does everybody else on earth want him?"

Anthony and Bear looked at each other. Bear shrugged. Anthony said, "All right, this has got to stay close, Coyle, okay? People's lives are on the line."

"Go for it."

"Did you hear the news last week? When the Secretary of Defense's daughter was kidnapped? Then his house got blown up, and his daughter's condo attacked, and now this guy here is your suspect for shooting at his wife?"

Coyle nodded.

"We're trying to track down who he's working for."

"News said it was rival drug lords or some crap like that."

Anthony shook his head. "You of all people know how the news gets things wrong."

Coyle nodded, thoughtfully. It had taken months before anyone in the unit had trusted Anthony, primarily because previous reporters they'd worked with got so many facts wrong.

"If it isn't drug lords, who is it?"

Bear leaned forward and said, "You know who I am?"

"Diplomatic Security. State Department, right?"

Bear nodded. "We're pretty sure the person behind all this works for a three letter agency."

Coyle's eyes widened. "Are you serious? It's a fed?" He looked at Anthony for confirmation.

Anthony nodded. "CIA."

"All right. So the FBI's going to be here at ten am to question him. So you've got until eight, then I need you out of here. All right? I kinda want to keep my job."

Anthony sighed in relief. Finally they might get some answers. Coyle stood and led them down the hall. Halfway down, he opened a door.

"You two can wait in here. We'll have him here in 5 minutes."

So they waited. Bear laid the newspaper on the table with the banner face down then sat down in one of the four small wood chairs arrayed around a table. He leaned the chair back against the wall, crossed his arms over his chest, and closed his eyes. Anthony felt unreasonable irritation. How could he possibly go to sleep that easily? Instead, he stood, bouncing on the balls of his feet and pacing. The room didn't look like he would have expected—a large one-way glass mirror. Instead, high in the ceiling, a black bubble was mounted in the ceiling—a camera.

After two minutes, Bear said, "Anthony, chill. You don't wanna be all nervous when Larsden gets in here. You're in command of the situation. Not the perp."

Anthony intellectually recognized the good sense of Bear's statement, but emotionally he was still tense. He wanted answers. He wanted to know who was gunning for Carrie and her family. Larsden had those answers.

His brow furrowed. Interesting that his mind had focused in on *Carrie* and her family.

Not that he disliked Carrie. He didn't. And she *was* the caretaker of what seemed to be an infinite number of sisters. But she was also a fairly recent widow, which made her off limits, and the subject of an ongoing investigation, which made her doubly off limits, and seriously what was he doing thinking about her when he was supposed to be thinking about—

The door opened. Coyle stepped back in the room, his arm cuffed around the bulging upper arm of a large man with a severe crew cut. The man—Nick Larsden, he presumed—had a network of tattoos scrawled up and down his arms. *Interesting*, Anthony thought. He recognized the US Army Special Forces motto— *De oppresso liber*—tattooed on Larsden's upper arm. But Larsden hadn't been Special Forces. In fact, he'd been a personnel clerk. Maybe that would be a wedge. A two-tour combat veteran like Coyle wouldn't think much of that either.

"Sit down," Coyle said. To emphasize his point, he pushed Larsden down into one of the chairs. Once Larsden was sitting,

Coyle unlocked one handcuff then locked it to the steel table. Only after that ritual was complete did he say, *"Mister* Larsden." His emphasis on the word Mister was a little ominous. "Allow me to introduce my colleagues from Washington, DC, Misters Wyden and Walker."

"Are you fuckin' serious?" Larsden said. "Is that like Laurel and Hardy?"

Bear leaned forward and slammed a fist on the table with a crash that hurt Anthony's ears. "You don't want to mess with me. I'm with the Diplomatic Security Services, and my normal interrogations are with al-Qaeda trained killers, not two-bit washed up personnel clerks like you."

Larsden immediately tensed up, his face turning red. "I ain't no personnel clerk—"

"Shut up!" Bear roared.

Anthony kept absolutely still. He'd never seen a police interrogation before, other than on television. He didn't have any gauge of whether or not Bear's methods were conventional or not. But the room went absolutely silent.

Bear leaned forward and said, "I want to make things absolutely clear to you, shitbag. The woman you were taking potshots at was the wife of the Secretary of Defense of the United States. Do you understand what I'm saying?"

Bear flipped the newspaper over. Right on the front page was a full-color photo of Richard and Adelina Thompson, underneath the headline, "ASSASSIN SHOOTS AT SECRETARY OF DEFENSE'S WIFE." Underneath that, in smaller but still bold letters, "Adelina Thompson demands political asylum in Canada."

"Motherfucker," Larsden muttered. "No one said she was ... what the hell?"

"You're mixed up in some bad shit, Larsden. This is way over your head. What were they offering you? Fifty thousand? A million? Whatever it was, it's not worth the electric chair."

Larsden jerked in his chair. "Electric chair! Hell no, I didn't hit her, she got away, right?"

Bear shouted, "Her teenage daughter's in the hospital, shitbag!"

Anthony didn't say a word. Technically what Bear said was true. Jessica Thompson was in the hospital, though not of a gunshot wound. Larsden didn't need to know that.

"What do you want from me?" Larsden demanded.

"I want to know who you're working for. I know you didn't think this stupid operation up yourself."

"I don't know!" he cried.

Bear leaned over the table, shouting in his face, "You better know, asshole!"

"Bear," Anthony said.

"WHAT?" Bear shouted at Anthony.

"Maybe I can ask him some questions?"

Bear shouted, "We're not asking him *shit* until he gives me a name!" But even as he shouted, apparently out of control, his right eye winked at Anthony, just out of Larsden's sight.

Christ, Bear was a hell of an actor.

"Seriously, let me try," Anthony said.

"If he doesn't talk he's *dead*," Bear shouted. "Do you know what they do to people in prison who kill little girls?"

"I'll talk!" Larsden said. "I'll tell you whatever you want to know. But I never met Oz! I don't know his name!"

Bear whirled toward Larsden. "Oz? Who the hell is Oz?"

"I don't know," Larsden said. "English, or maybe Irish. Real bastard. This job was supposed to be a simple bounty, going after a couple of fugitives. Then when I caught up with them, it turned into murder. And the bastard said if I didn't follow through, he'd make sure *I* ended up dead."

Anthony said in a calm voice, "So you decided to murder a woman and her child to save your own skin?"

"Wouldn't you?" Larsden said. "No bullshit. I took the job, but I didn't know it was going to turn into all this."

"What was the payoff?" Anthony asked.

"One million," Larsden replied. "When he announced I had to kill them to keep them from crossing the border, I told him he had to make it three. He didn't even blink."

Bear said, "Did you meet this *Oz* in person?"

"No," Larsden replied. "Phone call only. An old Army buddy put me in touch with him."

"*What* old Army buddy?" Bear asked.

"Marky Lovecchio. I knew him in Germany."

Anthony leaned in. "How many jobs have you done for this guy?"

"Oz? This was the first one. And let me tell you, I'm regretting it."

"Little late for that," Bear said. "You should have thought of that before you took out a rifle and started shooting at people."

"Yeah..."

"Where's Marky Lovecchio from?" Bear asked.

"Boston."

Anthony said, "Did you see a phone number? When Oz called?"

Larsden shook his head. "Nah. It always said unknown caller."

"English accent?" Anthony said.

"I don't know. English. Scottish maybe. Irish. I don't know. He sounded like that actor ... the old one ... Liam Neeson?"

That's not very useful, Anthony thought. "What else did he tell you? Anything?"

"He was pissed she got so close to the border. He said I had to do *whatever it took* to make sure she didn't get into Canada."

"Well you blew that, motherfucker," Bear said.

"So what's next? Do I get immunity if you catch him?"

Bear snorted. "Are you serious? You haven't given us anything yet. Immunity is something you *trade* for."

"I've told you everything I know."

"Yeah? I don't believe it."

For the first time in the interview, Coyle interrupted. "Anthony. Time's up."

"All right, asshole," Bear said. "You're about to go through the ringer. IRS and FBI and Border Patrol and I don't know who all else wants a piece of you. They'll mess you up so bad you won't even know your name. So you better think it through. We're the only ones who can protect you. You better come up with some answers. We'll be back in the morning."

## Adelina. May 6.

Adelina Ramos Thompson slowly opened her eyes. She was in a reclining chair, her feet up in the air, and she felt groggy and more than a little exhausted.

As always, her eyes immediately darted to her daughter.

Jessica had awoken from the previous evening, for about three hours. She was lucid, aware of her surroundings, and bitterly spiteful. Adelina withstood the onslaught of verbal abuse for almost an hour before she finally slipped out to the waiting room. Under the influence of medication, Jessica had fallen back asleep. Only then did Adelina return to her daughter's room.

She felt like a coward. She should have stayed, no matter what Jessica had said. But ... she was human.

*I hate you*, Jessica had said. *You were a whore. You cheated on our father. I don't believe your lies.*

It had gone on and on, until Jessica finally turned away from her. Time passed and the verbal attacks began again. Adelina sat there, not hiding the tears that ran down her face, but also not replying in kind. Jessica's words hurt. They wounded, like bloody stab wounds left open, but Adelina reminded herself that Jessica didn't know what she was saying. She didn't have the facts, and she was going through hideous and painful addiction withdrawals. Worse, her speech was slurred, the left side of her mouth drooping almost imperceptibly.

While Jessica was asleep, Adelina got on her knees in the corner of the room and prayed for Jessica's recovery. She prayed that one day her daughters might forgive her—or, if they couldn't do that, that they would at least find peace.

She'd finally fallen into a fitful sleep, still on her knees. A nurse found her there and helped her stand on unsteady legs, pain radiating up through her knees. She had stumbled to the chair and collapsed.

Now, Jessica looked better. Her skin wasn't so sallow, and her breathing was steadier than it had been the night before. And that was a blessing. For the first time in days, she knew where all of her daughters were. Julia, Carrie and Sarah had all moved back to the condo the night before, and hired armed guards for protection. Alexandra and Andrea were at the British Embassy in Washington, DC, along with Dylan. She didn't dare hope to see George-Phillip again—she'd hurt him too much to ever expect that—but she knew that unless he'd changed profoundly in the last sixteen years, he would do everything he could to protect her daughters.

Adelina would never forget those months. Never. She had lost hope in Belgium, lost all pretenses that she could ever have a life.

Her hospitalization in Spain, initially just a few days, extended to weeks in Belgium after she'd woken up in a panic attack and the doctors had to restrain her to keep from clawing her own skin off. Weeks she'd spent in a drugged haze, while they tried antipsychotic medications on her. *Clozapine*, which gave her dizziness the first three days, then caused seizures on the fourth day. *Risperidone*, which took away the terror but caused uncontrollable trembling and insomnia and the worst migraine she'd ever had. It was four weeks before she'd stabilized on *imipramine* and low doses of *risperidone*, which reduced the anxiety but also made her listless and vacant, with frequent trembling. Better that than another panic attack.

Almost ten weeks after her hospitalization, she returned to the Embassy in Brussels in mid-September. Julia had been cold on her return, turning her nose up and walking away. Carrie, always the sweetest of children, had come to her and hugged her, whispering, "I missed you, Mommy." Alexandra, almost four, had been full of nonsensical questions.

The months following her hospitalization were hazy to Adelina. She vaguely remembered packing as the tour in Brussels was coming to an end, but the memories were confused and unfocused. She'd tried to reach out to Julia, but the poor girl had been so hurt and confused that she'd refused any contact, spending all of her time in the garage with Corporal Lewis, who Adelina thanked God for every day. At least *someone* was watching out for her, because it was clear that during her hospitalization, Richard had barely seen the children.

The drugged haze continued as they spent several months in Washington, DC in 1995—months Adelina could barely remember now, except that it was one of the very rare times in their marriage where Richard had insisted she sleep with him. Those occasions, no more often than every few weeks, had filled Adelina with rage and self-loathing as she lay there, unmoving, disassociated. One night in May, in the room in the condo, he'd cursed at her when she winced at their painful intercourse.

*You're a dried up old whore,* he'd said in response to her body's inability to lubricate.

*Maybe if I didn't hate you with every fiber of my being, my body would respond differently.*

His response had been immediate and violent. But his attempts to have sex with her began to become less and less often, and the very last time had been in September 1995, just before he left for China.

By that time, she knew she was pregnant with twins.

The children had to switch schools in the fall when Richard was assigned as Ambassador to the People's Republic of China. The panic attacks and anxiety had returned in full when she'd stopped her medication due to the pregnancy.

The flight over had been miserable. Richard had flown separately, as he often did, leaving Adelina to handle the travel arrangements for the children. Twenty-four hours travel time, seventeen of them in the air, with a teenager, a pre-teen and a toddler, made the stuff of nightmares. She'd been in the bathrooms on the planes half a dozen times vomiting. Julia was sullen, almost never taking her headphones off long enough to help. Carrie had been a godsend, holding hands with then four-year-old Alexandra as Adelina juggled the luggage while they made their way through the connecting stop in Los Angeles. Then, in Narita International Airport in Tokyo, everything went to hell in an instant. They'd stepped off a moving sidewalk into the crowded terminal, hundreds of people moving in every direction. Adelina had been awake more than twenty-four hours, and she stumbled, setting the bags down and searching for information about their connecting flight.

Then a chill had gone down her spine when Carrie screamed, "Alexandra! Momma, I can't find her!"

Adelina shouted, "What?"

Carrie was standing there, eyes wide, panicking. They were surrounded by people and Alexandra was nowhere in sight. Julia had taken up a position against a wall, headphones on.

"Alexandra!" Adelina screamed out the name in a voice loud enough to be heard across that part of the terminal. "Alexandra!"

She'd turned to Julia and pulled the headset off. "Help me find your sister!"

Julia, not fully aware of the situation, shouted, "Leave me *alone!*"

A mix of panic and rage swept over Adelina. She reached out and slapped Julia full across the face. Julia's face jerked back at the slap, and Adelina shouted, "*Don't* you talk to me that way. Help me find your sister!"

Julia looked stunned. It was the first time Adelina ever struck one of her children, and remorse and horror instantly swept over her.

"Alexandra!" Carrie cried, not seeing what had happened behind her. A red mark had bloomed up on Julia's face. Adelina turned away, calling Alexandra's name again.

It took forty-five minutes before airport security found her. She'd wandered into one of the smoking lounges, where she'd panicked, crying in the corner.

They'd missed their connecting flight.

The next few months were a nightmare for Adelina. This pregnancy was *different* than her first three. She was older, of course, thirty-one years old, but that wasn't old to have a baby. But it was

her fourth, and twins, *and* she'd just been taken off powerful antipsychotic and antidepressant medications. Almost instantly after
coming off the meds, the fear and anxiety returned, her mind constantly wrapped around itself, twisting in fear. She took to writing
in the margins of her Bible, and in a tight scrawl in her journal, filling every page right out to the margin, desperately trying to contain
the uncontrollable emotions which were tearing her apart.

She remembered meeting with Charlotte Kelly, the only west-
ern obstetrician working in Beijing.

*This pregnancy will be different than your others, Adelina. The hor-
mones are twice as much or more. And as you get further along, you're
going to be much larger. I want you to get as much rest as you can. Are
you staying off your feet?*

Adelina had laughed. *As much as any parent of three children can.
My youngest is four.*

*Get some help. You're going to need it. I want you back every two
weeks. We're going to consider this a high-risk pregnancy.*

High-risk pregnancy. Everything about her life was high-risk.
She wasn't ready to have another child, much less two more. She
knew she was a terrible mother—every time she saw the sullen rage
in Julia's face she knew it. Julia became so involved with school
activities that fall that Adelina rarely saw her. It felt as if Julia was
more and more withdrawn, but she wouldn't talk with her mother,
and Adelina had no idea how to help. She was overwhelmed and
terrified.

*Shouldn't the morning sickness be over?* She'd asked Doctor Kelly
late in the fifth month of her pregnancy, just before Christmas.

*It's not always predictable, especially with multiples.*

Predictable. It felt as if she spent half of each day vomiting.

One night in late January, Julia didn't come home from school.
At first Adelina didn't worry. Julia had been late often this year,

and usually got rides from her friends—Lana, the daughter of the Australian Consul-General, and Harry Easton, the son of the British Ambassador. But that night, she didn't appear *at all*.

She had called Lana's parents: the girl had been home for hours. Ronald Easton had answered and verified that Harry was home and hadn't seen Julia since he'd left school that day.

*Where was she?* For that matter, where was Richard? As he often did, he hadn't come home that evening. Usually she was glad when he gave his attention to whores and massage parlor girls instead of her, it meant that she would be left alone. But with their oldest daughter missing, things were different. Adelina lay on the couch, clutching her chest, unable to breathe, her chest tight with tension. What if she lost the babies? What if Julia didn't come home? What if Richard had finally lost it and done something to their daughter? *WHERE WAS SHE?*

At ten o'clock that night, Julia stumbled in, half covered in snow, her eyes wet with tears. She was pale, strung out as if on drugs, her eyes dilated. Adelina pulled herself up, barely able to move with the weight of the twins, and half stood, half rolled off the couch.

"Where were you?" she had screamed. "Julia! Where were you?"

Julia's eyes had widened, and she'd instantly screamed back. "Why don't you ask me *how* I am, Mother? Don't you care? Don't you care about *me?*"

Adelina back, "You can't just run off anywhere you want, Julia! You can't just do whatever you want! It's dangerous! *Don't* you turn your back on me!"

In the other room, Alexandra began to cry—a little at first, then a loud scream.

"See what you've done, you bitch!" Julia shouted. "Leave me alone!"

Without thought, rage swept over Adelina. For the second time as a parent, she hit one of her children—a loud, stinging slap that knocked Julia to the floor.

Stunned, Julia stared up at her, her face horrified and grief-stricken. Then she screamed, "I hate you! I hate you!" She stumbled to her feet and ran out of the room, slamming her bedroom door shut so hard the frame rattled. The next morning she was running a fever, and stayed home from school for a week.

Seven years passed before she learned what had really happened to Julia that night. Julia confronted her in their dining room in San Francisco demanding to know why Adelina hadn't been there for her daughter's darkest moment, when the fourteen-year-old Julia had come home from a back-room abortion.

The winter of 1995-96 had been the culmination of years of suffering. Finally, on the first of April, the twins were delivered. She took her first dose of risperidone in nine months less than twenty minutes after their delivery. Almost immediately she began to come out of her emotional tailspin.

Then, at the beginning of May, George-Phillip appeared in her life for the second time, and once again changed everything. His arrival was no less transformative than the sunrise after a long night, and despite herself Adelina quickly fell for him again. He was everything she'd ever wanted or cared about—loving, caring, respectful. He asked her what he thought and genuinely listened to the answers.

She hadn't planned to see him again. She hadn't planned to fall in love with him again. When she saw him at the Embassy reception, her first intention had been to avoid him entirely. Adelina was in the back of the ballroom, talking with Julia and Carrie. Both girls wore well-tailored dresses, with their hair and makeup professionally applied. It was Carrie's first official function.

"You've both done a very nice job tonight," Adelina was saying, knowing that the words would be ignored by Julia, who had barely spoken with her in the last six months. Carrie, however, brightened at the words.

"Does this mean I can do it again?" Carrie asked.

Adelina didn't answer. She'd stiffened, her heart suddenly racing, despite the heavy medications she'd been taking again since the birth of the twins. She froze, staring in the mirror at the front entrance to the hall. George-Phillip was there, unmistakably him despite the dozen years since they'd seen each other. He was accompanied by a slightly younger Chinese woman. A girlfriend? It didn't seem likely—her posture looked like that of a colleague, not a lover.

"Mother?" Carrie asked.

Adelina didn't answer. Her eyes were on the man she'd loved— and sent away. The memories were still fresh. Finding out she was pregnant. She'd provoked Richard into raping her, so that he wouldn't suspect adultery. Then she sent George-Phillip away, unable to cope with the hideous shame of the repeated rapes, the adultery, the ugliness of her own life.

The subterfuge had worked for several years, but Carrie looked so different from Richard, and was so tall even by the age of eight, that he'd secretly gotten DNA testing for both of them. He'd stayed away for a couple of days right before Valentine's that year then showed up unexpectedly. With flowers. She'd taken them, suspicious, but didn't understand the danger that was coming. When she sniffed the flowers, his fist came out of nowhere, knocking her down. By the time it was over, she had two broken ribs and was pregnant again.

She'd told herself that she was over George-Phillip. That she didn't love him anymore. Maybe even that she'd never loved him at all.

But one sight of him in the mirror swept those lies away.

"Mother?" Carrie had asked again.

"What?" she had responded.

"Oh, never mind!" Carrie said, her eyes watering. Julia shook her head slowly. Adelina didn't need to translate the look of contempt that her oldest daughter gave her.

"Go," Adelina said. "Just go."

The two girls walked away, and Adelina promised herself she'd stay away from him, she wouldn't put herself into harm's way, that she wouldn't put her *heart* at risk again. Her resolve lasted less than twenty-minutes when she saw him walk to the back hallway.

A month later she saw him again, and this time, she did something she knew was wrong.

"I miss you," she had said.

He had closed his eyes. Then whispered, "You broke my heart, Adelina."

"I broke my own," she had replied, her voice toneless.

Two weeks later, she told the nanny that she was going out, found a pay phone and called the British Embassy.

"I need to see you," she had said.

"I don't think that would be a good idea," he had responded, his voice redolent with pain.

"I'm begging you," she whispered. "There are things you do not know."

And so it had started again. Now—seventeen years later—she sometimes had to ask herself—did she regret it? Any of it? What if she'd never met Richard Thompson? What if she'd never been raped, and gone on to audition for the National Symphony, what if her father had lived?

The problem was, all of those dreams meant that her daughters would never have lived. And as she looked at Jessica—sick, weak, in danger—she knew she'd never make that trade. They were worth *anything*.

Her thoughts were interrupted by a knocking on the doorframe of the hospital room. Her eyes shifted to the door.

A tall man in a well fitted but off-the-rack suit stood in the doorway. "Mrs. Thompson?"

"Yes?"

"My name is Wolfram Schmidt. I'm a Special Agent with the Internal Revenue Service, and I'd like to ask you some questions."

# CHAPTER NINE
## Isn't it obvious?

Adelina. May 6.

"I 'm sorry, you're who? From where?" Adelina's response wasn't particularly useful, but it stalled for a moment while she collected herself.

"My name is Wolfram Schmidt. I'm a Special Agent with the Internal Revenue Service."

Adelina's heart was thumping. She stared at Schmidt. She was stunned he was even here. After all, she was outside the borders of the United States. He had no jurisdiction.

"What can I do for you, Mr. Schmidt?"

Schmidt took the question as an invitation. He stepped into the room, and she stood, unsteadily, before he could say anything.

"Let's step outside," she said. "I don't want to wake my daughter."

He assented, and she stepped outside the room directly behind him. Once outside, he stepped across the hall. Adelina followed, staying a little more than arm's length from him.

"Mrs. Thompson ... first of all, I'm aware from the headlines that you've applied for asylum in Canada. I want to be clear that I've got no power here. I can't arrest you, or force you to come back. I can't make you do anything. You could call the police if I'm bothering you."

She studied him. His little speech was obviously a ploy to mollify her, to gain her trust. The problem was it worked, at least a little.

"I'm not quite ready to call the police. What exactly *is* it you're here for?"

"Well, I'm hoping you'll cooperate voluntarily. As you may know, the Justice Department has appointed a special prosecutor to investigate your husband's activities. Among others, the FBI and Internal Revenue Service are part of that investigation—I'm the lead for the IRS side of the investigation."

"You're also investigating my daughters."

Schmidt nodded, slowly. "One of them. Specifically Julia Wilson and her husband."

"Tell me why?"

Schmidt said, "First, you're aware that the President first raised the possibility of your husband—"

Adelina interrupted. "Please don't call him that."

Schmidt's eyes widened and his nostrils flared slightly. He was surprised, Adelina thought. "All right," he continued. "The President first contacted Ambassador Thompson in December to discuss the possibility of him becoming Secretary of Defense. It was already clear that his predecessor's health was failing."

Adelina nodded, encouraging him to continue.

He said, "The initial background checks cleared, of course, though there were some curious gaps in his resume. Those fairly quickly came to light, however, when we learned that Ambassador Thompson had been affiliated with the Central Intelligence Agency for many years. Effectively, he was on loan to the State Department."

*What? The CIA?* Adelina was stunned. She shook her head, slowly. "I—how is that possible?"

"You didn't know?"

"I know virtually nothing of him beyond the little he chose to reveal over the years. We are not close."

"You managed to have six children with him."

"Not with my consent," she said in a flat tone.

Schmidt was taken aback—his eyes widening, his nostrils flaring slightly. "I see. You understand that's immaterial to this investigation."

She shrugged. "The investigation is your problem, not mine."

"It might become yours, of course." He frowned. "After all, your name is on the tax returns."

"My name, but you certainly won't find my signature. I've never signed a tax return in my life. Mister Schmidt—tell me what I can do to help. I promise you, Richard is no friend of mine, nor is he a husband. Now that I'm finally safe from him, I'll be filing for divorce as soon as humanly possible. I'll gladly testify against him if that's what you need. But I can tell you, without question, that Julia had nothing to do with his schemes."

"Mrs. Thompson—your husband has half a dozen accounts in the Caymans, and there may be more elsewhere that we haven't uncovered yet. He has unreported assets in those accounts in excess of ten million dollars."

"I'm not surprised," she responded. "He's a snake and a liar."

"Were you aware of the accounts?"

"No," she replied.

Schmidt leaned forward and looked her closely in the eye. "Mrs. Thompson—please answer this carefully. Last Friday night, just before armed gunmen attacked your daughter's condominium in Bethesda, you placed a call to the condominium. That call lasted for less than 30 seconds and it was moments before the first shots were fired. Tell me why you placed that call."

Adelina felt her heart thump. Of course they would have pulled the phone records by now. Did her phone show an incoming call? Perhaps it might, perhaps it might not. She'd been stunned to learn, four years before, that George-Phillip had moved from Britain's Ambassador to the United Nations post and taken over the Secret Intelligence Service. Had he been an intelligence agent all along?

Like Richard?

She swallowed and said, "I can't answer that just yet."

Schmidt raised his eyebrows. "Why not?"

"I cannot."

"Mrs. Thompson, it appears from the sequence of phone calls that you had some advance warning of the attack, and you were trying to warn your daughter. Is that the case?"

She shook her head. She hadn't planned on contacting George-Phillip. But now there was no choice.

"Mrs. Thompson. You understand how this looks?"

"Ask me again tomorrow."

"I don't understand."

"Not all secrets are mine to reveal, Mr. Schmidt."

"Do you plead the Fifth Amendment, Mrs. Thompson?"

"We're outside the borders of the United States, Mr. Schmidt. You have no jurisdiction here. I promise I'll tell you when I can."

"Why did you apply for asylum?" he asked.

She smiled bitterly. "Because my *husband* sent armed assassins to kill me. As you may know, he is a high government official. I have nothing I can do to protect myself other than run."

Schmidt sighed. He reached in his pocket and took out a business card. "I have business this afternoon in Bellingham. The man who shot at you is in jail there, and I'll be questioning him this afternoon. In the meantime, if there is anything you can think of—please call me."

"I will. Thank you, Mister Schmidt."

He turned and walked away. Adelina's shoulders sagged. She needed to call George-Phillip now. She had no choice. Time to talk to the nurses and find out where she could make that call. But, as she turned away, she heard the words, "Momma?"

Adelina ran back to Jessica's room. George-Phillip and the IRS could wait.

## Sarah. May 6.

Sarah grinned. The sky was slowly turning from black to rose, highlighting the trees in silhouette as they continued down Interstate 76. She was exhausted and ready to stop. She could feel the vibration of the bike in her bones.

*There.* The first exit in Ohio. They'd driven for five hours, stopping only for gas and coffee, their goal to place as much distance between them and Washington, DC as possible. As they approached the exit, she nudged the bike over into the next lane, slowing down to fifty miles per hour. They'd carefully stayed between five and ten miles over the speed limit and avoided high traffic areas, not wanting to be flattened by a long haul trucker. But for the last two hours, they'd mostly had the highway to themselves.

Sarah did not relish the idea of dying in a motorcycle accident. But even as she drove up the exit ramp, slowing to a stop, she exulted a little. Eddie wouldn't be happy she'd stolen his bike, but he'd understand. And she was finally *free*. For more than ten months she'd been confined to the hospital and then the condo. A cripple. She'd nearly lost her leg to her injuries and the later infection, which kept her in a wheelchair for months, then on crutches for more months. But she'd been completely on her feet since early March, and worked out every day, performing the exercises her physical therapist had assigned, then doubling up on that.

Carrie would have a conniption, of course. She drove a gigantic armored SUV, the biggest and heaviest vehicle she could find, ever since the accident. Sarah understood it, of course. Fear could make you act out in strange ways. For Sarah, that had meant pursuing an obnoxious, in your face recovery. For Carrie, it meant ordering her life into such a tight structure that nothing could impede the walls of the little prison she was constructing for herself.

Sarah wouldn't accept any walls, not Carrie's, not her mother's, not even her own.

Andrea, hunched over behind her on the bike, pointed to their right. A sign that had clearly been erected sometime in the 1970s read *Pamela's Diner*. The light in the letter E had burned out. Behind the diner, a Motel 6. They would accept cash for sure. She goosed the bike forward, trailing her toes on the concrete until their speed picked up enough to balance them. She was almost too short to manage the bike, but Eddie had taught her how to drive it a week before Andrea came to the United States.

*Bet he regrets that now*, she thought, her internal voice a little smug.

When she cut the engine, silence instantly fell over them. It was jarring, the silence seeming louder than the 1340cc engine that powered the bike, a 2003 Sportster with metallic blue and chrome trim. Andrea climbed off behind her, stretching her impossibly long frame as Sarah slipped off the motorcycle. Both of them took off their helmets.

"We made good progress," Andrea said.

"Yeah. Long way to go, though." Sarah's response felt stiff. "Let's get some breakfast."

Andrea nodded and turned toward the diner. Sarah followed, her thoughts suddenly circling around the fact that she didn't know what she had to say to Andrea. They'd talked a little bit about boyfriends a few days before—before killers had attacked the condominium and Andrea went on the run. Before they knew that an English prince was Andrea's father (something Sarah thought was a gigantic laugh). But really she didn't know her sister. Andrea had effectively stopped living with them when Sarah was in the second grade, and her visits home had become infrequent. She knew Jessica and Andrea had once been close. But now? She didn't think anyone was close to Andrea.

Could she blame Andrea for having strong armor? Sarah couldn't even imagine what it must have felt like to believe that your parents didn't want you. She knew Julia and Carrie had uncovered a lot of things about their mother recently ... that she'd lied about her age, and that she'd been effectively raped and kidnapped from her home. But even so, *both* of their parents had a lot to answer for when it came to Andrea.

Sarah paused to stretch again before they entered the restaurant. Her muscles felt compressed, and her legs still hadn't stopped vibrating. Worse, her left leg—the one that had been badly injured and broken in the accident—*ached* like it hadn't in a very long time. Of course, she had more hardware in her leg than a Home Depot, with all those pins and screws rattling around on the bike it was no wonder she hurt.

Andrea opened the door for her, and Sarah limped into the restaurant. Then the two of them waited at the front door.

Immediately she saw herself in the large mirror near the hostess station at the front of the restaurant. Both of them with dark hair, almost black, with streaks, Sarah's white and Andrea's turquoise. Both of them wore mostly black, though Sarah's skirt was plaid over black leggings. In the mirror, they looked a little comical— Andrea was a full foot taller than Sarah.

Andrea grinned at Sarah in the mirror as the hostess led them to a table. For the next several minutes, they both studied the menu, ordered their food and drinks, then sat back and looked at each other.

Sarah said, "I feel kind of awkward. I mean, we're sisters, but we don't know each other very well, do we?"

Andrea nodded, her expression a little sad.

Sarah said, "Thanks for calling every week after I got hurt. It meant a lot to me."

Andrea shrugged. "You needed it. I could tell."

"I felt so alone. Especially at first, when I thought I was going to lose my leg. And I thought I was going crazy sometimes, with just me and Carrie and Mother. Your calls helped ground me."

Andrea said, "I wish we could have spent more time together. You know—growing up."

Sarah said, "Me too."

"Do you remember going to the zoo? When we were little?"

"Yeah. Carrie used to take us all the time. And to Golden Gate Park." Sarah studied her sister for a moment. They both shared facial features from their mother—the same small, slightly upturned nose, the green eyes and nearly black hair. But Andrea and Carrie had gotten some serious mutant tall genes from their father.

It felt weird to say that word in reference to someone else. "What was it like? Meeting your ... your dad?"

Andrea sighed. "I don't know really. He seemed really nice. But you can't trust that, can you?"

Sarah said, "I don't know. Maybe sometimes you have to trust something."

Andrea stared at her sister, letting her big green eyes stare. Then she nodded, once. "Maybe you're right. But how do you know when?"

Sarah shrugged. "I've got a lot of questions for Mother."

"Me too."

"There are a lot of things I feel like I should know about you. What's your favorite color?"

"Blue," Andrea replied. "You?"

"Isn't it obvious?" Sarah asked, gesturing to her all black clothes.

Andrea chuckled. "How come you and Jessica are so different now?"

Sarah's mouth turned up in a half-smile. "We always were. I think she felt like she had to somehow compensate for ... something. I don't know what. It seemed like I constantly got in more trouble while she constantly became more prim."

Andrea said, "I don't see how she got mixed up with drugs."

Sarah shook her head. "I don't either. I feel like I missed something crucial, and it pisses me off. We haven't gotten along the last couple years, but she's still my twin. I should have known."

The waitress arrived with their breakfast. They stayed silent as their food was arranged, then Andrea said, "I don't want to stop long. Let's sleep a couple hours then get on the road again, okay?"

Sarah nodded. "Yeah. It's a long way before we'll get there."

"You could have picked a more practical mode of transportation," Andrea said.

"More practical than a Harley?" Sarah asked. She grinned. "What country have you been living in?"

Two hours later, they were driving west again.

## George-Phillip. May 6.

It was a little after four in the morning when George-Phillip awoke, fully awake though it was still very dark. He was already an early riser, and the addition of jet lag guaranteed insufficient sleep for the next several days. He stumbled out of bed and took care of his morning routine, then glanced into Jane's room. His daughter—*youngest daughter*—thankfully could sleep anywhere, any time. She would still be out for at least a couple more hours.

He closed the door, then stepped out of the suite, intending to head downstairs for a cup of coffee, a habit he'd picked up during his first time in Washington, DC thirty years before.

A Captain of the Royal Marines was waiting for him along with O'Leary when he got downstairs.

"Your Highness," the Captain said, coming to attention.

"Good morning, Captain," George-Phillip said, his eyes moving to O'Leary in question.

"George-Phillip, I'm afraid we have bad news," O'Leary said.

"Sir, the young lady ran last night. She climbed over the fence and ran."

Stunned, George-Phillip asked, "*Which* young lady?"

"Andrea Thompson, sir," O'Leary said.

George-Phillip shook his head. "When did this happen?"

"Just after midnight, sir."

*"And you're just telling me now?"* George-Phillip shouted.

The Captain looked at O'Leary, confused. O'Leary looked uncomfortable. "Sir, that was my order—we couldn't get her, someone met her with a motorcycle and she was gone before our men even made it to the gate. Nor could we pursue her—after all, she wasn't a prisoner."

"She is my daughter!" George-Phillip shouted

The Captain's eyes widened and he took a step back. O'Leary, however, stepped forward, placing a hand on George-Phillip's arm. "Your Highness, I'm well aware of that. But you are also the Chief of the Secret Intelligence Service. You can't allow your personal considerations to interfere with that, sir."

Rage gripped George-Phillip. His response was delivered in an icy tone. "You take too much liberty, Oswald. I can't even imagine what you were thinking. Do we have *any* idea where she went? Who she went with? Why she left?"

The Royal Marine Captain shook his head. "No, Your Highness. Her room was locked from the inside, and while the bedclothes were a mess, there's no sign of a struggle. She took her bag and went out the window, sir, then ran for the fence."

George-Phillip said to the Marine Captain, "Go wake up Dylan Paris. And I want to see the video from the security cameras. Has anyone told the Ambassador?"

O'Leary said, "Is that wise, sir?"

George-Phillip said, "Twice now, a sixteen-year-old girl has evaded our security. Think about it, Oswald. I want to know why she ran. We just had dinner last evening and agreed that it would be safest for her to remain on the Embassy grounds."

He half turned away from O'Leary, but O'Leary grasped his arm. "Sir—have you considered that maybe some of what they are saying in the media about her is true?"

George-Phillip said, "I'm well aware that you always opposed my involvement with Adelina Ramos—"

"*Thompson*, Your Highness. Her last name is *Thompson*."

George-Phillip turned back to O'Leary, jamming his index finger into O'Leary's chest. "O'Leary, we've been friends and colleagues for thirty years. But I'm telling you now that you are pushing this too far."

"Yes, Your Highness. Of course."

"You may go. I want an update as soon as possible. O'Leary—don't fail me. I want my daughter found and protected."

O'Leary said, "Yes, Your Highness." Then he turned away. He stumbled once as he stepped away.

"Oswald? Are you all right?"

O'Leary looked back. "Of course, sir. I turned my ankle when I was inspecting where she went over the fence."

# CHAPTER TEN
# Evil empire.

Richard. May 6.

**The** Central Hearing Facility in the Hart Senate Office building was the largest hearing room on Capitol Hill, with seating for up to several hundred spectators. The seal of the United States Senate, which displayed a flag with thirteen stars over a ribbon labeled *E Pluribus Unum*, dominated the marble wall at the head of the room behind the dais where thirteen Senators were seated. On either side, wood paneled walls were punctuated with openings behind which reporters with cameras were preparing to film the hearing.

The room was full, every single seat taken. Unlike the typical Congressional hearing where one or two members of Congress showed up to make a few comments for the cameras, for this hearing every single Senator was already seated and ready to begin their questioning.

"The hearing is about to come to order, sir," said the nameless intern who had accompanied Richard Thompson to the anteroom. "You can go in now."

Richard didn't bother answering. Instead, back straight, head high, he walked down the aisle at the center of the hearing room. A hush fell on the room as the hundreds of spectators realized he was approaching the witness desk that faced the Senators on the dais. Much as had been the case fourteen years before, when Senator Chuck Rainsley sat at the head of the Senate Foreign Relations Committee blocking Richard's appointment to Moscow, Rainsley was back, now as head of the Senate Armed Services committee. The turncoat had even politically survived the switch from Republican to Democrat in 2003, just after the invasion of Iraq, and despite his obvious leftist leanings, had managed to claw his way to the head of the most important and most powerful committee in Congress. Richard remembered all too well the political circus of his confirmation hearings as Ambassador to Russia more than a decade ago. Rainsley had put every possible obstacle in his way, dug deep into his personal life and then blindsided him with closed, classified hearings where his CIA career was examined.

Richard *hated* this oppressive, noxious room and the chairman who sat at the head of the table. For thirty years Chuck Rainsley had been his nemesis. Richard didn't allow himself to blink as he walked up the aisle, meeting Rainsley's eyes defiantly. Despite the flashes of dozens—possibly hundreds of cameras—Richard made his way up the center of the aisle without pausing or even noticing the barrage. None of the people out there really mattered. Now it was between him and Rainsley.

"All right," Rainsley said, his appalling Texas drawl elongated for the cameras. He looked at the other Senators and said, "Y'all all right?"

When there was no response, Rainsley banged a gavel on the table. "Good morning, everybody. This committee was originally scheduled to consider the nomination of Ambassador Richard Thompson to be Secretary of Defense. As I'm sure y'all are aware, yesterday the President withdrew the nomination. However, this committee still has business to address with Ambassador Thompson. Now, for the moment, we're going to skip right over the reports of drug money laundering and corruption, as well as the reports of millions of dollars of assets secreted away in the Caymans."

Richard seethed at Rainsley's response. In one sentence, Rainsley had dismissed any possible discussion of the lies he'd been accused of, even as he gave credence in a public hearing to those accusations. Rainsley, once a straight shooting Marine (or so he claimed) had become familiar with the wily, slippery ways of Washington. It made Richard sick enough that he wanted to walk out and go wash his hands.

"Today," Rainsley said, "we will begin by addressing a report which appeared in *The Guardian* newspaper in London the day before yesterday."

Rainsley paused for a full twenty seconds to allow the reporters to get a better angle with their cameras. Then he said, as dramatically as possible, "Thirty years ago, in one of the bloodiest incidents of the Soviet invasion of Afghanistan, a tiny village in an out of the way corner of the furthest province from the Afghan capitol was gassed with sarin, the deadliest nerve gas ever invented."

Richard felt his lip turning up in contempt of Rainsley. He forced it down. It was essential to maintain his diplomatic facade.

"For those of you not familiar with the military," Rainsley said, emphasizing (for the three people left in remote rural Alaska who didn't know) that he'd once been a Marine, "just a single drop of sarin is deadly enough to kill a person instantly. In this incident in Afghanistan, two helicopters delivered the chemical weapon in the dead of night and dropped it on unsuspecting villagers. According to Human Rights Watch, more than two hundred and thirty men, women and children were killed. Even the *dogs* died, as did a Human Rights Watch investigator who came into contact with the poison three months later."

The room was silent. Rainsley had absolute mastery over his audience, his words articulate and persuasive. Those words were being broadcast across the nation and the world. If Richard couldn't counter them effectively, it didn't matter what he did. His career would be over irrevocably.

Rainsley spoke again, this time his voice loud, outraged. "Ladies and Gentlemen, colleagues of the Senate—for thirty years we have believed that the Soviet Union was responsible for this massacre of innocents. Who here doesn't remember President Reagan citing the massacre when he described the Soviet Union as an *evil empire?* And yet ... how shocked we would all be to learn that it wasn't the Soviet Union at all who was responsible for the massacre. Instead—a rogue CIA operative, operating with little or no oversight."

Richard normally had complete control over his facial expressions and responses. But at the phrase "rogue CIA operative," he shook his head with contempt.

Rainsley pointed a finger. "According to a report leaked this week to a British newspaper, *this* man, former Ambassador, most recently acting Secretary of Defense, was responsible for procuring the weapons. He was responsible for delivering them to the Afghan militia, which then dropped them on unsuspecting civilians. Instead of protecting the civilians of Afghanistan, we did just the opposite. We laid waste to them."

Rainsley shook his head, sadly. Then, just in case no one knew, he said, "When I served in the Marine Corps, we knew a different kind of war. We learned to face our enemies. We learned to protect innocent civilians. The deadliest mission I ever served on, our job was to *keep the peace*, not to make things worse."

Rainsley was working himself up into one of his trademark tantrums, his face turning bright red. One of these days, he'd have a stroke. When that day came, Richard hoped he'd be there, to help Rainsley along to the other side. For the time being, he tried not to roll his eyes.

"I must not go on," Rainsley said. "My outrage knows no boundaries."

*Your morals know no boundaries,* Richard thought, staring at the man who had violated his wife, *impregnated her* not once but *twice.* He should have insisted Andrea be aborted. Adelina would have refused, but enough sedatives could approximate consent.

Rainsley yielded to the ranking member, a nonentity from the minority party. The tea party might hold sway in the House of Representatives, but here in the Senate, liberal democrats had a grip on all of the gears of government, especially the most powerful committees. Richard listened to Lewis's opening statement with complete indifference. This committee might think it was important, but in fact all it did was rubber stamp the President's nominations. Instead of listening, Richard looked up at the ceiling. The room had acoustical tiles in the ceiling to ensure those in the back could hear. Unlike the ancient hearing rooms in the other office buildings on Capitol Hill, this one was modern, sleek, as was the building that housed it. Richard preferred the original buildings. Whoever had commissioned this glass and concrete monstrosity ought to have been shot.

An interminable period of time later, Richard glanced at his watch. It was almost 11 am, and the members of the committee still hadn't finished their opening statements. He reminded himself that the entire purpose of this hearing was to show the constituents back home that the Senators were doing something. That's why they were taking all the time. He looked behind him for a moment, at the large crowd.

Richard blinked. In the front row, in the rows reserved for journalists ... it was that bitch Maria Clawson. No longer a too-thin social climbing gossip columnist, she was now old, angry and bitter. When she saw Richard looking at her she raised her notebook in the air, just slightly, then smiled at him, as if to say, *I'm going to screw you all over again.* Yeah, he remembered her. He remembered her poison pen, her sourceless blogs that implicated him in supposedly forcing Julia to get an abortion. As if he'd had any clue the girl had gotten herself pregnant. He'd made it clear to Adelina thirty years ago that his name should never again appear in one of Clawson's columns, and she failed to prevent it. He'd made sure Adelina regretted that failure. But the satisfaction of seeing her cringe, the pleasure of her capitulation, had done nothing to relieve the seething anger and blackness that stirred inside of him.

He turned back to the front, taking his eyes from the noxious woman.

*Finally.* Richard snapped back to reality as Rainsley was saying, "Richard Isaiah Thompson, raise your right hand and repeat after me. Do you swear to tell the truth..."

Richard repeated the words mechanically. He didn't care for the use of his middle name. The name Isaiah was marble and ice, it was murder, it was *private.* Never in his life had he used his middle name. He didn't even know how Rainsley knew his middle name, unless Adelina had told him during one of their trysts.

"Do you have an opening statement, Mister Thompson?" Rainsley said. Dispensing with the honorifics.

"I do, Senator." Richard's voice was cold as he spoke.

"Please proceed."

Richard stared up at the dais. Rainsley was in the center. To his left and right were six Senators on each side. This committee (like all of them) tended to be white, male and wealthy. Richard's natural constituency. But he couldn't discount the fact that 7 out of 13 members of the committee were Democrats, who would gladly throw him to the wolves if it meant they could extort one more dollar out of the government. The Republicans on the committee weren't allies either—they were weak, ineffectual, divided and terrified of losing their seats to Tea Party insurgents.

"Mister Chairman, distinguished members of the committee, please allow me to state, first of all, that the charge I was in any way involved in the Wakhan massacre is not only unfounded, but a grave injustice. In my detailed comments I will make it clear to you that not only am I completely innocent of these charges, but, in fact, I tried to prevent the massacre *and* reported it through official channels after the fact. *Second.* I will demonstrate that the ludicrous charges currently being examined by the grand jury and the special prosecutor are manufactured by the very man who committed the massacre and is now attempting to destroy me in order to save face."

"That will be quite the feat, Mister Thompson," Rainsley said. "However, your money laundering activities, or lack thereof, are not of interest to this committee. I'm certain the grand jury will take care of *that.* This committee *is* interested in those matters that affect the national security of the United States. Clearly, the provision of weapons banned under the Geneva conventions to terrorist organizations is one of those matters. You'll restrict your answers to that."

*Terrorists?* Rainsley managed to escalate with every word he spoke. The mujahideen of the early 1980s were American allies, regardless of the atrocities they committed in 2001. Richard leaned forward and said, "Senator, official US policy in the 1980s was to assist the mujahideen. While I gave no one chemical weapons, you can hardly retroactively label them terrorists."

Rainsley smiled, as if to say, *Checkmate*. "Mister Thompson, the same allies you speak of killed thousands of Americans on September 11. Call them whatever you like, but the fact is those Americans are dead."

"Mister Chairman," called out the ranking member, Senator Lewis. "In the interest of time, can we skip the bandying of words back and forth and deal with facts?"

Rainsley nodded. "Of course, Senator. I will concede to you—please ask the first question."

Lewis nodded, then leaned forward. Based on the opening statements, it appeared that the Republicans on the committee were tentatively supporting him—most likely because doing so allowed them to oppose the administration, which had dumped him like a piece of garbage. Lewis's glasses hung at the end of his nose, his bald head glaring under the bright lights. His blue eyes looked at Richard over the top of his glasses.

"Ambassador Thompson ... I'd like to begin by recognizing that all of us on this committee are aware of your long and distinguished history in service to this country. And even if some other members of this committee have forgotten, I remember that the United States armed the mujahideen specifically to defend against the invading Soviet Union. That said, chemical weapons are a serious matter. Please answer for the committee the following question. Did you take part, in any way, in the provision of chemical weapons to the Afghan militia?"

Soft ball, Richard thought. Perfect. "I did not, Senator."

Lewis nodded, his eyes scanning over a sheet of paper. Then he looked back up at Richard. "Do you know who did?"

"Yes, Senator. I reported the crime in 1983. The perpetrator was Leslie Collins, the current Director of Operations of the Central Intelligence Agency."

Julia. May 6.

Martin Barrymore was the quintessential Long Island WASP lawyer. Five foot eight, grey haired, balding, and deep inside his very small heart, he had a little bit of murder in him. As general counsel of Morbid Enterprises, Inc., Julia and Crank's holding company, he'd tackled a lot of issues. Copyright and trademark violation, contract negotiation, mergers and acquisitions. Taxes were never an issue, because the company was scrupulous about paying them. But now, he was heading up the team of tax attorneys who were preparing to deal with the Internal Revenue Service, and Julia was grateful for him.

The two of them, along with two tax attorneys who reported to Barrymore, rode up the elevator to the ninth floor of the IRS headquarters in Washington, DC. Julia was relieved Crank hadn't come—he'd have been far too likely to make flippant comments about how they might not escape from the building alive.

All the same, he'd insisted on something useful to do.

*Look, Julia—I don't feel like I'm pulling my weight. All I do is write songs and sing. You're doing everything for us.*

*But Crank,* she'd said, *that's what we've always done. I'm okay with that, I want you to be able to write your music and not worry.*

He'd grinned and said, *This is a crisis, babe. You take amazing care of me. But you gotta let me help.*

So they'd discussed it, and Crank had flown up to Boston first thing that morning. He would be meeting with the staff of the Boston office, and dispensing three weeks pay—in cash. It's all they had in their personal bank accounts, and the possibility of checks bouncing had resulted in a large cash withdrawal. That might be all the staff would get unless Barrymore could get the IRS to agree to free up some money.

Crank would be good at that. He didn't realize it, but over the years, he'd become a natural leader. Confident, bold, but warm and approachable. Everyone felt comfortable approaching him—whether it was network anchors, overenthusiastic fans or roadies who'd been working for the tour for a week. Sometimes she had to step in the way just so he could get some songs written. He didn't like to say no, didn't like to disappoint people.

For now, he'd be fine. A small pit of anxiety turned in her stomach. If she couldn't get the money freed up, then their fifty employees and their families would be out of luck. No severance pay, no nothing. It was grossly unfair, and according to Barrymore, it was also likely illegal. She was counting on his ability to fix that situation quickly. He'd already drawn up papers to file suit in Federal District Court if this meeting didn't go well.

"This way, please," said their escort, a youngish looking woman who had introduced herself as Jayna McCloud. An intern probably; Julia would have put her at twenty-one at the most.

She led Julia, Barrymore and the tax attorneys to a conference room at the end of the hall. The conference room was cheaply appointed. Painted walls, a pressboard conference table (attractive and functional, but cheaply made), chairs that looked half decent but were not ergonomically sound. She guessed if the IRS used these chairs throughout the headquarters, there were a lot of people out with bad backs.

At the table sat three people. The first, at the head of the table, Julia recognized. Emma Smith had been one of the agents who had questioned her in San Francisco what seemed like a lifetime ago, but was in fact just a few days.

"Mrs. Wilson, thank you for coming today. Allow me to introduce Cliff Shriver from the FBI."

To her right, Shriver was a man in a decently tailored grey suit. His jacket was open, and his sidearm, a gleaming black pistol in a shoulder holster, was clearly visible. A badge hung from his jacket lapel.

"And this is Scott Kelly from Diplomatic Security Services. Scott isn't here on an official basis, but he's asked to be in on this meeting because he said he has information that may be helpful to us all. It's up to you whether or not he stays."

"Pleasure to meet ya," Kelly said, his voice a clear Boston accent. He had dark circles under his eyes, the kind you got from years of sleep shortages. He reminded her a lot of her father-in-law Jack, a retired Boston cop.

"I think that will be fine," Julia murmured.

"Julia?" Barrymore asked quietly.

"It's fine," she said. "I want to clear this up as quickly as we can."

Emma Smith nodded in approval. "Please have a seat then."

Julia sat at the end of the table opposite Smith and studied her adversary. Her two in the morning impression of the woman hadn't changed—her skin was smooth, unblemished and free of makeup. She looked to be in her late twenties, or would, but her hair was white. Not bleached, not blonde, but prematurely gray and white. *Interesting*, Julia thought.

Smith said, "Mrs. Wilson, this is an informal meeting. It's not a hearing, and you're free to go at any time. Your attorney is here to advise you on your rights, of course, but I want to make it clear that while you have the right to not say anything at all, if you *do* say anything, we might use it in our investigation."

Julia leaned toward Barrymore, who said, "It's standard. I'll watch out for you here." She nodded.

"Thanks," Julia said. Barrymore responded to Smith. "We're looking forward to clearing this up."

"All right. I want to start with the accounts in the Caymans."

Julia nodded, not saying anything. She'd heard the reports in the media, but that's all she knew. "I'm not actually aware of any such accounts."

Smith opened a folder and slid half a dozen sheets of paper down the table. Barrymore retrieved them and showed them to Julia.

"These are powers of attorney, registered with HSBC, Butterfield Bank, Cayman National Bank, First Caribbean and the Royal Bank of Canada, all operating on Grand Cayman. They authorize you to establish accounts on behalf of your father. Do you recognize them?"

Julia shook her head. They were, in fact, powers of attorney. More disturbing, they all bore her signature. They were all dated December 19 and 20, 2013. Which was alarming. She and Crank had stayed overnight on Grand Cayman en route from Europe to Washington, DC.

"I've never seen these," she said. "That looks like my signature, but I didn't sign these documents."

"Where were you on December 19th and 20th, Mrs. Wilson?"

"I suspect you know the answer to that question," she replied.

"Were you on Grand Cayman Island with your husband?"

"Yes. We were on our way to the States to spend Christmas with my sisters."

"How do you explain your signature on these notarized documents?"

"I can't explain them. This is the first I've ever heard of them."

Smith nodded.

Kelly leaned forward and said, "Can you think of any reason why someone would go to this much trouble and expense? After these accounts were established, more than twenty million dollars was deposited into them. We haven't been able to trace the source."

Julia frowned. Then she said, "Do you know when my father was first approached about taking the Secretary of Defense job?"

The three federal agents looked at each other, mystified.

Julia nodded once. "From what I've been told, it was in December 2013. Right around the same time these documents were signed."

## Bear. May 6.

Neither Anthony Walker, not Bear Wyden were accustomed to staying in luxurious accommodations. So after they left the county jail, Bear suggested they check into the local Days Inn there in Bellingham and make that their base of operations for the next couple of days.

"Sure," Anthony had said. An hour later, they had checked in. Anthony went to work on his laptop, making phone calls and generally making a nuisance of himself.

At one point, he looked up from his laptop, his eyebrows scrunched together and a line running down his forehead. "Didn't you say you ran the security detail for the Thompsons in the nineties?"

"Yeah," Bear had replied.

"What were the girls like? Julia and Carrie?"

Bear shrugged. "Kids. Julia was the oldest; she was typical eighth grader. Pissed at the world and especially her mother. Carrie was a sweetheart. Why do you ask?"

Anthony shrugged. "Just wondering."

"Yeah, well wonder quietly." Bear, who had an incurable sleep deficit, lay down to take a nap. He closed his eyes, lulled by the clickety-click sound of Anthony's keys on the laptop.

It was tranquil for a change, and Bear found himself drifting off shortly after noon. That made it all the more alarming when the door to the hotel suddenly burst inward and someone shouted, "Freeze, FBI!"

Bear froze. So did Anthony, his fingers still poised on his laptop, cell phone at his ear.

Five seconds later the room was full of fully armed and pissed off federal agents. Bear was thrown rudely to the floor, where his hands were cuffed with zip ties behind his back and his sidearm was taken away. Anthony was also face down in the carpet, his cell phone beside him face down. Bear instantly found himself wondering—was it still connected to whoever Anthony had been talking to? Hopefully they were connecting a recorder.

Footsteps. He craned his neck as far as he could, but he could only make out a pair of not very well polished wingtips and grey suit pants.

"Let him up," a voice said.

He was hauled upward by his arms and came to rest face to face with a tall man with swept back salt-and-pepper hair and a hawk nose.

"Agent Wyden," the man boomed. "I'm Wolfram Schmidt. Internal Revenue Service—and I'm in charge of the Thompson investigation."

*Crap. That was quick.*

"Hey," Bear said, giving Schmidt a disarming grin. "Great to finally meet you!"

Schmidt narrowed his eyes. "It's not that nice to meet you, Wyden. You're suspended. And no longer associated with this investigation. What brings you to Washington?" His eyes flitted toward Anthony. "And in the company of a journalist, I see."

"Well, you know, you can't always pick your friends..."

"Shut up. What the hell are you doing here, Wyden?"

"Officially?" Bear asked.

Schmidt rolled his eyes. "Yeah."

"Nothing. Nothing at all, officially. I'm suspended. But, the thing is—"

"Shut up."

"It's hard to answer your questions if I shut up."

"Jesus," Schmidt said. "Untie them. Wyden, sit down."

An agent cut the zip ties holding his wrists. Bear didn't argue—he just sat down on the end of one of the beds. Anthony was maneuvered to sit next to him, and Wolfram Schmidt with his swept back hair sat down opposite them.

"Seriously, Wyden. Quit screwing around and answer my question or you'll find yourself arrested for obstructing justice. You showed up before anybody else to question Larsden, and now he's dead."

# CHAPTER ELEVEN
## That poor boy

Anthony. May 6.

**Y**ou *showed up before anybody else to question Larsden, and now he's dead.*

What the hell? "What happened to him?" he blurted out.

Anthony's mind crowded with questions. If Larsden was dead, then their only link to Oz was Marky Lovecchio, and they still hadn't identified him. Was that actually the guy's name? If so, they should be able to find him on Google or some public records. Facebook, some other social networking, credit checks. No one was completely invisible.

Schmidt gave Anthony a withering look. "I don't even know why you're part of this discussion. This is an ongoing investigation and—"

Bear interrupted Schmidt. "Yeah, I get it, ongoing investigation, can't comment, yada yada yada. What the hell happened to Larsden? He was the picture of health four hours ago."

Schmidt said, "Off the record, someone shanked him, and naturally no one saw anything. He bled out in the county jail before anyone even knew what happened."

"Son of a bitch," Bear said. He looked at Anthony and both said the same word at the same time: "Oz."

Schmidt blinked. His response was sarcastic. "Oz? Are we going on a trip?"

Bear looked at Schmidt. "I'll tell you everything I've got. I mean everything. But I need you to know, I know for a fact the sisters weren't involved in whatever is happening here. Their father is a complete slime bag, but they weren't involved."

"Yeah? What about Julia Wilson? She's got an enormous stake in whatever the hell is going on."

Anthony shook his head. He was certain Carrie and her sisters weren't involved. "I'd stake my reputation on it. They've been set up. The question in my mind is when did you start your investigation? When did this whole thing kick off?"

Schmidt looked back and forth between Bear and Anthony. Then his posture changed, very subtly—his shoulders lowered just a fraction of an inch, as if he'd relaxed just slightly. His eyes darted back and forth between Bear and Anthony. "For the record, our investigation began officially in January."

"What kicked it off?"

Schmidt said, "Banks are required to report suspicious activity. We received a notice in January of what looked like a strange pattern of activity in a set of corporate accounts in Atlanta. We followed up and what we found was money churning. Small deposits and withdrawals, all of them less than a few hundred dollars to a few thousand, but many of them a day. Someone was funneling a busload of money through these accounts. The company we were looking at didn't even really exist. Shell company, owned by another shell company, and none of the officers and directors were real people.

Bear asked, "When were these accounts opened?"

"All of them in December and January."

"And how did it lead back to Thompson?"

"Stock transactions. There were half a dozen equity sales in one of Julia Wilson's accounts, which had already been flagged by the IRS, but only for verification. But then we saw a large cash transfer from one of Wilson's corporate accounts to the Caymans. That led us to pull records there, and they matched up. The accounts in the Caymans were the destination of the cash transfers out of Atlanta. But the only link we had was to Julia Wilson. And there wasn't enough there."

Anthony asked, "How do you get from there to seizing their assets?"

"No more," Schmidt said. "I've got questions for you. What is Oz? Or who?"

Bear said, "Oz is British or Irish. We don't know anything else about him, except that he hired Larsden." Bear summarized the questioning for Schmidt, including the news that Oz had been introduced to Larsden by an Army buddy named Marky Lovecchio.

"That ought to be easy enough to follow up," Schmidt said. "We know when and where Larsden was in the Army—process of elimination from there. He can't have served around many people with a name like Lovecchio."

Bear said, "So, now that we're working together—"

Schmidt shook his head. "Nobody is *working* together. I'm conducting an investigation. You're obstructing justice."

"Bullshit," Bear said. "You haven't even looked at *why*. Why would someone with a forty million dollar successful company get involved with cheap money laundering? Or for that matter, why would Richard Thompson?"

"Greed. Simple as that. Who the hell knows why any people do this stuff?"

Anthony shook his head. "Not Thompson. He's greedy for power—not money. I think you need to ask what happened here. Because it looks to me like someone duped you in an effort to discredit Thompson."

Schmidt shook his head. "I don't buy it. I'm willing to explore it, but I don't buy it. What I do know, Wyden, is that *you* aren't on this case anymore. And I don't want to get wind that you're going around questioning my witnesses, or butting your fat head into this investigation. Larsden was an *essential* witness and now he's dead. I've got half a mind to arrest you right now."

Bear growled, "You'd be better off putting your resources into finding out who the hell had him killed."

"I intend to do that. But you stay a thousand miles away from this investigation. Do you understand me?"

"Yeah, Schmidt. I get it. Just tell me one thing first."

"What?"

"What was your mother thinking when she named you?"

Schmidt stood up, irritation on his face. "My father and grandfather were named Wolfram, thank you. Once again, Wyden, I'll thank you to mind your own business." He looked at his compatriots and said, "Let's go."

Schmidt and his bevy of IRS and FBI agents left the room. One overenthusiastic FBI agent gave Bear the finger on his way out. Bear shook his head.

So much for interagency cooperation, Anthony thought. "Was that smart?"

Bear shrugged. "It's the IRS. What else can you do?"

Anthony chuckled then shook his head. "What now? Larsden was our best lead. Who the hell is Oz?"

Bear sighed. Then he said, "I think we go see Adelina Thompson now. Otherwise, I'm out of options."

Anthony thought about how Carrie and her sisters reacted every time their mother was mentioned—an almost palpable tension. He hadn't been able to work out why they were so sensitive about their mother. But now it looked like he was going to get the chance.

"Sounds good," he said.

Anthony thought back to his last sight of Carrie, calmly going through the disaster of her ransacked home, baby strapped in a sling at her side. She'd been calm, collected and organized, even in the midst of disaster. She had lines of strain and stress around her eyes, but she was a beautiful woman.

He shook his head. He didn't have time to be thinking about Carrie, nor would she be interested in the midst of her grief and worry about her daughter.

But still.

## Alexandra. May 6.

Dylan spun around after pacing the length of the room for the five hundredth time. His back was a line of strain and anger, his hair still tousled from sleep.

"What I don't understand is why she didn't say anything. Or leave a note. Are you sure something didn't happen?"

Alexandra sank into a chair as Prince George-Phillip answered Dylan's question. George Phillip was sitting in a chair across from Alexandra. "Of course I'm not sure. How could I be? All I know is that she went out the back window shortly before one am and ran across the grounds, climbed a tree and went over the wall before anyone could get to her."

"Something must have happened," Dylan said. "Don't you have security cameras?"

"Outside. Not in the residence. But nothing unusual showed up. No one came or went."

"Then it must have been someone in the residence, sir. That's the only option. She wouldn't run on her own." Dylan's voice was sharp, unpleasant. "I need to go find her."

"I wouldn't advise that," George-Phillip said. "You're still a fugitive. The moment you leave the Embassy you'll find yourself in jail until they finish the investigation. You did kill a federal agent."

Dylan shook his head. "I can't just stay here and do nothing."

"Dylan," Alexandra said. Why did he have to be so stubborn? There was nothing he could do. She was just as worried about Andrea as he was, but *someone* needed to keep a cool head.

"Stop," he said. "I *have* to do something. Can you imagine Ray just standing around waiting?"

"Dylan," Alexandra whispered, her heart sinking. "Stop. If Ray were here, there'd be nothing he could do either. We don't have enough information. She could be anywhere."

Dylan stopped and stared at the ceiling and sighed. "This is so frustrating," he groaned.

"I agree," George-Phillip said. "But I'll tell you that I've got all possible assets looking for her, and the search is being run directly by my assistant, who is the most competent man I know. If anyone can find her, O'Leary can. And there's absolutely nothing you can do to help Andrea or Alexandra or their sisters if you are in jail."

Dylan nodded. "I know," he said in a tense voice. Then he exhaled, and in a slower, lower tone he said, "I know. In the meantime, what *can* I do?"

"I want you talk with O'Leary. Let him know what you can about what she knows, where she might go. You two were on the run for a short period—did you use cash? How did you communicate?"

"Cash, gift cards, burner phones. She can stay hidden if she wants, she knows how. But it's dangerous out there."

Alexandra sighed. "You're forgetting Sarah's with her."

Dylan said, "Sarah's a kid. They both are."

"I wouldn't underestimate either one of them, Dylan."

"It's not a question of underestimating them. You didn't see the people who came after her, Alex. They were killers." His voice was fierce, the tension behind his words as sharp as a straight-razor.

She closed her eyes. How was she ever going to get her husband back? It was as if the war had reached out and swallowed him back up, just like it did Ray. He was here, and completely alert and aware. But he wasn't. As she watched him, she thought about the long months of recovery from his injuries. Walking, and later running beside him around Central Park as he healed his body. But healing his mind was another thing entirely. That wouldn't be finished in a week or a month or a year. She could almost see he was on the edge of a meltdown.

Alexandra stood up and put her hands on his shoulders, effectively stopping him midstride.

"Dylan," she said.

"Look, I just *can't* not do—"

"Dylan!" she said. "*Stop*. She's going to be okay. You can't fix this. Please let it go." Then she wrapped her arms around him as tight as she could.

For a second, he didn't move. Then his shoulder sagged, and his arms wrapped around her, and he said, "I'm sorry. Shit. I'm sorry."

They stood and swayed together for a few moments, slowly calming down. Then she stirred when she heard a throat clearing behind her.

*Shit!* Prince George-Phillip was still standing there.

"Forgive me," George-Phillip said.

"No … forgive me," Dylan said. "I'm just not used to sitting around."

George-Phillip gave him a disarming smile. "I understand completely. You've got a very smart woman here, Dylan. Listen to her."

Dylan hung his head. "Yes, sir."

"I really must step away," George-Phillip said. "I promise I'll let you know the moment I hear anything."

"Thank you, Your Highness," Alexandra said. She knew for Dylan words like that must be incredibly awkward, but she'd grown up around diplomats. Titles were routine. She waited for George-Phillip to leave, then turned back to Dylan.

"I love you, Dylan."

"I love you," he whispered back.


## Carrie. May 6.

Carrie looked at the phone sitting on the table in front of her. Forty minutes before, she'd taken Rachel, who seemed to be running a slight fever, and put her down for her nap. Rachel was listless, and didn't want to drink, which left Carrie with swollen and painful breasts. She'd pump in a few minutes, but right now she was trying to decide what to do about her cell phone. In the background, the television was turned to CSPAN, where Richard Thompson was live on television, testifying before the Senate Armed Services Committee.

She'd missed two phone calls while putting Rachel down. One from Sarah, who hadn't come home the night before. She'd also sent a text message: **I'm with Andrea, headed west. Don't worry about us.**

The other call was from an unknown number, but the voice-mail was from her mother.

She sighed and closed her eyes. Deal with Sarah first. She sat on the couch, tucking her feet under her and facing the silent television. The cameras were focused on Senator Chuck Rainsley, his grey hair looking white under the bright lights. When had she met with him? Two days ago? Three?

She wondered if Richard had been lying to her about Rainsley, or did her mother lie to him? Was he sitting there in front of that committee now, thinking that the man who had cuckolded him was the same man questioning him?

Carrie shrugged. The web of lies was so complicated that she had no idea what to think.

*You were five before I knew. We'd already ... bonded.*

The subtext, of course, was that had he known she wasn't his daughter, he would have shoved her aside, disregarded her, maybe sent her away *just like he did with Andrea.*

Richard Thompson didn't deserve this much of her attention. She picked up the remote and turned the television off, then dialed Sarah's number.

The call went straight to voicemail. Of course. Carrie's stomach twisted a little, realizing there was no putting this phone call off. She thought about the last time she'd seen her mother, five months ago. She'd never gone so long without seeing her, but they'd still spoken regularly. She'd never been close to her mother—a lifetime of hurt prevented that. But she'd never, ever forget how her mother had stood up for her at the hospital, how she'd hugged Ray and burst into tears when she learned of their secret marriage. She'd never forget those black days after he died, days when she couldn't even get out of bed. Days when she wanted to die. Despite their painful past, their conflicts and sometimes their hate, her mother had been there for her and Sarah.

Her hand shook as she reached out and picked up the cell phone again. She dialed the unfamiliar number slowly, each digit heavier than the last, until it felt like she couldn't possibly dial the last number. But then she did.

She put the phone to her ear, trying to ignore the twisted feeling in her stomach. She didn't know the woman she was calling. Except that she'd suffered unspeakably, and Carrie—along with *all five* of her sisters—hadn't known, hadn't guessed, and for a lifetime they'd blamed her for it.

One ring. Then a second. Click. Then the voice she knew so well, high pitched, the very faint Spanish accent. "Hello? Carrie?"

Carrie's throat closed and she leaned forward, left hand across her stomach. She tried to say something. Anything. But no words came out.

"Carrie? Are you all right?"

"Mother," she whispered.

"Carrie, what's wrong?"

"I'm so sorry," Carrie whispered. Tears began running uncontrollably down her face. *Goddamn it!* She hadn't meant to fall apart. "I'm so, so sorry, Mother."

"What? Whatever for? Carrie, you must tell me what's wrong."

Carrie sniffed and blinked her eyes, rolling them up toward the ceiling to try to control the tears. But she couldn't, they just kept coming. She felt desolate. She whispered, "Julia found the police report, Mother. And the pictures. From Valentine's day."

Her mother sucked in a breath, and Carrie spoke again. "She found the diary. We would never have looked at it, not in a million years, but you were *missing*."

"*Madre de Dios*," Adelina whispered.

Carrie said, "I didn't know. *We* didn't know. We thought … we thought you were … crazy. That you hated us. We thought … we thought *he* was the sane one."

Adelina whispered, "All I ever wanted was to protect you."

Carrie sobbed. "You did. You did the best you could. Mom … I met my father. My real father. He seems like a good man. He told me … about you two. About … what happened to you in Spain. It wasn't perfect, Mom, but you *did* protect us. We just didn't know. I'm so sorry. I'm sorry I hated you."

"Carrie, you don't have to—"

"Please forgive me?" Carrie whispered.

"Of course. Carrie, you're my daughter. I'm the one who … I'm the one who needs forgiveness. From all of you."

"No," Carrie said. "It's…" She closed her eyes. Her mother sounded—she sounded as if the weight of her remorse would crush her. "I forgive you. You did the best you could, Mom. And … you don't know how much it meant to me. After Ray died. You saved my life. I wanted to die. And you gave me the courage to go on."

At the other end of the line, she heard her mother's voice catch, then sniffing. More tears. She waited, taking a deep breath.

Carrie felt … empty. Drained. The tears still ran down her face, but they weren't tears of grief. They weren't the desolate, awful tears and emptiness and death she'd felt after Ray died. They were tears of … relief. Of redemption. Of … joy? She'd lost a lot … but she'd gained something too. A father she'd never known. And a mother she'd never known either.

Both of them took some time to pull themselves together. Adelina was the first to speak.

"So you met Prince George-Phillip? Where?"

"He's in Washington, Mother. I don't know exactly why, but I understand he had a meeting with the President."

Silence at the other end of the line, except for her mother breathing.

"Mother, what is it?"

Her mother sniffed. Then she said, "I never stopped loving him, you know. I'd have given anything to have had a life with him. Except for you girls. That was the one price I couldn't pay."

Carrie closed her eyes. The tears threatened to overflow again. She thought about the unspeakable suffering her mother had been through. To protect her daughters. To protect *Carrie.* She whispered, "It's not too late."

In a sad voice, Adelina said, "I broke his heart, Carrie. Twice."

Carrie closed her eyes. Then in as forceful a voice as she could muster, she said, "Mother. It's *not too late.*"

Adelina sighed. Then she changed the subject. "Tell me—where are your sisters? I've been out of touch too long."

"You first," Carrie said. "How is Jessica?"

Adelina sighed. "She's stable and in recovery. It was ... you can't imagine, Carrie. You're a mother now ... but to see your daughter go through that ... she was addicted to meth, Carrie."

Carrie sucked in a breath. "How?"

"Grief and neglect and the wrong crowd all at once. After she and Richard came back to San Francisco last fall he retreated to his study and more or less ignored her. What he didn't know ... what none of us knew ... was that her girlfriend had killed herself."

"Oh no," Carrie gasped. "Which friend? Who?"

"Her girlfriend, Carrie. Jessica was in love with the poor girl."

"Oh..." Carrie said.

Adelina sobbed, then said, "She was afraid to tell me. She thought I'd hate her because she was a lesbian. My own daughter. That's how badly I've failed."

"*You didn't fail,*" Carrie said. "Mother ... you didn't. You're human, and there's only so much any of us could do. And ... none of us were there for her. None of us."

Abruptly Carrie remembered the Christmas before last. When she'd fallen in love with Ray (a stab of pain that they'd never celebrated Christmas together) and the morning when she'd gone downstairs and found her mother in tears.

*Was I that terrible a mother to you girls?*

Carrie remembered that she hadn't been able to say anything reassuring. She'd merely said, *You've mellowed out a lot over the years.* As if that did anything but dig the wounds in deeper. A few minutes later, Adelina had said, *I know you've always watched out for your sisters, you've always tried to fix things for them. And I'm grateful for that ... especially ... during those times when I couldn't be a good mother. You were a mother to them.*

Carrie sighed. Now it all made sense, it made a kind of terrible and heartbreaking sense.

"So ... Jessica fell in love. And the girl committed suicide. And she was all alone and got mixed up in drugs." The prompt steered her mother back onto the subject.

Adelina began speaking again. "When I got out here I got her into therapy. But I didn't realize how serious it was, until a few weeks ago. She came home late after going out without permission. She had blood on her forehead from a fall, and then she started vomiting. Carrie ... I was ... in a rage at first. Screaming at her. But then she had a seizure."

With the last word, Adelina's voice dropped to a tortured whisper and she continued. "She fell to the floor and her arms and legs were moving uncontrollably, and ... it was the most terrifying thing I'd ever seen. I called 911 and an ambulance came and got her to the emergency room."

Carrie closed her eyes. That explained the scene Julia had described at the house. There simply hadn't been time to clean up.

"Where are the rest of my daughters, Carrie?"

Carrie sighed. "Julia and Crank are staying at the condo with me for the time being, but Crank had to fly up to Boston this morning. The IRS has ... well, they've frozen their assets. He went up there to pay their employees in cash, and Julia is here dealing with the IRS. She'll be back this afternoon, I think."

Adelina sighed then said, "I met the lead investigator from the IRS. He seemed reasonable."

Carrie raised an eyebrow. "Really? When?"

"He left here a couple of hours ago."

Carrie let out a breath and said, "I'll let Julia know."

"And the others?" Adelina asked.

"Well, Dylan is trapped at the British Embassy for the time being. So Alexandra is there with him. I don't know how long that will last, though. The media picked up on it this morning. He ... well, there's no making it softer. When the condo was attacked on Friday, he killed two of the gunmen. One of them was a federal agent."

As Carrie said the words, her eyes involuntarily darted to the hallway floor. The carpet had been ripped out there by the FBI forensics lab. She presumed because it had blood on it.

Adelina sighed. "That poor boy. He already had a heavy enough burden on his soul."

Carrie whispered, "Yeah. He does. So that leaves Andrea and Sarah. Andrea *was* at the British embassy as well, but apparently last night she ran—jumped over the fence. George-Phillip called me this morning."

"Why?" Adelina cried.

"I don't know," Carrie said. "But Sarah stole Eddie's motorcycle and apparently picked up Andrea. Sarah sent me a text saying to not worry. But she didn't answer when I called. I'll try again as soon as I can."

Carrie looked around and said, "It's weird, really. Rachel's asleep. It's the first time I've been alone since last August. Since … well, since Ray died."

Adelina spoke quickly. "You're alone? Do you have any protection there?"

Carrie nodded. "Julia hired bodyguards. I think we're as well protected as we can possibly be."

Adelina sniffed again. Then she said, "Will you send this number to the rest of the girls? It's a prepaid cell phone."

"Yes, of course," Carrie said.

"And kiss your lovely daughter for me," Adelina said. "I'm sorry I haven't been able to meet her yet."

Carrie nodded, more tears beginning to slide down her face. "I will. And Mother, you stay safe. Please? Can Julia send *you* bodyguards?"

"We'll see. I think I'm okay for now. It's unlikely even Richard could find someone willing to murder publicly in a hospital."

*Even Richard?* Did her mother think it was he who had attacked them?

They said goodbye and Carrie walked in the other room to check on Rachel. Her daughter looked a little flushed, hair damp. She touched Rachel's forehead. She was hot to the touch. Troubled, Carrie went in search of a thermometer.

# CHAPTER TWELVE

## Perfect love casts out fear

Sarah. May 6.

**A**s they rode northwest, the sun setting in a blaze of reds and yellows, Sarah's eyes burned and she felt a heavy blanket of fatigue drape her body. Sixteen hard hours of driving on just two hours of sleep, and she was ready to collapse.

All around them, nothing but trees, grass, green and more green. The air was noticeably cooler and less soupy than late spring in Washington, DC, and the air was cleaner too. But even the cool air, the new scenery and the constant vibration of the motorcycle weren't enough to keep her awake.

She tapped Andrea on the shoulder. Her younger sister had been driving for most of the day, and seemed to have unlimited energy. But, even though it had been nine months, Sarah was still recovering from a horrific injury.

And then there was the Jeep.

It happened not long after they'd switched driving at two in the afternoon. Andrea had been driving most of the morning, with just two stops for the bathroom and then a quick fast food lunch.

"I'll drive," Sarah had said.

"You sure?" Andrea asked. "You look tired."

"I'm fine," she responded. She *was* tired, but she wasn't going to let her younger sister shoulder the entire burden of this drive, injury or not. It had been many months since the car accident. She should be able to manage this now. So she got on the bike, determined to do her share.

The first twenty minutes were completely uneventful. Not too much traffic, and it was a beautiful day. Sarah felt confident and happy.

And then there was the Jeep.

It was large, forest green with a chrome grill, and appeared in her rearview mirror. The license plate was blue and red, almost like the Virginia plates she'd once seen emblazoned with the letters GR8 DAD. Sarah felt her throat close up, the muscles in her arms and chest tense. She began to breathe rapidly and felt a pain in the center of her chest.

She accelerated and switched lanes to try to move away from the Jeep as unspeakable terror rose in her throat. She knew it wasn't *that* Jeep, the one that had ended Ray's life and nearly her own. She knew it couldn't be. After all, Sergeant James Hicks, the man who had gotten behind the wheel of that Jeep with murder in his heart—he was dead.

That didn't make it any easier. Because she felt tears in her eyes and her vision went slightly blurry.

The Jeep appeared again. One lane over, no more than ten feet away from her. Sarah panicked, jerking the bike over slightly, running them almost into the truck in the left lane. That only increased the panic, her heart suddenly beating wildly, and she twisted the accelerator in her right hand.

The bike responded instantly, and they leapt forward. Sarah leaned forward, even as Andrea tightened her arms around Sarah's waist. She sped the bike forward, switched lanes, then switched again, weaving around the cars ahead of them.

Andrea tapped on her shoulder, hard, then screamed almost in her ear, "What are you doing?"

Sarah's panic hadn't subsided. The Jeep was no longer in the mirror, but it was still in her chest, and she pulled to the side of the road, letting the bike coast the last few feet, then she shut it off.

"What's wrong?" Andrea had asked.

Sarah hadn't answered, just pushed herself off the bike as quickly as she could, walking to the grass on the shoulder. She threw her helmet on the ground and fell to her knees, then puked, acid and bile splattering the grass.

Then the thought struck Sarah. Is this what her mother had felt like all those years? If so, no wonder Adelina Thompson had seemed crazy, because Sarah couldn't breathe.

Andrea had knelt beside her and put a hand on her shoulder. "What happened?" she had whispered.

"Nothing," Sarah said, tears springing unbidden to her eyes. "Nothing at all. Everything."

"It's okay," Andrea responded.

After that, Andrea drove.

At the next stop, just outside Minneapolis, they sat down to discuss the route.

"It's still another 26 hours driving time," Sarah said, her face glum. She looked up at Andrea, then said, "I can't make it. Not without a lot of rest. I'm sorry, Andrea. I'm just not—"

"It's okay," Andrea responded. "You're still recovering. What are our options?"

"I think Amtrak has a northern route. I don't know if they go through here. Or we could fly?"

Andrea shook her head. "My identification is fake. I don't even have a passport, the police took it when I was kidnapped."

Sarah sighed. Her eyebrows furrowed, then she said, "What about a charter flight? How much of that money do you have left?"

"I can't imagine what that costs," Andrea said.

"A lot," Sarah responded. "I think. Julia and Crank have to hire one on contract, they said individual charters were way too much."

Andrea winced. "Train then."

They got lucky. At ten pm, they boarded the westbound Amtrak Empire Builder bound for Seattle, Washington. They'd be there at ten in the morning on Thursday, a lot sooner—and more refreshed—than if they'd ridden the Harley the entire distance.

Sarah sent a text to Eddie: **Please forgive me. I left the hog in Minneapolis. I promise I'll get it back to you.**

She waited nervously. Thirty seconds later, he texted back. **You're really going to make me choose between you and my bike?**

Sarah let out a nervous laugh. If he could joke, then it wasn't *too* bad. She texted back: Is there any doubt of the outcome?

This time the reply took a lot longer. Long enough to start making her nervous. But then it came: **No. I'd choose you.**

Well, *shit*, she thought. Unfamiliar emotion washed over her. Affection. Maybe even love. When she thought about Eddie, it gave her chills sometimes.

He'd once said to her, *I think I fell in love with you the moment I saw you.* That was a neat trick, considering that when he first saw her she was unconscious with her left leg crushed between the driver's seat and door panel of Carrie's Mercedes.

Eddie had seen her at her worst, cursing in rage and pain when the morphine wore off, filthy and covered in vomit and in so much pain she hated the world. She didn't understand why he'd stayed through all that. And when she asked, he just shrugged and said, *It's all good, I got nothin' else to do.*

Which was bullshit. He was pre-med at George Washington University, and worked part time as an EMT, and was heavily involved on campus as well.

Well, she wasn't going to complain.

As exhausted as they both were, Andrea and Sarah began to drift to sleep almost immediately after the car pulled out of the station, the car rocking a little as the wheels clicked on the tracks. Sarah felt her eyes getting heavier and heavier, and she fell straight into a dream.

She was still in the train car, and Andrea was curled up asleep next to her, her long legs curled up almost to her chest. But no one else was in the long car. Sarah stood and looked around. It was dark outside, the sky the color of India ink, no lights or passing houses or streets. Nothing. The car rocked under her feet, unsteady, and she carefully stepped down the aisle toward the next car. Instead of the black rubber mat she thought the train had as its floor, it was cold, hard stone or marble, polished to a high shine. The reflection of the floor reminded her somehow of a promise she'd made, but she couldn't remember what it was.

She knelt down, tracing the hard floor with her fingertips. What had she promised?

She didn't know. It felt like it was a million years ago. She stood, and walked down the hallway toward the sliding doors ahead. It was silent in the hospital corridor, the walls the same tan fabric she remembered from the previous summer, artwork engineered to be offensive to no one spaced evenly along the walls.

Beyond the door it would be plainer, the walls simple off-white, the waiting room opening into the intensive care unit. She didn't want to go in there—too many bad memories. Too much terror. But even so, she felt herself drawn toward the sliding double doors. She felt herself shiver. It was cold—the kind of cold that claws its way into your bones and won't let go no matter how hard you fight. She wanted to go anywhere else but this antiseptic place where the smells assaulted her nostrils and burned into her brain.

But she kept going. As she walked closer, the doors slid open, and a little boy ran by with a Spider-Man T-shirt and a blue and orange baseball cap. She turned to say something, but he was already gone before she could take a breath.

She shivered. Something about that boy was important. But what? She didn't know. She shook her head and turned back toward the doors and walked through.

Her brow furrowed. It wasn't at all what she expected. Instead of a cold and antiseptic intensive care unit, the room beyond was ... well ... not a room. It was almost a jungle. Lush tropical plants were everywhere, growing under the bright sunshine. Sparrows were scattered about on the ground, pecking at it, and high up in one of the trees, a sloth hung from a branch, basking in the sunshine.

Then she saw him. In a clearing surrounded by half a dozen trees was an Adirondack chair covered in peeling white paint. Ray Sherman sat in the chair, inexplicably wearing khaki shorts and a grey Army T-shirt. His feet, resting on a tree stump, were bare. Another taller tree stump acted as a table, and a green drink in a martini glass rested on it. Ray wore a floppy canvas hat and was reading a book.

Confused emotions flooded through Sarah as she realized this must be a dream. Ray was dead, after all, and it really wasn't fair that Sarah should see him in a dream. That should be Carrie.

Not that she was making any sense at all. It's not like she had any control over her dreams. But she stood there and studied him anyway. He looked different than the last time she'd seen him. For one thing, he was relaxed and was wearing civilian clothes instead of his camouflage uniform.

That made no sense. Sarah had never seen him in his duty uniform, just the dress uniform he'd worn to the wedding. Or had she? Why would she expect him to be wearing that? She shook her head, because she didn't understand. But he was clearly there, his stubble making it clear he hadn't shaved that morning. He reached out and took a sip from the martini glass.

She shook her head then cleared her throat.

Ray glanced up from his book and smiled.

"Hey," he said. "I was wondering if you were ever going to come by."

"Come by? What is this place?"

He shrugged. "I don't know exactly. It's a good place, though. Have a seat?"

She started to say, "There aren't any seats," but before the words came out of her mouth, she saw that there was one, another Adirondack chair complete with a footstool and a drink.

Bemused, she sat down. The chair was solid enough.

She sighed, and said, "Carrie misses you terribly. It's been hard for her."

He nodded. "I know. I miss her, too. Heaven is nice and all ... but seriously, it won't be complete until I know she's safe. Until then I just hang out here. I've been catching up on my reading. You ... you can't imagine how beautiful it is here."

"Oh, yeah?" she asked, feeling like an idiot.

"Yeah. You know how it is, there's never enough time to read everything you want when you're alive. But now I've got all the time in the world."

Ray might be dead, but he was still weird.

"You know things have been pretty crazy. Rachel's sick. And they don't know if she's going to get better."

At that, he looked troubled. "I know," he said. "Sometimes I wish I could ... you know ... do something. But I can't ... well ... it's complicated. In the end, she'll be okay. We all will."

Sarah closed her eyes. He didn't understand. They were all in tremendous danger. "Ray ... things are bad."

He nodded. "I know. But you know what to do. You always have."

She shook her head. "I don't. Can you show yourself to Carrie? Even in a dream?"

He sighed. "I ... I can't. It makes it harder for her. I tried to stick around last fall, you know. I did for a long time. You were a terror for your mom." His face sobered. "Carrie was so sad, it broke my heart. But then one day I knew it was time. I said goodbye when you guys were at the zoo."

He didn't make sense at all. Sarah wanted to shake him. "Ray ... what do I do?"

He took his feet off the stump, leaning forward and planting his bare feet on the ground. He looked her closely in the eyes, studying her for a moment. It was unnerving, his eyes boring into hers. This didn't feel like a dream at all, and her heart began to beat rapidly, almost as if another panic attack were coming. Even the thought made her muscles tense.

"It's okay," he whispered. He rested a hand on her shoulder. "What you do is love." He looked around then waved his hands vaguely toward the trees and jungle that surrounded them. "All of this ... all of us ... everything. You love. You ... forgive."

She took in a deep, shuddering breath. She thought again about her mother and the panic attacks and how much they hurt and terrified her.

"I'm afraid, Ray. I'm afraid."

He smiled, and said, "Well, perfect love casts out fear, Sarah." He reached out and with a bare fingertip, touched her cheek. "You can do it. Everything you need is right here. In your heart."

She closed her eyes. For just a second, a tendril of memory took her back to the hospital, to a moment of crisis, when Ray had saved her life.

She didn't understand. That never happened. She drifted, and opened her eyes, and Ray was gone, and she was in her seat on the train, rocking back and forth as the tracks rattled beneath her, and she heard his words, *Perfect love casts out fear.*

She let her eyes close again and drifted into a deep sleep.

# CHAPTER THIRTEEN
# CALL ME, URGENT

"**M**rs. Wilson, I want to tell you I appreciate your cooperation. I'm going to instruct the bank to free up your operating accounts so that you can make payroll."

Julia sagged in her seat in relief. The operating account wouldn't last long—maybe three months—but at least she'd be able to pay her employees. She closed her eyes for a moment, rubbing the bridge of her nose with two fingers and a thumb, then looked back up. "Thank you, Miss Smith."

Barrymore—Julia's lawyer—leaned back and said, "We've provided you with full financial records of the company—with all the information you could possibly need. What else can we do to help here? As I stated this morning, my client is innocent of any wrongdoing and we want to help this investigation succeed just as much as you do."

The IRS investigator, Emma Smith, said, "I'll have my team look over the documents and we'll get back with you. I do appreciate your cooperation."

Smith stood, followed by Kelly and Shriver from Diplomatic Security and the FBI. Julia and Barrymore, with their assistant attorneys, also stood. In an awkward exchange, Smith, Kelly and Shriver all passed business cards to both Julia and Barrymore, then they all shook hands. It felt like the end of a standard business meeting or negotiation. Not a near apocalypse. Her mind was unfocused for a moment as Emma Smith made small talk.

Julia had never been much for idle chatter. But she couldn't vent her frustration until she was out of the IRS headquarters and on her way. In the elevator, she said, "Marty, do you need a ride back to your office?"

"Nah," he said. "I walked over, it's only a few blocks."

As he spoke, he was turning his phone back on. He gave her a sideways look, and opened his mouth as if he were going to ask what had happened during the brief period she'd met alone with the investigators. Julia started to turn her phone on, pointedly ignoring his unstated question then realized she was still holding the business cards. She glanced at them. Standard government business cards—the seal of the agency they worked for, name, phone number. But Scott Kelly's had a short handwritten note on the back. It said, "Call me for anything." A 703 area code number was handwritten below it. 703 was Northern Virginia—Kelly probably commuted to DC from Virginia. That would be his cell phone then. She put the card in her purse. Allies were necessary, wherever they could be found.

The elevator opened just as her phone finished booting up, and as they walked out the door of the building, the chime of several text messages rang out. She ignored them, dialing the Pinkerton driver instead. Moments later, a sleek black Escalade pulled up to the curb. A bodyguard jumped out of the passenger seat and opened the door. Julia slid into the car and turned toward Marty, standing outside.

"At least you're well protected," he said.

"It's costing enough. I'll catch up with you later. Let me know if you hear anything." He waved and walked away, and the driver closed the door. She glanced at the text messages on her phone. Four of them were routine business related messages. One from Crank said: **All okay in Boston! The team is confident. On my way back, see you about nine. Love you, babe.**

She smiled wryly as she texted him back: **IRS went well. Update later, but we'll be able to stay open for now.**

Then she looked at the last message. It was from Mike DeMint, the band's publicist. **CALL ME, URGENT.**

Mike didn't use hyperbole, and an all caps message with the word urgent in it meant just that. She dialed the number.

"Julia?" he answered immediately. "Problems."

"Mike, what's up?"

"Okay, so you're gonna be pissed. Are you sitting down?"

"Yes, Mike, I'm sitting down. What is going on?"

"It looks like Maria Clawson is making a comeback. She was all over Fox News this afternoon as an official commentator on your father's hearings, which aren't going very well."

Julia burst out into language that would have made Crank blush if he'd heard it. When she calmed down, she asked, "What else?"

"That's not the worst of it. She's trying to tie it all up with the IRS investigation into your company. You're going to have to respond."

She found herself shaking her head as the car pulled out into traffic.

"I'm not responding to anything, Mike. Not without a lot more information. What exactly did she say?"

"She's got a long blog post today. It digs back into your father's hearings as Ambassador to Russia back around 2000. And mentions you and … your past. When you were in high school."

Another string of curses from Julia.

"Anyway ... looks like she's trying to make a comeback—at your expense. The blog post was ... sensationalist. Stupid. And it stops short of libelous; you're going to have a very difficult time doing anything about it. And it was big enough that she's out there now in public."

Julia closed her eyes and took a breath, then said, "Let me look at her blog, I need to get caught up."

She disconnected the phone. Moments later she was on Maria Clawson's website, which had been inactive for three years.

Now it had a sensational headline at the top.

### UH OH: RICHARD THOMPSON AND JULIA WILSON BACK IN THE NEWS WITH NEW AND IMPROVED SCANDAL: WILSON MUM ABOUT ACCUSATIONS OF DRUG MONEY LAUNDERING

Julia felt bile in her throat. Side by side photos at the top of the page, which was designed like a late 1990s Geocities website with flashing icons and multicolored text, showed her father at the witness table, right hand raised in the air, and an incredibly un-flattering photo of Julia and Crank which had graced the cover of *National Enquirer* two months ago. In the photo of her and Crank, she was leaning over to pick her cell phone off the ground where she'd dropped it on the sidewalk. The asshole photographer had manned to get a shot right up her shirt at a particularly graceless moment.

Crank had stopped making a habit of punching photographers ten years ago, but there were times when she wished he'd start again.

The first three paragraphs of the blog post held no surprises— a recap of the hearing. She scanned through it, interested in how it had gone, but still incredibly resentful of her father's lies. From the tone of the article, the Armed Services committee had raked her father over the coals.

But the third paragraph started to get interesting.

**Not surprisingly, unnamed sources within the Special Prosecutor's office have named Julia Wilson (wife and manager of obnoxious rocker Crank Wilson) as her father's primary accomplice, by funneling millions of dollars through a network of shell companies and hidden accounts in the Caymans.**

**Loyal readers will recall that this is not the first time the two have been linked in scandal. Suspicions that Thompson had arranged a secret abortion for his then fourteen-year-old party-girl daughter delayed Thompson's nomination as Ambassador to Russia.**

*Party-girl.* The accusation didn't have the frightening sting it once held. During the first period of Clawson's campaign against her father, Julia had been under eighteen, and Clawson never identified her by name. But a photograph that should never have been taken surfaced on the Internet—a photograph of Julia, fourteen, lying across the laps of two boys.

She'd been fourteen, scared, abused and desperately lonely and afraid. Harry Easton, now an attaché at the British Embassy in Washington, DC, had been her much older boyfriend back then.

She closed her eyes and shoved the old fears and resentments back. She didn't have time for this. She could not fall apart. Carrie and her other sisters needed her. Her employees needed her.

She moved on from the blog post to *The Washington Post*.

Front and center on the paper was the same photo of her father at the witness table. She scanned through the article and winced. Twelve paragraphs in—far down in the article, but still present—Maria Clawson surfaced:

Media critic Maria Clawson linked the current outrage to a series of past scandals involving the Thompson family, including an accusation that Ambassador Thompson arranged a secret abortion for his then fourteen-year-old daughter Julia. In an interview on Fox News, Clawson said, "Before she started managing her drug-promoting counter-culture punk band, Julia had a history of drunken and drugged outbursts which scandalized the diplomatic community. It's common really—the overprivileged kids of the rich and famous going crazy is almost a stereotype. It's a shame, really, because with her platform, Julia Wilson could do some real good in the world."

Julia wanted to kill someone. Starting with that bitch Clawson.

She dialed Mike DeMint back. He answered on the first ring.

"Mike, I want a strategy. We need to hit back and hard. What do I do?"

He didn't hesitate. "You go on the air. Take her on directly. Tell your side of the story, especially the impact her blog had on your life. I'd suggest something like Barbara Walters. She's retiring in a couple weeks, I bet she'll do it. You're a huge catch."

Julia shook her head, feeling nauseous. Then she said, "All right. You make the arrangements and let me know. We'll take it all public. Let me just get permission from my sisters. Some of the story is theirs."

"Yeah, whatever. Just let me know quick. Your window to strike back is short."

"How short?"

"With media cycles the way they are? I think you need to move tonight and probably interview tomorrow. I'll do a brief statement tonight and get it on the website and social media."

Julia closed her eyes and counted to five thousand. Or maybe five. She *hated* dealing with the media. "All right," she said. "Do your worst."

She disconnected the phone. Traffic was unusually light for DC. Of course, their interview with the IRS had run very late, a marathon session. The clock on the dashboard reported 8:30 pm, which was past time for rush hour. As the driver sped up Wisconsin Avenue toward Bethesda, she texted each of her sisters, telling them her plans. If they were going to survive this, all of this, they had to be there for each other like they'd never managed before.

Fifteen minutes later, the SUV came to a stop in front of the condo.

"Wait a moment," the driver said. The bodyguard got out of the car and joined two more who were working the lobby.

What felt like thirty minutes later, but was actually only thirty seconds, one of the guards opened the door. "Mrs. Wilson, I'll escort you inside."

As she got out of the car, her phone started to ring. She took it out and answered without looking at the caller ID as she followed the guard to the front door.

"Julia." She felt a chill. It was her father. Her gut reaction was to hang up the phone.

*You've never done anything but lie to me.*

Those were the last words she'd said to her father. When was it ... four days ago? He'd tried to make excuses, to avoid taking responsibility for what he'd done to her mother. *Her mother.* Adelina Thompson had been the most hideous figure in her life. Frantic. Often crazy. Screaming attacks and rage and bitter, hurtful comments.

*I woke up to find you on Maria Clawson's website nearly having sex with a drug addict.*

Julia had responded, *No, Mother, we were just kissing. Believe me, I know the difference.*

*I'm sure you do.* Her mother's barbed response had wounded.

*I didn't raise my daughter to be a slut.*

The words still bled, no matter how many years had passed.

Alexandra lost in the airport. *Can't you do anything right?*

Alexandra hurt when she fell down the steps. *I can't turn my back on you for thirty seconds!*

Yes, the words still hurt, but she saw new scenes now, heard new words. Carrie, six years old, throwing a fit because their mother couldn't play with them. Adelina had been black and blue. She hadn't gotten off the couch in days.

*The police report.*

The words had been stark. Incredibly damaging.

*Contusions around neck.*

*Third, fourth and fifth ribs on the right side cracked.*

*Blunt force trauma.*

Her father had been the suspect. The attack had happened *one day* after the report came back showing Carrie wasn't related to him.

She walked forward into the lobby of the condo, her heels clicking on the floor, and it felt as if she were running a gauntlet.

His voice sounded ragged. Exhausted.

"Hello, Father," she said. Cautious.

"Julia. Darling."

She blinked then said, "What do you want?"

"I wanted to talk to my daughters. And Carrie won't even answer my calls."

She sighed. "Yet you think I will?"

"You're my oldest daughter, Julia. We've always understood each other."

She took a breath. "I think you presume a lot more than you ought to. I think you've left a lot to be explained."

"Of course," he said. "And I'll answer whatever questions you have. Julia ... you and the other girls ... you're all I have."

She let out a breath. "Not Mother?"

"Your mother is unstable. You *know* that."

"I don't know what to believe from you."

His response was firm. "Believe this. I've had the worst day of my life today. I've faced the most brutal Senate hearing you can imagine. And I'm devastated that you girls would believe *her* over *me*. After all she's ... done. Julia ... please. All I ask is that you listen. Meet me for a drink and we'll talk. You'll see. You're the only one who will listen to me."

Her mind went to the photos in the police report. Her mother black and blue. The DNA results. The lies about her mother's age. But then she knew he was right about some things. Her mother *was* unstable. Her mother *had* lied to them all, over and over again. And he was her father. He'd always been the stable one. What if there was a real explanation?

"I don't know what good it will do."

"Julia, you're my daughter. You and I ... we've always been the closest. I'm begging you. Hear me out."

She sighed. Then slowly, she said, "All right. Let me tell Crank, and we'll meet. Where?"

# CHAPTER FOURTEEN
## A six-foot-deep hole

Julia. May 6.

**T**he lounge in the Bethesda Hyatt Regency was small and elegant, sitting just to the side of the open atrium that towered above them. On the other side of the bar, a young man, possibly twenty-five, gently played a highly polished grand piano. It was Tuesday evening, so the lounge wasn't very crowded, but it was relatively dark. Julia and her father sat at a table in the back corner, far away from the other patrons.

"All right," she said as the waitress walked away with their drink orders—double whiskey sour for her father and club soda for Julia. She craved a drink right then. But this wasn't the time. "You wanted to talk. I'm listening."

He frowned and loosened his tie. Julia blinked then glanced at her purse, resting on the seat of the chair to her left. Her father was one of the most stilted and anal-retentive men she'd ever met. For him to do anything so human as to loosen his tie in public showed a level of discomfort that stunned her. But she kept that reaction to herself. Julia had learned a great deal from both of her parents, and one thing she knew how to do expertly was out-WASP her father. She betrayed no reaction to his discomfort.

"First of all—Julia ... I need you to know I'm disappointed. Disappointed that after all I've done for you ... as close as we've been ... that you would assume the worst without even giving me an opportunity to explain or defend myself."

Julia didn't respond. How could he possibly think his actions were defensible? What could he possibly say?

"Well?" he asked.

She shrugged minutely. "What do you want me to say? I saw the police report. You both lied about Mother's age. You both lied about Carrie and Andrea's birth. Dad ... the police report ... she had broken ribs. She was beaten and raped."

Richard closed his eyes and exhaled. He didn't answer right away, but the skin between his eyes formed a furrow just above his nose. He rubbed the bridge of his nose between his thumb and fingers. Julia looked away. She was well aware she had the exact same mannerism when confronted with extreme stress.

"First of all—yes, your mother and I lied about her age. We were ... young, and in love. And in Spain it didn't matter at all that she was seventeen when we married. But I knew full well that would be frowned upon when we went back to the United States. So we publicly fudged the numbers. It never occurred to me it would become a big deal. Who could have predicted how wrong everything has gone in our lives, Julia?"

"And Carrie and Andrea? Dad ... that's not exactly a small lie. She had an affair with a British Prince? For fifteen years or more? Dad, I don't know about the rest of my sisters, but I feel betrayed. Why did we never know? And the police report? What happened? Why?" She shook her head, speechless. At the word *Prince* his eyes had widened slightly.

"What's this about a Prince?"

She raised her eyebrows. "Surely..."

Richard shook his head in disgust. "You see? This is just one more example of her lies. She swore to me that Senator Rainsley was the father. It almost destroyed our marriage, you know. I mean ... I wasn't perfect. And as I told you before, when we were in

China, I ... was briefly involved with another woman. I made my amends. But this ... I assume you're referring to Prince George-Phillip?"

Julia nodded slowly.

His response was fierce. "She never told me *that*. She lied to me about who she'd had the affair with. Or perhaps she slept with both of them. I wouldn't put anything past her. Julia, I don't know how you can sit there and make accusations against me when you *know* how unstable she is."

Julia flinched. Of course she knew her mother was unstable. Not just unstable, but downright crazy sometimes. She closed her eyes, mind drifting back to that awful night in Spain when her mother had collapsed, gibbering in fear. Carrie and Alexandra had been too young to do anything, both of them panicking. They'd arrived in Calella late, it was dark and the streets had been crowded with men and women out partying and drinking. Julia hadn't known what to do. She didn't know their grandmother's address, she didn't speak Spanish, she didn't know *anything*. Her mother hadn't been able to do anything at all to protect her daughters, then or ever.

*Why would I want to know? Why would I ask when my oldest daughter had become a drunken slut?*

It didn't matter how much time had passed, or how many times they had nice Friday afternoon chats on the phone. It didn't matter how much Adelina Thompson had done for Carrie and Sarah after the accident. Those words couldn't be taken back, ever. She didn't believe her father, but she didn't believe her mother either. She didn't believe anything at all.

Julia slowly nodded. "Yes. I know she's unstable. But how else am I to interpret that police report? And it happened the day after you found out about Carrie."

"Julia, yes, I had a paternity test. I'd suspected for a long time that your mother had an affair with Chuck Rainsley. The first time he ever came to our house for dinner, she spent the entire time blushing and chatting with him. I spent a lot of time that spring overseas, mostly in Pakistan and Afghanistan—"

"Anthony Walker said you were probably CIA and not State Department. Is that true?"

Her father blinked and his mouth tightened. "The Post reporter?"

She nodded.

"He's astute. I was an employee of the CIA for many years, Julia, under deep cover as a diplomat. It's not all that uncommon. And don't talk to me about hiding things from you. No intelligence agent tells their children what they do for a living. That would have put you all in significant danger."

"So why tell me now?"

He shrugged. "I retired twelve years ago. I can't discuss specific operations with you or anyone, but my employment with the CIA will be widely public by morning. It was disclosed at the hearing today."

"So back to ... the affair. And the police report."

"Right," he said, taking a deep breath. "So, I suspected the affair. It was little things. Unexpected moodiness. Did you know that one time she smashed her violin? And left it in pieces on my pillow?"

A sudden flash of memory, one of Julia's earliest. Carrie was a baby, sitting in her highchair screaming, her little face bright red. She might have been a year old? Julia had been ... four? She'd been sitting in the corner, tearing the pages out of a book she'd found. Julia didn't know if they'd had a nanny then, but she must not have been there that day, because Adelina had seen her and screamed.

*Julia, what are you doing?* The scream had startled her, and then Adelina snatched the book out of her hands. Julia remembered blood suddenly on her hands, pouring out of two of her fingers. Paper cuts, she realized now. She'd started to shriek, and Carrie was shrieking, and her mother had grabbed her by the wrist and dragged her toward the kitchen doorway where Carrie's highchair was. The screaming got louder and somehow they shuffled and Julia could still remember the slow motion when Carrie's highchair tipped over backward, the terrifying smack as it hit the hardwood floor.

Julia shuddered. Yes. She could easily imagine her mother leaving a broken and smashed violin on her husband's pillow. Adelina Thompson had been dangerously unstable their entire life. In retrospect, she realized that it was a lucky thing Carrie hadn't fractured her skull that day.

She redirected her attention to her father, who was still speaking.

"...when the report came in, I confronted your mother. She'd *lied* to me, Julia. *For years.* So, of course, I confronted her. Adelina was hysterical ... she went berserk. She screamed at me and threw things. Julia, I swear to you, I would never lay a hand on your mother. I loved her. I always loved her. And you know that. I stayed with her despite her *years* of infidelity. The fact is, Adelina is mentally ill. She always has been. What kind of husband would I be to leave her when she was sick?"

Julia grimaced, shifting uncomfortably. What her father said was true. Her mother *was* clearly mentally ill. Julia had witnessed too many years of panic attacks and anxiety driven freak-outs to come to any other conclusion.

"So what happened?" she whispered.

"She ran. Out the door, and out into the street. I confess, I thought she was just angry, and going for a walk to cool down. Sometimes she did that ... Adelina is a passionate woman, but not one who deals with personal confrontation very well."

*No kidding.*

"When she didn't come back after an hour, I called Melissa Brewer and sent you girls over there, and I drove, looking for her. We didn't have cell phones then, of course, so all I could do was search, then check back at home every once in a while to see if she'd come home. I was frantic."

As he told the story, Julia found herself nodding. Unfortunately, so far it was completely believable.

"So ... by ten that night, I was panicking. I called the police, but they told me they couldn't do anything until she was gone for twenty-four hours."

"So what happened?" Julia asked.

"At one am the phone rang. It was Adelina. She was calling from ... from a pay phone in the Tenderloin."

Julia sucked in a breath. Her father looked ashen as he continued his story.

"I immediately went to her. I don't know if you know what it was like back then—San Francisco now isn't what it was twenty-five years ago. Back then the whole district was ... massage parlors and cabarets. Whores and pimps and drug dealers. Homeless men sleeping in doorways. Junkies and transvestites and derelicts. I found your mother at a bus stop on this filthy street corner. Her clothes were torn and she was glassy eyed—drunk or drugged or I don't know what. She was battered and bruised and..."

He stopped speaking and stared off into space. Julia didn't react.

He swallowed and looked back at her. "I don't tell you this to bullshit you, Julia. It's what it was. She was in bad shape. I took her to the hospital, and we were hours waiting in the emergency room. Finally they saw her, and that took hours more. It was about three in the morning when the police questioned me. It was routine— they *always* question the husband when a woman is assaulted."

He sighed and shrugged. "It was awful. Just ... awful. Julia ... I love your mother. And I second-guessed myself for years. Should I have just let it go and not confronted her? I felt responsible. It's not as if I didn't know that she was unstable. And it just got worse. We went to Belgium and ... well ... you remember her hospitalization."

Julia stared at the table. Of course she remembered. She remembered every slap, every bitter word.

"Julia, I swear to you, I never laid a hand on your mother. And I'd do anything for her to be healthy again. We once loved each other ... surely you know that. She was ... so beautiful when we met. Young and happy and full of life. I know things were awful when you were a teenager, but don't you remember when you were little? She used to take you to church, and sometimes we'd have lunch afterward?"

"I remember," Julia said. Her eyes watered.

## Richard. May 6.

When Julia's eyes watered, he knew he had her. Julia had always been his closest daughter, the most loyal. From the time she was a toddler, he'd done everything he could to ensure her loyalty and love. And done just as much to ensure that she felt nothing but fear of her mother.

"Of course I remember." She stared at the table, as if she were reviewing memories in her mind. And he knew that many of those memories were of hugs from him. Throwing her up in the air as they laughed. Embracing her as she came off the stage at her first piano recital.

"Do you think that's why she went so crazy and distant when we were in Belgium and China? Because of the assault?"

He shrugged, but inside, he was filled with glee. He needed Julia as his ally, and it was clear he'd won her over, or at least begun to. "I don't know. Her psychiatrists suggested that it might be some post-traumatic stress. But some of the instability was there even before."

Julia sighed. "What about Andrea?"

"What about her?"

Julia winced. "Why was she ... why did she spend so much time in Spain growing up?"

*Careful.* Julia and her sisters had almost fanatical loyalty to each other. If she detected any hint of hostility toward Andrea, he would lose her. So, he drove another nail into Adelina's coffin. "I should never have given in to her on that. Adelina wanted it. She said that at least one of her daughters should grow up Spanish. It was irrational."

"But you told Carrie that it was ... you hadn't ... bonded with Andrea."

He leaned forward and looked at her with a serious expression. "It's true, I guess, though I'm ashamed to admit it. Would I have allowed Adelina to send her away if she were mine? I guess ... I wouldn't have. But it's what your mother wanted. And, I guess the truth is, sometimes I found it was easier to give in to her rather than have to deal with months of hysteria."

He ran a hand through his hair, knowing the gesture of insecurity would help persuade her, and that his self-deprecation would come across as honesty. Disarm her suspicion.

She shook her head, then said, "Is that why you never protected us from her? Because it was ... easier?"

He closed his eyes. Better to take the hit on this one and win her over. He spoke in a low tone. "I suppose it was. And I'll regret that to the end of my days."

"I know you did the best you could," she said. *Excellent.* She continued. "But I've still got questions. Why the kidnapping? The IRS investigation? What the hell is happening? And why did you have that file in your office? The one with the pictures of the ... dead bodies from Afghanistan?"

He cursed at himself for the instinct that had led him to keep those photos, to keep that file. Nothing in it had been classified. Nothing in it that hadn't made the papers. But those photos— they showed a power that had awed him. A single bottle, tightly secured inside a steel container. That was all it had taken to kill the entire village. And that power had been in *his* hands. But that, he could never admit to. He might feel his own thrill—much as he'd felt when the truck he'd driven had smacked into the body of Manuel Ramos, smashing the pompous old man's body and cracking his skull open like a rotted watermelon.

"You should never have seen that. It wasn't classified anymore, but it ought to be. Back in 1983 Afghan militia attacked a village with chemical weapons and killed everyone."

"I know about the incident, I've read a fair amount about it."

Of course she had. She was his daughter far more than Adelina's, and he knew she wouldn't walk into a meeting like this without being prepared. But he was ten laps ahead of her—no matter how fast she was, she wouldn't be able to gain control of the situation.

He said, "Then you probably know that at the time, the United States blamed the Soviet Union for it. But what no one knew was that Leslie Collins was responsible for it."

"Leslie Collins? As in the Leslie Collins you used to have over for dinner all the time?"

"Yes. I didn't find that out until much later, of course, and reported it as soon as I knew. But the higher ups in the Agency at the time decided to cover it up instead. Because it was in the interest of national security."

"And you went along with that?"

"I had no choice, Julia."

"So why all the stuff that's happening now?"

He looked at his daughter. Time to plant a seed that would drive a wedge between his daughters and George-Phillip. The thought of that man made him seethe. How the hell had Adelina managed to keep a secret like that all those years? He remembered how many times over three decades he'd had meetings with George-Phillip. Talked over drinks at Embassy functions in different countries. How many times he'd *touched his hands*. Richard wanted to vomit at the thought of it. He wanted to kill. Instead, he spoke in a calm and rational manner.

"Actually I think there are two things happening here. And you gave me the last puzzle piece."

"What piece?" she asked, arching both eyebrows.

"Well, first, I think Collins knew that if I took over as Secretary of Defense, I'd move to have the cover up of Wakhan declassified finally. That would end his career and likely see him in prison. I believe he engineered the secret accounts to discredit me. And you, unfortunately, are an innocent bystander. I assumed he was behind the kidnapping as well. It certainly made the drug money angle more convincing. But now I wonder if something else entirely happened with Andrea."

"What?" She tilted her head. She was hooked.

"Prince George-Phillip, of course. Can you imagine what a scandal it would be if it became public that he'd had a long-standing affair with Adelina? With two children? The easiest way to handle that would be to ensure that those children no longer existed, wouldn't it?"

Julia winced, a slight furrow appearing between her eyebrows. She reached into her purse and took out a tattered, tightly bound book.

"One more thing. What about this, Dad? It's Mother's journal. And it says you raped her."

*Christ, that crazy bitch kept a journal?* He cursed at himself. How had he missed that? He knew for sure she hadn't kept one in the eighties—he'd thoroughly searched her room, more than once, when she was at church. Carefully, he tilted his head. Then he said, "It's not true, obviously. Let me see it."

She stared at him, her face obviously reluctant.

"Come on, Julia. It's me. You *know* me," he said.

She closed her eyes and sighed. "I don't think you should read it," she said. "It's private."

"Julia, you know I have her best interests in mind. I'm deeply concerned about her."

Her hands shook as she passed the book to him. He studied it. Black leather cover. It was *old*, the paper slightly browning, the entire book slightly curved, as if it had been bound up inside a vase and bent permanently. *Where had she kept it?*

He looked at Julia and raised an eyebrow. Her expression was skeptical. But it was also hungry. Julia *needed* an answer that made sense. Her desperation for order in her life, her desperation for approval—it was plainly obvious. Just as plainly obvious that he was the only one who could provide her with that. Her nothing of a husband couldn't. She'd married him because she could control him. Crank wasn't her equal in determination or in intelligence, and his education was worse than third-rate. Only his freak talent with the guitar, and the business management she'd learned from her father, gave Crank the massive success he so richly did not deserve.

Richard flipped open the journal. He grimaced. The journal was a densely packed block of letters starting on the first page, the handwriting deeply slanted and barely legible. Good God.

"It's worse than I thought," he muttered.

"What?" Julia asked.

"Isn't it obvious? There's no paragraph marks here. No margins. This is the journal of a crazy person." He flipped through the first few pages. Richard was fluent in Spanish—after all, he'd been stationed there and helped assist the organizers of the February 23rd coup.

He stopped on the sixth or seventh page, and the words leapt out at him. *Richard murdered my father.* He kept flipping through. Pages and pages of rambling about God and the devil. He turned the journal to Julia, who he knew full well couldn't read Spanish fluently.

"Look here," he said. "She rambles on for pages and pages about the devil. It makes me wonder if she was hallucinating."

Julia shook her head sadly. Richard took the book back and continued flipping through. An account of her hospitalization. On another page, she wrote, *I hate myself for breaking George-Phillip's heart. But what else could I do?* He grunted in disgust and passed the journal back to Julia.

She should have done what she was told. Richard wanted nothing more than to punish her. Instead, he looked up at Julia and said,

"Julia. I know you've—you've had a difficult relationship with your mother in the past. But I need your help."

He leaned close and looked at her with the most sincere eyes he could. "Julia, I don't know if you can forgive her. But you have to recognize that she was sick. We need to help your mother, Julia. We need to get her back to the United States. I ... I hesitate to say this ... but I'm starting to think that it's time we considered some inpatient options for her."

Julia flinched. "Like ... a mental hospital?"

*Like a six foot deep hole in the ground.* "Yes. She needs competent medical care, and I've never believed that quack she goes to knows what he's doing." He looked down at the table and ran his hands through his hair again. He didn't want to overplay his cards. But he also knew that this conversation was *essential.* He looked back up at Julia and said, "Julia. Can you forgive your mother? Will you help me?"

She met his eyes. He could see the vulnerability in her eyes. The desperate need for approval which had driven her career and her life. She would do as he asked. She *would.*

Then she nodded. "Of course I'll help."

# CHAPTER FIFTEEN
# No, ma'am.
# He's dead.

**T**he nurse at the desk looked irritated when Bear asked for Adelina Thompson. She waved down the hallway and said, "You'll find her at the end of the hall with the security guards. Room 201."

Bear smiled and said, "Thank you, ma'am." He walked on, Anthony at his left side. Immediately, the correct room became apparent. Two men in black quasi-military uniforms flanked the door in an uneasy triangle with an officer of the Royal Canadian Mounted Police.

One of the men saw them coming and approached. His sidearm was visible in a shoulder holster. *That* was unusual for Canada.

"Can I help you?" the man asked.

Anthony said, "We're here to see Adelina Thompson."

"And you are?"

"You can tell her it's an old friend," Bear interjected. "Bear Wyden. She'll remember me from Belgium. And let her know we come with news from Carrie and Julia."

The guard looked at him suspiciously and consulted a sheet of paper. Then he said, "Your name isn't on the list of permitted visitors. Wait here." Then he waved at the other guard, who took a blocking position in the hall as the first one went back to the door.

The badges on the uniform looked almost official, unless you looked closely. The center showed an eye, like the CBS logo, with a triangular shape spreading out from the center. Like an all-seeing eye. Creepy. The words on the badge said Pinkerton Security Services.

Bear waited impatiently. It had been one long as hell day, starting with a crack of dawn flight west. Once they'd finished here, they were headed back east on a red-eye from Vancouver to Washington, DC. Thank God *The Washington Post* was paying for the flight. Finally, the guard came back.

"All right, you're cleared. You carrying?"

Bear shook his head. He wasn't officially on duty. The last thing he needed to be doing was carrying his service weapon across international borders.

The guard patted them both down—not a perfunctory search, but really looking. Finally he waved them in.

Inside the room, an emaciated teenager lay on the hospital bed, the back of the bed configured to allow her to sit up comfortably. Her eyes were hollow, but Bear could see that she had the potential for real beauty if she gained a little weight. As it was, she clearly wasn't healthy. He recognized her from the portrait in Richard Thompson's office at the Pentagon, as well as many photos displayed in Carrie's condominium. Jessica, who had been born after Bear last saw Adelina Thompson.

His eyes shifted from the daughter to the mother. Adelina was still an attractive woman. He'd guess she was fifty years old now. Over the years she'd put on some weight, and giving birth to six children had changed her body significantly. But her eyes were still wide, her hair black and twisted carelessly into a knot over her shoulder. She stood as Bear and Anthony entered the room.

"Bear," she said, walking forward with a half smile.

He smiled at her. "You remember me," he said. "It's been a long time."

"A long time, but how could I forget the man who protected my family and my daughters?"

"You're still as lovely as always," he responded.

Adelina said, "Jessica, this is Bear Wyden. He headed our security detail in Belgium in the nineties. It must have been nearly twenty years ago."

"Almost exactly," he responded. "This is Anthony Walker. He's a friend of Julia's, and a reporter for *The Washington Post*."

Adelina's eyes widened. "A reporter? Friends with Julia? I find that ... surprising."

"Friends may be an overstatement," Anthony said. "But we've been working together. Julia's come around to the idea that it's time to shed some public light on what's been happening to your family."

Adelina's eyes darted back and forth between the two men. Then she said, "You have my undivided attention. I never expected you to pop up out of the woodwork. What brings you to Canada, exactly?"

Bear said, "I know you were away, so you may not know the extent of the details. But when your daughter Andrea arrived in the United States last Monday, I was assigned to investigate her kidnapping. I'm still with Diplomatic Security, of course. I assigned a protective detail to guard your daughters, but they were attacked again on Friday night. I've been doing everything I can to track down those responsible for the attacks. Our best lead was Nick Larsden, the man who shot at you and your daughter as you were trying to cross the border."

"Was?" she asked nervously. "He's not free, is he?"

"No, ma'am. He's dead."

Adelina blanched.

He went on, "Someone in the jail knifed him. We don't know who, or whether it was for hire or just a bizarre coincidence. Anthony and I interviewed him early this morning, but we didn't get a chance to finish."

"Why not?"

Bear looked at Anthony, as if to ask Anthony's opinion. Should he tell her the truth? Anthony raised an eyebrow. That was the opposite of helpful. He turned back to Adelina and laid his cards on the table.

"We're not here in any official capacity, Adelina. Secretary Perry *officially* relieved me of duty a couple days ago."

She raised an eyebrow. "And unofficially?"

"Unofficially, he's very suspicious of ... the entire situation. So when the IRS and the special counsel took over the investigation, he cut me loose to find out what I could find out."

She nodded slowly then said, "That sounds like him. I appreciate your candor."

"You know the Secretary?"

"Of course," she said. "He and Chuck Rainsley are very close friends. And I was once friends with Brianna Rainsley. So we came into contact with each other a great deal in the 1980s."

Bear and Anthony looked at each other. Well, that verified one question. But they still had plenty more. "All right," Bear said. "Will you talk with us?"

"I'll be happy to. On the record or off. If Anthony here wants to print my story in *The Washington Post* I couldn't be more pleased."

Anthony grinned. "I'd *love* to get your story."

"In the meantime," Bear said, "I've got a number of very specific questions I'm hoping you could help us with."

She nodded. "Please, go ahead."

"Would you rather talk in private somewhere?" He nodded meaningfully toward Jessica.

Adelina looked at her daughter. Something unspoken passed between them, then Adelina looked back at Bear. "It's fine. We can talk in front of Jessica."

Bear raised his eyebrows. "All right. I'd like to start with Nick Larsden. Have you heard of him before? Had any encounter with him?"

"No." Her tone was flat as she answered the question.

Anthony said, "Mrs. Thompson ... I was with Julia when she broke into your husband's office. I saw the police report. And ... I saw the diary."

Adelina winced. Then she said, "Then you know what he did to me."

Anthony nodded. "It's true?" he asked.

"Yes. I was sixteen when he raped me the first time."

"Have you ever heard of anyone who went by the name of Oz?" Anthony asked.

Adelina froze at the name. Her eyes widened and her skin went pale. "Oz?" she asked.

## Adelina. May 6.

*Oz.*

Of course. Why hadn't she realized it before? The name sent chills down her spine.

Jessica looked at her, as did the two men, and it was obvious they could see her reaction.

She sighed and said, "Yes, I've heard the name. How did it come up?"

Anthony and Bear looked at each other, then Bear said, "Nick Larsden said he was hired by someone named Oz."

Adelina swayed on her feet, then said, "I need to sit." She stumbled across the room to one of the chairs and fell into her seat. Anthony and Bear followed her in, taking the two wooden visitor chairs.

"Mrs. Thompson? What can you tell us?"

The first time she'd heard the voice, she hadn't known he went by that name. It was just a voice. A guttural, mean sounding voice. It sounded as if the owner of that voice just wanted to reach out and *shake* someone. It was a voice you didn't want to cross. And back then, Adelina had already been terrified every minute of every day. She didn't need any more fears. But she got them anyway.

It happened in 1984. A few days before, she'd manipulated Richard into losing his temper. Into *raping* her. Her purpose, of course, was to have a plausible date when she could have become pregnant, because the two of them hadn't touched each other since the move to Washington.

She'd never felt so dirty. Not even the first time he'd done it. Because this time it was to conceal a lie. A lie she was responsible for. And no matter the reason, no matter how horrible he was, she felt in her heart that she was the one who was wrong. She was the one who was defiled. She was the one who God would judge.

She'd already decided that she wouldn't see George-Phillip again. She *couldn't*. She loved him like she'd never loved anybody. Every time she thought of him, her heart ached—her whole body ached. But if she continued to see him, it would still be in secret. It would still be dirty. And eventually, she knew, Richard would find out the truth. And then he would kill her, or the baby she had inside of her.

She'd already decided, but then came Oz.

It was almost two in the morning when it happened. Richard had flown to London for a meeting, and she and Julia were blessedly alone in the condominium. When the phone rang, the bell was harsh in the darkness.

She stumbled out of bed to the kitchen grasping for the phone, her heart suddenly racing. No one called at two in the morning. Certainly not Richard. It had to be something awful. Had something happened to Luis? Had that bastard finally followed through on his threats and done something to her baby brother?

"Hello? Thompson residence," she gasped into the phone.

"Mrs. Thompson," a voice said. A voice that sounded like the gravel at the end of a long dirt road. Irish accent.

"Who is this?"

"A friend," came the reply. "We have a mutual friend. The Prince is returning to Washington, Adelina. Stay away from him. Do you understand me? You stay away from him, or you'll suffer for it."

Rage flooded through her. It didn't matter that she'd made the decision to say goodbye. Suddenly awake and alert, she spit into the phone, "Who is this?"

"You heard my warning, Adelina. Stay away from him. Don't answer his calls. Don't see him. Or you and I will have a personal problem."

Angry beyond words, Adelina said, "And what exactly does a personal problem entail?"

"Why don't you check young Julia's bedroom to find out?"

Adelina threw the phone at the floor and ran for Julia's room, her feet slipping on the kitchen floor. She screamed silently as she went down on the floor. She scrambled back to her feet, down the hall, opened Julia's door, and snatched her daughter out of the Snuffleupagus toddler bed Richard had bought for her a few weeks before. Immediately Julia began wailing, startled out of a deep sleep in the middle of the night.

Adelina switched on the light and checked Julia for injuries and marks of any kind, even as the girl screamed, her hair tangled in her face.

"It's okay," she whispered, holding Julia to her.

Then her eyes fell on the wall.

A large sheet of white poster board was pinned to the wall ... directly above the toddler bed. A crude, hand drawn representation of Snuffleupagus, Julia's favorite Sesame Street character, had been drawn on the poster board.

A red letter X was scrawled across the creature's chest. In red letters beneath the children's show character were words, printed in large block letters. The message said:

**HEED MY WARNING. OZ.**

Now, as Adelina told the story to Anthony and Bear, the full weight of the fear swept over her again and she began to shake. "Whoever Oz is ... he, or someone who worked for him, was *inside the condo* and put that poster board up, then left, before calling me. They could have killed us. Or taken Julia. Anything. I wouldn't have been able to do anything to stop them."

"What did you do?" Bear asked.

"The only thing I could do. I broke it off with George-Phillip. I gave him no explanation—I didn't even give him the opportunity to talk about it. I broke his heart."

To her left, sitting in the bed, Jessica listened with wide eyes. Adelina hadn't told her about Oz yet, or why she'd broken it off with George-Phillip. Now her daughter sat there with tears freely running down her face.

Bear asked, "Did you ever hear from him again?"

"Once," Adelina said. "In November 1996. I was pregnant with Andrea at the time."

"What happened?" Bear asked.

"The last time I saw George-Phillip was at an Embassy dinner. For several months we'd been secretly seeing each other. He would ... he would sneak into the compound with false identification in the middle of the day and we'd go off together. I kept fooling myself that it would be all right, that somehow we wouldn't be found out, that somehow I could protect my daughters and still have him. But then two things happened."

The first, of course, was when she missed her period. They had been careful to use contraception despite Adelina's religious qualms, but due to the heavy medication she was taking already, her doctor had flat out refused to prescribe birth control.

She knew. Her last pregnancy with the twins had been extremely difficult and she knew exactly what morning sickness felt like. For three weeks she'd been nauseous, but she'd pushed that to the side, wanting to ignore it, wanting it to be anything but what it was. But when she missed her period, there was no way to ignore it. She bought a home pregnancy test and the result was positive.

Adelina was pregnant and it was impossible that the baby was Richard's. She would sooner die than kill her own baby, and she had no desire to touch Richard ever again. He had no desire for her.

For a week after she discovered the pregnancy, she was paralyzed. She didn't return George-Phillip's phone calls. She thought, she wrote in her journal, and she prayed. Useless prayers, she'd believed at the time. But she couldn't hide forever, and a few days later the US Embassy hosted a dinner for the officers of the Australian and British Embassies. Such affairs were common, and as wife of the Ambassador, she had no excuse for not attending.

Protocol placed her at her husband's left hand, directly across from George-Phillip, who sat to Richard's right. Through the meal she barely spoke, keeping her eyes on her plate.

At one point Richard said in a tone only she would identify as deeply sarcastic, "Not feeling well, darling?"

She simply shook her head. He leaned over and gripped her arm and she flinched.

"Your job is to entertain our guests, Adelina," he whispered.

She attempted a smile, then stood up and said, "Excuse me."

She hid in the restrooms, but of course that didn't last lone. Before long, she was circulating in the room, attempting unsuccessfully to make conversation. After escaping from a conversation with the Australian Consul-General, she heard George-Phillip's voice behind her.

"Hello, Adelina, how are you?"

His voice made her heart sink. For days she'd been debating what and how much to tell him. She looked at him and felt her eyes water. She wanted so badly to collapse into his arms, to sink into his love. She wanted so badly to run away with him.

"You haven't called," he said. His eyebrows were sunken close to his eyes in consternation.

She wanted to make an excuse. She wanted to tell him … she'd been busy, she'd been taking care of the kids, she'd been washing her hair. Instead, she blurted out in a whisper, "I'm pregnant."

His Adam's apple bounced in his throat as he swallowed. "Is the baby mine?"

"Of course. I'd never touch him unless he forced me."

He looked so sad her heart broke. "Adelina, you *must* leave him. He's destroying you and your children."

She thought about the photos she'd received every year on Luis's birthday. Photos taken surreptitiously. Luis at school. Luis eating ice cream. Luis at his first job waiting tables. His eighteenth birthday party. Every single year. Richard wanted to remind her. And then, of course, there was the man he sent from London all those years before. *Oz*. If Richard's goal had been to cow and terrify her, he had succeeded.

"You don't know what you're asking. If you did, you wouldn't say that. I'd lose my children. I'd lose everything." Anxiety twisted through her as Richard approached from behind George-Phillip.

"Of course, I enjoyed the show very much! I'm hoping we can take Julia to it, you know she loves music."

Richard casually clapped a hand on George-Phillip's shoulder. His voice was jovial, suspecting nothing. "I didn't get to tell you at dinner, Your Highness, how much a pleasure it is to see you again."

"And you, Ambassador," George-Phillip said.

He smiled, an insincere diplomatic smile. Adelina knew what his *real* smiles looked like. And she was terrified she'd never see that smile again.

"Please excuse me," she said. "I must find Julia."

That night, she had confronted Richard in his office. All five of their daughters were home, which meant this was the safest time. He was unlikely to assault her with Julia and Carrie in earshot. He looked up at her puzzled when she walked in. She never entered his office.

"What is it, *darling?*" he asked, his tone nasty.

Her chest tightened up, pain curling like smoke across her sternum, and she found herself short of breath.

Richard's chin set. "What is it, Adelina? You've interrupted me. Explain yourself."

She closed her eyes. And then she said the words that she thought might end with her death. "I'm pregnant."

He stood, his face suddenly red, eyes wide, mouth twisted in a rictus of rage. "Pregnant," he said, his voice a curse. "I would think that would be biologically impossible."

He stood and walked around his desk. Her eyes followed him, never wavering, because he held a brass letter opener in his hand. She began to shake as he reached her side of the table. Then she saw it. *He* was also shaking. But not with fear or rage. Almost with excitement.

Her eyes followed the letter opener. He held it toward her stomach then pressed it against her. Not hard. Just enough to slightly hurt.

"Is this an immaculate conception, Adelina? Did your God plant a baby in you to save us all?" His tongue lightly licked against his lower lip as he spoke. Anticipation. He was going to hurt her badly.

Then he leaned close, his lips right next to her ear. "Or did Senator Rainsley plant this baby in you too? Is that where you were running off to during the day lately instead of paying attention to our daughters? I wouldn't have thought he was in China long enough to make you pregnant."

He brought his forehead to hers, leaning against her. "What would you do with your poor Catholic morals if I order you to abort your fucking baby? If I tell you to have it *cut out of you?* What would you do if I told you that if you didn't, I'd take Carrie and sell her to the highest bidder? I'm sure some of those perverts in the Yakuza would love a twelve-year-old white girl, huh? Would you kill this baby to save that one?"

Adelina shuddered. Involuntarily, tears began to run down her face. She closed her eyes. She couldn't show weakness. He fed on fear. He fed on weakness. He was *evil.*

"Answer me, you cheating whore," he demanded. "Shall I cut the baby out of you right here?" He pressed the letter opener against her again, harder this time, hard enough to really hurt.

"No," she gasped.

Abruptly he turned away. He strode away from her and stood behind the desk. "Have your baby," he said. "Maybe I'll smother it in its sleep. Maybe it's time I paid a visit to Luis. Or maybe I'll just torture you until you finally end your own worthless life. Get out of my office."

She had done as he ordered. But that wasn't the end of it. Because two days later, she woke up in her bedroom with a hand over her mouth. She struggled, but realized she was pinned down somehow. She couldn't move her limbs at all.

Hot stinking breath blew on her face, smelling of rot and mud and tobacco. Then the intruder spoke. She recognized the voice, even all those years later. It was Oz.

He spoke in a guttural Irish accent. "I told you to stay away from the Prince. And you disobeyed."

"Please don't hurt me," she whispered.

"This is your last chance. I'm not going to kill you this time. But if you ever see him again, you *and* your daughters will die."

The weight had lifted off of her. "Last chance, Adelina. Make the right decision."

Then he had run out of the room. Moments later, she had stumbled out of bed, running to check on her daughters.

They were in their beds, and safe.

As she finished telling the story, Bear shook his head. "Did you ever find out who Oz was?"

"No," she replied.

"Did you ever talk with George-Phillip about it?"

She closed her eyes. Then whispered, "I never spoke with him again. I had to protect my daughters."

She heard the sympathy in Anthony's voice as he asked her the next question. "Did Richard get his revenge, Adelina?"

She slowly nodded and tears ran down her face. "He did. I don't want to talk about what he did. He made my life miserable for a long time. And the older Andrea got, the clearer it became that she wasn't his daughter. I finally sent her away for her safety. I was afraid he'd lose his temper some day and kill her."

She opened her eyes. Then she said, "It was at its worst when we lived in Bethesda after we got back from China. On a few occasions he physically hurt me. Especially when Maria Clawson began to write about him regularly. Write about *us*. Poor Julia had gotten mixed up with some very bad stuff in China, and a photo circulated amongst the students. She got her hands on it."

She looked down at the floor. Unable to say it. Unable to forgive herself. She whispered, "He ... tortured me. Every time she wrote a new column, it was more ... more vitriol from him. More pain. More threats. I thought more than once about just throwing myself off the balcony."

Anthony said, "Adelina. I don't know if you'll ever be able to get a legal judgment against him. But I want to bury Richard. I want him to be thrown down so low that he never gets back up again. I want to tell your story."

Adelina shuddered. She didn't speak, but an unexpected voice did. To her left, in a vicious tone, Jessica said, "Do it. Bury him. Don't ever let him hurt her again."

Anthony looked at his watch. "We've got about four hours before we have to leave. Bear, are you up for this?"

Bear shrugged. "Do what you gotta do. We aren't getting an earlier flight."

Anthony said, "First, you need to understand—I need people who can corroborate your story, or parts of it. Will George-Phillip admit the affair?"

"I don't know. You'll have to ask him."

Anthony nodded. "Your daughters will remember some things. What about Chuck Rainsley?"

Adelina swallowed. "Maybe Brianna Rainsley. She didn't know the extent of it, though. But there is one person who did, if he's still alive and you can find him."

"Who?"

"Father Dennis from the Saint Jane Frances de Chantal church in Bethesda. I'm sure he's moved on somewhere else by now."

"Will he talk?"

"I'll give you a letter from me, with written permission."

"Okay. One other thing. Can you think of anyone who knows about what happened in Afghanistan?"

She shook her head. "Leslie Collins, I'm sure. And Prince Roshan. If I had to guess, it was the three of them. They were thick in the eighties. They thought I was too stupid to understand they were up to something."

"Anyone else?" Anthony asked.

"There was another name ... Karat ... Karak..."

"Karatygin? Vasily Karatygin?"

"Yes! I'm sure that's it. You've heard of him?"

"I have," he said. "He was a Russian special forces major, he converted to Islam and defected in the 1980s, then was the second-in-command of one of the Afghan militias for a long time. He's still there ... keeps a low profile, mostly involved in opium smuggling, I think now."

She nodded. "I know I heard his name more than once. But I can't guarantee it's him. Nor do I know if he'd talk to you."

"Well, we might have to find out. Do me one favor though."

"Yes?"

"Prince George-Phillip I have to see. I've interviewed him before, but if I go through official channels, it will take weeks. Can you get me in to see him?"

She looked distressed. "We haven't seen each other in seventeen years. I'm certain he hates me. I broke his heart and never explained why."

Anthony shook his head. "All right. Maybe through your daughters. I believe Carrie met him yesterday."

Adelina whispered, "Yes. She told me."

"All right. I'll start there. Can we get started with some questions?"

"Yes. But one thing first."

Anthony raised an eyebrow. "Yes?"

She whispered, "When you talk to him ... tell him ... tell him I'm sorry."


## Marky Lovecchio. May 7.

The phone ringing was harsh in Marky Lovecchio's ear. Who the *fuck* was calling him at six o'clock in the morning?

He took his hand off the tits of the stripper he'd brought back from the bar the night before. He'd flashed several hundred-dollar bills at the club, enough to get the attention of several of the girls. Then he'd made his pick and brought her back to the cheap and nasty motel room.

She was hot, but a lousy lay. Fucking tease. He decided he was going to wake her up with a good fucking whether she liked it or not.

He untangled himself from her then picked up his phone.

"What?"

It was Oz. "Lovecchio. I trust you're having a good time spending my money?"

"It's my money now. I took care of him, didn't I?"

"You did. And that was good work. But I have another job for you."

Lovecchio muttered a curse. The girl was stirring; bleach blonde hair stringy along her back.

"I'm not in the market right now, Oz. I need a little time to relax."

"You can relax after you're finished, Lovecchio. The woman who Larsden let get away? She's with her daughter at the hospital in Abbotsford."

"Canada?" Lovecchio blurted.

The girl was definitely stirring now. She slid out of the bed and walked toward the bathroom.

"Yes, Lovecchio. Canada. The woman is in room 201. I don't care what happens to the daughter, but kill the woman."

Christ. He said, "How much?"

"We'll call it half a million. That's what I was going to pay your friend before he fucked it up."

"Whatever. Fine. I'll do it. How soon?"

"By tonight."

He started to respond, but Oz hung up.

"Hey," he called to the girl in the bathroom. "Come here!"

She muttered something incoherent. He looked around. Her skimpy dress was on the floor.

A second later she came out of the bathroom. He looked at her, his eyes grazing over her obvious implants, the curve of her hip. He didn't care if she couldn't fuck. He'd do the work. "Come here," he said.

She shook her head, a cigarette dangling out of her mouth. She reached for her dress. Bitch. He stood and walked toward her. "You're not finished yet."

PART TWO

# CHAPTER SIXTEEN
## Here's my theory

"**You** look exhausted." Given that Carrie was pouring a fresh cup of coffee as she said the words, Anthony decided he could forgive her.

"We flew back on the red-eye," he said. "I came straight here from the airport."

She nodded. "Cream and sugar are over here. Meet you on the balcony, it's beautiful today."

"Okay," he said.

He put too much sugar in his coffee then noticed the mug. It bore the logo of the United States Army, which reminded Anthony once again that Carrie was a widow, and a fairly recent one at that. The shelves and walls displayed a number of photos, including two from Carrie and Ray's wedding. From the look on both of their faces, you could tell they were deeply in love. And he'd died only a few months later.

Anthony leaned a little to see out of the kitchen toward the balcony doors. Carrie and Julia were sitting together at a cast iron table. He walked down the hall to the restroom and slipped inside. Out of curiosity and little more he opened the medicine cabinet.

The top shelf had several prescription bottles, including a Xanax prescription for Carrie filled only a few days before. He closed the door to the cabinet. He needed to mind his own business. He was a reporter, but he was also human, and needed to treat people decently.

Two minutes later, he joined Julia, Carrie and Rachel outside. The women sat across from each other as they sipped their coffee. As he seated himself he couldn't help but notice the contrast between them.

Their appearance, of course, was quite different. Julia was average height for a woman, about five feet four inches. He was used to seeing her brown curly hair tied in a businesslike bun, but here, in her family home, she had her hair down, draping both shoulders. She wore faded jeans and a *Trampled by Turtles* T-shirt. A rock band of some kind? He didn't know. Her hair was relaxed, but she didn't seem to be. Her back was straight, feet flat on the ground, and occasionally she drummed her fingers on the side of her mug.

Carrie, on the other hand, was slouched in her chair. The baby lay in a seat next to her chair, and Carrie's knees were drawn up in front of her. Her dark hair, almost black, draped over her shoulders.

"So tell me about your trip. Did you learn anything?" Carrie lifted her coffee cup to her lips after she finished speaking. She closed her eyes and inhaled, taking in the rich smell of the coffee, then sipping it slowly, her slightly pink lips touching the mug.

Anthony tore his eyes away from her. "Well ... we've got a name. But it's almost certainly a pseudonym. Oz. Your mother's encountered him twice before, once in the eighties, then again when you all were living in China. We've got good reason to believe the same man is responsible for hiring Nick Larsden to kill your mother. Unfortunately, we couldn't question Larsden any more ... he's dead."

Julia said, "I thought he was captured. I didn't hear anything about him being wounded in the news."

"He wasn't wounded by the police, he was knifed in the jail. I doubt it's a coincidence. He'd already told us about Oz though. We'll track down who he is."

Carrie sucked in a breath. "So … I don't get it."

"Well, here's my theory," Anthony said.

"Your theory?" Julia asked.

He nodded. "You've got two sets of killers, operating with different but similar motives. One *was* trying to keep a lid on who is behind the massacre at Wakhan in the eighties. Whoever that was—and my working theory is that it's Leslie Collins at the CIA, or possibly the head of the Saudi intelligence service—they moved to discredit your father and anything he might say as soon as his name was floated as Secretary of Defense."

"Okay," Carrie said. "And the second?"

"Oz. I'm guessing unrelated to the first set of killers. Whoever Oz is, he *twice* did everything short of killing your mother to keep her away from Prince George-Phillip. I'm guessing those attacks, and Andrea's kidnapping, have something to do with hiding your parentage, Carrie, and Andrea's."

Carrie sat up straight, color appearing on her cheeks. "It's not George-Phillip."

He shook his head. "No. I'm certain it isn't. For one thing, why would he have to threaten her to keep her away?"

"Richard, then," she said. Apparently she'd settled on calling him that instead of *Father.*

"That's what your mother thinks," Anthony said.

Julia started to speak, then stopped and seemed to reconsider whatever it was she was going to say. Finally, she said, "How does Jessica seem?"

Anthony raised his eyebrows. "Honestly?"

Julia bit her lip. Then nodded. "Yes."

"She's really sick. She's way too thin, and looks ... washed out. I think she's going to be a long time recovering."

"And Mother?" Carrie asked.

"My impression?" Anthony asked. "That's a woman on a mission, and I wouldn't want to be Richard Thompson right now."

At his response, Julia pursed her lips a little. Her reaction seemed off, and Anthony didn't understand it. He kept his mouth shut.

"So what's next?" Carrie asked. He met her eyes. Blue-green. Large, framed by long eyelashes. No wonder her soldier had fallen for her.

"Well, part of it depends on you. I need to get in to see Prince George-Phillip. There are a bunch of points in Adelina's story he can corroborate. I need at least two sources to run this stuff when it's this sensitive. I'm going to try to track down your mother's confessor from the 1980s. She gave me a letter for him with written permission to discuss her. And then I'm off to Kabul to see Vasily Karatygin, who may or may not be able to give me the information I need about what happened in Wakhan."

"You're going to Afghanistan?" Carrie asked, her tone a little shrill.

"Yeah. I need sources, I can't run this story on speculation."

She looked away, her lips tightly closed. When she turned back to him, her eyes had lost their warmth. Anthony frowned, suddenly feeling off balance. He said, "You've got a lot of bad associations with Afghanistan."

She shook her head in disgust. "Afghanistan reached out and destroyed my life. It took my husband and broke his best friend. It's still coming back. With all the news that's been coming out,

Ray's back in the news cycle. Did he do it or didn't he? CNN called me at *midnight* to ask if I'd comment on the special report they're doing on war crimes in Afghanistan. They're tying Ray in with Robert Bales, who killed all those civilians in 2012, and including a story about Wakhan. As if Ray could have been responsible for something that happened before he was even born. *I hate them!*"

She said the last few words with such ferocious intensity that Rachel's eyes popped wide open beside her. The baby immediately began protesting with loud gurgling noises.

"I have to go." Carrie's voice cracked, as if she were on the verge of tears. She snatched up the baby and slipped inside the condo.

Anthony exhaled. He hadn't realized that he'd stopped breathing during her brief monologue. He was shaken by the force of her emotion—and his own reaction to it.

Then Julia said in a low, threatening voice. "I don't know what kind of game you're playing, Anthony. But if you mess with my sister, I'll destroy you." Then she stood too, leaving Anthony sitting alone on the balcony.

## Carrie. May 7.

In the room she'd once shared with Ray Sherman, Carrie sat on the edge of her bed looking down at her daughter. Carrie had tears in her eyes, unbidden tears that did nothing but infuriate her.

Rachel lay on her back on the bed. She was still hot this morning and seemed listless. Carrie sighed. She'd take Rachel's temperature in a few minutes. She leaned forward and cooed at her baby, then kissed her on the cheek.

Rachel gave her a big toothless smile. Carrie smiled back, ignoring the tears that were threatening to spill over, and kissed Rachel's other cheek. Rachel gave a small laugh. That escalated to a shower of kisses and loud, happy laughing and gurgling.

Carrie sighed. She was frustrated and confused and more than a little bit angry. Angry because she shouldn't have reacted that way to Anthony's announcement he was going to Afghanistan. He was a journalist, and she barely knew him, and it wasn't really any of her business anyway. But her instant reaction to his news was—fear. Anxiety that he would be hurt.

She sighed a little as she lifted her daughter's arms, evoking more baby laughs.

Anthony Walker.

She shook her head. He was a foreign correspondent for Christ's sake, which was just about as dangerous—or even more—as being a soldier. She'd *read* Anthony's dispatches from Iraq when he was embedded with a US Army platoon. His life was dangerous, no life for someone with a family, and on top of that, he wasn't even that good looking. Ray hadn't even been dead a year and she felt *incredibly* disloyal to even be thinking of Anthony that way.

Ray hadn't even been dead for a year! What was wrong with her?

She lifted Rachel to her chest and let the tears spill over. She knew exactly what was wrong with her. She was hideously lonely. She'd met her soulmate and married him and lost him all in the course of nine months. And nothing would ever be the same.

# CHAPTER SEVENTEEN
## Small breakthrough

Bear. May 7.

**B**ear grumbled to himself as he crept forward twenty feet then stopped again. I-66 out of Washington was a parking lot. As far as he could see there was no accident—these were just normal traffic conditions for this early in the morning, just another day in Washington.

Bear *hated* Washington. But he also knew he was never leaving, because this was where his kids lived. He was going to be here for the indefinite future anyway. His appointment to the Joint Terrorism Task Force hadn't been endangered yet by his supposed suspension, or the loss of classified documents—but that didn't mean it wasn't coming soon.

Ten more feet. Stop. At this rate he wouldn't get to Leah's place until ten or ten-thirty. He was exhausted and wore rumpled clothes, eyelids heavy after taking the red-eye back to Washington. But what else could he do? After their arrival at Washington Reagan National Airport at six am, he and Anthony went their separate ways—Bear had gone back to his apartment just long enough to shower and change then get back out on the road.

His phone rang. He fumbled for it.

*Scott Kelly.*

He answered. "Kelly, what's up?"

Kelly's Boston Irish accented voice sounded out of the car speakers. "I hear you had a run-in with the IRS yesterday."

Bear chuckled. "Yeah, you could say that. Schmidt is not happy that I'm on the case. Not happy at all. What's up at your end?"

"Small breakthrough actually. Or a big one, maybe."

"Tell me."

In the right lane just ahead of him, a rusted red pickup pulled ahead. The driver to Bear's right—driving a Prius no less—was staring at his phone, probably watching porn or reading a Russian novel. Either way he didn't move fast enough. Bear launched his car into the opening, achieving nearly forty feet in one stretch.

Kelly continued yammering on, unaware of the deadly combat Bear was engaged in.

"All right. First, you remember kidnapper two? The one Andrea Thompson said was American?"

"Yeah. She said he called himself Dan."

"Right. We couldn't get a match on his prints, nothing. Nothing in the FBI database, nothing anywhere. Anyway, on Thursday the Pocatello, Idaho police put out a missing persons report. Thirty-one year old Army veteran missing. His mother called it in, but the local police took forty-eight hours to put out an alert. They must have figured he went hunting or something."

"Yeah?" Bear asked. His reply was laced with sarcasm. "That's our guy? Some guy who used to be in the Army just randomly hooks up with one of the most dangerous mercenaries in the world to kidnap Andrea Thompson? I need more, Kelly."

Kelly lashed back. "Let me finish the story, Bear."

The guy in the Prius was honking his horn. Bear didn't flip him off, even though he wanted to. But he did goose the car forward. Morning commutes were only won with guts of steel and the instincts of a hunter. Bear laughed at his own idiocy.

"All right," Kelly said. "So we went to the Army. It was a match. Picture matched. But the Army's pissed, because kidnapper Dan's fingerprints don't show up in their database. And his DNA didn't match up either."

"He wasn't actually in the Army?"

"No, he was. That's where it gets interesting. His name's Tyler Coleman. I went and talked to his company commander. Someone deleted the records, Bear. They deleted the computer records, but there are still paper records of his enlistment. This was our guy for sure. He was Special Forces for one enlistment, 2001 to 2005. Then he disappeared, apparently taking his permanent military record with him."

Bear squeezed the steering wheel. "Fucking CIA."

"That's it. Emma Smith—she's the IRS second-in-command—pulled his social security and tax records. From 2006 until 2011, he supposedly worked as a technical specialist for an outfit called Brennan Holdings in Northern Virginia."

"Bullshit," Bear said.

"Yeah, exactly. Brennan Holdings is a CIA front company. We're trying to find out what he did for them, but during that five-year period Customs and Immigration shows two *dozen* times he left and entered the United States. And then nothing. In 2001 he paid cash for a big house in Idaho, bought some vicious dogs and basically retired."

Bear grunted. He was driving at least four miles an hour now—maybe even five. "At twenty-something years old? I must be in the wrong line of work."

He thought through the implications. Tyler Coleman "retired" from the CIA in 2011. Something stank. "What did the IRS say about his income since 2011?"

Kelly replied, "He reported less than thirty thousand in income in 2012 and 2013. The IRS might have never noticed—we're talking about rural Idaho, the median income out there is pretty low. But here's the kicker, Bear. I talked with the Sheriff out there. Coleman's been arrested for disorderly conduct, public drunkenness and assault in the last three years. He beat up some guy in a bar and did three months in the county jail. His fingerprints should have come up in the National Crime Information Center, Bear. But his record was wiped from there too. And that was *after* he left the Agency."

Bear gripped the steering wheel with both hands. He was moving at a good clip now, almost as fast as a bicyclist. Uphill. With a flat tire.

Maybe not. Brake lights came on in front of him again. Bear sighed as he came to a stop. He was a tenth of a mile from the exit. He could walk faster than this.

"Okay. So the CIA was somehow involved in kidnapping Andrea. Or maybe a rogue element inside CIA. What else?"

Kelly said, "You won't like the next part."

"I didn't like the last part. What is it?"

"The guy Leah tagged the other day, before—" Kelly didn't finish the sentence. *Before she got shot.*

"Yeah," Bear said. "Go on." Kelly was talking about the bizarre melee that had happened in the street in Bethesda the day before the condominium was attacked. A British tourist had been shot, and one of the shooters killed. The other one was tackled by Dylan Paris and then arrested by Diplomatic Security.

Kelly said. "Two things. First, the British tourist? He wasn't a tourist."

"Who was he?"

"Name is Charlie Frazier. We're certain he's MI6."

Bear let out a curse. "What the hell?"

"Yeah, exactly. And here's where it gets really strange, Bear."

"It's not strange yet?"

"The shooter was Saudi Mukhabarat."

Bear didn't answer. He just sat breathing. In his mind, he thought back to the photograph. 1983. Leslie Collins, Prince Ro-shan, Richard Thompson. All three were in Afghanistan together.

"Kelly. Listen to me. I got it. I know what's happening now."

"Well don't keep it to yourself."

"It's not one group of bad guys here, Kelly. It's two. Or more. One side is Collins and Roshan and Thompson. They were involved in the Wakhan massacre, Kelly. I bet they engineered it. And now, their mutual paranoia is taking them down. Collins thought if An-drea Thompson's parentage came out, it would be enough of a scan-dal to bust the whole story open. But his actions precipitated that instead of preventing it."

"What would her parentage have anything to do with it? She's a bastard child of a prince. It's not unique."

"Her father conducted the formal investigation into Wakhan for the British government, Kelly."

Bear was missing something. Who the hell was Oz? Did he work for Thompson like Adelina thought? Or worse, did he work for George-Phillip? Maybe Adelina was all wrong about her former lover. Maybe he'd kill his own children to keep a scandal from hap-pening.

"Kelly, you ever hear of an intelligence operative who goes by the name Oz?"

"Oz? Like the Wizard?"

"Yeah."

"Nah."

*Yes!* Bear had a clear path to the exit. Or close enough. Less than two hundred yards down the emergency lane. He slipped the car into the emergency lane and sped up, ten miles an hour, then twenty, then thirty, the cars to his left flashing by.

Bear spoke again. "Kelly, look into it. This guy's nasty, and he's been trying to keep Adelina Thompson away from Prince George-Phillip for thirty years. I don't know what else he's done, but he's the guy who hired the gunman who went after her on the border."

"All right. I'm on it."

Blue flashes. *Shit!* Bear saw the lights in his rearview mirror as he pulled off onto the exit. The police car rode up right on his bumper. Damn it. Looks like a State trooper.

"Kelly, I'm being pulled over."

On the other end of the line, Kelly let out a guffaw. He silenced himself for just a moment then burst into heavy belly laughter.

"Shut up, Kelly." Bear pulled to a stop, then reached for his wallet and folded it to show his diplomatic security ID and badge.

Then he waited. The cop was still sitting there behind the wheel, probably watching the end of his movie on the computer in the car.

Bear waited another very long minute, then opened the car door and started to step out.

"Sir! Get back in the car!"

"I'm with Diplomatic Security—" He raised his hands in the air, one of them holding the badge and ID.

"I don't care who you're with, get back—is that a gun?"

Instantly the situation became much more serious. The State trooper pulled his sidearm and pointed it at Bear. Bear didn't move a muscle.

"I want you to place your hands on the roof of the vehicle sir. Do *not* make any sudden movements."

Bear rolled his eyes, then slowly turned to the car and put his hands on it. "I'm not dangerous, officer. I'm an agent of the Diplomatic Security Service. My ID and badge are in my—"

"Shut up."

"Well, that's not polite," Bear muttered.

The officer took Bear's pistol from his shoulder holster then took the badge and ID from his right hand.

Then he left Bear standing there and walked back to his cruiser. Bear started to grumble, but then another cruiser pulled up, lights flashing. What the hell?

From the inside of the car, Kelly's disembodied voice sounded out.

"Bear, you still alive?"

Bear didn't dare move. But he shouted into the car. "I think I'm under arrest!"

Kelly didn't answer, instead bursting into laughter. Again.

Bear sighed. Then he called into the car, "Look into Oz, will you? I'm on my way to Leah's if the cops ever let me go."

"I'm on it!" Kelly replied, chuckling.

With friends like that, who needed enemies?

## George-Phillip. May 7.

Wednesday morning's *Guardian* carried a giant headline.

# AFGHAN GOVERNMENT FILES COMPLAINT WITH WORLD COURT

## Prime Minister tells Guardian, "Being a Royal won't protect Prince George-Phillip from prosecution."

The article was filled with dozens of manifest falsehoods. Some were simply from ignorance—such as mistaking the International Criminal Court with the World Court—two very different bodies with very different jurisdictions. But some of the mistakes in the article were clearly otherwise motivated. Whoever had leaked information to *The Guardian* had a copy of the report George-Phillip had filed in 1984, but it was clearly filled with distortions.

George-Phillip was considering leaking the actual report. He wasn't sure what else would accomplish the job of clearing the air. And he couldn't very well protect his daughters if he was facing a trial.

He set the paper down on the expansive desk. The office in the family quarters at the Embassy was quite nice, bigger than George-Phillip's office in London and certainly far more traditional. He'd never cared for the steel and glass headquarters of MI6. Outside the window, he could see the crowd of protesters outside the fence. Dozens of them, and the crowd was growing every minute.

*Justice for Afghan Civilians*, one sign read. *Civilian Blood is on Your Hands!* said another.

He studied the protestors for a moment. They were young and old. Big and small. A broad range of people who were genuinely outraged that the facts of the murder of hundreds of civilians had been covered up for so many years. He felt sympathy for them. He'd felt the same outrage. He remembered that day in Miss Thatcher's office. Shaking.

*It's a miscarriage of justice. Prime Minister, if we sit on this it will tell the world we approve.*

Prime Minister Thatcher had merely shook her head. *No, Your Highness. As it is, the world believes the Soviets are responsible. If they learn the truth, it will be a massive victory for Chernenko.*

*Chernenko is an old man!* George Phillip had replied. *He'll likely be dead within the year.*

*But the Soviet Union will still be there, Your Highness. For now, the truth must stay hidden.*

George-Phillip had collapsed into a chair. In a quiet voice, he'd said, *And what of Richard Thompson and Leslie Collins? Prince Roshan and Vasily Karatygin? They'll just go free after such a massive crime?*

She'd shrugged then said, *God will deal with them.*

*Perhaps God would*, George-Phillip thought. But he also thought that God mostly worked through human agencies.

A knock on the door. George-Phillip turned away from the protestors and said in a loud voice, "Come in."

The door opened. It was Oswald O'Leary.

"Come in, old friend," George-Phillip said. "I suppose you've heard the news I'm recalled to London."

"I have, Your Highness. No doubt you'll put an end to all of this when you arrive."

"Do you see them out there?" he asked, pointing to the street.

O'Leary's nose wrinkled, as if he smelled something bad. "It means nothing. There's a protest every day in Washington."

"It means something," George-Phillip said. "Those people in that village. Their blood cries out from the ground."

"Very poetic, sir. But not practical."

George-Phillip shook his head. "Always practical, my friend. I've known you thirty years and little changes."

"Always the idealist, sir. I've protected you from yourself for more years than you know. What will you do now?"

"I will tell the truth. My daughter called me not long ago. She's asked me to speak with a reporter from *The Washington Post*."

O'Leary's eyes widened. "Your daughter, sir?"

"Carrie, of course."

"I wouldn't advise it, sir. I truly wouldn't. I know Carrie and Andrea are your daughters, but clearly Andrea doesn't want to be. She ran away when you provided her shelter. And the other one … she was married to a war criminal."

"Oswald," George-Phillip said, an edge forming in his voice.

"Sir, you know I've never approved of your affair with Adelina Thompson. If she knew, the Queen would—"

"You go too far, Oswald."

O'Leary faced him without flinching. "I look out for your best interests, Your Highness. I always have. You realize that *none* of this would be an issue if you hadn't had that affair in the first place. Sir, I'm begging you. *Do not* talk to this reporter."

George-Phillip shook his head. "I admire your conviction, but this is the course I must take. In the meantime, I have a task for you, O'Leary. And there could be none more important."

O'Leary sighed heavily. Then he said, "Yes, sir. What is it?"

"Oswald, I'd like you to go to British Columbia, to carry my best wishes to Adelina. I want you to ask her and her daughter—all of them, if she wishes—to join me in London. And if she agrees, I want you to escort her and keep her safe."

O'Leary looked stunned. "Sir? You can't be serious—"

"I've never been so serious, Oswald. I know you don't approve of her. I know you disagree with me. But you're also my most trusted aide. You're my most trusted *friend*, Oswald."

O'Leary closed his eyes. Then he nodded, once. "Of course, Your Highness. Whatever you wish."

# CHAPTER EIGHTEEN
## Leave them alone!

Adelina. May 7.

**A**delina Thompson stared at her temporary cell phone as if it were a snake about to betray her. It lay on the plastic tray table, amidst the debris of Jessica's breakfast. Adelina had bought coffee and a croissant at the coffee shop in the lobby of the hospital. After days here, she was ready for a hotel room, a bed and a shower. But she wouldn't leave Jessica alone here. Not after all that had happened.

Jessica didn't appreciate it, of course. She was eighteen, and what eighteen-year-old appreciates their mother? Certainly none of Adelina's daughters had. Except Sarah. Sarah, who had surprised her. Sarah, who had pulled through such incredible and excruciating pain and become a stronger woman for it.

Sarah … who had whispered in her mother's ear, just before Adelina left for California after Christmas, "I'll miss you, Mom. Thanks for everything."

One day, though, Jessica would understand. Jessica wanted nothing more than to be left alone. But the fact was, she'd been left alone too much, too long.

So, for the time being, they were staying here. They had the security guards Julia had hired, and Jessica was recovering in a safe place now. Safe physically, anyway. Every few minutes she looked back at the phone.

Carrie had sent her a text that morning. It was brief and to the point.

**Mom. Prince George Phillip would like to speak with you.**

Following that sentence was a telephone number. 202 area code. Washington, DC. George-Phillip was staying at the Embassy. Her daughters had visited him.

She wanted to call. She didn't dare.

Except for the phone call before she fled the Bay Area, they'd exchanged no words since before Andrea was born. What reason did he have to call her now? And what would she have to say to him? She still loved him, but what did that really mean, when she'd rejected him in order to protect her children so many years before?

He'd married. Adelina had watched from afar, but even minor royalty had media coverage of their weddings—especially when they were prominent diplomats. His wedding to Anne Davies had been covered in the celebrity magazines and gossip blogs, and Adelina had read every word, studied every picture.

Lady Anne was much younger than George-Phillip. She had blonde hair and blue eyes and was nothing like Adelina. She looked … wholesome. Beautiful, well-bred, almost certainly well educated. Adelina felt a painful mix of emotions when she looked at the photographs. Pain. A vague warm happiness for George-Phillip that he had finally found someone to love. But also a stabbing pain. All those years he'd stayed single … more than twenty years after they'd met. But marriage. Marriage meant he'd given up. That he'd moved on. That he'd finally let go of their shared dream together. The night of the wedding, after spending hours locked in her room looking at the photos online, she'd collapsed into her bed and wept, because that was it. She'd lost all hope.

Two and a half years later, the poor woman succumbed to pancreatic cancer. A hideous and aggressive disease.

He must have been heartbroken. The news media had reported they had a single daughter, Jane. But she'd been unable to find a single photograph of the girl. George-Phillip must keep her tightly under wraps.

Adelina picked up the phone. She turned it over in her hands, trying to decide. She should call. She wanted to call. But she was terrified. Would he only talk to her out of some sense of duty to the past? She couldn't imagine it would be anything else. But she couldn't let her life be driven by fear anymore. She dialed 1-2-0-2-

Then one of the security guards knocked. A moment later he ducked his head into the room.

"Mrs. Thompson? Two young ladies here, they said they're your daughters."

Adelina gasped and stood up. "Let them in, please."

A few seconds later Andrea and Sarah walked into the room. Andrea wore tough blue jeans and a T-shirt. Her hair had been dyed, black and turquoise. Sarah wore her customary black, with fishnet stockings and combat boots.

The three of them stood, frozen, the two girls facing their mother. To the side, not forgotten, Jessica slept peacefully.

"Hello, Mother," Andrea said.

Adelina sniffled, trying to hold back tears. She approached Sarah and Andrea and said, "I'm so glad you're here. I've missed you terribly."

Sarah approached and put her arms around Adelina. "I've missed you too, Mom."

Adelina squeezed her arms around Sarah tightly. Then she looked up at Andrea. Her youngest daughter. The daughter who had born the price, more than any of the others, of Richard's sickness and violence and Adelina's terror. She whispered, "Andrea."

Andrea walked toward her and put her arms around both Sarah and her mother. They stayed that way for a long time, swaying slightly, until Andrea broke off the hug and stepped back. Sarah followed suit.

"Have a seat," Adelina said. "How did you get here?"

The two girls looked at each other and exchanged a secret look. Then Sarah said, "The first half by Harley, but we took Amtrak for the second half."

Adelina looked at Andrea. "I understood you were safe at the British Embassy. Why did you leave?"

"Someone attacked me … and … I had a lot of questions."

Adelina sat up. "In the Embassy?"

Andrea nodded. "Yeah. I was getting ready for bed and texting with Sarah. A man came in and tried to—I don't know if he was trying to hurt me or kill me or what. But I pushed him off, and Sarah picked me up."

Adelina closed her eyes. "I'm so sorry, Andrea. For everything. But especially for you being in that kind of danger. Everything I ever did was to protect you girls. But I've not exactly succeeded there, have I? Tell me what you remember about the attack."

Andrea began to describe what happened. What the room was like. The man's smell. Then she said, "He had a thick Irish accent. Deep voice."

"Oz," Adelina whispered.

"What?" Sarah asked.

Adelina explained. As she finished telling the story, she said, "I always thought he worked for Richard. But now I'm beginning to doubt."

Andrea said, "Do you think it's possible it was the Prince? That's what the man said."

*George-Phillip? No.* Adelina shook her head. "No, I don't think it's possible he's changed that much."

"Well, he came from *somewhere*," Andrea interjected. "And there can't be that many people who have access to the royal residence at the Embassy."

Adelina sighed. "The man who shot at us at the border worked for Oz. I'm afraid he won't rest until I'm dead."

"I don't understand," Andrea said. Her eyes were watering, and she spoke at a whisper. For just a moment, the standoffish, armored young woman looked like the little girl she'd once been, and it felt like a stab through Adelina's heart. "I don't understand any of this. I wish none of it had ever happened."

## Marky Lovecchio. May 7.

Making it over the border had been a breeze. Marky had shown his driver's license to the Canadian border guards and they'd passed him into the country. Simple as that. They hadn't even searched his Challenger, almost a disappointment since he'd stashed his guns. There was no point in taking unnecessary chances, and he knew a guy in Vancouver who got him a pistol. It wasn't ideal—a .32 calibre popgun. But it ought to be enough to do the job.

He was disappointed he hadn't been able to stick around in Seattle. That stripper had been a live one, and he'd wanted to stick around with her in the hotel room for another day or two. But no such luck. He wasn't fucking with Oz.

The hospital didn't look much like private hospitals in the United States, or at least not like the ones Marky had been to. This was more like a VA or Army hospital—everything worked, everything necessary was there, but it wasn't lushly appointed with expensive carpets and artwork. Marky was grateful the morning had been chilly. It was May, and wearing a jacket would have raised questions if it were hot. As it was, he was easily able to conceal his weapon underneath his jacket.

He wandered down the second floor wing, his sneakers occasionally squeaking against the institutional floor. He'd passed the cancer ward and pediatrics. Ahead, a crowded nurses' station. His target was in room 201, which would be down the hallway to the left if he was right.

There. The nurses' station was at the intersection of two hallways. To the left and right, patients' rooms. Ahead, more hallway, and probably more rooms.

Marky had been through this before. All you had to do was look like you knew where you were going, look like you knew what you were doing. Nobody questioned you if you were confident and bold. He turned left. At the end of the hall were two security guards. One was sitting in a chair, his telephone out, sending a text message. The other was across the hall from him, leaning against a door frame. A nurse was walking toward him, and behind her a teenage girl with black and turquoise hair. She was hot, and he leered at her as she passed him going in the opposite direction. But he didn't have time to screw around. He looked back toward the guards. Neither of them had stirred, the one at the door lazily looking in his direction.

That was going to be a fatal mistake. Marky wasn't lazy, and he was prepared for these two. He should be able to take down the first before the guy sitting down texting even knew what was happening. He passed another room, the smell of ammonia and an underlying earthy smell wafting out of the room. Some old person dying maybe?

Marky casually slid a hand into the back of his waistband as he got to within twenty feet of the inert guards. The standing one started to move, but he was too late. Marky squeezed the pistol, firing a .32 calibre bullet straight into the guard's eye.

## Sarah. May 7.

As Andrea left the room, almost in tears, her mother started to stand.

"Let her go," Sarah said. "I think it's going to take some time. Everything she thought she knew has changed."

Her mother sighed, then sank back into her seat. Jessica was beginning to stir.

"You know I would have done anything to keep her. Except risk her life. Richard would have killed her. He told me that, and I believed him."

Sarah shrugged. The words made her feel—bleak. Empty inside. "I've spent the last two weeks taking in a lot of things, Mother. I learned about how you and Dad met ... what he did to you. I learned two of my sisters had a different father. I learned a *lot*. But ... that just makes things harder, you know? What used to make sense doesn't."

Her mother nodded, her face lined. Adelina looked sad. *Old*.

Sarah reached over and took her mother's hand. Then she said, "I know this, Mother. All of us are your daughters. It might not be easy ... but that will never change."

Her mother's eyes misted over. Sarah didn't know what might have happened next, because she froze at the sudden loud *pop* just outside their room, loud enough her ears instantly started ringing. A second one, then a third. *Gunshots*. It couldn't be anything else. Sarah fought her suddenly rising panic.

Jessica jerked up in the bed. Sarah grabbed her around the waist and lifted her off the bed as if she were a rag doll, even as her mother came to her aid. They dumped the now screaming Jessica on the floor.

The doorknob turned. Sarah didn't stop to think. She dove over the bed, grabbing for the door, and leaned against it.

"Sarah!" her mother screamed.

The door pushed inward, pushing Sarah back. She let out a howl, her boots scrambling for purchase as she tried to close the door. She tried to force it closed, but couldn't. Then suddenly the pressure let off the door and she flew forward, losing her footing. Her vision went black when her head connected with the heavy wood panel, then she was thrown back, the door bursting inward.

Sarah landed half on her left leg, the one she'd injured the year before, and immediately collapsed, the muscles in that leg not strong enough for sustained work.

A man wearing jeans and a Black Sabbath T-shirt and a black jacket filled the doorway and raised his pistol, aiming at her mother.

## Adelina. May 7.

"What..." Jessica asked in a half scream as she tried to get to her feet.

Adelina pushed her daughter down. "Stay down!" she screamed.

The room had filled with smoke and noise, Sarah howling with what sounded like rage, and Adelina turned back toward the door just as it burst open, throwing Sarah back against the bed with a loud thump.

Terror filled Adelina at that moment, terror that she wouldn't be able to protect her daughters, that she wouldn't be able to see them grow up and get married and have the lives they all deserved.

Terror that she wouldn't be able to make amends to her daughters, that she wouldn't live long enough to beg for their forgiveness.

The man in the doorway was large and muscular. A black leather jacket over a T-shirt and blue jeans. Smoke clouded the room from the gunshots he'd already fired, but that was nothing to the gaping black hole of the pistol he lifted up and aimed directly at Adelina.

Everything seemed to slow down to a sickening slowness. Jessica started to move again and Adelina held her left hand out as if to signal *stay*.

Then two arms and two legs were suddenly wrapped around the killer from behind, one hand grabbing at his gun. A flash of black and turquoise and arms and legs moving everywhere and Adelina realized that Andrea had jumped on the killer's back. Her daughter let out a feral shriek and screamed, "Leave them *alone!*"

Andrea had one hand on the guy's gun arm and another wrapped around his face. The pistol was aimed slightly toward the ceiling, and it went off, once, twice, then Sarah ran headfirst at the man, hitting him in the gut with her head. He let out a scream as one of Andrea's fingers sank into his left eye, blood bursting out and down his face. Then Sarah stood in front of him and grabbing at his gun hand with her two hands, she kicked him hard, in the knee.

He collapsed with a scream as Adelina's daughters swarmed over him. Andrea took his gun away then tied his wrists behind his back.

Only then did Andrea, still on her hands and knees, look up and call out. "Mother! Are you okay? Is Jessica?"

Adelina collapsed into her seat.

# CHAPTER NINETEEN
# Realpolitik

Richard. May 7.

**T**he first thing Richard Thompson saw when he entered the Senate Central Hearing Facility for the second day in a row was that even more people packed the room today than had the day before. Industrious Senate aids had added more rows of chairs, all the way to the back doors. Along each wall on the left and right side of the room were television crews, and additional cameras were crowded on the floor area between the dais and the witness table.

It was officially a media circus. The morning papers had been clear enough. *The New York Times*—always reliably liberal—had called for a public trial of both Thompson and Leslie Collins. The conservative *Washington Times*, on the other hand, had landed squarely behind both Thompson and Collins, labeling them as heroes for taking the war to the Soviet Union. CNN and Fox News talked of nothing else, with pundits on both sides of the aisle calling each other traitors, liberals and a host of other names. The news coverage was ubiquitous, with reporters digging into everything they could find about his history, his family's history.

The networks were digging up archive footage of his Senate hearings in 2000, his diplomatic mission to Iraq just before the invasion in 2003, and even footage of the February 23rd Coup. Left wing commentators openly speculated that Thompson and the CIA had been behind the right-wing paramilitary units that had taken over the Spanish capital. His entire career was being sifted with a fine-toothed comb, right alongside Julia's. He'd also seen coverage of her career—Morbid Obesity's first appearance on television, their first album going platinum, Julia speaking to reporters from Hollywood to Moscow. The reporters took the accusations in the IRS investigation as fact, and clearly someone on the grand jury was leaking information to the press.

None of the reporters had any real facts to speak of.

But they didn't need any, did they? Richard knew that well enough from the debacle of his nomination as Ambassador to Russia.

Consequently, it was with considerable trepidation that Richard now entered the hearing room and walked, head high, between the massive crowd. Toward the front of the hearing room were the officials, journalists and lobbyists who could afford to hire line-sitters to wait in the hours before the hearing. In the middle and back of the room were the members of the public who'd been lucky enough to get close to the front of the line. They were probably a mix of activists and others who were affiliated with left-wing organizations. But sprinkled in the crowd were at least a dozen men and women in military uniforms. Perhaps people who had served in Afghanistan? Who knew why these people were all here.

He was halfway up the aisle when two men stood up. Both of them were dressed in ridiculous looking baggy sweatshirts and pants and had unkempt hair. They held up a banner between them. It read "Justice for Afghan Blood."

Next to them a young woman stood up. If she'd bothered showering she might have been attractive, but as it was her hair looked a little greasy, her face pockmarked with pimples and scars from old pimples. She shouted, "Justice!" then reached into her purse and swung her left hand back, as if she were a baseball pitcher, and *threw* something across the room directly at Richard.

He jerked back and away from the projectile even as someone in the audience screamed, and his eyes tracked on the object. A balloon. A *water balloon*. It splashed down into the crowd to Richard's right, and dark red liquid exploded across half a dozen people, who began shouting and yelling.

Capitol police rushed into the now roiling crowd and hustled the activists away, even as others assisted those who had been splashed.

With blood. Real blood. Richard could smell it. Half a dozen drops had hit him, a few in the face and his hands and probably a few more on his suit. He took out a handkerchief and wiped his face and hands then turned back toward the front of the hearing room, where the witness table faced the gathered Senators.

The smell was awful. He had almost reached the front of the room when his eyes locked on Maria Clawson's.

*That whore.*

Richard was certain that somewhere along the way she had probably been involved with Chuck Rainsley. Nothing else could explain her long standing hostility to him. He'd felt glee when Julia had funded the lawsuit that wiped out Clawson's career. But now, the witch was back. She was making a comeback of her career on the back of Richard's disgrace.

*Disgrace.*

That was the word his father, Cyrus Thompson, had once used. Richard shuddered and continued his walk down the gauntlet toward his waiting execution.

He grunted as he reached the front row. Three seats from the aisle on the left side, studiously ignoring Richard, was Leslie Collins. Deputy Director of Operations of the Central Intelligence Agency. His former *friend*. Richard thought it was laughable that Collins would show up here in person to watch Richard crash and burn. Two seats down from Collins was a thirty-year-old Saudi in a dark suit and wearing the traditional white *keffiyeh*. He recognized the man, Prince Roshan's eldest son Ahmed.

Ahmed had the courage to nod at Richard. More courage than that snake Collins showed. Richard turned toward the front of the room. The Senators were all seated, waiting for him, fangs drawn and dripping with his blood.

Richard might be losing, but he would take some of them down with him.

That was something else Cyrus Thompson had taught him. Even as the old bastard was dying, he'd held on to his grudges, his hatreds, his contempt, including his hate and contempt for his own son.

Richard took a seat at the table and looked at his watch. If they started on time, the hearing would begin in three minutes. In the meantime, he sat up, his back straight, pride in every line of his body.

*Disgrace.*

Yes, that's what his father had said. *Disgrace.*

The word had been his response to the death of Cyrus Thompson IV—Richard's elder brother.

It was the summer after Richard's freshman year at Harvard. Cyrus, two years ahead of him, was entering his final year. Something had always been different about Cyrus. He was thinner than Richard, smaller. Where Richard played rugby and lacrosse and joined the rowing team when they were at Exeter, his older brother had been bookish and introspective.

One night just a few weeks before Cyrus's death, they'd sat on the roof of Kirkland House, four blocks south of Harvard Yard.

"You know Father hates me," Cyrus had said.

Richard had remained silent, just looking up at the stars.

"It's true," Cyrus had said. "I'm a joke. He wanted someone to take over his businesses and his life. Instead he got me. I'm scrawny and read books and what I really want is to be a professor. Right here. But even this ... Father selected Kirkland House. The *jock* house, as if I would ever fit in here. It was his, so it had to be ours."

Richard sighed and took a drink from his hip flask. He had a warm glow growing in his stomach.

"I just give him what he wants," Richard said. "It's easier."

"That's easy for you to say. You want the same things he does."

Richard shook his head. "No. I'm going away. Far away. Screw him. I'll be on the other side of the world, and Father can find someone else to take over his metal shavings or whatever the hell it is he makes."

Cyrus sat up, startled. "Where are you going?"

Richard said, "Can I tell you a secret? A real secret—you can't say anything to anybody."

"Of course."

Richard looked over his shoulder, even though he knew no one else was up on the roof. He whispered, "Last month I met a recruiter for the CIA."

"*What?*"

Richard nodded. "They won't do anything until I graduate, of course. But he said they're looking for people with language talents and who can move around with rich people. Diplomats. Whatever."

Cyrus was dumbfounded. "But ... but ... what if you end up in some place like Vietnam?"

Richard shrugged. "Better with the CIA than as a draftee. Speaking of which ... how are your grades?"

Cyrus had been placed on academic probation during the first semester. One more failed class and he'd be booted out of Harvard—and would lose his draft deferment. There were always ways around such things, of course, but Richard and Cyrus both knew that their bastard of a father wouldn't use them. He'd sooner send his older son off to be killed in some jungle than he would recognize that he wasn't a clone of his father.

Cyrus sighed at the question. Then he whispered, "I'm failing."

"*Why?*" Richard said. "You're just as smart as I am. Smarter."

Cyrus shrugged and looked away. "I don't know. Sometimes it's just hard to care."

Three weeks later final grades had been published and it became official. Cyrus was kicked out. His draft lottery number had already been called, and only the student deferment kept him out of the Army.

They'd returned home to San Francisco, and both brothers had been called into their father's office—the same room that once became Richard's office after the old bastard died. Father had hugged Richard and smiled at him, complimenting his grades and his lacrosse trophy.

Then he turned to his elder son. "I'm ashamed of you, Cyrus. You're ... a disgrace to your family."

"Father ... what should I do?"

Cyrus Thompson III just stuck his nose in the air and looked away from his son. "I suppose you'll have to go to war. Maybe it will finally turn you into a man. Get out of my sight. You disgust me."

Cyrus fled. Richard stood there without responding. His father turned toward him and said, "Your brother isn't capable of leading a squad of mice out of a paper bag. You'll take over the business when I retire."

Richard shrugged. "Don't count on it, Father. I may have other plans."

His father's face had turned red, and he shouted, "You'll make plans I approve of and none other!" he'd thundered.

The next morning, Richard had found his brother, swinging from the rafter in the attic.

Days later, at the funeral, his father had repeated himself, but in a new and more hideous way. "His death was just as much a disgrace as his life."

Richard retained that word. *Disgrace.* He remembered it, kept it, used it, felt it. For the next decade he ignored his father's entreaties to return to San Francisco, instead embarking on his career with the Foreign Service and his much more secretive career with the Central Intelligence Agency.

They spoke, regularly, on Christmas and Easter. But Richard didn't return to San Francisco. He didn't witness the slow deterioration of his family's four-story Victorian in San Francisco. He didn't witness the slow deterioration of his father. It wasn't until 1983, more than ten years after the death of his brother, that he returned to the city he'd once called *home.*

It was during a short leave from Spain. He'd been under intense pressure from his superiors—both because of the failed coup, which *would* have put in place a sympathetic government, as well as his involvement with the underage daughter of a deposed Marquis. The Agency's position was clear—don't make waves. Don't do anything that could call attention to the Agency. Marry the girl and shut her family up.

He did. And when he arrived in San Francisco, it was in preparation for sending his new wife home. He found his father bedridden. His health wrecked by syphilis, which had gone untreated and undetected until it was too late. Partially paralyzed and blind, the old man's internal organs were failing and he likely only had a few weeks to live.

*Married, are you?* His father had raged. *To some Spanish slut?*

Richard had responded with disdain. *She's the daughter of Spanish nobility, if you care, Father. I don't. What I do care about is that she comes to live here when I go back overseas. I can't cart a pregnant seventeen-year-old around the globe.*

His father had replied with venom. "I'll allow no such thing. In fact, if you don't dump the girl I'll disinherit you. You ungrateful little bastard. You're just as much a disgrace to this family as your brother was!"

Richard had responded with rage. But not the kind of rage Adelina would later evoke in him. No, it was a cold rage, a rage that resulted in a response that was worthy of his father. After a few phone calls, and the passing of a considerable amount of money, Cyrus Thompson III, the former shipping and manufacturing magnate, was declared incompetent and his affairs placed in the hands of his loving son.

No Last Will and Testament ever appeared to disinherit Richard Thompson. When he returned to Spain it was with a clear conscience and conviction that his father would be dead within a few weeks.

A terrible shame.

A few months later Richard installed his new young wife and daughter in the four-story house where his mother and brother had died. His mother's bedroom he turned over to Adelina. Perhaps the ghosts in there would haunt the superstitious bitch. He had the attic converted to a bedroom, which later became Julia's, and much later Sarah's.

Now, as he folded his hands in front of him and waited for the hearing to begin, Richard thanked whatever fates were out there that he'd made peace with Julia. He'd invested way too much time and energy over the years into ensuring her loyalty, and now it was paying off. That morning, before the hearing began, they'd discussed strategy. Finally, at one point, she looked dead across the table at him.

"Dad ... I want you to level with me. I know it was the Cold War and bad stuff happened. I know people had to do things that look ugly in today's light. Did you do it? Did you give them the chemical weapons?"

Richard quickly calculated the correct response. Then concluded that he needed to tie Julia ever closer to him. The rest of his daughters would take their mother's side, he was sure of it. But his Julia had been too badly damaged by Adelina to *ever* take her side.

He had nodded. "I did. It was horrible. But also necessary."

She had closed her eyes and took a deep breath, her cheeks going a bit pale.

"Julia ... you know better than anyone about foreign policy. You know how these things work. I didn't want to do it, and I certainly didn't know they would use it on innocent villagers. We actually provided the militia with satellite photos of the Russian training camp, as well as an advisor who was a Soviet defector. Vasily Karatygin—he'd converted to Islam and went over to the side of the mujahideen. But they didn't use it on the military ... it was on civilians. I'd have done anything to prevent it."

She gave him a knowing look. "But since it did happen, you had to blame it on the Soviets. *Realpolitik.*"

He grimaced. "Sadly, yes."

She had taken the bait. So now he had at least one ally. Julia had promised to turn her attorneys loose on defeating the IRS—

she'd met with them the previous day. And she promised to go after Maria Clawson. Richard, meanwhile, would take on Leslie Collins and the Senate Armed Services Committee.

His attention was jerked back to the front of the room when Senator Chuck Rainsley banged his gavel on the table.

"Mister Thompson, have you heard a single word I've said? I asked you a question." Rainsley's face was red.

Richard sighed. Then he did something that he thought might win over some of the media and the public, who looked at Rainsley as a giant blowhard.

"I'm sorry, Senator, I really hadn't noticed you were talking. What was that?"

A long moment of silence in the room was punctuated only by the clicking of digital cameras. First a titter in the back of the room, then a guffaw, and then a loud laugh from the audience.

Rainsley was infuriated. "Perhaps you'll hear better if you are declared in contempt of Congress."

Richard stared at Rainsley, knowing that at this point, the only thing that mattered was the court of public opinion and the grand jury. This Senate committee had no significant bite.

"I will repeat my question, Mister Thompson. You claim that CIA Deputy Director Collins was responsible for the massacre, and that you reported it. Do you have evidence? Copies of this report? Did you tell anyone, for example, during his confirmation hearings?"

"The information was classified. Of course I didn't keep copies of the report—keeping classified information is a felony."

Rainsley leaned forward, his face beginning to turn red. "Mister Thompson, isn't it true that you were one of the agents of the Central Intelligence Agency who aided and abetted the coup organizers in Spain in 1983?"

His face cold, Richard replied, "I cannot discuss classified information in an open hearing, Senator."

"Then tell me this!" Rainsley thundered. "You met your then sixteen-year-old wife in Spain during that coup. Why is it that she is now requesting political asylum in an allied country?"

Richard felt his face flush red. *That. Fucking. Whore.*

## Anthony. May 7.

"This way," the aide said. He was clearly more than a servant or doorman. In his fifties, the man had the face of a pug and a thick Irish accent. "My name is Oswald O'Leary, I'm the Prince's chief aide. He's in his office upstairs."

Anthony followed the man up a set of marble stairs. "His chief aide? What does that job entail, if I might ask?"

O'Leary chuckled. "Whatever is necessary to preserve the standing of the crown, sir. I was actually assigned to the Queen's security escort many years ago, then seconded to Prince George-Phillip."

Something about O'Leary bothered Anthony. He tried to shut it out of his mind. Adelina's account of Oz disturbed him, but he could hardly suspect every man with an Irish accent.

On the other hand, O'Leary was close to the Prince.

"How did you meet the Prince?"

O'Leary said, smoothly, "His first real assignment with MI6, I was assigned to work with him. That would have been ... oh ... the spring of 1984. We were here in Washington, DC."

Anthony felt a chill. Carefully, he said, "And your assignment came from the Queen? Isn't that unusual?"

He asked the question as they reached the second floor and began walking down a long hallway.

O'Leary smirked. "Not really. My primary role was to protect the Crown from scandal. Those were rough years—Princess Margaret and Lord Snowden had nearly public affairs and divorced, Prince Andrew got involved with an American girl who turned out to be a porn star. There was concern the monarchy itself might be brought down. Here we are."

Anthony didn't have time to react as O'Leary opened the door. His mind was rushing over O'Leary's words. Concern the monarchy might be brought down? Assigned to watch over George-Phillip in the spring of 1984? That was when George-Phillip and Adelina first met.

That was when Oz made his first appearance.

Anthony looked back at O'Leary, keeping his face unnaturally still, tight, because he didn't want to give away what he'd realized. The pug-faced man looked back at him. Was this Oz? The man who had threatened Adelina? Who had entered her house? It would explain a great deal. Including the attack on Andrea which had taken place in the Embassy, where no one should have had access.

He had to jerk his attention away from O'Leary to Prince George-Phillip, who rose from his desk and approached, right hand out to shake.

"Anthony Walker. A pleasure to meet you again. I've followed your career with some interest since our first interview."

Anthony took George-Phillip's hand. The resemblance with Carrie and Andrea was startling. He wondered how no one had ever noticed before. "No doubt you know about my exile, then."

George-Phillip chuckled. "Indeed I do. I admire a man who risks all for his convictions. Have a seat, please. Carrie Sherman ... well, I suppose you know she's my daughter ... asked me to agree to meet with you. I'd like to hear what this is all about."

Anthony took the proffered seat, one of a pair of matching red leather Queen Anne chairs that faced each other by a side table. Tea had already been set on the table.

"Please ... have some tea, Mister Walker."

Anthony smiled. "Anthony, please, Your Highness."

George-Phillip smiled. "Anthony, then. And you can call me George-Phillip."

Anthony glanced back at the door. O'Leary was gone. But what were the chances he was listening to whatever happened in this room?

Strong, Anthony thought. Very strong.

"Please," George-Phillip said. "Tell me more about your assignment."

Anthony nodded. "There are several layers to the story. The first thing you should know is, I was originally assigned to do a fluff piece on *Morbid Obesity*. Are you familiar with the rock band?"

"Not my style of music, but I know of them. Carrie's older sister runs a fairly large entertainment empire from what I understand."

"Correct. But the story quickly grew when the IRS and the grand jury opened their investigation into Secretary Thompson."

At the mention of Richard Thompson, George-Phillip's face soured. Not surprising. Anthony continued. "My interest here has expanded. You probably know I did a retrospective story on the Wakhan Corridor last year."

"I read it. You had most of it right."

Anthony scowled. "Except for the perpetrators, of course. Like everyone else, I thought it was the Soviets."

"I'll be frank with you, Anthony. I'm familiar in detail with what happened, *and* who was responsible."

Anthony nodded. "I thought so. Is *The Guardian's* story anywhere close to accurate?"

"Some of it," George-Phillip replied. "Although my recommendation at the time was that we go public. The Prime Minister and the then director of MI6 ordered that my investigation be squashed. Despite my distant royal status, I was very low on the bureaucratic food chain in those days. However, as of this morning, my investigation from 1984 has been declassified. I'm turning a copy over to you."

Anthony closed his eyes. That was more than he'd hoped for. "Thank you, sir. There's more."

George-Phillip raised his eyebrows. "Oh?"

Anthony swallowed. If he was wrong, and George-Phillip wasn't the man he thought he was—Anthony might be thrown out now and lose any possibility of doing this story.

He didn't think he was wrong. "Your Highness, yesterday morning I interviewed Adelina Thompson. Among other things, she told me how she came to marry Richard Thompson, and the nature of their thirty-year marriage. She also told me a great deal about your affair."

George-Phillip vaguely waved a hand. "I never liked that word. I loved Adelina as I have never loved another."

"Not even Lady Anne?"

George-Phillip closed his eyes. "Anne and I were comfortable together. And happy. But we did not have that ... that passion. We shared a quiet and happy life, and a wonderful daughter."

"I'm sorry for your loss," Anthony said. "Your Highness, I'll be honest with you. I want to crucify Richard Thompson. I've got *almost* enough details to do it. I'm putting together a major story. But I need corroboration. I need details. Will you go public? Will you tell me your story?"

For the next three hours, Anthony sat across from George-Phillip, as the tea grew cold and they ignored the refreshments brought by Embassy employees. When George-Phillip produced the Wakhan file, they moved to the desk as George-Phillip spread out the contents, going over his conclusions.

Then they moved on. George-Phillip described his first meeting with Adelina. How swiftly they fell in love. As he spoke, his face took on a longing, wistful quality. He looked at Anthony and said, "I've never experienced anything quite like it. I would have done anything for her. Anything. But she didn't want it. She broke it off with me, without explanation."

"That must have been difficult," Anthony said, his tone noncommittal.

"It was devastating."

Anthony winced. Unlike, George-Phillip, Anthony knew exactly why she had broken it off. She'd told him of the shame of Richard's rape. The self-loathing she'd experienced. And then Oz.

He sighed. "Your Highness—"

"George-Phillip," the Prince corrected.

"Normally I wouldn't do this. But ... I know why she broke it off with you. Then, and later in China."

"Dear God, man. Why?"

Anthony took a deep breath. Then he told George-Phillip what he'd learned from Adelina. The nocturnal visit and the note left in Julia's room. The assault that came much later. And now, the assassins hired to chase down Adelina, including the attack in the hospital in Abbotsford just a few hours before.

As he spoke, George-Phillip's face took on an expression of rage.

"Does she know who this person is?"

"We know he has an Irish accent. And ... we know he's been involved in this affair for more than thirty years. Whoever it is, he wanted Adelina to stay far away from you, and he's become willing to kill to prevent that. And ... we know he has access to this Embassy compound ... to this residence?"

"*What?*" George-Phillip's tone was sharp. "Explain," he ordered.

"Andrea Thompson was attacked in her room here in the Embassy. That's why she ran. The man who attacked her said that he was giving her a gift from her father. Then he tried to smother her. She stabbed him with a pen and he ran."

George-Phillip's face paled in shock. Then he said, "O'Leary... he's was opposed to my involvement with Adelina from the beginning. And he's been the *only* person I've been around since the beginning. He was limping after she disappeared...."

He picked up the phone at his desk and dialed a number. "Captain, this is Prince George-Phillip. I'm giving you an order which I expect to be carried out instantly and quietly. Detain Oswald O'Leary and bring him to me." George-Phillip was silent for a moment, listening. Then he said, "I'll explain later. It is imperative you detain him now."

He hung up the phone and turned to Anthony, rage on his face. "I only have two hours before my flight leaves for London. I'll bring O'Leary with me and we'll get to the bottom of this. There's no one else it could be."

# CHAPTER TWENTY
# Contingency plans

Leslie Collins. May 7.

**L**eslie Collins sat frozen in his seat, staring straight ahead and trying not to meet anyone's eyes. He held his right wrist in his left hand ... discreetly, but to take his own pulse as his doctor had taught him to do. Right now his pulse was nearly 160, dangerously high for a man his age and condition. The hearing would be over soon, thank God.

He'd received multiple messages from the office—first his secretary, several times. Then from the Director of Central Intelligence himself, which was not a call you ignored—but he had done so. Finally, the last call, twenty minutes before, came from the White House.

He'd ignored that one too.

As the hearing had progressed through the day, Collins had thought through everything he knew, everything he'd done. Soon enough the grand jury would be investigating him too. Somehow the investigators had gotten wind of Tyler Coleman's identity, which had led them back to Brennan Holdings, the shell company Leslie had operated for more than ten years to hide his own activities. Activities which were necessary for national security, but which politicians didn't have the stomach to approve of.

Soon enough Brennan Holdings would lead directly back to Collins. He'd be like Richard—pale and sweating in front of days long Senate hearings, followed by a trial and possibly incarceration. The investigation might even turn over his role in setting up the secret accounts in Thompson's name. If that happened then it might be the worst case: Thompson falsely exonerated while Collins took the fall for everything.

If he even survived that long. It wasn't lost on him that Ahmed al-Saud—Prince Roshan's eldest son—had also attended the hearing, sat down two seats from Leslie, then leaned over and said, "My father requested I inquire about your health, Mister Collins."

Everything was out of control. Collins had ordered Andrea Thompson's kidnapping in an effort to prevent the story from breaking, and yet his employees had fucked it up beyond all recognition. But now he'd realized that in no way was he the only player in this game. Who had tried to shoot Prince George-Phillip? Was it Thompson, because he'd found out the Prince had actually been the man screwing his wife? Was it Prince Roshan, trying to tie up loose ends, which might lead to him being identified as one of the Wakhan perpetrators?

For that matter, who had hunted down Adelina Thompson and tried to kill her not once, but *twice?* Had Thompson finally grown tired of her and decided to have her killed? Was it more sinister, and he was somehow trying to frame Collins?

Everything was falling apart. Collins stood, inevitably attracting the attention of the legion of reporters and photographers who were encamped on the floor between the dais and Richard Thompson.

It didn't matter anymore. He was shaking as he walked out of the hearing room. He needed to somehow get a grip on this situation. Maybe it was time to flush out Roshan. Or have him killed before he somehow dodged responsibility and tried to blame Collins for his activities.

Outside the hearing room, he was mobbed by reporters shouting unacceptable questions.

*Were you responsible for the massacre at Wakhan?*

*Who kidnapped Andrea Thompson?*

*What was your role in the cover up, Director?*

Collins pushed his way through. How dare they? No one understood. They didn't understand that you couldn't make an omelette without breaking some eggs. You can't defend a nation without doing some things that nice calm people in their living rooms couldn't stomach. Right after September 11, Americans had cried for blood. But they had no strength, and when they saw *actual* blood, they shied back.

It took men of Collins' stature, willing to do whatever it took, to keep the nation safe.

He left the crowd of reporters behind, making his way to the underground garage. He would go home and get some rest. He would plan. He would get through the rest of this awful week, and go forward with dignity.

But he would also start making contingency plans.

## George-Phillip. May 7.

As the small twin-engine jet left the tarmac at Washington Reagan National Airport, brilliant red and orange light flooded through the small windows. The sun was setting over Washington, DC and the view from the air was amazing.

Jane was excited. She sat in a window seat this time, looking far down at the ground as the plane banked to the right, staying on a course over the Potomac River.

George-Phillip leaned forward next to her and pointed out the Washington Monument and the White House. Jane clapped her hands and bounced in her seat. Ahead of them, through the open door of the cockpit, he could see the crew managing the instruments.

Her pure joy in the view helped assuage some of the sting of O'Leary's betrayal and escape.

Less than ten minutes after he'd ordered O'Leary's detention, the captain of the Royal Marines guarding the Embassy returned with the news. Oswald O'Leary had driven out of the Embassy grounds less than one minute before George-Phillip placed the call. Where had he gone? And *why?* Why all of it? The story Anthony Walker had told, of secret phone calls and threats, attacks in the middle of the night—it was alarming in the extreme. He would never have suspected O'Leary, who he'd trusted for more than thirty years.

O'Leary had never hidden his disdain for her. As far back as 1984, he'd said, *You should stay away from that Thompson woman. The Queen would not be happy*. But disdain was a far cry from murder.

George-Phillip leaned toward the window again. He could see the heavy Washington traffic below, swollen like something alive. Clogged arteries, a disease-ridden old man.

The flight attendant, a young woman who likely had only recently graduated secondary school, approached their seat. "Please continue to keep your seat belts fastened until we reach cruising altitude. In the meantime, can I get you a drink, sir?"

"Orange juice for both of us, please."

"Why are *you* having juice, Daddy?" Jane asked.

"Because I want to," he replied, casually. Jane was at a stage where she asked a lot of nonsensical questions.

The flight attendant turned away and began walking toward the front of the plane when a sudden jerk of the jet seemed to lift her into the air for just a second, then she fell flat to the floor. George-Phillip felt intense G-forces pulling at his stomach as the plane banked hard to the right. Below, facing the window, George-Phillip could see Northern Virginia countryside spread out perpendicular to the plane. They were tilted up almost vertically. He twisted his neck, trying to see what was going on, and then caught sight of it.

Behind them, coming up fast. A bright light with a white contrail.

A *missile.*

Adriana and Jane screamed.

## Dylan. May 7.

Dylan Paris looked up from the textbook he'd been studying when the Captain of the Royal Marines walked into the room. After four days basically hiding at the Embassy he'd grown restless, and despite all appearances to the contrary, he'd held out hope that he and Alex would make it back to Columbia in time for final exams.

That increasingly seemed less likely. All the same, yesterday she'd taken the metro out to Bethesda and picked up their textbooks and brought them back to the Embassy. For the time being, he was still in legal limbo. Not officially a refugee or asylum seeker—nor would he be willing to become one. He'd served his country in wartime, and all he'd done the previous Friday night was protect his family from attackers.

However, the fact was, one of those attackers was an armed federal agent. Never mind that Ralph Myers had been shot by a *defending* federal agent, Leah Simpson. Never mind that Dylan Paris had taken on the other two attackers—both criminals—with nothing more than a knife. The fact was, Dylan was a suspect in the killing of a federal agent, and when he walked out the doors of the Embassy—*if* he walked out—he was subject to arrest.

Alex had left an hour before, not long after Prince George-Phillip hastily made his exit for the airport. He knew she would be back later, but for now her trips outside the Embassy were their only real contact with the outside world.

*I only expect to be in London for a few days. Just stay here until we manage to sort out what is happening. You're safe here.*

But was he? A killer had attacked Adelina and three of her daughters as far away as Abbotsford, British Columbia just that morning. Only after that had he learned why Andrea had so abruptly—and secretly—fled the Embassy earlier in the week. She'd been attacked in her room by a man George-Phillip said was his longtime personal aide.

*Why?*

Dylan didn't know. But he knew he was restless. Being cooped up in the Embassy, with nothing to do and nowhere to go, was driving him over the edge.

Consequently, it was with more than a little interest that he looked up when the Marine Captain entered the room. Over the previous days Dylan had gotten to know some of the Royal Marines, several of whom had served in Afghanistan. They spoke the same language he did.

"Mister Paris," the Captain said.

"Hey," Dylan responded.

Visibly disturbed, the Captain said, "I'm afraid the Ambassador has ordered your eviction from the Embassy, sir. If you'll gather your things and accompany me, I would appreciate it."

## George-Phillip. May 7.

When the obsolete Stinger missile hit the right engine of the jet, it felt as if a giant had grabbed hold of the plane in its fist like a toy, then slammed them into the ground. George-Phillip felt his neck wrench and his head hit the back of the seat hard and his vision went dark for a moment.

The engine, mounted on the right side of the tail of the plane, instantly exploded, sending hundreds of metal shards ripping through the rear cabin of the plane. George-Phillip grabbed for his daughter as a fragment of shrapnel punched a fist sized hole in the cabin no more than a foot in front of him. The screaming from Adriana and Jane didn't stop as the plane tipped over, the ground now above their heads, now below them, as the plane went into a dangerous spin and began to dive for the ground.

The flight attendant didn't scream. Thrown to the floor of the cabin by the intense G-forces, her neck was broken.

Air bellowed through the cabin, an animal cry of pain and rage as the plane strained to keep itself intact as it raced for the ground. George-Phillip floundered for breath. Next to him, Jane's head was canted forward and her hands were covering her face. She shrieked in short, extremely high-pitched bursts with gasps of air in between.

He leaned toward her, wrapping his arms around her and began to sing the first thing that popped into his mind, a lullaby his governess had once sung to soothe him.

*Bah, Bah a black Sheep,*
*Have you any Wool?*
*Yes merry have I,*
*Three Bags full,*
*One for my master,*
*One for my Dame,*
*One for the little Boy*
*Who lives down the lane.*

The words came out naturally and he sang them in a strong voice, desperate to overcome the terror that gripped Jane. Her shrieking continued, but it began to abate as he sang the lyrics as loud as he could.

Then the air masks popped out of the ceiling compartment and began flapping around in the air, buffeted by the terrible winds and crosswinds as the plane tilted this way and that. George-Phillip could see the ground getting closer and closer outside the plane, but it was no longer spinning around them. Rather, the plane had stabilized upright, more or less, pitching and yawing to the left and right drunkenly. Jane's shrieking subsided, though Adriana's hadn't.

But the ground was getting closer and closer, trees and houses and swimming pools and schools and shop racing by below, first on one side of the plane, then the other. George-Phillip thought he was going to vomit, but then a loud thump threw the cabin again.

## Dylan. May 7.

Dylan was calm, though his mind raced, as he stuffed his books, cash and medication into a bag. The Captain had already informed him that federal agents were at the gate of the Embassy, ready to take custody of Dylan.

Once he finished packing his bag, he turned to the Captain.

"May I call my wife?"

"Of course." The Captain's expression wavered. He looked at the door, then to the window, then to Dylan. He met Dylan's eyes. "Do I have your word you won't try to escape? That you won't attempt to go out the window?"

Dylan met his eyes. Then nodded. "Yes."

"Then I'll leave you some privacy." He stepped outside into the hall, closing the door behind him.

Dylan took out his cell phone and dialed Alex's number. It went directly to voicemail. She must still be on the metro.

"Alex, it's Dylan. Listen to me carefully. The Embassy is turning me over to the feds. That's happening right now. I'll call you as soon as I know anything, but I don't know how long that will take. Have Carrie call Bear and Prince George-Phillip as soon as possible."

He paused, eyes darting to the window. He'd promised.

"I love you," he said. Then he hung up the phone and opened the door.

The Captain stood there, waiting for him. His face was unreadable, but Dylan was grateful he'd been given a chance to make a phone call.

"I'm ready," Dylan said.

He felt grim as he followed the Royal Marine out of the residence and toward the front of the ground, the reverse of the walk he'd made escorted by other Marines just a few days before.

Outside the Embassy gates, he saw a man and a woman, both in suits. On the left, the man was stout, his face almost chiseled, an unmistakably Irish face. Beside him a woman, taller, with almost-white hair.

"Dylan Paris?" the man said as the Marines opened the gate and escorted him outside.

Dylan said, "Yes."

"I'm Scott Kelly. Diplomatic Security Service. You're under arrest."

## George-Phillip. May 7.

George-Phillip's teeth collided as the plane lurched up with a loud bump, and a rush of blood poured into his mouth. He'd bitten his tongue. Outside, the world swung wildly as the plane continued to swing left and right.

"We're going to attempt an emergency landing. Everybody make sure your belts are tight. Take the brace position, hands on your heads, lean forward and touch the seat in front of you, feet flat on the floor. Landing in seconds."

George-Phillip pushed Jane forward, helping her into the position, then leaned his own head against the back of the seat in front of him. The plane had leveled out, and outside he could see lights flashing by. The sky was still rose above them, but it was noticeably darker this close to the ground. Then the lights disappeared, and he could see water, racing underneath the jet.

He felt an inhuman thrust as the plane hit the water, nearly throwing him from his seat, belt or not. A crash, then another crash, the plane went skipping along the water like a flat stone thrown against the surface of the pond.

The plane hit the water again, tilting to the right as the nose swung left. A moment later the plane was stopped.

The pilot was in the doorway immediately. "Everybody to the front door!"

Ahead of him, Adriana unbuckled her seat and lurched toward him. "Jane!" she called.

George-Phillip had already unbuckled Jane's belt and swung her to his hip. "She's all right. We have to go before this thing sinks."

Water was already pouring into the cabin from a dozen or more holes in the aft of the cabin. The flight attendant's body was nearly covered with water now.

The pilot threw open the front door and a moment later a large yellow raft filled with air just below the door.

"Come on, then!" the pilot shouted. "Go! Go! Get on the boat!"

Adriana went first, then George-Phillip strained to pass Jane to her. Jane wasn't moving, she seemed almost catatonic, her eyes wide open, her face frozen. He leaned forward, holding the girl out the door of the plane to the life raft. A wave separated them for a moment, leaving a gap of black river water beneath Jane just as he began to lose his grip.

Then Adriana was there, her arms glued around the little girl. She sank to her knees in the center of the boat.

George-Phillip boarded next, followed by the navigator, two other crewmen, and finally the captain.

"Row, sir. Row." That was the captain, who was holding an oar out to George-Phillip. The Prince took the oar and began to paddle, opposite the crewmen across from him. Not far upriver, a huge bridge, and to their left George-Phillip could see emergency vehicles, lights flashing, along the edge of the water. The pilot had managed to maneuver them not only to the river, but back toward the airport.

Behind them, the plane sank into the river, marked only by a gush of bubbles as water rushed into the cabin of the plane.

# CHAPTER TWENTY-ONE
# He was the devil

**D** reams.

Adelina knew she was asleep in the dead of night, even as she stared around her at the fog clouding her world. She hadn't slept well, nightmare visions of her daughters attacking an assassin from behind flashing repeatedly in her brain.

*Andrea. Sarah.* The two girls had acted instinctively and viciously to protect their mother and sister.

She tossed and turned, the painful crick in her neck taking on titanic proportions, a swollen red throbbing welt of rage flooding from her heart to her soul.

The rage would never dissipate. It would never scatter or melt away. Thirty years was too long to contain the lies. Thirty years was too long to hold that rage. Now was the time for her rage to become vengeance.

A flash of memory.

George-Phillip, twenty-one years old. A baby, younger than three of her daughters were now. He'd swept her up in his arms. They'd been stupidly reckless, stupidly open.

The Cherry Blossom Festival, spring of 1984. She'd worn a scarf over her hair and he'd worn sunglasses, but neither of them took any other steps to hide their identity. In a haze of drugged love they'd walked around the tidal basin near the Jefferson Memorial, hand in hand as the beautiful white and pink petals rained down around them. He'd pinned a flower in her hair, and they stood looking out to the water.

In her dream they lay down in the grass and he ran his fingers through her hair. She closed her eyes, a shiver of goose bumps running down the back of her neck as he kissed her.

Oblivious. *Stupid.*

Because it was an outing like that which had brought the attention of Oz.

George-Phillip was swept away, and she was walking barefoot along the cracked sidewalk in Bethesda, the condominium she'd hated so much towering above her. Her prison. The place she'd given in to despair. She walked up the stairs of the building, her feet moving through sludge and dirt, until she reached the penthouse floor. Walking down the hall, her footsteps left thick black footprints on the carpet.

The front door was open, and she walked into the condo like it was the gateway to hell. Julia was on the floor, two years old, her curly brown hair hanging in her eyes, wailing, and her face red. Above her, pinned to the wall with a steak knife, a note.

*I told you to stay away from him!*

Without transition she was in the formal dining room of the San Francisco home. Julia was older now, standing across from Adelina, her face twisted in rage, her teeth visible.

*Yes, you do! You've treated me like dirt for the last eight years!* Her shout was a dagger. *When I came home from that hideous abortion clinic in Beijing, you never even asked me what was wrong or where I'd been! Didn't you notice all the blood on the sheets, Mom? Didn't you notice how sick I got? I needed a mother and all I had was...*

Adelina wanted to cry, *I didn't know! I didn't know!*

Her eldest daughter, her first love, shook her head. *Nothing. Not once were you there when I needed you. When Lana sent that pic-*

*ture out, you didn't offer to help. You didn't hug me, and tell me it was going to get better. Someone in Bethesda Chevy Chase made copies and stuffed them in people's lockers at school. They tortured me, Mother. To the point where I couldn't see any way out but suicide. And what I've never understood, to this day, was why? Why wouldn't you help me? Why weren't you there when I needed you?*

Every word felt like another punch through her heart. Adelina stared at her daughter in shock. *Suicide?* She'd known all along that Julia was hurting, was isolated, but every time Adelina reached out to her, she jerked back. Her little girl had tried to commit suicide! Because of her. Because she was a failure. Because as hard as she'd tried to protect her daughters, she'd failed every single one of them.

Adelina started to cry. *I* ... she whispered. *I didn't know it was so bad for you. You're my daughter. I just wanted ... I wanted you to be better.*

Bitterly, Julia had replied, *You wanted to protect yourself.*

Adelina shook her head, clutching her hand to her chest, trying to soothe the pain that was radiating from her sternum. She couldn't tell Julia the truth. Richard would—no ... she couldn't even think of what he might do. What he might say. How he might hurt Adelina or one of the children. She remembered his horrible voice.

*I'll take Carrie and sell her to the highest bidder.*

*Would you kill this baby to save that one?*

She scrambled for words that would express part of the truth, but would protect the awful secrets at the heart of their marriage. *No ... that's not it at all. Your father and I ... we went through a really rough time in Belgium and in China. We thought ... we'd fallen out of love. And he had an affair in Belgium. And ... yes. I did in China.*

Julia's face twisted in disgust and contempt, and Adelina swayed on her feet. *So you were just too preoccupied.*

*Julia ... what happened in China?*

Then her daughter told the awful story, of getting involved with Harry Easton, the British Ambassador's son. That she'd been pushed into sex far too early, that she'd gotten pregnant. That the awful night she came home hours late, covered in snow, had been after an abortion. That the illness Adelina had believed was the flu had been the effects of too much bleeding. Adelina had kept her own secrets, and her daughter had learned to do the same.

It was hell, that they both could say so many words and at the same time obscure the real meaning behind them.

The blackness swept over Adelina. It swallowed everything, every thought and emotion and even her sight. Because Julia was right. No one had helped her. No one had been there for her. Her sociopath father had so effectively isolated Adelina from her own daughters that they *hated* her.

That was confirmed when Carrie, the daughter Adelina had always depended on, the one she knew she could count on no matter what, dismissively looked away from her.

Carrie murmured to Julia, "You've got family now. You've got me."

And that was right. Because, after all, it was Carrie who took care of Adelina's daughters. The grief she felt at that moment was greater than she'd ever felt before. Greater than the loss of her father. Greater than the loss of her own life when Richard so carelessly enslaved her. Because what she'd lost wasn't a *thing*, it was *her daughters*. The pain was so bad that she knew if she didn't get away *right then* she was never going to stop screaming.

So she ran. Adelina ran from her daughters because she could no longer face them. She ran into her room and locked the door and buried her face in a pillow and screamed her rage and pain and loss at God. God didn't answer. She'd lost the ability to feel

Him, and even *that* loss didn't compare with the pain of losing her daughters.

In the dream, Richard somehow came *into her room*, he stood there above her, his face bright, his lips curled up in cruel amusement, as he said, *You see? None of them will ever believe you. You think they do, but they're mine. Just as you are.*

In the strange way dreams do, her room grew and lengthened. It became the ballroom at the Embassy in Beijing. Richard stood in front of her, hate and contempt in his eyes. Julia and Carrie were behind him, and they were tied up in a web of spit and lies, while George-Phillip pleaded with her. *Leave him, Adelina.*

*Leave him!*

*I can't!* Her daughters were behind Richard, and he would do anything to keep her enslaved, he would do anything to win. He turned to Julia and Carrie and began to whisper and croon in their ears, even as his hand behind his back crept forward, a wicked curved knife curling from his palm.

He was the devil. She was married to the devil. And she would never be free.

The violence of her screaming shook the walls and windows of the tiny motel in Abbotsford and awakened all three of her daughters. Jessica moved sluggishly, bringing her knees to her chest, her eyes wide as Adelina thrashed, terror in her eyes, as she scrambled back to the head of the bed, eyes searching everywhere for Richard.

It was Sarah who ran to her, followed shortly by Andrea. Then all three of them had their arms around her, and her screaming subsided into unfettered sobs.

Bear. May 8.

When Bear arrived at the house in suburban Virginia, he was, as always, startled by how neat the landscaping was, how precise the rows of flowers and rock beds were, how neatly the mulch surrounded the trees. Bear had never been suited for a life in the suburbs, and when he and Leah had lived together, their yard always had the ragged look of a bad haircut too many weeks in the past. Now, she lived in a home where the Kentucky bluegrass lawn was cut precisely two and a quarter inches long, where the flowers were nourished into a parade of colors.

It was days like this when Bear hated the man who had married his ex-wife.

He walked up the steps (which had obviously been swept that morning) and knocked on the door.

Gary Simpson answered. Of course. He looked much better than he had the last time they saw each other, a few hours after Leah was shot.

"Bear," Gary said.

"Gary. How is she?"

Gary said, "Come on in. The kids have been asking for you." He moved into the house, his huge frame surprisingly delicate.

Before Bear even made it in the door, a flash of brown hair and blue eyes raced to him, and then his daughter Rebecca's arms were around him. He lifted her up; arms wrapped around her, and breathed in the scent of her hair.

"Daddy," she whispered.

"Hey, sweetheart. How are things?"

He set her down. A few feet away, Jimmy, her fourteen-year-old younger brother, eyed Bear with a wary expression.

"I missed you," Rebecca said.

"Missed you too," Bear said. He blinked his eyes and rubbed them. Damn allergies. "How's your mom?"

"She's getting better," Jimmy said in a serious tone. "Have you caught the people who shot her?"

Bear walked in and sat down on the couch. "I'm working on it. Getting closer."

Jimmy frowned. "Why are you here, then?"

Bear sighed.

"Leave him alone, Jimmy." Rebecca's tone was contemptuous. "He came to check on us. And Mom."

"Shut up." Jimmy's tone was curt.

"*You* shut up."

Bear grimaced, then reached out and grabbed both of his surviving children and pulled them into a rough hug. "*Both* of you shut up. You don't need to fight."

Jimmy struggled for a moment, but Bear didn't relent. Finally the boy sighed and let his arms down. Only then did Bear let him go. He stood and said, "All right. Let me talk to your mother."

"She's in the back," Rebecca said. "I'll show you."

Bear felt distinctly uncomfortable as his daughter led him down the hall to the bedroom Leah shared with Gary. He didn't especially want to see the room. But he wanted to know she was okay. *Ex*-wife or not, he wanted her to be okay. It's not like they had parted in a wave of recrimination and rage. Their marriage just died, right alongside Leanna, their eldest daughter.

Rebecca knocked on the door and opened it at Leah's prompt.

Leah was sitting up on the bed, a pile of pillows propping her up. She had a book laying face down on the bed next to her, and a copy of *Guns and Ammo* was on the nightstand on her side of the bed.

"Hey, Leah. You've looked better."

She snorted. "I looked worse a few days ago. They let me out of the hospital yesterday. But it still doesn't feel good to have a hole in my side."

"When are you gonna be back at work?"

"Doctors say thirty days at least. I might have to do physical therapy. So light duty for the next few months."

Bear's face fixed on a large painting on the wall. It was three feet by four feet. Oil on stretched canvas. A mostly tan background, cloudy, as if up in the sky. Or in *heaven*. Because stretched across the canvas in a joyous pose was an angel, wings swept back. The angel bore the face of Leanne.

He choked a little and felt his eyes tear up. He looked away from the painting, then back to it. "Ahhh, *crap*," he muttered. "Where did that come from?"

Leah said in a near whisper, "Rebecca painted it for me. Sometimes it helps. You know. To remember she's happy now."

"Shit," Bear whispered. Then he did something no self-respecting lawman did. He choked back a sob. Suddenly he felt his younger daughter's arms around him.

"We miss her too, Dad," she whispered.

"You painted that?" he asked.

She nodded, her face sober. "Last year."

"Well." He took a deep breath, trying to get a hold of himself. He wiped the back of a fist against his eye, smashing the tear before it had a chance to roll down. He looked at Leah. "You know it's not too late to leave that scrawny accountant and come back."

Leah gave him a sad smile. "You know it is, Bear. Don't start that again."

He nodded. "Yeah I know. Joking."

"How's the case going?" she asked.

He shook his head. "You wouldn't believe it. You been watching the news?"

"A little. I watch it, but I don't understand it. Someone shot down Prince George-Phillip's plane last night? Fox News is going insane, they're talking about bombing Syria."

"Keep watching. And check the *Post*. Anthony Walker. I think the whole story's going to be out there soon. But I'll tell you this. It's nothing like we thought it was when that girl was kidnapped two weeks ago. And it sure isn't what the news thinks it is."

"You'll solve it if anyone can."

"I've got some help," he said. His voice was steadier now that they were talking work and cases. "Look ... I just wanted to check on you. I'm gonna get the sons of bitches who did this. I promise."

Her reply was a whisper. "Thanks."

He stood. Then awkwardly, he rested a hand on hers for a second. Then he jerked back. Rebecca was still near the door.

He said, "All right, kiddo, I'll catch you later. You take good care of your mom. And your brother."

"I always do," Rebecca said, her lips curling up in a grin.

Their goodbyes were brief and awkward, as always. Then he got back on the road, headed into the city. He still had a lot of work to do. But emblazoned on the back of his mind was the painting Rebecca had created, showing her older sister in heaven.

## Richard. May 8.

The hearings had adjourned for a couple of days, though they were due to resume on Monday, with Leslie Collins testifying. In the meantime, Richard Thompson received a call from the White House, requesting his presence at a meeting at the State Department.

The White House Chief of Staff, Denis McCullough, had said to him, "Given the sensitivity of the situation, we'd like you to come in the back entrance at the loading dock. Be there at eleven and you'll be met."

Richard had nearly refused. You didn't ask a US Ambassador and former acting Secretary of Defense to meet at the back door like a criminal or servant. At the same time, a request from the White House wasn't a request; it was an order.

So at eleven that morning he'd approached the loading dock entrance of the State Department. A young man in a plain suit stood there next to the armed security guards. "Ambassador Thompson? I'm Rick Nabors, with Diplomatic Security. Please follow me."

Richard followed him. Down the ramp and into the cavernous garage at the back end of the Main State building. In the heat, he smelled the stench of garbage coming from a dumpster. Two delivery trucks were backed up against a filthy loading dock. Richard felt his rage building as he followed the arrogant young man up the stairs to the loading dock. They cleared another guard then he followed down the hall of the basement.

Despite his thirty-year diplomatic career, he'd only once been in the basement of this building. The bowels of the State Department were reserved for functionaries and mechanics, computer administrators and transportation functionaries. The cogs who made sure the organization functioned, but not the leaders, not the men and women who made the decisions.

Consequently, he was livid when Rick Nabors stopped at a bare door halfway down the hall. Richard could still smell the dumpster outside.

Nabors opened the door and said, "Please have a seat. You'll be joined in a few minutes. I'll be just outside the door if you need anything."

Richard stood and eyed the tiny conference room with a jaundiced eye. A *metal* conference table, painted steel grey, sat at the center of the room. Six cheap looking chairs with fabric cushions surrounded the table. Against the wall was a wall of metal shelving stacked with various kinds of equipment Richard had no name for. Circuit boards and boxes and wires. It was dusty in here.

A pitcher of water with ice sat in the center of the table with four glasses.

This was appalling. It was as if the meeting had been engineered solely to tell Richard that he was no longer in good graces. He took out his phone, ready to fire off an angry email to the Chief of Staff at the White House, when he realized he didn't even have a cell phone signal in here.

Then the door opened. He didn't need to call the Chief of Staff.

James Perry, the former Massachusetts Senator turned Secretary of State, entered the room first. Behind him was Denis McCullough, the White House Chief of Staff, responsible for the political survival of the President. Stout and grey haired, McCullough looked ridiculous standing next to the lanky James Perry. The third man to enter was Admiral Barry McFarlane, the National Security Advisor.

Richard came to his feet.

McCullough spoke first. His voice was jovial, friendly, despite the fact that they were meeting secretly in the basement of the State Department. "Richard! So nice you could make it."

The men shook hands and McCullough said, "Why don't we get started."

Interesting. Of the three men, McCullough technically had the lowest rank. The fact that he seemed to be leading the meeting made it clear that this was more political in nature than it was related to national security.

"All right," Richard answered.

McCullough leaned forward. "Ambassador Thompson—"

"Richard. Please." Richard tossed out the pleasantry automatically.

McCullough's face soured a little. "Ambassador Thompson—we've got a few issues we need to discuss with you. As I'm sure you can imagine, the President never imagined when he tapped you as Secretary of State that we'd be facing corruption investigations, kidnappings and murders."

Richard leaned forward and said, "Those are hardly my fault—"

McCullough said with a straight face, "Please do not interrupt me again." He picked an imaginary piece of lint from his coat sleeve.

*Don't interrupt me again.* Richard felt those words rush down his spine like poison. If a low level political functionary like Denis McCullough could speak to him like that, then he was sunk. It was over.

McCullough went on. "As I was saying, the President never imagined this series of events would take place. Fox News is having a field day. Afghanistan has lodged a complaint with the International Criminal Court. And the Chief of the SIS was *shot down* over American territory last night."

*Good riddance,* Richard thought.

"In short, Ambassador Thompson, you're embarrassing the President and the Administration. We're losing approval ratings in the polls. We need to find out how to put a stop to that bleeding. Now."

Perry looked at McCullough as if he'd discovered he was sitting next to a giant bug. His nostrils were flared and his eyes narrowed. He turned away from McCullough and leaned forward. "I have one question for you, Thompson. Were you responsible for procuring the chemical weapons which were used against the civilians in Afghanistan?"

"No. I was not."

Admiral McFarlane just sat there, not saying a word. It was disturbing.

Perry said, "Do you have any way of corroborating that? Any evidence? You told the Senate committee that you filed an official report. But there's no evidence of that."

"Collins probably destroyed it long ago. He's the deputy director of the CIA. If anyone could do it, he could."

McCullough interrupted. "We want you to fall on your own sword. The President will guarantee you'll never see the inside of a courtroom or jail cell. But this needs to end. We want you to take full responsibility, tell the world that you lied and that the President knew nothing."

Richard leaned forward and said, "And what about justice for those civilians? Does Leslie Collins walk away free?"

Perry shook his head. "You are the most cynical human being I've ever encountered, Thompson."

McCullough said, "Do it. We'll guarantee your immunity, Thompson."

Richard shook his head, then spoke, his voice rising in volume as he continued. "Never. Those banks accounts were frauds set up by Leslie Collins, and he's the one responsible for killing the civilians. I've been in government service for thirty years. I've been Ambassador to China and Russia and was President Bush's envoy to Iraq to try to stop the war from happening. I've been through a thousand background checks and there's never been a breath of scandal. How *dare* you?"

McCullough looked at Perry first, then the Admiral. Both shook their heads.

Then he looked back to Richard. "In that case, Ambassador, you can count on the President's opposition. You'll be crushed, and still held responsible for your crimes. We're done here."

The three men stood, and Perry led the way out. Richard sat in his seat, stunned at the sudden reversal. Unless he could get the Republican leadership to back him, then he had no hope. Right now, that didn't seem likely at all.

The door opened again, and the young Diplomatic Security Agent stuck his head in the room. "Ambassador? I'm to lead you out the back door."

# CHAPTER TWENTY-TWO
## Wear your seatbelt

Anthony. May 8.

**I**n the ten years of Anthony's career as a reporter, he'd been through a lot of rundown and messy airports.

But Kabul International Airport took the crown. It was stifling hot inside the airport, where the air conditioning had apparently failed. Crowds of Afghani men competed for space with soldiers from half a dozen nations, most of them armed with automatic weapons, which they displayed with surprising casualness.

He cleared Customs surprisingly easily. He'd only brought one change of clothing, an audio recorder, his phone and laptop. He would wear the same clothes for the entire trip, which would, with any luck, see him departing again in less than twenty-four hours.

That's if he didn't get delayed in the war zone, held up by Customs or local officials. And assuming Karatygin would even meet with him. And if Karatygin did, assuming he let Anthony leave alive.

A lot of assumptions.

As he left the secured area and walked toward the baggage claim, he saw a man holding up a sign with his name. Soldier. Former soldier, rather, now with a private military contractor. His uniform was indistinguishable from the US Army Combat Uniform, although it bore no insignia. A pistol was holstered at his right hip and a rifle slung over his shoulder. The Kevlar vest he wore looked heavy.

"Anthony Walker? I'm Iggy Mann. You got any bags?" His voice was the thick molasses of northern Alabama.

Anthony lifted the bag on his shoulder, saying, "Nice to meet you. This is all I've got."

"All right. Let's get going. We want to get to Charikar fairly quickly if you want to see Karatygin. Word has it his people are pulling out tonight."

Anthony cursed under his breath. He waved Iggy onward then followed him.

A small convoy of vehicles sat in the sun outside the building. Black sports utility vehicles with wide wheelbases and shaded windows.

"We're in the middle vehicle. You get in the back."

Anthony followed. *The Washington Post* was paying a fortune for this escort. It was unusual, but then again, Afghanistan was a very dangerous country. He opened the back door of the SUV and tossed his bag in, then took one last look at the airport.

Several signs were above the doorways, the largest one reading WELCOME TO KABUL in English. Armored vehicles with large mounted machine guns were at each end of the terminal, and two tanks flanked the road.

"Get in," Iggy said from the front passenger seat. His tone was irritated. "I don't need you getting shot before we even get there."

Anthony nodded, sliding over the seat and pulling the door closed behind him. Immediately, all three vehicles in the small convoy started moving. The first one stayed fifty meters ahead of them, and as it left the airport, he saw a man pop up through the sunroof, assault rifle in hand.

"All right," Iggy said. "I don't know how much they briefed you before you left the States."

"Nothing. I don't know anything." Anthony's tone was nervous.

Iggy shook his head. "Great. Whatever. Here's the deal. If everything goes right, it's an hour drive. If it goes wrong, it might be tomorrow. Soon as we get out of the airport we go down Russia Road through the city. That's the most dangerous part, because parts of the drive, we don't have any distance view or open fields of fire. We'll be going balls to the walls, moving through traffic as fast as we can to clear the city. All right?"

"Yeah."

"Wear your seatbelt," Iggy said, a smirk on his face. "Once we clear the city, it's a straight shot up A76 until we get there."

"And Karatygin is still there?"

Iggy shrugged. "Last night he was. I hear they're getting restless. The Russians still got a price on Karatygin's head, and the US wouldn't mind seeing him die too. On the highway we've got to worry about the Taliban hitting us, but once we're in Karatygin's camp, it's US drones. Either way you end up dead. So every step of the way, you listen to me. Clear?"

Anthony nodded.

Iggy turned back to the front. "This must be a pretty big story for you to risk this much."

*It was*, Anthony thought. It was the biggest story.

The moment they pulled out of the airport, traffic was dense. Buildings crowded both sides of the street, both the streets and the sidewalks crowded with people. The overriding impression color wise wasn't that different from Baghdad—dun colored buildings surroundings dun colored streets and people with dun colored clothing. Colorful signs decorated many of the buildings, but the general impression was one of disrepair. Trash littered the street, in some places piled up deeply in corners of buildings. Clearly the city had little in the way of sanitation workers.

A white pickup truck pulled in between the front and middle vehicles of the column. Four men wearing turbans and sporting Kalashnikov rifles lounged in the back of the truck, which had no license plate.

"Mother fucker," Iggy said. He gripped his rifle and gave directions into the radio. "Casey, let the white truck mosey on by."

Moments later, the SUV ahead of them moved to the left side of the road—blocking oncoming traffic—and let the white pickup go by. Once it was gone, they sped up, racing through traffic.

At one point in the ride, they were caught in a square full of pedestrians. The truck in front inched forward, honking its horn, with the two behind pushing their way. Iggy squirmed around in his seat, trying to look in every direction at once. He spoke into the radio again. "Casey, you need to move it a little faster. We're sitting ducks right here."

Anthony didn't hear the response. But the brake lights were still showing on the vehicle in front of them. Until the man in the sunroof raised his rifle high in the air. He fired a short burst, the staccato sound echoing across the square. Immediately the crowd scattered, everyone running as quickly as they could away from the vehicles.

The tiny convoy sped up, the road ahead of them completely clear. Less and less buildings to the right, and then they were headed out of Kabul into the open countryside of Afghanistan.

"How dangerous is this road?"

Iggy looked back at Anthony and smirked in response to the question. "From one day to the next it's peaceful as a cow farm or deadly as a snake's nest. All depends on how the Taliban is feeling today."

Anthony nodded. "How are they feeling today?"

Iggy lit a cigarette, filling the cab with acrid smelling smoke. "Pretty cranky, I guess. With US troops withdrawing, it's a matter of time. Taliban's been probing, attacking new areas. Ganging up on the roads around Kabul. It's like they's a vulture hovering, waitin' to dive in the minute the mountain lion is gone." He winked at Anthony. "Kabul's the carcass."

Anthony shuddered. Iggy was almost certainly right. It wasn't hard to see what was happening in Afghanistan, and from what he'd seen, violent incidents were up nearly twice as much the year before. The main difference was the ongoing withdrawal of US troops. Before long, Afghanistan might be a Taliban stronghold all over again.

"Anyways," Iggy continued, "we got a pretty good system. We don't like driving this highway if we can avoid it, but when we do, we usually make it without any losses. That's our job."

*Usually.* That was reassuring. Anthony decided to go over his notes for his story. If he could keep himself occupied, maybe he wouldn't have to think about the possibility of getting blown up in the Afghan countryside. The SUVs were moving quickly now, very quickly. But they didn't have to worry about traffic, because there wasn't any.

Anthony slid his laptop out of his bag. He had a lot of notes, and a lot of loose ends to track down.

George-Phillip's interview had lined up perfectly with Adelina Thompson's, which was incredibly valuable. What it gave him was a clear timeline of when Richard Thompson was out of the country and events surrounding her marriage and Carrie and Andrea's parentage. He had a copy of the police report, provided by Julia, and a scan of portions of Adelina's diary, also thanks to Julia. He had their brief interview with Nick Larsden before his death, naming Oz. He had George-Phillip's *suspicion* that Oz was Oswald O'Leary—his longtime aide and assistant.

He scanned over his notes. George-Phillip's original investigation report fingered Richard Thompson as the primary mover in the Wakhan massacre, aided by Prince Roshan, Leslie Collins and Vasily Karatygin. Roshan and Collins had everything to lose if the truth came out. But Karatygin might not. He'd once been a major in the Soviet *Spetznaz,* or Special Forces. He'd converted to Islam and joined the mujahideen in the early 1980s, and because of his knowledge of Soviet tactics, training, and equipment he'd quickly moved to the top of Ahmad Shah Massoud's militia.

Except now, Massoud was a provincial governor. And he'd long since disassociated from his former ally. Karatygin had surfaced after the US invasion in 2001. He now ran an "import-export" operation, which Anthony took to mean smuggling. Probably weapons and heroin. Anthony didn't think the odds were very good that Karatygin would be willing to talk. But it was a possibility. Maybe he'd been sitting in the desert for the last thirty years as Collins and Thompson and Roshan rose to the top of their nation's security organizations, while Karatygin hid out in caves from the Taliban. Maybe he was a little bit resentful. Or maybe he was worried about what would happen when and if the Taliban took over again. Anthony didn't know *what* he might be worried about, but he hoped that by the time he asked Karatygin the operative questions, he'd have figured something out. Karatygin had agreed to meet, but he hadn't raised the issue of the Wakhan massacre—yet.

Some things just didn't make sense. Oswald O'Leary might be Oz, but *why?* He'd been George-Phillip's confidante for thirty years. Why would he betray George-Phillip? What possible reason did he have? Was he somehow linked to Richard Thompson? Or was it something even more insidious?

At the sound of a gunshot, Anthony looked up suddenly. The vehicle swerved, accelerating suddenly.

Iggy turned around, his rifle at the ready and his eyes scanning everywhere. "Sniper fire," he said. "Probably from the village off to the left. Don't worry about it; the odds of a hit are pretty slim. The bigger issue is making sure we don't slow down or panic."

To Anthony's eyes, the headlong rush down the twisting highway appeared to be panic. But he wasn't in a position to say anything at all. He knew little about the country and even less about current on-the-ground conditions.

A few minutes later they reached an indefinable moment where Iggy and the driver appeared to relax. In the distance, Anthony could see a cluster of buildings too small to be considered a town and too large to be a village. Buildings made from cinderblocks and tan stone abutted each other in a tangled and unrecognizable jumble. The only color were clotheslines scattered through the village, brilliant greens, reds and blues waving in the air, brightly colored pennants of resistance against the chaos and grim fundamentalism sweeping the nation once again.

Before they reached the village, the small convoy turned on a road slightly to the left then circled around. On a hill a quarter mile from the town was a walled compound.

Iggy pointed. "Karatygin's camp."

Anthony stared in fascination. Men—obviously armed—were positioned along the tops of the walls and in a tower overlooking the entire area. It wasn't a camp; it was a fortification. He felt a chill as he wondered if he'd leave this compound alive. The only thing protecting him was the GPS tracking device he carried and the fact that the *Post* knew exactly where he was.

The convoy pulled to a stop at the gate of the compound. Two guards armed with what appeared to be US military issue M16 rifles guarded the gate. But these men were clearly not Americans. They wore linen trousers and tunics, loosely fitting, with combat boots and no helmets. Both had long unkempt beards. Anthony watched helplessly as the guards questioned the men in the front vehicle of the convoy. There was nothing he could do to influence the situation right now other than sit tight and wait. And hope they didn't all get shot. There were six armed guards in the convoy, but Anthony didn't think they'd last long if Karatygin's compound was full of hostile people.

The gate opened, and the guards waved them in. The driver started the SUV moving, and Anthony stuffed his notebook away.

Iggy turned around in his seat. "Keep your mouth shut until I tell you it's okay. These guys are dangerous."

Coming from Iggy and his crew of armed veterans, that was saying something.

Inside the compound were half a dozen small buildings clustered around one larger building in the center. As they pulled to a stop, Anthony could see that armed guards were stationed all around the square, weapons at the ready. Iggy and the driver got out. Anthony followed suit. The ground was uneven rock.

The various guards stirred, then went silent, as a tall Afghani walked out of the center building. He was dressed in traditional Pashtun clothing, loose linen pants and a tunic that hung to his knees. Nothing about his clothing indicated anything unusual about his position. But the guards looked slightly more alert, held their weapons a little higher, and stood a little closer to the convoy.

"Which one of you is the reporter?" the man asked.

Anthony swallowed. "I am."

The man approached and looked him over. "Anthony Walker." The words were a statement.

"Yes."

"Come this way. Vasily would like to meet you."

This was it. Anthony shrugged his bag higher on his shoulder and followed the man into the darkness of the largest building. They moved through a darkened foyer, down the hall and into a brightly lit whitewashed room. A large window opened into a courtyard, lush with palms and other vegetation. The room had hardwood floors—highly unusual in Afghanistan—and lush Persian rugs. Colorful wall hangings in bright patterns hung from three walls.

A reupholstered couch was against the opposite wall, with two bare wooden chairs facing it. A man lay on the couch, his back propped up on pillows. He was pale and gaunt, with wispy white hair, and held a paperback book with bright red Cyrillic letters across the front. His eyes were sunken, with nearly black circles under them, and one eye was pale with a cataract.

Clearly this was Vasily Karatygin. And just as clearly, he was sick or dying. His obvious illness, however, didn't reduce the man's size—he was *extremely* large and muscular, with a lip swollen on one side and a crooked nose. Both clearly the result of a fight probably decades in the past.

The man looked up from his book as Anthony entered. He spoke some words—in Pashto, Anthony presumed—to the man escorting him inside, who answered in a subservient tone.

Finally Karatygin said, in English, "So, you're the reporter who wishes to question me about Richard Thompson. Have a seat."

Anthony was jolted by the words. Nowhere in his remote communication with Karatygin's representatives had he specified the reason for his visit. He swallowed nervously, hoping that Karatygin had no plans to have him murdered.

Then he took a seat and said, "Yes. I'm Anthony Walker with *The Washington Post.*" Anthony took his recorder out of his bag and displayed it for Karatygin.

Karatygin smiled, curling his lower lip back, revealing a long black scar on his lip and several missing teeth. Anthony pressed *record*.

"I am Vasily Karatygin."

"I never mentioned Richard Thompson," Anthony said. "Why do you believe he's the reason I'm here?"

"You obviously would never make much of a spy, Mister Walker. It's obvious. Thompson is in the news a great deal these days—as is the massacre at Wakhan. I can only presume that you are here to ask me questions about both."

Anthony stared at Karatygin. Of course he was right, and in retrospect, it *was* obvious. He shrugged and said, "Yes. That's what I'm here for."

Karatygin stared at him for a moment. The smile was curving back into a menacing snarl. "At one time I would have simply had you killed for your presumption."

Anthony looked back. He didn't want to push right now.

Karatygin's face softened. "You are a lucky man, Walker. Lucky indeed."

Anthony didn't respond. Instead, he simply waited, not knowing what Karatygin was getting at.

He didn't have to wait long. Karatygin said, "When I was a boy, Walker, it was a different world. I was a good communist, raised in a good communist family. None of that drugged religion for me. But one day I was in a fistfight at school. I was fourteen years old."

Karatygin's face looked wistful as he spoke. "My mother was at work, and my father long dead. So when I arrived home our tiny flat was empty. I do not know what was in my head, but I took the opportunity to search through my mother's things. Perhaps I thought I would learn something of my father. Instead, I found the medal of my namesake."

Anthony raised an eyebrow. Karatygin immediately answered. "Vasily is a Russian form of Basil. She had a Saint Basil medallion in her dresser."

"I don't know much about religion," Anthony said.

Karatygin chuckled. "And you think I did, growing up in the Soviet Union? Hah. It was years before I found out anything. Basil was a father of the Church—a supporter of the Nicene Creed. A man who fed the poor and helped prostitutes and thieves. A saint. This was my mother's ambition for me."

"And what now?"

"Now I'm dying. I have a tumor in my lung, and more in my bones, and soon I'll be more tumor than man."

"Can you not seek treatment?"

Karatygin gave a short shake of his head. "It's far too late for that. My mother's God wishes me to come home, and I am afraid."

If half the things Anthony had heard about Vasily Karatygin were true, then he *should* be afraid. Anthony didn't say so, however. Instead, he said, "You had no religion, but you became a defector. How did that happen?"

"The invasion of Afghanistan was *durak* ... ehhh ... stupid. Criminal even. We killed civilians on a grand scale, we tortured and murdered. All in the name of winning the Cold War. I was disaffected well before I left. You see not long after I finished school, I found a biography of Basil in an antique store. Hidden. I bought it. I wanted to know what it was my mother had seen in my future. And the more I read, the more vicious the fighting became. The more I learned of this man of peace, the more I watched my country murder. But even *that* wasn't the end."

Anthony listened, fascinated. He nodded, encouraging Karatygin to go on.

"In 1979 I was a Major in the *Spetznaz*—what you would call Special Forces or commandos. We were ambushed not far from Fayzabad. I was wounded and left for dead. It took me *one year* to recover. *One year* to regain my health. I was brought back to help thanks to the hospitality of the villagers and the protection of Ahmad Massoud's *mujahideen*." Karatygin shrugged. "I regained my health. I converted to Islam. That didn't take. But it took long enough for me to become the enemy of my country. I fought against them until the Soviets withdrew."

"And now?"

Karatygin laughed. "Now I try to stay alive. I'm lucky this bunch does not abandon me. Instead, they keep nursing me back to health every time my illness worsens. They won't do that once your story is told."

"Why not?"

Karatygin smiled, the dark gaps in his teeth a nightmare. "Because in my zeal to carry the fight to my countrymen, I murdered. Not a few. Not a dozen. Hundreds."

Anthony swallowed. Then he said, "What was your role in the Wakhan massacre?"

Karatygin grimaced. Then he said, "I was the perpetrator. I organized it. I went to Thompson and asked him to help me procure the weapons."

"The sarin?"

Karatygin nodded. "They were Soviet stocks. A mujahideen raid near Kandahar captured them, and they ended up in CIA hands. Leslie Collins—I'm certain you are familiar with him—ran the CIA operation out of Pakistan. Thompson was his right hand man."

"Where does Prince Roshan fit into this?"

Karatygin smiled. "He was their confederate, of course. Roshan was highly interested in the effectiveness of the weapons. At the time, the three of them had the idea that they could use them on a large scale against Soviet troops. I was happy to help. But we had to test them first to assess the effectiveness."

Anthony shuddered. "The incident in Wakhan was a test?"

Karatygin nodded. His eyes were wide. Frightening. "It was. A successful one, wouldn't you say? Everyone in the village died. Even the dogs and the sheep died. When we realized how deadly it was, Collins and Thompson wanted to do it again, against a Soviet base. But by the time we returned back to our base, we realized we had a bigger problem."

"What?" Anthony asked.

"The weapons were stored in a cave in Badakhshan. After filling the tanks on the helicopters, the fumes slowly spread through the cave, and killed everyone. We abandoned the cave, and the men who were there."

"Jesus," Anthony said. "How many?"

"Twenty or so. Not as many as the civilians we murdered."

"And what happened to the cave?"

Karatygin gave Anthony a toothy smile. "It's still there. The barrels are still there, although the sarin is long since gone. Everything is still there. Even the skeletons."

*Dear God*, Anthony thought. He would have done almost anything to get a look at it. But the trip would take hours—or days really, given the road conditions and the violence. If he even survived the trip.

Karatygin leaned forward and said, "You want to see it. Don't you? I can tell."

Anthony nodded. Then he said, "I've been in the village. I did a story for *The Washington Post* about the massacre three years ago. It's ominous. Skeletons everywhere. Nobody even went back and buried the bodies. The skeletons of children, in the street."

Karatygin said, "Sometimes I think those children will come back. I see them coming at me in my sleep."

Anthony stared at the man across from him. This man, along with the others, had committed a truly evil act.

Anthony said, "Why are you telling me all of this now? I don't understand. Why?"

Karatygin looked away from Anthony. In a low voice he said, "I'm not fool enough to ever ask for forgiveness. Not for the people I've killed. But someone must speak the truth. Shouldn't they? How are Thompson and Roshan and Collins any different from the men who sent me to Afghanistan to die in the first place? How are they better?"

He looked at Anthony with naked rage in his eyes. "They aren't different *at all*. For them it is all about power and pride and position. Every one of them went on to become a man of power. It's time someone brought them down."

Karatygin shouted in Pashto. A moment later, one of his men appeared. A burst of words from each, then Karatygin began to struggle to stand. He reached for a cane then finally got to his feet, tottering.

He looked at Anthony and said, "The helicopter is on the way. I will show you. You must come."

Anthony stood. Then he nodded. "Let's go."

# CHAPTER TWENTY-THREE
# Big fish

**B**ear's apartment looked much the same as it had for days. Tiny. Empty. Alone.

He slumped into the seat at the tiny table where he'd scanned through Richard Thompson's personnel file days before. The file had been stolen, and he still didn't know who had done it. Perhaps Thompson himself. Or Leslie Collins. Whoever it was, this case had moved on from there. Bear didn't even know where to go or what to do next.

Anthony had left for Afghanistan the previous evening, leaving only a message stating that he'd gotten what he wanted from his talk with George-Phillip. It might have been helpful to know what that was. Marky Lovecchio had been captured in Canada—Bear didn't know the details behind that, other than the fact that it happened during an attack against Adelina Thompson and her daughters. *Oz*—Oswald O'Leary—had gone missing. At Prince George-Phillip's request, the National Crime Information Center had issued an alert asking local law enforcement to be on the lookout for O'Leary.

Bear sighed, walked to the refrigerator, and looked inside. No beer. *Crap.*

That's when the phone rang. He walked back to the table and picked up his cell phone. It was an unfamiliar number.

"Bear Wyden."

"Mister Wyden—this is Wolfram Schmidt."

For almost a full second, Bear thought, *who the hell is Wolfram Schmidt?* But that didn't last long. All he had to think of was the humiliation of being *arrested* by the Internal Revenue Service.

"What can I do for you, Schmidt? Is this a friendly call?"

A grunt at the other end, and the fastidious IRS agent said, "It is, Wyden. Actually, I'm calling because I'm boarding a flight back to Washington in a few minutes and I'd like to meet with you this evening. I think we may have information that might be useful to each other. I presume you know Scott Kelly?"

"From DSS? Of course."

"At Agent Kelly's recommendation, we'd like to invite you back onto the investigation."

Bear's mouth ran away with him. "I'm not doing anything to railroad those girls. They've had enough."

Schmidt said, "I'm not either. It's clear to me that much more is going on here."

Bear took a breath. He'd been ready to say something nasty to the IRS agent and hang up the phone, but now he had to pause. "I'm listening," he said.

"The grand jury is ... broadening the scope of our investigation. We're preparing to offer immunity to Adelina and Andrea Thompson in return for their testimony."

"Oh yeah? Their testimony against who?"

"Richard Thompson and Leslie Collins."

"Big fish," Bear said. "Collins, in particular.

"Mister Wyden, there are no fish too big for the Internal Revenue Service."

*Jesus.* Bear could almost see the evil grin on Schmidt's face.

"Okay. So you offer them immunity. You're expanding the scope of the investigation. To what? Thompson raping Adelina when she was a kid? The Wakhan massacre? What's your plan here?"

"You've been paying attention," Schmidt said.

"I was wondering if you had been."

"At this point we don't have enough to make anything stick for Wakhan, at least not for Collins. But we've got solid evidence of Thompson's involvement."

"Yeah? What evidence?"

"Given that one of our suspects is deputy director of the CIA, I don't want to discuss that over the phone."

Bear didn't answer. Instead, he thought about his missing file. Then he said, "All right. Let's say he's listening right now. What would you tell him?"

"I'd tell him he's as good as convicted."

Bear grinned. "I like you, Schmidt. When does your flight get in?"

"Eight o'clock at National."

"I'll meet you. But I've got one other question. What about Julia Wilson? She's been hounded by you guys. And I don't believe for a minute that she did it."

Bear didn't like the uncomfortable pause that followed. Schmidt finally said, "If this goes where I think it will, Julia will probably be in the clear anyway. But I can't promise anything."

Bear sighed. "I guess that's the best I can ask for. But I gotta tell you. It seems thin."

"We'll talk more later."

## Carrie. May 8.

"I don't know what to do, Carrie! You *know* what it was like when he got arrested in New York."

Carrie half-listened as Alexandra talked. Rachel was listless this afternoon, and her fever had stayed steady at one hundred and one degrees. She'd spoken on Wednesday with the pediatric nurse, who reassured Carrie that the low-grade fever wasn't that unusual.

"If there's a change, I want you to let me know," the nurse had said.

Carrie wanted to demand a battery of tests. She wanted to take her daughter to the hospital and make sure *everything possible* was being done. The nurse brushing Rachel's fever off had nearly enraged her. But she'd calmed herself and not said anything offensive.

On an intellectual level, Carrie knew the nurse was right. Children got fevers, chills, coughs and colds. They got rashes and stuffed up noses and diarrhea. You had to pay attention and focus on good nutrition and keeping them warm and hydrated and covered up. But not every fever was a sign of severe illness. And not every illness required hospitalization.

That's what Carrie knew intellectually. She was a scientist, after all.

But what she knew in her heart and in her gut was something else entirely. In her gut, she knew that a series of hideous circumstances had ripped her husband right out of her life before their daughter was born. Before she was even sure that she was pregnant.

She couldn't lose Rachel too.

So her thoughts were wound deeply around her daughter. She was listless, but was she *too* listless? She had a fever, but was it too high? Rachel had spots of color on her cheeks and hadn't nursed much.

All Carrie could see was the worst. What if the nurse was wrong? What if she had some horrible exotic disease and the nurse had misdiagnosed over the phone? After all, she hadn't *examined*

Rachel, and what were her credentials to diagnose her daughter anyway? When she closed her eyes all she could see was Ray, his body pale, as with a snap and click, one after the other, the monitors turned off and he was taken from her forever. All she could see when she closed her eyes was losing her daughter.

She remembered talking with Ray, right before he passed. She'd made a lot of promises. *I promise I'll be a good mother to our child. I'll be there for her, and tell her the right things. I'll listen to her problems and sing her songs at night and I'll teach her to be strong. I'll tell her about you. I'll tell her that her father did the right thing, always. That when it really counted, you told the truth, and you inspired other people to do the right thing too.*

That wasn't all she'd promised him. She'd promised not to smother their daughter with her fears, because she knew that might happen. *And I promise I won't be like ... I won't make her miserable either. I'll teach her to love you and remember you but not to let it overshadow her life. Because I know you wouldn't do that. You'd want her to be strong.*

That was a lot easier to say than do. And Rachel was only six weeks old. How hard would it be when she was six? Or sixteen? How would she deal with it when her little girl got a *driver's license,* or started dating, or—

"Are you even listening to me?"

Alexandra's question made Carrie jerk. She hadn't been listening. She'd completely forgotten her sister was there. Alexandra looked—not quite offended—she looked ... hurt. Vulnerable and wounded.

"I'm sorry, Alexandra, I just ... I'm so worried..." The words didn't even make it out of her mouth before she started to sob. She choked it back viciously. But she couldn't force back the tears that had already escaped.

Alexandra sighed. "I'm sorry, Carrie. I'm sorry. I'm scared. I'm really scared. I've called the FBI and the IRS and the DC police and no one will tell me where he is, and he hasn't called and..." Her face looked broken.

Carrie closed her eyes. She needed to pull it together. She whispered, "Look. We'll figure it out. Maybe Bear knows. Or ... or ... *shit*."

Alexandra whispered, "I don't know how much more I can take."

## Dylan. May 8.

Dylan Paris ran his hands through his hair and looked around the room for what felt like the ten thousandth time.

No exits had magically appeared. Instead, he was waiting for the return of the two cops who had been questioning him. He didn't know what agency they were from—Justice Department or FBI or CIA or IRS or whatever—but he did know he'd answered the same questions over and over and over again.

At least it wasn't like that awful night he'd spent in a holding cell in the New York City jail, crammed in with drug dealers and rapists and God only knew who else. They'd let him take his anti-seizure meds, which was good, because no wanted to see him flopping around on the floor choking on his own vomit.

Dylan sighed. He needed to go home. Badly.

The door opened, and in walked two people. He instantly recognized one of them—the man who had arrested him the previous night. He looked like Crank's dad, Jack, Irish, with dark hair and a friendly countenance. His partner, though, she didn't look so friendly.

The man sat down across from Dylan. The woman, with her black suit and silver hair, stood slightly behind the man. Dylan thought she might be prematurely grey. Her skin was smooth, not flawless, but youthful.

"Dylan, how ya' doing? I'm Scott Kelly, with Diplomatic Security Services. This is my temporary boss, Emma Smith. She's from hell. I mean the IRS."

The woman frowned, but didn't respond otherwise to Kelly's joke.

Dylan didn't respond.

"You doing all right?" Kelly asked again.

Dylan shrugged. "I'm in a jail cell. How good do you expect me to be?"

Kelly nodded. "Yeah. I get it. But you gotta understand, when you kill a federal agent, there are some questions that have to be asked."

Dylan shook his head. "I thought the agent who died was in the hallway. And was shot by Leah Simpson."

Kelly nodded. "Smart guy. That's true, Leah was the one who took him down."

"She didn't like me much," Dylan said. "At least I didn't think so. What happened to her? Did she have kids?"

Kelly said, "She does. She'll survive the gunshot wounds. In fact, she's been sent home."

Dylan closed his eyes. Good. *Good.* He opened them. "That's a relief, I'm grateful to hear it."

Scott Kelly's face immediately softened. "Well, she's not out of the woods yet. But yeah. Anyway. We've got some questions for you."

Without inflection, Dylan said, "No, I didn't know the attackers. I don't know where the drugs or the money came from. It can't possibly be Andrea's, because everything she had was lost when she was kidnapped. I don't know where she is now, or why she left the Embassy. Does that answer your questions?"

The woman standing behind Kelly—Emma Smith—said, "Mister Paris, I suggest you cooperate."

Kelly's response was much more visceral. "Don't be a wiseass."

Dylan leaned forward. "I'm not being a wiseass. I've been asked all the same questions over and over again since late last night. What the hell is this? Why don't you go look at the recordings?"

Kelly said, "Because we need to know who the hell is trying to kill people in your wife's family, asshole."

That instantly deflated Dylan. He sighed and said, "All right. Sorry. Look, I'm just frustrated. I don't know why I'm locked up when all I did was try to protect my sister-in-law."

Kelly shrugged. "It is what it is. I don't have a lot of say about that."

Silence. Dylan's eyes flickered to Smith, still standing behind Kelly. She didn't respond or clarify, which meant that she *did* have some say about it. Whatever. He would cooperate.

"Ask your questions. I'll answer."

"Why did you take the money with you?"

"I took *some* of the money," Dylan corrected.

"Why?" Kelly demanded.

"People were trying to kill Andrea. By that time she'd been attacked three times. I knew we were in danger and it was clear Diplomatic Security couldn't protect us. So I grabbed as much of the money as I could, along with one of the guns, and I met Andrea where we had agreed to rendezvous."

"Why did she go over the side of the balcony? That was a stupid stunt out of the movies."

Dylan shrugged. "Isn't it better to die trying to survive? Instead of rolling over and letting them take you out?"

Kelly nodded, his expression showing a trace of approval. The boss lady from the IRS didn't like that.

She leaned forward and said, "Where did the money come from in the first place?"

Dylan shrugged. "I don't know. Not long before the attack, Andrea called me in and showed it to me. She was confused—she said it was in the same closet she'd gone in that morning. Which meant someone planted the stuff during the day."

"Where was she that day?" Smith demanded.

Dylan closed his eyes and thought back through events. He'd been in class in New York when Alex urgently texted him that Andrea had been kidnapped. They left for Washington that night. The attack in Bethesda later that week. Adelina's phone call. The assault on the condo. The hideous hotel they'd stayed in, and the days of running after.

He shook his head. "It's all a blur. Too much has happened in the last week, I honestly don't have a clue."

Kelly spoke. "Take me through the events of that night. Starting with the money and the drugs."

Dylan closed his eyes. He tried to remember the details. How the room looked. How it smelled. The fear on Andrea's face.

*Dylan? Can you come here a second?*

He'd walked down the hall and into the bedroom she'd been using. In the closet, underneath a pile of clothes was a cardboard box. Full of drugs and money.

*Those weren't in here yesterday, or this morning. I know—I went through the closet before I left to get the blood test this morning. Who was in here?*

After he finished telling that part of the story, he said, "Then the phone rang. The house phone."

"Who was it?" Smith asked.

"The girls' mom. Adelina Thompson. She said … she said that Andrea was in danger. She told me to get her out of the building. The shooting started seconds later."

Smith and Kelly looked at each other, then back at him. Kelly said, "Did you know the attackers?"

Dylan shook his head. Then he said, "I didn't get a chance to see them really. Lot of shooting. A *lot*. Andrea went over the side of the balcony, and I hid behind the door. Leah was shooting at the attackers, but then she went down. I had a couple of knives and…"

He closed his eyes. He didn't want to think about it. He didn't want to see it.

Smith asked in a harsh tone, "You had a couple of knives and what?"

"Take it easy, Smith," Kelly responded. "He's talking. Let him talk."

Dylan said, "I had a big heavy meat cleaver and a long kitchen knife. The first guy came in dumb and fast, not paying enough attention. I got his gun hand with the meat cleaver. The other one came in right behind him … he was disoriented, and I stabbed him in the back. I'm pretty sure it severed his spine, he went down instantly."

Kelly nodded and said, "I understand you're a veteran. Afghanistan? Iraq?"

"Afghanistan."

"Purple heart? How bad was it?"

Dylan grimaced. "I nearly lost my leg. It took a long time before I was able to walk again."

"PTSD?" Kelly asked.

Dylan leaned forward and said, "Are you suggesting my mental state somehow made me hunt down these guys and kill them? I assure you I was fully conscious of what I was doing."

Kelly's mouth twitched up slightly on one side. "What exactly were you doing?"

"Defending my home and my sister-in-law. I'd do it all over again in a heartbeat."

Kelly said, "All right. Let's move on—"

"Wait," Smith ordered.

"What?" Kelly asked.

"You killed them both. What was next? Is that when you left?"

Dylan shook his head. "No. First I grabbed as much of the money as I could fit in a bag. My meds and phone and wallet and stuff. Then I ran. The balcony door was still open, and I could hear sirens coming."

Smith moved to Kelly's side and leaned on the table with two hands, forcing Dylan to look up at her. "What about the drugs? Did you take any of those?"

Dylan recoiled. "Hell, no."

"Come on, Dylan," Kelly said. "You can tell us. We know the VA had you heavily medicated for a long time. You weren't even tempted?"

Dylan leaned forward and spoke slowly and clearly. "No. I did not take any of the drugs."

"All right," Kelly said. "Which way did you go out?"

Dylan sighed. "Down the hall toward the elevators. Leah was out there—I thought she was dead. Along with two other guys."

"Did you know Ralph Myers?"

Dylan shook his head. "No."

"Did you know *any* of the people outside?"

"Leah, of course. I thought she was dead. The guy about halfway down the hall, I didn't know. And the one closest to the elevators was part of the guard detail."

"Did you take the elevator down?"

Dylan shook his head. "No. Stairs. I figured the cops would be coming up through the lobby and elevators, and the stairwell opens out to the alley instead of the lobby."

Smith and Kelly looked at each other. "How did you know that?" Smith asked.

"When Ray was still alive, we used to sneak out that way when there were reporters out front."

Kelly said, "Okay. That clears up some things. What happened—"

Dylan interrupted. "How long am I going to be in here?"

"As long as it takes," Smith responded.

"Look. I want to help you. I want to nail whoever it is hurting my family. But keeping me locked up isn't—"

"We'll decide when to let you go," Kelly said. "And it's not right now. Tell me what you know about Richard Thompson."

Dylan shifted uncomfortably. Then he said, "He's a complete bastard."

For the first time in the interview, Emma Smith half-smiled. She said, "Go on. When was the first time you met him?"

Dylan leaned back in his chair. "I guess ... about four years ago. Before I joined the Army. Alex and I had met on a foreign exchange program my senior year in high school. Richard had a background check run on me. He called me into his office to make sure I knew how worthless I was. Then later on, when I was recovering in the hospital, he sent me an email. Told me to stay away from his daughter. To let her believe I'd died in Afghanistan."

Dylan thought back to those days. Recovering in the hospital, sometimes wishing he were dead, the pain was so bad. He'd gotten through it, but just barely. He said, "Without Alex I wouldn't be anything, you know. She was with me through most of my recovery. Running with me. Helping me train. She ... she means every-thing to me. Her dad didn't give a flying fuck about any of that."

"What else?" Smith said. "What else do you know about him?"

"What? You mean like his career? I don't know shit about that. I watched the hearings on TV while I was cooped up in the Embassy, so I know he was really CIA. That's about it."

"What about Julia and Crank Wilson? How well do you know them?"

Dylan sighed. "Pretty well. They're family. I mean, they're al-ways on the road, but for the last couple years it's been holidays ... and disasters. When Ray was in the hospital Julia basically took charge, got everything managed. She helped organized my wed-ding too. Crank's a great guy. They stop by and have dinner with us every time they're in New York."

"What about money? Do you think she was hiding anything?"

"Hell, no," Dylan said. "Why would she need to? Every single album Crank's put out went platinum. They're rock stars. And she's invested the money from that all over the world. But it's not like ... not like being friends with a rock star. He's just my brother-in-law. We hang out and smoke and talk bullshit."

Kelly said, "All right. We're going to break and grab some lunch. We'll be back later to ask you some more questions."

Dylan sighed in relief. The two agents left, and he was escorted back to his cell.

## George-Phillip. May 8.

"And you just turned him over to the US authorities?" George-Phillip shouted. "Why? And why wasn't I informed?"

Ambassador Stephen Easton backed up a step toward his desk. The corpulent old fool had spots of color on his cheeks as he said,

"Your Highness, I am the Ambassador here. Not you. You don't determine what happens—"

"I made a promise, Ambassador. There was no reason at all for you to do that."

"Other than the law and for our relationship with the United States. If the boy is innocent then they'll let him go."

George-Phillip leaned closer to the Ambassador. "Don't you understand that the person orchestrating these attacks is a senior official in their government?"

Easton licked his upper lip. Then he turned away, without answering, and sat in the heavy leather chair behind his desk. He wheezed a little as he sat.

"Please have a seat, Your Highness. I understand you are upset, but there are things we must discuss. And the Prime Minister is expecting our call in less than five minutes."

George-Phillip wanted to shake the old fool. Instead, he calmly sat down in the chair.

"That's a serious accusation," Easton said.

"It's a serious situation."

"Please explain Oswald O'Leary's part in all of this."

George-Phillip sighed. "I'm not entirely clear on it. Apparently Adelina Thompson—"

"The woman you had an illicit affair with. The wife of an American diplomat."

George-Phillip starred back at Easton. Then he said, simply, "Yes."

Easton blinked several times. "Go on."

"Apparently O'Leary was opposed to my involvement with her..."

"No wonder," muttered Easton.

"Shall I continue without interruption?"

Easton frowned. Then he casually waved a hand. "Continue."

George-Phillip told the Ambassador what he had learned of the mysterious Oz. "I don't know what his motivation was."

The phone on Easton's desk rang, interrupting George-Phillip's narrative.

Easton pursed his lips. "It's the Prime Minister." He reached out and pressed a button on the phone.

"Hullo!" he nearly shouted. "Prime Minister? Ambassador Easton and Prince George-Phillip here, sir."

George-Phillip exchanged greetings with Duncan Howard, the Prime Minister of England. He'd never liked the man, a career politician who had climbed his way into his chair over the backs of his friends. But George-Phillip didn't have to like the Prime Minister. All he had to do was tolerate him and for now, work with him.

"George-Phillip, I was incredibly relieved to learn you survived the plane crash."

"Thank you, Prime Minister. Though I should correct you on a minor issue—it wasn't a crash. We were shot down, and lucky to survive."

On the other end of the line, the Prime Minister coughed. "I understood that is not firmly established as of yet."

"Prime Minister, believe me. It was a surface to air missile of some kind."

"It's quite interesting," the Prime Minister said. "I spoke with the Home Secretary not long ago. The National Crime Agency identified who fired at your home last week."

George-Phillip jerked forward in his seat, his attention suddenly riveted. The NCA, or National Crime Agency, was the national policing agency responsible for border policing, among other things. "I'm listening, Prime Minister."

"It seems that a Saudi national named ... let's see ... Hakim Silsilah. Odd name, that. The border police discovered a weapon secreted away in the trunk of his vehicle during a random inspection as he was heading to the Chunnel. The weapon matches the ballistics of the bullets we found in your house. So Silsilah was brought in and questioned. And you're going to be intrigued by what we found."

George-Phillip said, "Please, sir. My daughter's safety is at stake here. *What have you learned?*"

"Your Highness, Silsilah worked for the Saudi Intelligence Agency. In exchange for an asylum and immunity offer, he's divulged that he was ordered to assassinate you."

"By *whom?*"

"Prince Roshan of Saudi Arabia."

# CHAPTER TWENTY-FOUR
# God Stuff

**A**fter the lights were switched off, all Dylan could see was the faint emergency light down the hall, flooding through the square, barred hole in the door.

Dylan had once, as a teenager, spent a memorable night in a holding cell in the Fulton County Jail in Atlanta as a result of a series of stupid decisions by him and his friends. No charges had been filed. A few years later, he spent a nightmarish night in the New York City jail. In that case charges were filed: after a drunken ex-boyfriend sexually assaulted Alex, Dylan had attacked him.

In both cases, the jails were old. They smelled of oil and grease and sweat. The odor of men who paced like caged animals, mixed with urine and vomit.

This was different. For one thing it was clean. Before the lights had gone out, he'd seen clearly that the concrete floor and steel walls were without blemish, the walls painted a grayish white, and the floor dark grey. The bed actually had linens, though the blanket was rough wool, something close to an Army blanket. He could live with that.

At least he was alone and he'd been able to call Alex. They'd given him that. Predictably she'd been distraught, and he'd only had a few minutes to speak before he was told to get off the phone. He supposed that was better than nothing.

He was restless, raging that he wasn't out there to protect his wife and her sisters. By the end of the interviews, he had been sure that they were going to let him go. Kelly had become more and more friendly, his body language clear that he believed Dylan. Smith seemed to stay more on the fence, but even she didn't seem as menacing by the end of the interrogation.

He needed to get out of here. Dylan had paced the room. He'd walked back and forth until his feet were exhausted, then lay on the bed, tossing and turning.

It wasn't the jail on his mind, or even the danger.

Instead, his mind kept turning back to the conversation he'd had with Alex days ago.

*Maybe you should consider AA like your mom?*

*I can't do all that God stuff. You know that.*

He couldn't. Because Dylan wanted nothing to do with a God who would allow children to be slaughtered. A God who allowed war, who allowed terrorists to destroy buildings and kill thousands of people. Dylan didn't want the God of his parents. Capricious. Sometimes overly harsh, sometimes overly permissive. They were drunks, until his mom cleaned up her act. She'd thrown Dylan's dad out and never saw him again.

Occasionally—especially when he was recovering from his injuries after the war—Dylan wondered what had happened to his father. But he'd never wondered enough to do anything about it. He'd never sought him out. He'd never done much of anything to change it, because he knew that his dad was still sick.

As was Dylan.

He couldn't hide it anymore. He couldn't hide *from* it. Since Ray's death he had been slowly sliding off into oblivion. At first it was one drink, then two, then two weeks later he was drinking to quell his anxiety and pain. He didn't get *drunk*. He didn't lose his capacity or ability to function. But after six months, he'd started drinking occasionally even in the morning.

Dylan knew what that meant. He'd turned into a drunk. He'd turned into his father.

*Maybe you should consider AA like your mom?*

It wasn't that simple. He knew a little about AA. After all, his mother had joined when he was still a teenager. They'd gone to war more than once after she cleaned up—she knew he was still drinking then and pushed him hard to quit. Eventually he had. But he never joined AA. Their emphasis on spiritual development and belief in God seemed little more than a cult to Dylan. His mother and father—drunk and erratic as they were—had at one time regularly dragged Dylan to church, before they fell apart completely. He didn't remember much from those days—he'd been very young. But he did remember the talk about hell. *Lots* of talk about hell. You'll go to hell for this and go to hell for that. You'll go to hell if you don't believe, you'll go to hell if you don't believe *enough*, you'll go to hell if you lie or cheat or steal or have sex or touch yourself or drink or dance too much or vote Democrat or make friends with people with brown skin.

Dylan wasn't interested in that kind of a God, and when his mother started harping about *love* and how her "Higher Power" had set her free from the bondage of drink, he'd just turned away. He didn't want to hear it.

But Dylan was beginning to wonder. Because in recent weeks he'd found himself more and more often staring into the bottom of a bottle. And for the last two weeks, ever since he and Alex had boarded a train for Washington, he'd found himself constantly craving a drink. Or four. It wasn't the tension and stress. He'd learned how to handle that in the Army. You just buckle down and keep going, no matter how much it hurts.

No. It was something more. He'd spent his whole life wrestling with feelings that he wasn't worth anything. That he'd never amount to anything. Every time he came into contact with Alex's family, it underscored that inferiority. Her sisters were scientists and ran their own companies and even the youngest was brilliantly talented. No wonder Alex's parents looked down their noses at him.

His old therapist at the VA had taught him mindfulness exercises, meditations he could do when he sat still and focused inward. Dylan had struggled with that for months. He'd get deeper and deeper, last longer and longer, but finally he felt like he pierced through and saw right into his center.

He didn't like what he saw. Inside Dylan Paris was a gaping wound, a hole. He'd once filled that hole with alcohol, then with overwork when he went back to school. He'd filled it with his concentration on being a soldier. And, unfortunately, he'd filled it with another person. With Alex. When he lost her, or thought he had, while he was in Afghanistan, it felt like his world had ended.

He loved Alex, and he would have done anything for her. But he'd slowly come to realize that she couldn't fill that hole either. And so he'd begun drinking again. He knew it wouldn't heal that raw wound. Nothing could do that. But it served as an anesthetic, for at least a little while.

Maybe his mother and Alex were right. But he didn't see how he could do it. He'd had quite enough of shame and self-hate. An angry, vengeful God on top of that?

He lay back on the bed, staring up at the ceiling, barely illuminated from the hallway. In a day or two at most, maybe a week, he'd be out of here. He'd done nothing but defend his family, and once that sank in they would let him go.

Dylan was afraid of when that came. He was afraid of what he would do when he got out. Because for the last twenty-four hours since he was taken into custody outside the British Embassy, he'd thought far less about Alex than he had thought about getting his hands on a bottle.

Ray would be disgusted. He could almost imagine him, sitting across the cell from him, leaning forward, and saying, *Get up, Paris. Your girl loves you and deserves better.*

He was right. But Dylan didn't know how he was going to do it on his own.

He *couldn't* do it on his own.

So Dylan Paris groaned as he got out of the bed. And for the first time in his life, he got on his knees. The floor was cold, the concrete unforgiving, and his knees and ankles hurt, especially the one that had sustained such heavy injures in Afghanistan.

Dylan closed his eyes and whispered, "I don't know what I'm doing here, but if you're really out there, and you really give a shit, then I ... need ... help." He began to shake. He felt a heaving in his stomach and the wound in his heart, the gaping hole felt exposed, naked. It felt *dirty*. It felt like *shame*.

"Please," he whispered. Then he slid down to the floor, overwhelmed with grief, grief for his childhood, grief for the violence he'd witnessed in Afghanistan, but most of all, grief for Roberts and Weber and even Hicks and above all, grief for Ray Sherman. His best friend and confidante and the only person other than Alex he'd ever trusted.

In truth, he'd trusted Ray more than Alex. And as the pain washed over him, he found himself, for the first time, weeping for the loss of his friend.

## Sarah. May 9.

Sarah Thompson sat in a chair next to the window of the hotel, looking out at Vancouver Harbor.

Initially they'd had some difficulty getting the suite. None of them had any credit cards except Andrea, who had a pocket full of pre-paid gift cards. After another attack, they didn't want to be in a traceable location anyway. But after the credit card fiasco the immigration officer who had temporarily approved Adelina's asylum request, Liam Tremblay, stepped in. The hotel opened its doors wide after that.

They were staying in a spacious suite, with a common living area and two bedrooms. Sarah and Andrea slept in one room, Jessica and Adelina in the other.

Now, as the sun slowly rose, the sky pink above the harbor, the buildings reflected in the water below, Sarah waited impatiently for Eddie to wake up and text her. He'd worked third shift the night before, so it would likely be some hours. It wasn't even nine in the morning back in Washington.

While she waited, she scrolled on her phone, commenting on the Facebook and Instagram feeds of her friends from San Francisco; friends she'd effectively lost when the accident happened. Instead of going home for her senior year, she'd stayed on the East coast and home schooled. Even the homeschooling had fallen to the side when her mother went back to the West Coast after Christmas. Sarah didn't know if she was going to graduate high school this year or not. She might have to go back and spend another year in school.

That was fine. She'd still stay in Bethesda. She was eighteen now, and her parents couldn't say squat about it, and she sure as hell wasn't going to leave Carrie behind. Or Eddie. If she had to go back to school she'd do it at Bethesda Chevy Chase, where Julia had gone *her* senior year, and maybe she'd kick some ass for her sister.

The opening, then closing of a door alerted Sarah.

It was her mother. Adelina Thompson walked out of the bedroom with a worn and sad expression on her face. She looked around, saw Sarah, and approached.

"Coffee's made," Sarah whispered.

Her mother did a detour, pouring herself a cup of coffee, then sat down in the chair next to Sarah.

"Beautiful, isn't it?" her mother said.

"Yeah. It is."

They sat in silence for several minutes. It wasn't an uncomfortable silence, but for Sarah, it was a little weird. All her life, her mother had directed everything. Sit here. Stand there. Wear this. Play that instrument. Sometimes Sarah had resented her mother, raged against her. But that was all washed away when her mother sat in bed with her, holding her as Sarah cried out in savage pain from her knee to her shin, desperately waiting for the time to come when she could take her morphine again.

Sarah spoke first. "How is Jessica?"

"She's recovering. The doctors were going to release her yesterday anyway, even if we hadn't been attacked. She'll always be at risk for another stroke, but ... she'll recover."

Sarah ran her fingers through her hair and said, "No ... I mean ... how is she *doing?*"

Adelina smiled. "You always get to the heart of things, don't you?"

Sarah shook her head. "Not always. I didn't know anything was wrong with Jessica. I didn't know ... anything at all."

Adelina reached over and took her daughter's hand. "She's doing better. In her heart. In her head. She hates me, but not as much as she hates herself. She's grieving for her girlfriend. But she didn't have a chance to properly grieve, because she was all alone."

"I don't think she hates you."

Her mother grimaced. "That's sweet of you to say, but it's not true. It's okay. I did my best to protect you all. I failed. But I did everything I could."

"I know," Sarah said. She squeezed her mother's hand. "I *know*."

Adelina's eyes widened a little, and she blinked, hard.

Sarah spoke again. "What can I do? For her?"

The answer wasn't what she had hoped for. "We pray. We love her. I'm going to accept the immunity offer. Saturday we'll fly to Washington. Then we take her home and let her know how much she means to us."

Sarah said, "I hate what he did to you. I *hate* him."

Adelina whispered, "No. Don't hate … if it hadn't happened, I wouldn't have you."

# CHAPTER TWENTY-FIVE

# Hey, Dad

George-Phillip. May 9.

"**B**ut why do you have to go?" Jane asked. She was still in her Hello Kitty pajamas, eyes blurry from sleep. Adriana hovered near the door of the room. It was four in the morning, and George-Phillip was dressed in a badly fitting Royal Air Force flight suit.

"Because the Queen and Prime Minister have asked me to, and you don't tell the Queen no," George-Phillip replied. "I'll be back by Sunday evening at the latest."

"But I'm scared," Jane said. Her face contorted. She was about to start crying.

George-Phillip kneeled beside Jane and put his arms around her. "Adriana will take good care of you. And so will Captain Forrester. I'll be back very soon."

"Can we go see my sisters soon?"

George-Phillip smiled. "Of course. I'll speak with Carrie about it as soon as I get back to Washington."

"Carrie's sad about the baby."

"She is. Rachel's very sick and that makes her mother frightened."

Jane pouted. "Can't she get her some medicine?"

"Well, Rachel needs a special kind of medicine that comes from another person."

Jane looked confused and skeptical. "Medicine comes from bottles."

Adriana chuckled.

George-Phillip smiled. "Some medicine comes from bottles. But Rachel needs a bone marrow transplant. That's something that comes from deep inside your bones, and there aren't many people who can give her what she needs."

"Would they die? The people who give their bones?"

George-Phillip felt his eyes water. "No, Jane. They don't give their bones, just part of the insides of them. They wouldn't die. Jane, I really have to go."

"I could give her some of my bones."

He winced. "No, Jane, I don't know about all that." He looked at Adriana, then back at Jane. "I must go now. The plane will be waiting for me."

He leaned close and kissed her on the forehead.

Thirty minutes later, he arrived at Joint Base Andrews just outside Washington, DC. The entire drive he fretted about Jane's declaration. For one thing, it was unlikely that she was a donor match anyway. Rachel was his granddaughter, and Jane his daughter with another woman. They didn't share much genetics.

On the other hand, George-Phillip would ensure he had himself tested as soon as he returned to Washington. The driver pulled to a stop at the gate and conferred with the US Air Force guard. Moments later they were moving again, following the careful directions of the guard.

He hadn't wanted to make this flight at all. Certainly not without Jane. But he had little choice. He'd done the best he could to ensure her safety, including substantially increasing the security detail at the Embassy. Unlike the charter flight which he had previously taken to Washington—and the one which was shot down—this

flight was being paid for out of public funds as a national security matter. The attempted assassination of the head of the Secret
Intelligence Service was a security crisis. The fact that a foreign
intelligence service had been responsible for that potentially made
it an act of war.

As a result, the Prime Minister had called for an emergency
cabinet meeting. He wanted George-Phillip there in person. A
grim George-Phillip had extracted one concession—he would be
flown back just as quickly as the trip over.

The car pulled to a stop in front of the main tower next to the
runway. A military officer in fatigues stood there with a small escort. One of the men in the escort approached and opened the car
door for George-Phillip. Fifty feet away, George-Phillip saw what
was almost certainly his plane—a Tornado Air Defense Fighter,
the long-range mainstay of the Royal Air Force.

"Prince George-Phillip? I'm General Hainey, US Air Force. I
wanted to extend my welcome to Joint Base Andrews, I'm the base
commander here."

"A pleasure to meet you, General. You didn't have to arise this
early to meet me."

The general smiled. "I'm always up this early, Your Highness.
Let me walk you to the plane."

"Of course."

George-Phillip turned toward the aircraft and walked beside
the Air Force general, who began speaking. "We've been running
a continuous combat air patrol since your flight was shot down the
other night, and the FBI is trying to track down who did it. In the
meantime, I want to let you know how grateful we all are that you
survived the crash."

"Thank you," George-Phillip replied.

They reached the aircraft. A crew was running through a series of checks, and the pilot approached.

"Your Highness? I'm Captain Warfield. You'll be riding in the back here. Climb on up, we're just finishing pre-flight checks."

George-Phillip climbed the rickety ladder up to the top of the aircraft. He'd never been this close to one, and was surprised to find how large the aircraft was close up. He threw one leg over the side, then the other, and slid into the bucket seat. He started to puzzle out the tangle of straps.

"Here, Your Highness, let me help."

Captain Warfield leaned over the side and attached the harness, then tightened the straps.

"Put your helmet on, sir, and we'll get going. The oxygen mask is here."

The captain showed George-Phillip how to get the helmet and oxygen mask adjusted then cautioned him not to touch any of the buttons in the back. "Those are the weapons systems, sir, so that would be a bad thing."

"I wasn't planning to, Captain."

The pilot had the audacity to wink at him. "You never know with passengers, sir. Or civilians."

George-Phillip grumbled, "I'll thank you to remember that I was a Royal Marine."

"You weren't eligible for the Air Force? So sorry, sir, that must have been disappointing." The pilot said the words in a deadpan voice as he dropped into the front seat and lowered the canopy. Before George-Phillip could think of an appropriate reply, the pilot said, "Have you ever flown in one of these, sir?"

George-Phillip coughed then said, "No."

"Just hold on tight then, sir. It's a little like flying with a jet up your arse." With that, the twin engines fired up, starting with a low moan, then a loud screaming roar that vibrated the interior of the fighter. For just a second, George-Phillip felt some level of panic. He was going to cross the Atlantic *in this?*

It was too late. The pilot continued to monologue as they taxied to the runway. "The flight will be about two and a half hours sir, we'll be traveling at a little over one thousand four hundred miles per hour, except during the mid-air refueling."

George-Phillip swallowed. "Mid-air refueling?" He was familiar with the concept, but had never seen the execution.

"That's right, sir. The yanks have a carrier group in the Atlantic right now, and they're being right hospitable."

With that, George-Phillip heard the words over the radio. "Royal Air Force One-oh-five, you are cleared for takeoff."

"There we are, sir," Captain Warfield said.

Then George-Phillip felt his entire body sinking into the thick padding in the bucket seat as the plane seemed to leap forward, the ground suddenly racing by beneath them. The plane bounced crazily on the tarmac until, fifteen seconds later, it left the ground.

"We'll be going to altitude right quickly, sir. Just relax."

The angle of the aircraft leaned further and further back, until it was almost climbing at a sixty degree angle from the earth. George-Phillip looked out. Already, the ground was far below, and ahead he could see the Atlantic Ocean. In three hours, he would be in London.

## Dylan. May 9.

Dylan placed his hand on the glass and spread his fingers out. On the other side of the window, Alex did the same.

"I think they're going to let me go soon," he said. "The questioning—they can't possibly believe I did anything wrong at this point."

Alex sniffed and said, "I miss you, Dylan."

"Hey … it's gonna be fine. I promise. I won't let you down."

She smiled.

"Time!" The jail guard in the public area outside shouted the word.

Alex jerked a little, and a tear ran down her face. "I love you, Dylan."

"Love you too," he said.

She stood, then leaned forward and blew him a kiss. He gave her a wry smile.

After his breakdown the night before, he somehow felt better than he had in—months, really. He felt calm and at peace. And he knew what he had to do when he got out of here. He stretched and stood up to turn away from the seat.

"Paris, wait there. You've got another visitor."

*Another visitor?*

He couldn't imagine who it could be. Dylan had finally been allowed to call Alex that morning, but he hadn't expected her to show up, and didn't know the routines for visits yet. But she had made the trek to the FBI's temporary holding facility in Greenbelt, Maryland to see him. She told him that the newspapers had somehow learned of his incarceration, and several confused news reports discussed his connection to the Thompson clan and what, if anything, he might be guilty of.

He sank back into the seat, wondering who the visitor could possibly be.

Dylan's eyes widened when he got his answer.

He was five-nine and a half inches. Hair a little longer than was in style these days, and greying at the temples. His face was weathered from years of too much drinking and too much smoking, and his hands had the rough look of a manual laborer. His clothes were clean, but threadbare—either very old, or he had gotten them at a thrift store. A bushy mustache, shot with grey, hung over his upper lip like a big furry caterpillar.

He smiled uncomfortably, revealing a gap between two of his teeth. "Hey, Dylan."

It was Larry Paris. Dylan's father.

It took Dylan almost twenty seconds to croak out the words, "Hey, Dad ... what are you doing here?"

"That ain't the way to greet your dad, Dylan."

Dylan started to stand, "I don't know why you're here."

"Now wait one second—give me a chance, boy."

Dylan paused. He felt rage like he hadn't experienced since the night Randy Brewer had assaulted Alex. He took a deep breath. And another. His therapist at the VA had said over and over again, *slow down your breathing and think before you react.* He sighed, then turned and sat back down.

"What do you want, Dad? I haven't seen or heard from you in almost ten years. Why are you here now?"

His father's mustache twitched. He said, "I miss you, boy. I've missed you horribly. But I didn't know where you was."

Dylan said, "Bullshit. You never even sent a letter. You never called."

"That's cause your mother kicked me out. Look ... Dylan. You're my son. I'm sorry. I wish I'd gotten in touch. After your mom kicked me out, I was in jail for a while, and I've been knocking around for a bit. I'm working now, though, I got a job landscaping in Manassas. I'm trying to clean up my act. I ain't had a drink in a year."

Dylan snorted. He found that hard to believe. Visions of his father swept through his brain. Larry Paris had been a nasty drunk, a *mean* drunk. He'd casually and regularly hurt Dylan's mom and sometimes Dylan. Jabs and twisted arms and slaps across the face weren't uncommon in his home. Nor were the kind of words you couldn't take back.

*I ain't had a drink in a year.*

The words sounded hollow, but they also reminded Dylan of the words he'd said to Alex. That he *would* get help. Was Dylan any better than the man who sat on the other side of the glass?

"I'm listening," Dylan said. He crossed his arms over his chest.

"I hear you live in New York City now. That you're going to some fancy college. Columbia? And you're married. That was in the paper."

"Yeah, I'm married. I love her."

"Paper said she's from a rich family—she the one paying for college?"

"No, Dad. The Army's paying for it."

His father's face fell. "You got hit in the Army. Paper said you were injured real bad."

Dylan was intensely uncomfortable that anything in the news was about him. Somehow he'd avoided much in the way of media coverage during Ray's court martial. But now anything and everything related to the Thompson family was being picked over by the media.

"Yeah, Dad. Roadside bomb. I nearly lost the leg."

"Well, it's a blessing you didn't, son. It's a blessing."

Dylan just nodded, waiting for his father to get to the point of his visit.

Larry Paris looked down at the floor, then back up at his son. "Son, I'd like to come back into your life, if you'll have me. I know I don't live in New York, but you could visit sometimes. I'd like to meet your wife one of these days."

Dylan shrugged. "I don't expect to be in this jail much longer. It was self-defense. But when I get out, I'm probably headed back to New York right away. We've missed exams and we're going to have to go beg for a second chance from the university."

"Well. Will you give me a call when you get out? I'll leave my number with you."

Dylan swallowed. He was trying to figure out if he had any feelings for this man other than disdain.

*Was this what he was headed for? Was he going to be like his father?*

His father spoke again. "Son, I got one other question for you."

Dylan sighed. "What's that?"

"Well, you see, I'm not comfortable with this, but I know you're married into a rich family and all. I'm—in a tight financial spot. You see, I lost my driver's license last year when I had a DUI. And I haven't been able to work much—"

"I thought you had a job landscaping."

"Well, I did until I lost the job. Anyways, I'm just wondering it you can maybe help—"

Dylan stood up. "Dad—"

"Now hold on—"

"Dad—"

"Dylan, I'm just asking for—"

"Dad! Stop! First of all, we probably don't have any money. If you'd bothered reading more in the papers, you'd know the IRS has been busy seizing everything the family has. And second—you haven't seen me in ten years. And you show up here asking for money? When I'm in trouble? Why don't you ask me how I am, Dad? Why don't you ask me how Mom is? Why don't you show me you give just one shit?"

Dylan turned away. Behind him, he heard his father shout, "Son! I'm asking you to forgive me. That's all in the past!"

Dylan looked back over his shoulder. The man who had once seemed so large looked small now. The man who had taught Dylan he was worthless had diminished to the point of ridiculousness. The man who had beaten Dylan and his mother in his drunken meanness was asking for forgiveness.

"Of course I forgive you. You're my father. But ... that doesn't mean you get to screw up my life a second time." Dylan turned and walked away.

## Anthony. May 9.

As Anthony sank into the backseat of the cab at Dulles International Airport in Northern Virginia, he closed his eyes. Everything was blurring together. It was nine o'clock at night in Washington, and he'd been on the flight for ... nineteen hours? He barely knew anymore.

"Where to?"

Anthony shook his head. "Sorry. Um ... Bethesda, please. Montgomery and Wisconsin."

The cab driver put the car in gear and sped away. It occurred to Anthony that he might not be welcome at Carrie's, at least not for a sudden drop-in. He wasn't thinking clearly. He'd been busy as hell Wednesday, including interviewing Prince George-Phillip, then flying halfway around the world for a twelve-hour visit in Afghanistan. Then he flew back. He'd been in the air for thirty-six out of the last forty-eight hours, and he was exhausted. He'd slept some on the flight, but it wasn't enough. And sleep hadn't come easily—the story was too much, too intense. He'd spent most of the flight outlining then writing. He'd emailed the story to Jackson Barlow, the executive editor, while on the plane.

Now he just wished he could go to sleep. But there was too much work to do. The story was shaping up—but he had an alarming number of open questions, and he had to have it together by Sunday morning. He badly wanted it to make the papers before the grand jury convened Monday morning.

He took out his phone to call Carrie. It was dead.

Damn it. He just had to hope she was there. He thought through his open questions. In the morning, he needed to talk to Bear and see if they could get at Wolfram Schmidt, the head of the investigation. From what little Anthony had been able to learn about the man—scrupulous to a fault—he wouldn't likely comment either on or off the record. But it was worth a try. He needed to ask Julia some questions, and Carrie.

His thoughts drifting over the questions, he didn't realize he'd fallen asleep until the driver shook him awake. Groggy, he paid the cab driver too much money and walked toward the high-rise condo.

Inside the lobby, building security was reinforced by armed guards hired by Julia Wilson. Anthony thought the other residents of the building couldn't be happy, because the guards were checking identification for everyone who entered the building.

Anthony identified himself, handed over his passport, and said, "I'm here to see Carrie Sherman."

"Please wait." The guard walked into the office behind the desk. Anthony could see him speaking into a phone, but couldn't hear what he said. When he returned, the guard said, "Arms out to your side, please."

Anthony swayed on his feet a little, then got his footing. The guards frisked him then searched his bag. Only then did one of them say, "I'll accompany you to the nineteenth floor, and Mrs. Sherman will step out and identify if you are who you say you are. If she gives the okay, you can go ahead. If not, then the Montgomery County Police will take you away."

"All right," Anthony said. He followed the guard to the elevator, then up. Carrie waved him in.

As he entered the condo, she gave him a curious look. "I thought you were in Afghanistan. Why didn't you call?" She led him in.

"I *was* in Afghanistan, but only for a few hours. I got what I needed. My phone was dead and I came straight from the airport." He swayed on his feet. "I've got a few more questions for you and Julia."

"You must be exhausted," Carrie said. She didn't mention Julia.

He nodded. "I am. After we're done, I'll head home and get some sleep."

She shook her head. "You should rest first."

He leaned forward. "Carrie, I can't. This story is huge. I just need verification from you about a couple of things. Please?"

She nodded. Her eyes were huge. "Yeah," she said.

"Okay. Um ... let me get my notes." He sank into the couch and opened the bag he'd carried all the way around the world and opened his notebook.

As he was rummaging in the bag, Alexandra came down the hall, already talking. "Carrie, Dylan just called. You're not going to believe who showed up—" She stopped talking suddenly when she saw Anthony.

"It's okay," he said. "Don't mind me."

Alexandra said, "Hello." Then she looked away from him, toward Carrie. "Anyway ... Dylan's *dad* showed up at the jail. It's the first time he's seen him in ten years and the first thing he did was ask for money." Her face twisted in distaste.

Carrie frowned. "Is Dylan okay?"

"Oddly enough—when I went to see him this morning, he looked better than he has in months. And he sounded better when I talked with him on the phone."

"Weird," Carrie replied. "We'll talk more about it in a bit, okay? Anthony's got some questions he wanted to ask."

Alexandra nodded. "I'm going to sit on the deck for a bit. It beautiful out tonight."

After fumbling a couple more minutes, Anthony said, "Okay. Here we go ... first ... I understand you met George-Phillip one time before."

"More than that, actually. But I didn't know he was my father. I met him a couple of times in China, in the mid and late nineties. I was a kid. And—he was kind of sneaky. He spoke at my graduation from Columbia."

Anthony grinned. "I kind of like that."

She met his smile with her own. "I do too. It ... felt good to think of him ... paying attention, even though he had to keep it all secret."

"Did you ever meet Leslie Collins?"

Carrie shook her head, slowly. "I probably did. Sometimes Dad or Mom had guests over, but they never actually introduced them. We would be paraded out, shown off for a moment then whisked away. Collins looks familiar though, so I think so."

"What about Prince Roshan?"

She nodded, more firmly this time. "I *do* remember him. He was here a few times. I was fascinated by his beard."

"You told me you remember your mother being sick on Valentine's of 1990."

"Just barely. I was really little. Julia remembered it though. She was ... bruised. Badly. She stayed on the couch for days, I remember that."

"What was it like growing up with her as your mother?"

Carrie sighed and leaned back, then pulled one knee up to her chin. "It was ... sometimes scary. Dad ... *shit!* Richard ... whatever … he was always remote. Stayed in his office, or at work. He showered me with things … lessons and instruments and tickets to the opera. Then when I was in college he gave me obscene amounts of money. I never really understood why, except—maybe it was to buy my loyalty. The one thing he had was calm. Mother was … distracted. Anxious. She would break down unpredictably. Scream at us. The worst was when I was … I don't know … seventeen?"

"What happened?"

"Okay, you know who Maria Clawson is?"

He nodded. "Yeah, she's making a comeback writing about Richard Thompson and Julia."

"Yeah, that's her. Well, back in 2002, when Julia and Crank met—there were sparks. They kissed, near the White House. And it turned out Maria had followed them. She got a photo that clearly showed Julia kissing Crank, and he was all spiked hair and leather jacket and torn up clothes. Mother went insane. See—Clawson was writing about our family for *years* at that point. *Richard's* nomination as Ambassador to Russia was held up, there were Senate hearings, it was ugly."

He nodded. "Go on."

"Anyway … when the photo ran on Clawson's blog, Mom blew up. I think … I think it was because of the pressure she was under. I don't know for sure, but I've been thinking over a lot of things. How he used to lean over and whisper in her ear, and she'd go pale. Anyway, that day she went nuts. Blew up, started throwing things. She came upstairs, and the twins were misbehaving—well, not really, but Sarah was a smartass—and she just lost it. She hit me. I hit her back. She ran off crying. It never happened again after that."

Anthony shook his head. The details matched up with what Adelina had told him. He took a deep breath and said, "All right.

Almost there." He took a deep breath. He was struggling to keep his eyes open. But he had to finish this.

"Is Julia around?" he asked. "I had a couple more for her."

Carrie shook her head, a troubled expression on her face. "Julia's been in Boston the last couple of days. I think she's trying to straighten out the mess the IRS left her. I haven't heard from her at all."

"Is that unusual?"

She sighed. "We normally talk every day. But things are ... different right now."

He nodded. "When will she be back?"

Pensive, she answered, "Sunday morning. You know it's Mother's Day, right? Crazy. Because we'll all be here."

"Adelina's coming back to Washington?"

She leaned forward and said, "You can run this, but *not* before Monday morning."

"Okay."

"She's been offered immunity. So has Andrea. They're going to testify for the grand jury."

Anthony smiled. "So she's coming back with Andrea, Jessica and Sarah."

Carrie nodded. Her eyes watered a little bit. "It'll be the first time we've all been together in a long time. Since Ray died."

He met her eyes. "It hurts, I know. I still miss my mom, badly."

"Your mom?"

Anthony murmured, "Yeah. Cancer. She passed last spring."

"I'm sorry. Well, you should just come here Sunday morning then. You can talk to Julia, and I'll be here."

"I wouldn't intrude..."

"No ... it's okay. Crank will be here too, and we're still holding out hope they'll release Dylan."

He said, "All right. That's it for now. Do you mind if I just email these quotes in from here? Then I'm going to catch a cab home."

Carrie said, "Go ahead. Of course."

He typed up his notes as quickly as possible, then inserted the quotes into his draft and emailed it to Jackson. They were small details, but made the story much stronger. The fact that Adelina, Julia, George-Phillip and Carrie's stories lined up so neatly helped a lot.

As he finished sending it, he leaned back and closed his eyes. For just a second, then he'd hit the road. In the morning he needed to track down Bear.

The moment his eyes closed, he was out. He didn't even feel when Carrie tucked a blanket around him and set his laptop on the coffee table.

# CHAPTER TWENTY-SIX
# Ulterior Motive

Anthony. May 10.

**I**t was seven on Saturday morning when Anthony woke up to the smell of fresh coffee. He sat up, rubbing his eyes, and realized that he had fallen asleep in Carrie's condo. He was alert instantly—Anthony typically slept well, was an early riser and didn't drink a lot of coffee. But after the week he'd had, and the long distance travel, he was still exhausted.

The door to the balcony slid open and Anthony realized that Carrie was on the porch with Rachel in her arms. Alexandra had slid the door open. "There's coffee in the kitchen."

"Thanks," he said. He stumbled to his feet, then walked down the hall to the bathroom and washed his face. Only then did he return, make a cup of coffee, then step out onto the balcony to join the two sisters.

"Good morning," Carrie said as he came out.

Her face looked strained. Rachel was in her lap and looked pale and listless, and Carrie tucked her in a little tighter. Alexandra was sitting across from her, leaning back in her chair.

"Morning," Anthony said. He sank into one of the cast iron chairs. "I didn't mean to fall asleep here. Thanks for the blanket."

Carrie shook her head. Odd. She seemed to be avoiding his eyes. "It's fine. You were exhausted."

"I guess you'll be busy today prepping for everyone coming into town?"

She nodded. "Alexandra is picking them up at the airport late tonight. I'm … not taking Rachel out today, she's been running a low fever for a couple days."

"Is it serious?"

She shook her head. "No … the nurse just said keep her hydrated. But I don't like seeing her this listless."

"How long has it been since her transfusion?"

"Just a few days."

Alexandra said, "I'll take care of getting everyone here, Carrie. You just take care of Rachel."

Anthony said, "Is there anything I can get you?"

"No, I'm fine. What are your plans anyway?"

"I've got to put in a call to Bear. I've got questions for him, and if we can get in to see him, I want to talk to the guy running the investigation for the IRS."

She said, "You're welcome to work out of here until you meet them. We've got a lot of room, you know that."

Anthony smiled. "Thanks," he said. "I really do appreciate you letting me stay last night."

Carrie studiously looked away from him, instead choosing to fuss with Rachel's blanket for the fortieth time.

Anthony finished his coffee and awkwardly said, "Well, let me get to those calls."

He felt extremely self-conscious as he slid the door open again and stepped inside. He picked up his phone. *Damn it.* He'd forgotten to charge it. He dug in his bag for his USB charger and connected it to his laptop and waited while he checked his email.

He'd received one marked urgent from Jackson.

TO: Anthony Walker
FROM: Jackson Barlow
SUBJECT: Karatygin
Anthony,
**Great job on the story. Got your updated notes. We're going to run this on the front page with a special report insert. The photographs are incredible.**

That was good news. Anthony thought that this meant he was definitely out of the doghouse at work. Only a few more loose ends to tie up.

As his phone finally booted up, he saw he had half a dozen messages. He dialed into his voicemail.

Two messages from bill collectors. One from Carrie—that was interesting—wishing him luck in Afghanistan. Two more from Jackson Barlow, demanding to know when he was coming back from Afghanistan. A final message from Bear. It was terse, giving an address in Falls Church, Virginia and a time: nine o'clock.

It was eight now. He jumped to his feet and slid open the door again. "Hey Carrie—can I borrow your shower? And would it be possible to get the concierge to call a cab? I've got to get to Falls Church."

Carrie looked up and said, "Sure. Maybe one of us can drive you? A cab to Falls Church is going to cost a fortune."

Alexandra said, "I'll watch Rachel."

Carrie said, "I don't know."

"Carrie, I've got it. You go—you could use a break. And Rachel's fine. I'll call you if her fever goes up."

Carrie sighed. Then she looked at Anthony. "All right. I'll take you."

He hadn't participated at all in that exchange. But he nodded and said, "Thanks. I'll be ready in ten minutes."

Anthony was surprised to learn that Carrie drove a giant black Chevy Suburban, one of the biggest sports utility vehicles on the road. But when he thought about it, it made sense. After all, Ray Sherman had been killed in a car accident. It would stand to reason that she would have a lot of residual anxiety about cars.

Regardless of that, she expertly drove them out of the crowded streets of Bethesda and on to the Capitol Beltway. Rush hour wasn't over, and they sat in the car nearly twenty-five minutes before they made it across the bridge and into Virginia.

Anthony said, "I can't tell you how much I appreciate the ride."

She looked at him and said, "I have an ulterior motive."

For just a second Anthony's heart seemed to skip a beat. But he looked at her as calm as he could and said, "And that would be?"

Carrie didn't look at him. She said, "I want in on the meeting."

"I don't know if they'll let you—"

"Let me try to persuade them. I've certainly got as much a right as you. And I probably have information they need."

Anthony opened his mouth to speak, then thought. And closed it. Because she was right. She had *more* right than he did. After all, it was her family being ripped apart.

"All right. Just bear in mind that Schmidt—he's the head of the IRS investigation—hasn't even agreed to see me. He doesn't know I'm coming. So you showing up might make things even worse."

Carrie was no fool. She changed the subject. "What did you find out in Afghanistan?"

"Few things that really surprised me," he replied. "But I got hard corroboration, both witness testimony and physical evidence, that Richard Thompson was involved in the acquisition of the weapons."

"Jesus," she whispered. "I kept hoping it wasn't true."

"I don't blame you," he said. "You've had—a lot of tough realizations in the last few days."

She nodded. "Yes. That's true."

"I wish it hadn't been that way," he said. Not that his wishes made any difference, or could do anything to help Carrie. But it was true. He wished she'd not had such a tough time. "You're strong, you know. Most people would have buckled under the pressures you've faced."

She gave him a wry smile. "My mother taught me to stand up to all kinds of pressure."

Anthony's admiration of Carrie Sherman only grew at that statement.

Thirty minutes later, they finally arrived at a nondescript suburban house in Northern Virginia. The first thing Anthony noted about it was the precision of the bushes, which had been trimmed in perfectly even lines. Even the grass looked freshly cut, with not a blade out of place. Whoever took care of the landscaping here was a fanatic.

Carrie pulled the SUV to a stop. Three other cars were in the driveway, including one with federal government license plates. She took a deep breath.

"You ready for this?" he asked.

She nodded, once.

They simultaneously opened the doors of the Suburban and stepped down to the driveway. Moments later a large man who looked like a former linebacker opened the door.

"You must be Anthony Walker?"

"Yeah. And this is Carrie Sherman."

"Come on in. I'm Gary Simpson. This is my house, but I'm not in on the meeting. You're a little late."

"Traffic."

Anthony and Carrie walked forward to the door, and had an awkward moment where he stepped back to let her go first, and she did the same thing, causing them to collide.

She stifled a laugh and he said, "After you. Please."

He followed her in. Carrie stopped almost immediately on entering the foyer, her eyes on a large photograph that dominated the entry. Her eyes jerked to Gary. "You're married to Leah?"

"Yeah," he replied.

Tears appeared in Carrie's eyes. "She was shot protecting my sister. I'm so sorry."

Gary sucked in a breath, briefly speechless. Then he said, "Thanks. She's going to recover." He seemed to bite back tears, then waved them on. "In the dining room."

Anthony followed Carrie into the room. The first thing he saw was a wall which was almost completely windows, framing a view of woods with a small stream running through them on the far side of the backyard. The backyard was as carefully manicured as the front, including a gravel path leading to a small wooden bridge over the stream.

A dark, most likely antique table with eight chairs dominated the dining room.

At the head of the table was Wolfram Schmidt from the Internal Revenue Service. The last time Anthony had seen Schmidt, the IRS agents had tied zip ties around Anthony's wrists in a hotel room on the West Coast. Schmidt wore jeans and a button down white shirt, and stood beside a large whiteboard. Halfway down the table, Bear Wyden sat. Files were open in front of him. Next to him, a youngish looking woman in a suit, with nearly white hair and an annoyed expression.

Leah Simpson sat in a recliner in one corner of the room, looking pale with her feet up. Another man Anthony didn't recognize sat across from Bear, who stood up as Anthony and Carrie entered the room.

"Folks, I want to introduce you to Anthony Walker ... and Carrie Sherman. Before you panic, Anthony is with *The Washington Post*, and I *asked* him to be here."

"Have you lost your mind?" the woman with white hair asked.

Bear grinned. "Anthony, let me introduce Emma Smith, from the Internal Revenue Service. Across from me is Scott Kelly, from Diplomatic Security. He's an old colleague of mine. In the corner nursing a grudge—and a bullet wound—is Leah Wy— um ... Leah Simpson."

Leah made a sour face at Bear.

Schmidt said, "I don't know that bringing the press into this is a good idea."

"Just hear me out for five minutes," Anthony said. "If you want to throw us out then, feel free."

Schmidt looked at his watch, making him the first person Anthony had seen in a year who actually wore one anymore. "You have five minutes. Talk."

Anthony swallowed. "I have information you need for the grand jury. Information that will put Richard Thompson and Leslie Collins away for a very long time."

Schmidt didn't respond, but Emma Smith looked skeptical. Anthony continued. "First—in the last few days I've interviewed Adelina Thompson and most of her daughters."

Emma shrugged her shoulders. "We've done the same, and probably got the same information."

"I'm guessing you haven't gotten in to see Prince George-Phillip."

Emma sat forward, and Schmidt looked interested. "Tell me more," he said.

"The Prince's story lines up with Adelina's. He is Carrie's father. And—here's the kicker. George-Phillip was responsible for the British investigation into the Wakhan massacre, and his conclusions and recommendations were very different from what was made public at the time. I have a copy of that report. And ... I got back in from Afghanistan last night. I met with Vasily Karatygin."

Bear grinned at that news. Schmidt merely raised an eyebrow.

Anthony looked at the others in the room and said, "On Monday morning, the *Post* is going to run a special report which will crucify Thompson and Collins. I've got hard evidence of their involvement in the procurement of chemical weapons." Anthony went on to discuss what he had seen and learned in Afghanistan.

Schmidt said, "All right. What about her? Why is she here?"

Carrie said, "I'm the only person who can tell you anything about the inside of my parents' marriage."

"Plus," Anthony said, "if she doesn't stay, neither do I."

Emma Smith closed her eyes. "Wolfram, this is all—"

"Yes, I know. It's irregular. It's ... all mixed up. On the other hand, we're taking on the CIA here. I think we might need some unusual allies. Walker—I can't give you everything we have. It's an ongoing investigation, and there are things we know that I cannot and will not tell you. But I can give you some information, off the record. In return, you give me everything you've got."

Anthony said, "This is exclusive? I don't want to find my information on CNN."

"Of course. Have a seat." Schmidt paused for just a moment then said, "Both of you."

Anthony glanced at Carrie, who flashed him a smile. Both of them took seats at the table.

Bear leaned forward and said, "Before you came in, we were actually trying to figure out—a timeline, I guess. Who did what and when. We've had multiple parties involved in this."

Anthony nodded.

Schmidt wrote on the white board in large letters:

*Who kidnapped Andrea Thompson? Why?
*Who opened the accounts in the Caymans in Richard Thompson's name?
*Who murdered Mitch Filner and why?
*Who is Oz?
*Who did Ralph Myers work for?
*Who was involved in the shooting in Bethesda?
*Who attacked GP, the Bethesda condo and the house in San Francisco?

When he finished writing, Schmidt said, "And the biggest question is why?"

Bear said, "Well, we know the answers to some of these questions already."

Schmidt said, "Let's take them from the top?"

Bear Kelly said, "Our kidnappers were Tyler Coleman and Tariq Koury. Koury is a fairly well-known mercenary; he did a lot of work for CIA and SIS over the years in Iraq and Saudi Arabia. Coleman was a US Special Forces veteran who worked for a shell company until 2011. Brennan Holdings."

Emma said, "Brennan Holdings is a CIA shell company. Leslie Collins set it up in the mid-2000s."

Bear said, "We can prove that?"

Emma nodded. "Yes, we've got him cold on that. The only question is, was it Collins' personal operation, or did it have official sanction? We don't have any way of knowing at this point."

Anthony said, "In the end, it doesn't matter. The Agency will deny it no matter what the real answer is." Anthony thought it was interesting that none of the federal agents in the room disagreed with him. "Can I use that? Off the record?"

Schmidt looked at Bear, who shrugged. Then he looked back at Anthony. "All right. How do you guys usually write it? An *unidentified source close to the investigation?* I'll verify that the kidnappers worked for Brennan and that Collins founded that organization."

Scott Kelly said, "We also know Mitch Filner worked with Collins, *and* with Brennan, and turned up dead last week with a stab wound. We've got video evidence of Filner and Collins eating lunch together the day after the kidnapping."

Anthony's eyes widened. It was a lot of coincidences, but serious ones. He took out his notebook and began making notes.

Carrie leaned forward and said, "Why would Collins want to kidnap Andrea?"

Anthony said, "I actually have a theory about that."

Schmidt replied in a droll tone, "Please enlighten us."

"Okay. Number one—Andrea and Carrie's birth father is Prince George-Phillip. Number two—George-Phillip conducted the British investigation into Wakhan. He fingered Thompson, Collins and Prince Roshan as the key players behind the massacre. *And* he recommended going public with the findings of the investigation. I have a copy here, which he personally handed to me. Number three—Prime Minister Thatcher personally squashed the findings because of the Cold War. Both the British and US Administrations wanted maximum propaganda value out of blaming the Soviets for the attack. I think Collins ordered the kidnapping assuming that it would go off without a hitch, Andrea's body would have been disposed of and her parentage would never come up. He assumed—correctly—that if it became public Thompson wasn't her father, then further examination of his life would end up exposing Wakhan."

Schmidt nodded. "So a public official ordered the kidnapping and murder of a US citizen—and a child—in order to preserve his own position."

Bear said, "It's consistent with everything we know."

"What about the accounts in the Caymans?" Schmidt said.

Emma leaned forward. "All right, what we know for sure is that Julia Wilson had nothing to do with it. After a lot of arm twisting, we obtained video from the banks in question. Yes, a woman opened the accounts, personally. No, it wasn't her. I'm guessing another contractor for Collins—the accounts were opened only a week after the White House settled on Thompson as the new SECDEF. Collins was laying the groundwork to discredit Thompson, in the event Thompson tried to blame Collins for Wakhan— which he did in the hearings this week."

"Some of the media's going along with it," Scott Kelly said.

"Exactly," Schmidt said. He looked at Anthony. "No offense. All of this is off the record until we say so, clear?"

"Yeah, I got you," Anthony said. "I'll clear anything I say with you guys unless it comes from somewhere else. Let's move on, we've been over that."

"All right. Next is—Mitch Filner. What happened to him?"

Emma said, "We know Filner worked for Collins in Southeast Asia, and lost his position with the CIA because of a rape accusation."

"That's ugly," Anthony said.

"It's fact, and at this point fairly widely known with the investigation team. You can go public with that. He lost his job and went to work for Brennan Holdings."

"Collins again," Schmidt said. "What if Collins was pissed off? Instead of a quiet kidnapping, a girl who just vanished, Collins ended up with a giant media fiasco and massive amounts of public scrutiny. Offing Filner was punishment."

Bear said, "Yeah, but is there anything we can make stick?"

Emma said, "Probably not with Filner."

Anthony continued to make notes. Carrie sat quietly next to him, listening, her eyes wide. This whole discussion must be a revelation for her. She'd been through the ringer—including dealing with media storm clouds. But this was an order of magnitude more difficult.

Bear said, "All right. What's the word from Joe Paretsky?"

Anthony perked up. He started to say something, but Carrie beat him to it. "Who's that?"

Bear said, "Your brother-in-law Dylan tackled him the other day. Paretsky shot a British guy named Charlie Frazier, who we are pretty sure is MI6. As in, he worked for your dad." The last words were said as he looked pointedly at Carrie.

"Why? I don't understand?" she said.

Leah interjected, "What I believe is that Prince George-Phillip assigned some agents to watch over you. They spied Paretsky and his now dead partner moving in on you and intervened. We didn't understand what was going down at the time because we didn't know the players. But my guess is, if Dylan hadn't jumped in, one of you might have been hit."

Carrie shivered.

Anthony shook his head. "If Collins didn't want a media fiasco, why blow up the house in San Francisco? Why attack the condo?"

Emma said, "He didn't."

"What do you mean?"

"Collins almost certainly blew up the townhouse. But we believe we found out who Ralph Myers was working for."

Bear sat up, his face intensely interested. "Who?"

"Saudi Arabia. Myers was badly in debt. College debt for his kid, then his wife got sick five years ago. Cancer. He was leveraged to the hilt. But about four years ago, his financial problems started getting better. Paid off his debts, got them under control, and everything's been fine since."

"Okay ... he got recruited by somebody. Why do you believe it was Saudi Arabia?"

Schmidt replied, "EZ Pass records. Over the last four years, on eight different occasions Myers drove from his house in Arlington to Manassas. Each time, it was one day after Ahmed al-Saud made the same drive."

"Roshan's son," Anthony said. "A dead-drop."

"A what?" Carrie asked.

Bear grunted. "It's spy talk. One person drops something—cash, or documents, or something else, in an inconspicuous place. The other party then picks it up at a different time. That way the two are never seen together."

"But in this case, you've got the traffic records recording their movement."

"It wouldn't pass in court," Bear said. "Not without photos or some other corroboration. But we know at least their vehicles made that trip."

Anthony said, "That makes sense. Roshan probably got sick of seeing Collins screw everything up. So he decides to end the whole thing. Sends a team to kill the Thompson family—all of you—and another to take out George-Phillip. I wonder if he knows."

Carrie said, "He knows. While you were on your way to Afghanistan, someone shot a surface to air missile at his plane. It crashed into the Potomac. Yesterday he flew to London for an emergency cabinet meeting. They took him by jet fighter."

Schmidt said, "You know an awful lot about his movement."

She smiled at him. "He's my father. We've been communicating quite a bit since that revelation. He told me last night that the British government had arrested the man who had fired on his house and connected him somehow to Saudi Arabia."

"So who the hell stole my files?" Bear asked.

Schmidt, for the first time, looked sheepish. He said, quietly, "That would be me. At that point in time, since one person in DSS turned out to be a traitor, we weren't counting on trusting anyone. So we seized the records." He reached into his briefcase and passed across a file.

"Mother fucker," Bear said.

Schmidt merely smiled.

"So the last question," Bear said. "Who is Oz?"

Anthony answered that. "We know who it is now. Oswald O'Leary. Prince George-Phillip's assistant. What we don't know is why."

"Where is he now?" Schmidt asked.

Carrie said, "He got away. George-Phillip gave me photos and descriptive information to pass on to our security people. In case he shows up."

Schmidt said, "So what next? Adelina Thompson and our other key witness are testifying on Monday morning for the grand jury."

"I'm running my story Monday morning," Anthony said. "We've got everything we need. I'd love it if I could get some quotes from you, even if they are anonymously attributes. But the story's happening no matter what."

Schmidt said, "We'll give you some quotes. Thompson and Collins are guilty of mass murder, but you and I both know they may never go to jail."

Anthony said in a calm voice, "I can still publicly hang them."

"You're all forgetting one thing," Carrie said. "What about Dylan? He's sitting in jail for killing a man who was attacking his family."

Schmidt said, "Mrs. Sherman—just before you got here, we'd already determined to let Mr. Paris go and drop any charges."

Carrie closed her eyes. "Thank you," she whispered.

# CHAPTER TWENTY-SEVEN
# Time's a wasting

Dylan. May 10.

**Dylan's** release from the federal lockup happened quickly and later he would remember little of it. What he did remember was when the guard escorted him to the front door, back in his street clothes. Alexandra was waiting outside, along with Bear Wyden.

She flew to him, a flash of brown hair and green eyes and then he was enveloped in her arms and Dylan knew that at least for that moment, *right now*, everything was going to be okay.

"God, I missed you," he whispered, ignoring the people who walked past on the sidewalk, some of them less savory than others.

"Come on, kids. Time's a wasting." Bear's tone was gentle as he said the words.

Dylan and Alex pulled away from each other, and Dylan said, "Do I owe you for getting me out?"

Bear shrugged. "Nah, I'm just the delivery boy. You can thank the IRS."

"Oh, well that's weird. Bear—thanks."

Bear grinned. "Let's get going."

Five minutes later, they were driving on the Capitol Beltway back to Bethesda. In the car, Bear kept up a running patter about his opinion of DC cabbies (low), his opinion of the federal government owned car they were driving (even lower) and especially his opinion of the increasingly humid weather (lowest). Alex sat in the front passenger seat, and Dylan leaned forward in the seat behind her, keeping a hand on her shoulder.

When Bear came up for air, Dylan said, "So am I in the clear?"

Bear glanced over his shoulder at Dylan for just a second, and then his eyes were back on the road. "Yeah. You're not going to face any charges. You did the right thing after all. What you did was heroic, and almost certainly saved Andrea's life. Twice really, because when you took down that guy in Bethesda, he was almost certainly gunning for her or Carrie."

Dylan said in a low voice, "Thanks."

The ride was nearly thirty minutes. Dylan never took his hand off of Alex.

After a long period of quiet, Bear said, "You know, Alexandra—for what it's worth—I'm sorry that things came down the way they did. That you had to learn the things you did about your father."

Dylan felt Alex's muscles tense as Bear spoke. Then, just like that, she sagged into her seat. "It's okay," she said. "I always knew something was wrong. Sending Andrea away never made any sense until this."

Dylan squeezed her arm. Traffic was getting heavier as they approached the center of Bethesda. The sun was going down, the sky brilliant reds and oranges.

They came to a stop in the parking area at the base of the building Dylan had last seen when he was walking away, blood still on his hands and the bottom of his shoes. He stepped out of the car almost unconsciously, and reached for Alex's hand when she got out. He tilted his head back, looking up the side of the building, at the balconies, all the way to the nineteenth floor. He didn't want to go up there. He didn't want to walk into the place where he'd killed two men.

He closed his eyes, took a deep breath, and said, "Let's go."

They rode up the elevator in silence, but it was a heavy silence. Dylan knew what he needed to do, but he was afraid. He was afraid to admit weakness. He was afraid to admit he'd lost control. He was afraid to admit to Alex that he'd failed again. But if there was anyone in the world who would understand and be there for him, it was Alex. He *knew* that.

He gripped her hand a little tighter and said, "What's the plan tonight? Who is here?"

"Just us and Carrie and Rachel. Julia and Crank are flying down from Boston in the morning, and—Mother and the others will be here very late tonight. Why? What do you need?"

Dylan swallowed. Then he said, "I need to call my mom."

"Yeah?" she said. Her voice cracked a little.

He nodded. "I'm gonna find out where to get to an AA meeting around here."

Instantly, Alex's eyes went red. She pulled Dylan close to her, and spoke in a broken voice. "Dylan. I'm so proud of you."

## Anthony. May 11.

After Anthony Walker handed the car keys to the valet at the entrance to the condominium, he turned around and stumbled face to face with Crank and Julia Wilson. She was dressed in a white A-line dress with deep red flowers splashed across it. He wore jeans and a black T-shirt with the words, "Bullet for my Valentine" written in gothic red letters.

Her eyes narrowed a little. Something was off with her expression. "I wasn't expecting to find you here, Anthony. Don't you think you could leave the story alone for Mother's Day?"

He grinned. "I'm here by invitation, actually." Then he followed her and Crank into the building, ignoring the flashes of cameras and the shouted questions of other reporters. The security guards at the door cleared the three of them in.

The elevator ride up was awkward. Anthony swallowed uncomfortably, pursed his lips, and looked at the ceiling.

Crank clapped him hard on the shoulder. "No need to be awkward, Anthony. If Carrie invited you, that's all that matters."

Anthony coughed and said, "I think she felt sorry for me. My mom passed away a few years ago so I didn't have any plans this morning."

"My condolences," Crank said.

"Thanks."

The elevator doors opened. Anthony waited until Julia and Crank stepped out then followed them. Their identification was checked again by another guard and then they walked down the hallway.

Julia knocked. Anthony heard a shout, and moments later the door was opened.

It was unmistakably Sarah Thompson who answered the door, right down to the dyed streak in her hair. But instead of the black and grey she normally wore, today she was in a bright yellow taffeta dress.

Julia and Crank both looked stunned. Sarah ignored their expression and simply grabbed Julia and hugged her, then did the same with Crank. She gave Anthony a look he was unable to interpret—almost like she was keeping some sort of secret, then turned and walked into the condominium.

"Come on in, there's coffee and orange juice. Breakfast isn't ready yet, but will be soon."

The first impression Anthony had was of minor chaos. Jessica—still looking pale, but not as bad as she had when he met her in British Columbia a few days before—sat on the couch, with her feet up on a coffee table. Alexandra sat in another chair holding the baby, who giggled periodically but looked pale. Anthony was no expert on babies, but he'd seen enough to know that Rachel did not look well. Standing near Alexandra was a stocky man with broad shoulders, neatly shaven but with hair grown just over his collar. Anthony recognized Dylan Paris from the many photos he'd seen in the news. It would be a long time before Dylan would be anonymous again. Right now he nervously flipped a small white disk between his fingers.

Julia and Carrie immediately embraced. Carrie wore a turquoise dress that nearly matched Sarah's. Anthony didn't catch the words that passed between them, but Carrie almost immediately turned to Anthony and took his hand. "I'm glad you could make it," she said. "Please don't be too uncomfortable."

Anthony shrugged. Of course he was uncomfortable—who wouldn't be, attending someone else's family's Mother's Day celebration. Especially when it was *this* family, with *this* mother.

There were two conspicuously missing women. Andrea. And her mother.

## Adelina. May 11.

Adelina's nerves were as taut as they'd ever been, the muscles in her neck stiff, her hands lightly shaking as she finished applying her mascara. The anxiety was a pit in her throat, slow burning and twisting like a rabbit on a spit. She was back in the same room she'd occupied off and on for more than thirty years. The room where she'd cried and wept. The room where she'd tried to nurture and protect her daughters, and the room where she gave up her dreams. The room where she'd waited all night after her 1 am arrival, tossing and turning, worried about what the morning would bring.

She sighed. She was afraid to go out there. Afraid to see all of her daughters. She was afraid of their judgment and their anger.

It didn't make any sense, really. She'd presided over a thousand family functions over the years. Birthdays and graduations, marriages, Christmas and Thanksgiving meals. She'd never been perfect, but she'd always done her best.

But inside, she was consumed by shame. Shame that she'd stayed married to Richard so long. Shame that she'd listened to his threats and his abuse. Shame that she'd let her daughters be exposed to such things.

Above all, shame that she had sent Andrea away. Even if it was to save her life.

So she stayed in her room and fretted. She prayed and wrote in the journal Julia had returned to her. She tried to build up the courage to face them.

And then, a knock on the door.

Adelina sat straight in her chair. "Yes?" she called. "I'll be ready in a moment."

Silence. Breathing outside the room. Then the words, "Mother, may I come in? It's Andrea."

Adelina sniffed. She looked at herself in the mirror. She was strong enough to do this. She could do it. She could do it.

"Come in," she said. Her voice cracked.

The door opened and Andrea slipped inside.

Andrea wore one of Carrie's dresses, a professional looking knee-length black affair with a wide belt.

She stepped into the room and said, "Won't you come out?"

Adelina swallowed. Then she whispered, "You know I didn't want to let you go. But I was afraid Richard would harm you. He told me he would, and I believed him."

Andrea nodded. "I know."

"Can you ever forgive me?"

Andrea walked close to her mother and rested her hands on her shoulders. Then she said, "Yes. I forgive you. You gave me my life. And my faith. Then you saved my life, and I didn't even know it. There's nothing to forgive, Mother. I'm your daughter and I always will be." As Andrea spoke, tears began to run down her face. Then she whispered, "I've always wanted to have my mother. And now I do. Now come out. The rest of your family is waiting for you."

Adelina whispered, "Okay."

Andrea turned and opened the bedroom door. Quivering with apprehension, Adelina followed. Out into the hallway, the hallway she'd walked through literally a thousand times. But never, not even during the worst of times with Richard, had she walked down the hallway with this much fear.

Her daughters were in the living room. As she entered, Julia came to her feet, followed by Carrie. Her two eldest daughters held hands and watched her with concern in their faces. Alexandra was close by, her husband's arm around her shoulders. Even Jessica came to her feet, Sarah beside her.

Carrie's eyes were wet. She reached out and took Adelina's hand. Julia said, "Mom ... welcome home."

# CHAPTER TWENTY-EIGHT
## Special Report

"**W**elcome back, Your Highness." The speaker was US Air Force General Hainey, who had arrived at Andrews Air Force Base once again to meet George-Phillip. This time, George-Phillip had just arrived on a return flight, which had raced the sun around the earth. He'd left London at 5 am—midnight in Washington—and arrived at Joint Air Base Andrews just before 3 am.

He shook hands with the General, the General's aids, and got in the car that had been provided by the Ambassador.

Inside the car was Linda Happer. Officially a translator with the Embassy, Linda was actually the MI6 Chief of Station in Washington, DC.

"Good morning, Chief," Linda said. "Nice flight suit."

"That's questionable," he replied. "What's the news?"

"That's the key question, sir. There's a lot—first this." She handed across a copy of *The Washington Post*. Splashed across the front page in two-inch high type was the headline: **GRAND JURY OPENS WAR CRIMES PROBE.** Beneath, the subheadline said: Richard Thompson, Leslie Collins implicated in poison gas massacre. Underneath the headline, taking up nearly half of the top half of the front page was a color photograph of the inside of a cave. Arm in arm, with wide grins on their faces, were a much younger Leslie Collins, Richard Thompson and Vasily Karatygin.

"Well. That's something," he said.

He scanned through the article, then flipped to the second page and his eyes widened. The headline on page two said, **Former headquarters of CIA officials became a crypt.** A photograph showed a cave scattered with bones and bodies. A cabinet was overturned, and papers were scattered about the room.

**The cave had been sealed for thirty years following the massacre.**

**"We used dynamite to blast the opening to the cave," said Vasily Karatygin, the former Soviet defector and conspirator who is now dying. "It was the only way guaranteed to keep the secret. Everyone who assisted us died. But the documents, and the weapons, were all left behind. It was death to go back in that cave."**

**By the time I entered the cave last week, the sarin had long since dissipated, leaving behind a monument to monstrosity. Inside the cave were twenty-two bodies, both men and women, all of whom presumably worked for the conspirators. I also photographed and examined dozens of documents and papers, which are depicted in this report. The most damning: a letter from Adelina Thompson to her husband. The letter is terse and unemotional, consistent with the background of their marriage (see A Marriage Forged in Revolution, page A6), and demands that Thompson release sufficient funds to pay for renovations to the Thompsons' San Francisco home and for their daughter to attend day care. The letter (pictured below) is the clearest and most damning evidence placing Richard Thompson at the scene of one of the most notorious war crimes of the twentieth century.**

"You're mentioned in the reporting, Your Highness. In the story about the Thompsons' marriage. You're discussed in there quite a bit. The Ambassador is livid."

George-Phillip murmured, "I'm sure he is." He felt at peace. If he had to resign his position today, he would be quite content.

She grinned.

"One more bit of news, sir."

"Yes?"

"The Virginia State Police caught up with Oswald O'Leary, sir. He's being held at a precinct in Alexandria for the time being. American Diplomatic Security is on their way to question them, but they gave me a courtesy call."

"I see. Are we invited, do you think?"

Linda nodded. "Yes, sir. If you'd like to question him, we can go right now."

"Let's go then. I have a meeting with the US Secretary of State at 10 am, so we'll need to make this quick and get back to the Embassy. I'm going to need a shower, that cockpit is cramped."

## Leslie Collins. May 12.

*This was a disaster.*

Leslie Collins sat in his office, still in his bathrobe, reading the special report in *The Washington Post*, which had been delivered less than twenty minutes before.

A disaster. Bad enough that his photograph was splashed across the front page. The interior of the special report was much worse. Photographs of bodies. Their headquarters in the mountains of Afghanistan, bodies still scattered inside the cave, along with gear and personal property that clearly belonged to both Collins and Richard Thompson.

A timeline of Andrea Thompson's kidnapping. Links between Leslie's holding company and the kidnappers.

He was finished. Destroyed.

He turned the pages, growing more and more distressed with each word he read. This morning his colleagues would be reading this report. His *children* would be reading it. The news media would circle like sharks, searching for weaknesses, smelling the blood, and then they would attack, sawing their teeth into his hide, ripping him limb from limb until there was nothing left.

The article was so damning.

**A senior source in the investigation told** The Washington Post **that investigators now have strong evidence Collins ordered the kidnapping and murder of Andrea Thompson. Sources speculate that Collins was concerned that once it became public that Andrea Thompson was not related to Richard Thompson, the resulting questions would quickly lead to the exposure of their involvement in the Wakhan Massacre.**

**Worried about that eventuality, Collins had a series of accounts opened in the Caymans in Richard Thompson's name. Initially, investigators believed the accounts were what they appeared to be, and opened an investigation into both Thompson and his eldest daughter Julia Wilson.**

**"The trail didn't make sense," said the** Post's **source in the investigation. "Once we obtained Julia Wilson's cooperation, the story quickly unraveled."**

**According to senior officials, Wilson will testify before the grand jury on Monday morning.**

He leaned forward and placed his forehead on the desk. There had to be a way to survive this. There had to. He'd survived worse. He'd controlled lives. He'd run spies in a dozen countries; he'd protected his nation for a career spanning forty years. *Why?* This was terrible.

Collins jerked in his seat when the phone rang.

The secure line.

Hand shaking, he reached out and picked it up and put the receiver to his ear. "Collins."

"Leslie, it's Ralph Williams."

Collins closed his eyes. Ralph Williams was former Senator Williams, former head of the Select Committee on Intelligence, and now Director of Central Intelligence. Williams was the highest ranking Intelligence official in the United States, and Collins' boss.

"Yes, sir."

"Don't come in this morning. I'll be sending around a classified documents officer to collect anything you have in your safe at home."

"Sir?" Collins let a little outrage creep into his voice.

"Let me be clear, Collins. You aren't coming back. Now, or ever. You'll be lucky if you don't land in prison, but I guarantee you'll never work in public office again. I suggest you get started writing your memoirs if you have any hope of protecting your reputation."

Williams didn't even use common courtesy. He simply hung up the phone, leaving Collins with a clicking silence.

Collins put the phone down.

He took a deep breath. Thompson was equally implicated in the story, which detailed far too much of what had happened over the years. There would be congressional hearings, and if the newspaper story was accurate, the grand jury might well indict Collins. But that wasn't the biggest danger.

Prince Roshan was the biggest danger. Collins knew that if Roshan saw this article, he would likely send assassins immedi-

ately, lest Collins or Thompson implicate him. Roshan was ambi-
tious—one day he hoped to be King. But there were more than 200
Royal Princes in Saudi Arabia—he was but one. A scandal would
wipe out his chances for good.

Killers might already be on the way.

*Christ.* Swallowing the lump in his throat, Collins picked up the
phone and dialed a number.

"Hello?" The answer at the other end of the line was terse.

Leslie coughed and his voice cracked when he spoke. "This is
Mister Collins. I know it's late, but I'm hoping to get a ride to see
my friend."

There was a long silence at the other end. The code phrase was
simple enough. It was a panic signal, a signal designed long ago to
allow for his quick departure from the country when and if needed.
He'd had that insurance set aside for more than ten years. Now it
was time to use it.

The man at the other end finally returned. "Ten am. Stafford."

*Damn it.* Stafford Regional Airport was forty miles south of
Washington, and rush hour would be coming soon. They needed
to get out of the house right away. He stood and walked out of his
office, shouting, "Meredith! Meredith!"

He stomped down the hall to their room, still shouting her
name. She let out a panicked shriek when he switched on the bedroom light, then she cried, "What? What is it?"

"Pack one bag with your most valuable possessions and get
dressed in something comfortable. Comfortable shoes. You've got
ten minutes and we're leaving."

"What?" she cried, sitting up in the bed.

He reached down and grasped her shoulders and leaned forward, nearly touching his nose to hers. "Pack. Bags. Get. Dressed.
I'm leaving in ten minutes. With you or without you."

When he let go, she sagged back onto the bed, horror on her face. He didn't care. He marched into the walk-in closet and tore off his bathrobe, then began getting dressed. He rarely wore them, but today he put on a pair of tough jeans and a thick shirt. Then he took a backpack off the top shelf and began stuffing clothes into it.

"Leslie, you must explain right now!" Meredith cried out.

"No time. We're in danger. We're leaving."

"What about the twins? What about Susan?"

"The kids will be fine. But we won't, if we don't get out now. Get. Dressed."

She started moving, throwing clothes on—her gardening clothes. Good. No heels or dainty dresses. Then she started packing a bag.

## George-Phillip. May 12.

"Prince George-Phillip? I'm Bear Wyden. Diplomatic Security Service."

The man who approached was of medium hight—considerably shorter than George-Phillip and stocky. George-Phillip suspected the *Bear* moniker came from the copious amount of hair the man seemed to have.

"Hello, Mister Wyden. I understand arrangements have been made for me to meet with O'Leary."

"Yes, sir. But—first—do you have a moment?"

George-Phillip raised his eyebrows. "Yes?"

"Sir, you should know I've been assigned to your daughter's case since the day she was kidnapped. Andrea's, that is. I've come to know her and Carrie pretty well, along with Adelina. I knew Adelina many years ago, too, in Belgium."

George-Phillip let out a sigh. "Yes ... I see. What can I do for you?"

Bear's mouth twisted a little. Then he said, "Those girls deserve a good father. They never had one. And Adelina Thompson has been tortured for decades. I don't trust anyone in the Intelligence business, but you seem like a decent sort. I just..."

George-Phillip let out a breath, then reached out and took Bear's shoulder. "I'll do my best, Mr. Wyden."

"Bear."

"I'll do my best. I promise."

"In that case, sir, I'll take you in to see O'Leary."

Minutes later, George-Phillip found himself in a room, accompanied by Wyden. O'Leary sat across from them. His feet were chained to a steel table. He had a serene expression on his face.

"Oswald," George-Phillip said.

O'Leary nodded. "Your Highness."

George-Phillip asked one question. "Why?"

O'Leary shook his head. "You still cannot see it? My job was to protect you and the Royal family, Your Highness. It always was."

"Protect me from what?"

"From scandal, sir. Surely you must realize. Prince Andrew was dating a porn star in 1982, and then that lunatic Fagan walked right into Buckingham Palace and sat down at the end of the Queen's bed. Princess Margaret and Lord Snowden divorced, and your own father died in a drunken accident. Is it any wonder the Queen wanted you protected?"

"The Queen?"

O'Leary nodded rapidly. "Of course, sir. I was detailed by the Queen herself to protect you from scandal."

George-Phillip sank into a chair across from O'Leary. *Oz.*

"You took it upon yourself, with this assignment, to break into Adelina's home. In 1983?"

"Of course, sir. To warn her away. I had no idea she was pregnant with your child sir, not then. But it wouldn't have made any difference."

"And you did it again in 1996, in China."

O'Leary nodded. "Yes, sir. For your own good."

"And you hired assassins to kill her. And her daughter."

O'Leary shrugged. "I'm loyal to the Crown, sir. Not to some whore you decided to sleep with."

Rage swept over George-Phillip. He stood and swept his hand back to strike O'Leary in the face, but Bear was quicker than he. Bear grabbed his wrist and said, "No, sir, I'm afraid you can't do that."

George-Phillip gasped. He took a deep breath, suddenly flooded with adrenalin. He couldn't believe the Queen would sanction murder. "O'Leary. When was the last time you spoke—with the Queen? Or anyone in her household? Anyone related to this ... *assignment*."

O'Leary said, "Why ... when you returned from Washington to London, sir. Officially the assignment was over then."

George-Phillip closed his eyes. Never in his life had he wanted to hurt someone as bad as he did right now. The betrayal shook him to his core.

He took a deep breath, his voice shaking, and said, "You are finished, O'Leary. I'll be speaking with the Home Office to have your diplomatic immunity revoked. You'll go to prison for hiring that assassin." He turned, still gasping for air.

"Your Highness! I only did what was right! What you didn't have the courage to do!" O'Leary's face was bright red. "I did everything to protect *you!*"

Without responding, George-Phillip stepped out into the hall, with Bear on his heels.

Outside, in the hallway, he saw Linda Happer. "Miss Happer. Please take me to the Embassy. I must get ready for my meeting with the Secretary of State."

Bear said, "I'm sorry about that, sir."

George-Phillip shook his head in disgust. "I—I'm appalled. And … incredibly disappointed. I've known O'Leary for thirty years."

Bear said nothing.

George-Phillip reached out and took his hand and shook. "Thank you, Mister Wyden."

"Yes, sir."

George-Phillip followed Happer out of the police station.

## Leslie Collins. May 12.

Ten minutes after he'd awakened Meredith, Leslie Collins jerked opened the side door; backpack slung over one shoulder, and walked toward his car. It was dark, but a waxing gibbous moon low in the sky illuminated the driveway and side of the house. Collins could hear birds beginning to chirp, even though the sun hadn't begun to rise. It would be sunrise soon enough. He needed to be well on his way toward Stafford before the sun was up—otherwise traffic would delay them past the departure time for his flight.

The car chirped when he disabled the alarm and unlocked it, and then reached out for the door.

Meredith let out a shriek. Movement. A man, stepping away from the shadows of the unused garage.

"Mister Collins."

Collins jerked back. The man who faced him in the darkness was short. Short cropped hair. Unshaven, unkempt. He had dark skin. His accent was clearly Arabic.

"Mister Collins, I have a parting gift from a mutual friend. *Bit-tawfiq.*" Collins recognized the words. Arabic for *best of luck.* The man moved quickly, raising a pistol to Collins' forehead.

The man pulled the trigger and everything went black.

# CHAPTER TWENTY-NINE
# Big fat bullets

Richard. May 12.

**R**ichard Thompson shook with the most powerful rage he'd ever felt as he continued reading the pages of the special report.

**According to a source in the Special Prosecutor's office, Julia Wilson has been cooperating with the IRS investigation. She wore a wire to her last meeting with her father, capturing an audio recording where he admitted to procuring the weapons for the massacre. Mrs. Wilson is scheduled to testify before the grand jury Monday morning, followed by her mother.**

*How could she?* Richard raged. His daughter. The one he'd cultivated. The only one he really loved. He felt a strange, twisted aching, an unfamiliar feeling; a feeling he hadn't really touched since his brother hung himself in the attic of their childhood home.

Grief.

He opened one of the cabinet doors and took out a glass. He hated this place. The President had given him two weeks to find a new place to live. He was being thrown out. Good riddance. These rat-infested quarters weren't fit for him. The building, formerly Quarters 2 at Fort Myers, had been the home of a two-star General before Richard was here. A large white structure with southern colonnades and French windows, Richard hated it. *Hated* it. He took out a glass from the cabinet, turned it in the light, and flung it across the room.

It shattered against the wall, a curiously satisfying sound. He took out another glass and flung it. Glass flew across the room, and a tiny fragment hit his arm.

On the top shelf was a set of wine glasses. He flung them, one after another, each of them shattering. Glass was now scattered all across the kitchen floor.

It was Adelina's fault. He was losing everything. He'd even lost his favorite daughter. And it was that Spanish whore's fault. He slid a drawer open and eyed the kitchen knives greedily.

No. Not sure enough. He had a gun in his study, a .45 calibre Colt M1911A1 pistol. Big fat bullets to shoot through her big fat head. There was nothing else to be done. As his father would say (if the old bastard were still alive), he was *a disgrace. Just like his brother.*

*Mrs. Wilson is scheduled to testify before the grand jury Monday morning, followed by her mother.*

He stalked toward his office to get his gun. Poor Julia was going to be an orphan in a few hours.

## Carrie. May 12.

"You're sure you're okay?" Carrie asked for the fifteenth time.

Alexandra nodded. "I'm *fine*. You stay with Julia and Mom, okay? They need you. I've got Andrea and the twins here, and I'm pretty sure Andrea can take on *anything*."

Carrie's eyes darted to her mother's, then Andrea's. Andrea's lips held the barest of smiles. As if she were thinking she *could* take on anything. Carrie turned back to Alexandra and handed over Rachel. The baby didn't stir. Her fever had dropped back to normal overnight.

"She'll likely be awake in another two hours. There are four bottles of breast milk in the freezer and one in the fridge, you can warm—"

"Carrie!" Alexandra said. "I've got this!"

Dylan pulled his phone out and checked the time. "Mrs. Thompson … Carrie and Julia. Time to go."

Carrie said, "I still don't think you need to come along, Dylan. We've got armed guards."

"Carrie," Alexandra said. "Shut up. Stop fretting."

She closed her eyes. "All right. In that case, let's go."

Dylan led the way out of the condominium, followed by Adelina and Julia. Carrie looked back at Alexandra and said, "Thank you. I don't know what's going on with you and him but … it's better. It's better, isn't it?"

Alexandra nodded, her eyes glistening. "It is," she whispered.

Carrie smiled and walked out the door, following her mother and sister down to the elevator. They still had ninety minutes before they had to be at the Federal Courthouse, but traffic in Washington was unpredictable. The four of them rode down the elevator in silence, flanked by two armed guards. In the lobby different guards took over and escorted them outside. Pale light shone down from a purple sky.

They climbed into a large SUV, Adelina in the center, her daughters on either side, and Dylan in the front passenger seat next to the driver. Guards loaded up in another vehicle. They weren't taking any chances. The small convoy set out into traffic, which was heavily snarled. Rush hour.

Carrie sat staring out the window as Julia and their mother spoke quietly. She half paid attention to the words. Mother and daughter were catching up on events of the last two weeks. Jessica's health, the assassination attempts, the IRS investigation. Julia had kept it secret that she'd worn a wire and met with her father.

Carrie sighed. *Why* had she kept it secret? She looked over at her sister. Julia's hair was natural again; it had been some time. Shoulder length, the brown locks curling around her face. She looked sad.

Then it hit her. She thought about what she knew about her sister. About Julia's high school experiences, both in China and in Bethesda. The harassment and teasing. *Her suicide attempt.*

Julia hadn't said anything because she was *ashamed.* Ashamed that somehow her sisters would think less of her. Ashamed that she'd done the wrong thing.

Carrie took a deep breath. "You did the right thing, you know," she said.

Julia looked at her, eyes suddenly wide. "What?"

"You heard me. You did the right thing. I know he's your father. But you did the right thing."

Julia swallowed, her face swimming with emotion.

Adelina took Julia's hand in her left and Carrie's in her right and said, "This will all be over soon."

## George-Phillip. May 12.

From the outside, Blair House consisted of four townhomes across the street from the White House, the central one of white brick and fronted with a columned portico. George-Phillip knew that inside, however, the four homes were seamlessly connected. With dozens of rooms and a large staff, the house served at the guesthouse of the President of the United States, and hosted visiting dignitaries and other events. George-Phillip had attended many events there over the decades.

This morning, he was met by a US Navy Commander.

"Your Highness. The Secretary is waiting for you in the dining room. Please follow me, sir."

George-Phillip was no longer in the flight suit he'd worn across the Atlantic and to the jail. He'd changed into a formal suit with highly polished shoes and cufflinks that had once been owned by his father. He'd had long enough while changing to have a very brief breakfast and a hand of Go Fish with Jane before he'd left again.

That wouldn't go on much longer. He'd handed his resignation to the Prime Minister while in London.

George-Phillip followed the Naval officer down the entry hall and to the small private dining room. As he entered, Secretary Perry stood. Both men were of similar height, though Perry, as always, looked dangerously gaunt.

Perry gestured to *The Washington Post*, spread out on the table amidst pitchers of orange juice and carafes of coffee.

"Have you seen this?" Perry asked.

"I have," George-Phillip said. "It's quite comprehensive."

"Have a seat, Your Highness. It's a pleasure seeing you this morning."

George-Phillip smiled. "And you, Secretary. Our mutual friend is on the way?"

"He is. But I asked him to be here a few minutes later so we could talk."

"Excellent," George-Phillip replied.

"I understand you're resigning."

George-Phillip smiled. "Word gets around fast, doesn't it? It's true. I need to spend more time with my children. Especially now that I have two more daughters I need to get to know. And several more ... surrogate daughters, I suppose. I feel equally responsible for them."

"Thompson was really a piece of work, wasn't he? I had no idea you were involved with Adelina, though. Is it true, what the article says?"

"That she was raped and basically held prisoner? Yes. Sadly, it is."

Perry grimaced and shook his head. "I always wondered. Have you seen her?"

George-Phillip shrugged. He felt an odd sort of pain at the question. "I don't know that she'd care to see me, Secretary."

Perry frowned. He looked at his watch, then said, "Prince Roshan will be here any minute … Your Highness … may I give you a bit of unsolicited personal advice?"

"Secretary?"

"Go see her. Not next week, or next year, or even tomorrow. Go see her today."

George-Phillip swallowed. He was saved from having to respond, however. The door opened, and the Navy Commander who had escorted him into the room opened the door.

"Mister Secretary? Prince George-Phillip? Prince Roshan has arrived."

The two men stood, and Perry said, "Please show him in, Commander."

## Julia. May 12.

*You heard me. You did the right thing. I know he's your father. But you did the right thing.*

Carrie's voice rang through Julia's mind as she sat down at the end of the long conference table. Twenty-three men and women were arrayed up and down the table. Some wore suits, some wore button down shirts, and two of the men wore jeans and T-shirts. All of them had serious expressions on their faces.

At the opposite end of the table was a man she recognized. Rory Armitage. Armitage was a former Congressman from Georgia, later appointed to the federal circuit as a judge by President Bush. A stern, puritan man with tightly clipped hair and an austere expression, Armitage had been appointed several weeks earlier by the President to examine accusations of corruption in the defense department. The probe had rapidly broadened to include Richard Thompson and was now broadening even further.

To the side of the room, the court reporter, a mousy looking woman, sat at a small desk.

Armitage didn't stand. He merely sat at the opposite end of the table, barely taking his eyes off the papers in front of him.

To his right, a woman in a blue dress spoke. "Hi, I'm Mary Cooley, the foreperson of the grand jury. Can you please identify yourself, and your place of residence and occupation?"

"Julia Wilson. Boston, Massachusetts. I'm Chief Executive Officer of Morbid Enterprises, Inc."

"Mrs. Wilson, do you swear to tell the truth, the whole truth, and nothing but the truth, so help you God?"

"I do."

The woman waved to Armitage. "She's your witness."

Armitage didn't move. He looked up, blue eyes gazing at her over his reading glasses, and said, "Mrs. Wilson, I'm about to play a tape, labeled Prosecution Exhibit 332. Please listen carefully."

She sat back and listened as Armitage tapped on a keyboard. The room was flooded with sound. With her voice.

*Dad ... I want you to level with me. I know it was the Cold War and bad stuff happened. I know people had to do things that look ugly in today's light. Did you do it? Did you give them the chemical weapons?*

There was a slight hiss in the background from the recording. Then she heard her father's voice. *I did. It was horrible. But also necessary.* A long pause, then, *Julia ... you know better than anyone about foreign policy. You know how these things work. I didn't want to do it, and I certainly didn't know they would use it on innocent villagers. We actually provided the militia with satellite photos of the Russian training camp, as well as an advisor who was a Soviet defector. Vasily Karatygin—he'd converted to Islam and went over to the side of the mujahideen. But they didn't use it on the military ... it was on civilians. I'd have done anything to prevent it.*

Her voice again. *But since it did happen, you had to blame it on the Soviets. Realpolitik.*

Her father: *Sadly, yes.*

Armitage typed something and the sound stopped. Then he spoke. "Mrs. Wilson, do you recognize the voices on that recording?"

"I do," she said. "Me. And my father."

"Please identify your father for the jury."

"Richard Thompson," she said. Inside, her stomach twisted. Her father had done—uncountable evil. But it still felt wrong.

*You did the right thing. I know he's your father. But you did the right thing.* Carrie's voice again.

"Mrs. Wilson, under what circumstances was this recording made?"

She looked down at the table. "In the days after my sister was kidnapped, I'd learned some horrible things. There was a police report, which showed my mother had been attacked, and that my father was the prime suspect. And my mother—she was missing at the time—had left a journal. I read some of it. It indicated she'd been—raped. By my father. She was sixteen when it happened. As my father became more embattled with the Administration, he reached out to me. In hopes of getting an ally. He talked about putting my mother away permanently, saying she was insane. And

... I needed to know if what they were saying was true. About him being involved in that massacre."

"So you agreed to wear a wire for the federal investigators?"

She looked down. Then she said, "Yes."

She reminded herself of her sister's words. *I know he's your father. But you did the right thing.*

"Mrs. Wilson—were any offers of immunity made to you?"

She nodded. "Yes. The IRS made that offer. I didn't accept."

"Why not?"

She felt her temper flare. "I won't have it said that I turned against my father in order to stay out of jail. I didn't. I wore the wire because it was ... it was the right thing to do. Because there were innocent people hurt. And they deserve some kind of justice. I ... I can't have babies. But if I could, if I ever did have children, I would want them to know that I did the right thing."

Armitage's mouth pursed and he nodded. Then he said, "A couple more questions. Then we're done. Did you open any secret accounts in the Caymans on behalf of your father?"

"No."

"Did you assist him in laundering any drug money?"

"No."

"To the best of your knowledge, was your father involved in any drug money laundering?"

"Nothing that I'm aware of. I don't believe that's true. My father's guilty of many crimes. But I don't think simple greed is one of them."

Armitage turned to the foreperson, Mary Cooley. "Miss Cooley, your witness."

Cooley said, "I don't have any questions."

"Very well then," Armitage said. "Mrs. Wilson, thank you very much for your time, you may go." Then he said, "Please bring in the next witness. Mrs. Adelina Thompson."

Julia stood. Her arms and legs were shaking. She met the eyes of Mary Cooley for just a second. Then she turned to the door. As she approached it, it was opened, and her mother stepped in. Julia touched her mother on the arm as she brushed past her, and whispered, "Be strong."

## George-Phillip. May 12.

Prince Roshan wore a conservative coal-grey business suit and a red keffiyeh. He smiled a broad toothy smile at the sight of George-Phillip.

"Prince George-Phillip. I wasn't expecting you this morning! What a pleasant surprise."

Somehow George-Phillip thought that Roshan wasn't at all pleasantly surprised.

"Come in, Your Highness," James Perry said. "Have a seat, please join us for breakfast. We have several *halal* dishes here."

Roshan eyed the plate of bacon and sausage and said, "You know my weaknesses, Mister Secretary. I hope Allah will forgive me for technical violations, but I must have a little of everything."

Perry waved for the servers to approach, and moments later the three of them were eating, with several minutes of companionable silence, punctuated only by the sounds of forks clinking against plates.

The silence was interrupted when Perry said, "Richard Thompson's grand jury meets today. You know he's sunk. So is Leslie Collins. Both of them have lost their careers, even if they don't find themselves imprisoned for war crimes."

"Yes," Roshan said. "It's a shame, really, I knew him once. I even had dinner with the two of them, many years ago. You remember, George."

George-Phillip grimaced. He didn't care for the familiarity. He said, "We know all about your role in the massacre, Prince Roshan. You should also know that we arrested your assassin in Britain. The one who shot at my home."

Roshan said, "Is this some strange British humor? You bring me here to insult me?"

Perry said, "Prince Roshan, yesterday the Virginia State Police found a Stinger missile casing not far from Great Falls Park. We've arrested your agent who fired it."

Roshan frowned, then wiped his lips with a linen napkin.

George-Phillip leaned forward. "The missile that you used to try to kill me and my daughter."

Perry said, "Prince Roshan, as I'm sure you are aware, shooting down a civilian aircraft bearing a cabinet member of the US ally could be considered an act of war. Britain and the United States are both members of NATO. We're allies. Did you really think we would stand by and allow you to fire missiles at airplanes in our country?"

Roshan said, "This is ludicrous. I object to this treatment."

Perry said, "If I could, I would see you in prison or executed for your crimes. As it is, I have to resort to diplomatic means. Go home, Roshan. You're no longer welcome in this country, or that of any of our allies. And please tell the King that if Saudi Arabia wishes to continue having the United States as an ally—as a *protector*—then you'll never serve in any official capacity again."

Roshan stood. "Arrogant Americans. You think you can tell us how to run our affairs?"

Perry said, "I'm sure you're aware of our armed drone program in the Middle East, Prince Roshan? If you don't do as I say, then I suggest you keep your eyes locked on the sky. Your days will be numbered."

Roshan threw his napkin down.

"Go home," George-Phillip said.

Prince Roshan marched out of the room.

"I wish we could do more," Perry said.

George-Phillip said, "MI6 is not as squeamish about assassinations as the United States is, James. Roshan's days *are* numbered. I've already spoken to the Prime Minister about it."

"Well, then. Your Highness ... don't you have an appointment at the Federal Courthouse?"

## Dylan. May 12.

When Adelina walked out of the chambers of the grand jury at nearly noon, she was pale and shaking. Dylan quickly moved to her side and took her arm. "You okay?" he murmured.

She smiled. "I'm not done for yet, Dylan."

Julia and Carrie both approached their mother. Julia's eyes were brimming with tears.

Adelina looked at them both, then said, "I'm proud of you both, you know."

Carrie said, "Will they indict him? Will he pay? I feel like he can never pay enough for what he did to you. Or what he did to those villagers."

Adelina put a hand on her daughter's shoulder. She whispered, "I wanted vengeance for the longest time. But ... that's not up to me. Or you. We're called on to continue our lives ... to forgive, if we can."

*Jesus Christ,* Dylan thought. We're called on to forgive? He thought about his father. His poor, weak and deluded father.

Carrie said, "Sometimes forgiveness is the hardest word in the world."

"You lost your husband. Then you lost your father." Adelina looked at her daughter with compassion in her eyes. "Of course it's hard. But I promise you … it will get easier."

Carrie grimaced. "Let's go, then. I might as well get started trying."

Adelina nodded, and the three women started walking toward the elevators. Dylan stayed ahead of them, watching for journalists, for threats of any kind. He'd spent the last three hours reading Anthony's reports in *The Washington Post* that morning, while Julia and then her mother testified. The report was—staggering. It revealed a level of corruption in the Central Intelligence Agency Dylan couldn't have imagined. Collins would go down, and so would Richard Thompson, but they wouldn't be the only ones.

The elevator opened and the four of them stepped inside.

"Probably going to be reporters downstairs," Dylan said. "The guards will be just outside waiting for us. Stay close until we get in the vehicles."

Adelina reached out and touched Dylan's hand. "Dylan. Thank you. For taking care of my daughters."

He gave her a sideways grin. "My pleasure, ma'am. I'd give my life for them."

He meant it. If he had to, he'd put himself between Alex and a bullet. Any of her sisters too. After all, that's what soldiers did. They put themselves in between their families and the desolation of war.

At least, that was the idea.

The elevator opened. The lobby of the courthouse was clear, armed guards and police everywhere. But outside, on the steps and blocking the street, were dozens of reporters and cameramen jostling for space. Beyond the reporters, hundreds of spectators, oddly drawn by the drama of a wife and daughter testifying against a former cabinet official.

"Here we go," Dylan said.

As they approached the doors, their security guards stepped inside. "This way, folks. This way!"

Out the revolving door they went. The crowd immediately pushed in toward them. Microphones shoved in their faces, reporters shouting and screaming. Their guards shoved the reporters back shouting, and Dylan joined in.

He yelled, "Give them some space!" while Julia called out, "No comment."

The gunshot came out of nowhere. Dylan heard it, his instincts suddenly kicking in as he swiveled on his feet and ducked down, searching out the source of the noise. One of their two guards fell to the ground, a giant hole in his face, and the other one suddenly screamed and fell backward, hitting Dylan, who tried to get out of the way.

He felt his reconstructed leg twist under him and he slipped, feeling the ankle snap. Dylan let out a scream of rage.

The crowd scattered, men and women, reporters and others screaming. As they ran, they revealed Richard Thompson, who had grabbed Carrie and was holding her by the neck. Richard's face was gaunt; dark circles under his eyes. He'd been awake for a long time. His face was unshaven, grey hair sprouting from his cheeks and neck. He had a pistol, a .45, trained on Adelina.

"I should have killed you long ago," he muttered. "I never should have let you live, you fucking whore."

"Let me *go!*" Carrie shouted, struggling.

"Shut up!" he shouted. He hit her with the butt of the pistol. "You aren't even my daughter. I'll kill you like a bug if you piss me off."

Carrie's eyes widened.

Dylan saw, running up the street, a tall man with dark hair. It was Prince George-Phillip. How did he know to come now? But he was too far away.

Julia strode forward, putting herself between her father and mother. In a low, cold voice, she said, "I am. I'm your daughter. And you're never hurting my mother again."

She reached out toward her disbelieving father and grasped the pistol, pulling it away from Carrie. "Now let her go," Julia ordered.

Dylan tried to struggle to his feet, but the shooting pain that lit up his leg like lightning told him he'd snapped something. *Goddamn it!* George-Phillip couldn't get here in time!

"Let her go," Julia said.

"You were my most beloved," Richard said. Almost casually, he let go of Carrie, who staggered away. His voice rose to a shout. "You were the one she hurt the most. *Her.* She's the one who called you names, and treated you like dirt, and ... she made your life miserable. Don't you want vengeance? You can have it!"

"Father. It's time to give up," she said. "You've lost. It's not time for vengeance. It's time to forgive."

"No. No. I can't lose. I can't. I won't be a disgrace. I won't be." He took a step back then raised the gun. "Goodbye, Julia."

Dylan and Julia screamed at the same instant, but no one could move fast enough.

Richard Thompson pulled the trigger.

# Epilogue

"**H**ave to let you off here, Your Highness. Street's blocked off by the Federal Courthouse."

George-Phillip leaned forward so he could see around the corner. The sidewalk and streets were packed with news vans and a large crowd of spectators and protesters.

"All right, then. Stay close. Go get a cup of coffee or something. I'll call you as soon as I'm finished."

The driver frowned. "Are you sure you want to get out here, Your Highness? That's a serious crowd, and you've already been attacked—"

"That threat's over. But thank you for your concern."

Without another word, George-Phillip opened the back door of the SUV and stepped out. A taxi driver, trapped behind the SUV, was laying on his horn continuously. What a snarled mess. Cars everywhere, pedestrians, reporters spilling all over the place. It wouldn't be surprising if he were mobbed by reporters—he'd been heavily profiled in that morning's article in the *Post*. But the unlikeliness of finding a British Royal Duke walking along the sidewalk in downtown DC probably protected him from that.

He began walking toward the crowd.

The crowd surged, as if a giant had swept a fist against them, and suddenly there was screaming—lots of it. People were pushing from the entrance of the federal building, fighting against the crowd. George-Phillip began to run toward the front of the courthouse, and caught a glimpse of his worst nightmare.

George-Phillip's eyes swept over the area even as he moved at a dead. What he saw was chaos. Richard Thompson, pistol in hand, holding Carrie by the throat. Julia reaching for him. Adelina rushing in his direction to protect her daughter. Dylan Paris was on the ground, his foot bent at an unbearable angle.

George-Phillip ran faster at the unmistakable sound of a gunshot, even as his brain tried to interpret what he was seeing. Richard had released Carrie, who spun away, and then he shouted words George-Phillip couldn't make out over the screaming.

Richard raised his pistol, and George-Phillip shouted, "Stop!" as the man's finger tightened on the trigger.

George-Phillip collided with Adelina, arms around her and knocked her to the ground as the shot went off. The screaming continued around him. He heard another shot, then several more. George-Phillip's reddened gaze went to Richard, who twitched like a marionette once, twice, then fell face-first to the ground, blood blooming across his back.

"George-Phillip!" Adelina screamed, terror on her face. She sounded far away, and his side was beginning to hurt terribly.

"Hello, love," he said. "I've missed you terribly. Are you all right?"

Then Carrie was at his side, and Julia was helping Dylan, and he heard sirens approaching.

They, too, sounded far, far away. But her sudden kisses on his face, her breath against his, was as close as his own soul. He closed his eyes, flooded by the warmth of home.

The Washington Post. May 13, 2014.

### Former Defense Secretary Charged With Attempted Murder of Britain's Prince George-Phillip

By Anthony Walker

Former Defense Secretary nominee Richard Thompson shot Great Britain's Prince George-Phillip in front of hundreds of witnesses Monday after an altercation with Thompson's wife and two of her daughters. Once US Ambassador to China and later Russia, Mister Thompson is under investigation for involvement in the delivery of chemical weapons to Afghan militia who used them on civilians. Additionally, his wife Adelina Thompson has accused the former Ambassador of raping her when she was sixteen years old. Thompson was shot by police after he fired on the Prince.

The shooting took place in front of Adelina Thompson and two of her daughters, Carrie Sherman and Julia Wilson. According to witnesses, Ambassador Thompson was attempting to murder his wife when Prince George-Phillip intervened.

The three women, with a brother-in-law, were taken with the Prince to Howard University Hospital Trauma Center. Ambassador Thompson was transported to George Washington University Hospital.

The embattled Ambassador faced Senate hearings only a week ago before the Senate Armed Services Committee, chaired by Senator Chuck Rainsley. During those hearings, it was revealed for the first time that Thompson was an active agent of the Central Intelligence Agency throughout his diplomatic career. Administration officials have refused to comment on Thompson's intelligence background.

White House spokesperson Kelly Daniels told *The Washington Post*, "We were distressed to learn of the very disturbing charges against Ambassador Thompson. As soon as the nature of those charges was revealed, his nomination was withdrawn. This Administration will not tolerate corruption or criminal activity. We wish a speedy recovery to the Prince, and the President asked me to convey his personal admiration for the Prince's heroism."

Ambassador Thompson is expected to recover, sources at George Washington University Medical Center told the *Post*, but it is likely he will never regain the use of his legs. Prince George-Phillip is expected to fully recover.

Rory Armitage, Justice Department Special Prosecutor, said, "Richard Thompson just added attempted murder of his wife to the long list of charges he faces. This investigation continues."

Accused co-conspirator and Deputy Director of Operations at CIA, Leslie Collins was murdered Monday morning while preparing to board a charter flight at Stafford Regional Airport. The pilot had registered a flight plan to Rio de Janeiro. Virginia State police are cooperating with the FBI to investigate the murder.

## Carrie. May 26, 2014.

It was seventy-six degrees at eleven am when Carrie parked her black Suburban near Section 60 of Arlington National Cemetery. The grass seemed to go on forever, as did the endless rows of gravestones. Near this section of the cemetery more than any other, cars and trucks of all shapes and sizes were parked. Carrie blinked back tears when she saw how many. You weren't allowed to drive down the carefully maintained roads inside the cemetery unless you were a surviving spouse.

Carrie almost never used her military ID, which identified her as a widow of a soldier who died while on Active Duty. But the ID had allowed her onto the cemetery grounds, thus avoiding the busy public lots. She opened the door of the SUV and got out.

On the passenger side, Dylan was negotiating his way out of his seat. He'd been frustrated the last couple of weeks—a broken ankle had resulted in crutches and more physical therapy. But he and Alexandra had been able to return to New York in time to plead with Columbia to allow them to make up the missed time and exams. Alexandra got out of the backseat and slipped her hand around Dylan's arm. It was the first time Carrie had ever seen Dylan wear his uniform. But today he was in his dress blues: his beret positioned on his head, the bright yellow Private First Class stripe on his arm, the blue braid around his right shoulder indicating his service in the infantry. Carrie recognized the Combat Infantryman's Badge—Ray had worn the same badge—along with his Bronze Star and Purple Heart. He carried a wreath.

Carrie opened the passenger compartment door and unbuckled Rachel from her bulky car seat, then slipped the sleepy baby into a sling at her hip. Rachel nuzzled against her mother, then settled in the sling.

"When's her next transfusion?" Dylan asked.

"Next week," Carrie answered. "Although…"

She trailed off.

"What is it?" he asked.

"My father—George-Phillip—is having a blood test this week. There's … you know … a possibility."

He grunted. She was well aware how slim the odds were, especially since Andrea hadn't been a match.

The three of them walked into section 60. Neither Dylan, nor Carrie, made it more than twenty feet into the grounds before tears were streaming down their faces. They walked down the row between the stones, barely seeing the other families, the mothers and fathers and widows who were making their own way, quietly, to their lost loved ones.

In every direction, as far as they could see, were the gravestones.

Carrie saw the names and the dates and struggled to maintain her composure. But Dylan had given up. Tears were streaming down his face and he sobbed once then bit it back savagely. Alexandra took his hand.

The names. The *names*. Carrie looked around them, staggered by the enormity of it.

**Scott Johnson. Sergeant. United States Army. March 2, 1987. July 12, 2005. Silver Star. Purple Heart. Operation Enduring Freedom.**

**Julie McIntosh. SSGT. United States Marine Corps. October 12, 1979. June 7, 2004. Purple Heart. Operation Iraqi Freedom.**

Every single name represented someone's child, someone's brother or sister, someone's father or mother. Every single one represented a life cut short, a life ended with a period in a country halfway around the world. Every single stone was a broken heart.

Dylan continued to walk on his crutches, with Carrie holding one arm and Alexandra the other. Carrie couldn't see clearly anymore, and didn't even realize it when they arrived at their destination.

**Raymond C. Sherman. SSGT. United States Army. April 13, 1986. August 19, 2013. Bronze Star. Purple Heart. Operation Enduring Freedom.**

"I miss him," Alexandra said. "I didn't know him that well ... not like you two did. But he was a good man. And a good friend."

"Yeah," Dylan whispered. He handed a crutch to Alexandra then knelt in front of them both, setting the wreath in front of his best friend's grave. He whispered something—Carrie couldn't quite make it out. Then he stuck out a fist—as if he were fist-bumping Ray—and said, "Miss you, bruh."

Then Dylan came to his feet, clumsily, and saluted the grave.

*Shit.* The tears were streaming down Carrie's face, but she didn't care. She said, "Do you guys—do you mind—I mean..."

"You need some time alone," Dylan said. "It's okay. You ... you need it. We'll be over near the car."

Carrie hugged Dylan, hard, almost knocking him off his crutches. Rachel protested, but settled in when Carrie let go.

"Hey, don't knock me down, woman."

Carrie laughed. Then she looked Alexandra and Dylan in the eyes and nodded. The two of them walked away.

She turned and knelt beside the stone, and rubbed her fingers along his name, feeling the engraved letters.

"Hey babe," she whispered. "I need to introduce you to someone." Then she had to stop talking, because for a few moments all she could do was sob.

"This is our daughter. Isn't she beautiful? I'm sorry I couldn't bring her here before. It's just—it's been a really hard time without you. Even harder than I would have thought."

She rocked back on her heels. "Rachel is sick, but I'm praying that we'll find her a bone marrow donor soon. In the meantime, we're watching out for her. I promised you I'd take care of our daughter, and I will. I sort of named her after you, you know. As close as I could get. You can't name a girl Raymond, that would be weird."

She sniffed, hard. "You wouldn't believe what's gone on the last few weeks. Or maybe you would. Maybe you've been around paying attention. I don't know. I have a new father, and ... I don't know if I can trust him. But I think maybe I can. He took a bullet for my mother—if that isn't the craziest thing I've ever heard. I'm going to try to get to know him, anyway. We'll see. Mom's ... well ... it's a long story. But I think she's going to be okay, and nothing in the world can make me happier."

She sniffed again, then muttered a curse, then took out a tissue and blew her nose, hard.

Rachel giggled. A loud baby giggle.

"What?" Carrie said. She blew her nose again.

Rachel laughed, louder this time. Her blue eyes shone wide and her little mouth was wide open. Baby laughs were the best in the world. This was Rachel's first.

Carrie blew her nose again, making a loud honking sound. Rachel cried out in delight, her little fists waving in the air.

"Do you see her, Ray? God, isn't she beautiful?"

He didn't answer, of course. She looked at his grave, and said, "I know ... I know somehow you can hear me. And I hope—I hope you can forgive me. No one can ever replace you Ray. No one. But ... I need to move on. I'm going to—I need you to let me go too. Because Rachel's going to need a dad." As she said the last few words, they came out faster and higher pitched and desperate.

She leaned close, her hands still rubbing the letters. She felt the smooth stone against her lips. "Baby, I'll miss you forever. I'll always, always love you. But I need to say goodbye now. I need to—I need to get on with my life, and with Rachel's. I don't know if anything's there with Anthony, but it ... it's worth a try, don't you think? I know you'd want me to be happy."

She paused, listening. She lay there for a long time, leaning against the grave. Then she said, "I love you, Ray. I'll be back to visit, and I'll bring Rachel back to visit. I hope ... I hope..." She sighed. "I love you, babe."

She slowly came to her feet. She kissed her hand, then pressed it against the gravestone and walked away.


## Carrie. August 5, 2014.

When the phone rang, Carrie Sherman was startled awake. She often fell asleep after breastfeeding Rachel, and today wasn't much different. She was lying sideways on the couch, her feet up, Rachel lying in the sling on her chest. The baby slept peacefully.

The phone rang again. Carrie reached over and picked it up off the coffee table.

*It was Doctor Gage.* In a panic, she hit the accept button and put the phone to her ear.

"Hello? Hello?"

"Carrie? It's Doctor Gage."

"Hi ... is everything okay?"

"Carrie, I've got news."

Carrie waited, her heart suddenly beating a thousand times a second.

"Your father is a match, Carrie. We've got a donor."

The tears began running down Carrie's face before she could say a word. Her eyes dropped to the baby peacefully sleeping across her chest, tiny fists bunched.

"Carrie, are you there?"

Joyful tears in her voice, Carrie said, "Yes. Yes. Thank you so much."

Rachel, the tiny baby who had no idea what had gone into this moment, slept peacefully. Just as she should. Carrie closed her eyes and sent a prayer up to heaven in thanks for protecting her daughter.

## Sarah. August 17, 2014.

Sarah sighed and leaned back in her chair. Carrie was out of the house, thank God, as was her mom. Right now it was just Jessica and Sarah, sitting on the balcony, a desk of cards between them. The breeze was nice, at a few degrees above seventy, making it the nicest day they'd experienced in a while.

Carrie had been restless that morning, fretting about Rachel's upcoming bone marrow transplant.

Prince George-Phillip was currently in London, but he would be flying to Washington next week for the painful bone marrow donation surgery. Sarah liked George-Phillip. She'd met him three times now, once at the Embassy, once at Blair House when the President had him stay as a guest there, and once for dinner at the condo. He was a funny man, and his ridiculous eyebrows made him even funnier. But his concern for his granddaughter was what won Sarah over.

Sarah stared out over the city and her eyes misted over.

"Do you remember how hot it was? Last year?"

Jessica nodded. It was August 17th the prior year, when they were in a car on the way to the zoo, that a jeep bearing death had come barreling through the intersection and cut Ray Sherman's life short and severely wounded Sarah. Indirectly, the accident had resulted in grave damage to Jessica as well.

"Yeah," Sarah said. "It was awful."

Jessica looked at Sarah and whispered, "I was awful to you. The year before the accident."

Sarah's mouth twitch to the right. She didn't say anything, except to slightly shake her head.

"No, really. I shouldn't have asked to change classes. We've been together all our lives. I should have talked to you."

Sarah closed her eyes, a cloud of emotion flooding through her. She whispered, "Why did you do it? I thought you hated me."

Jessica shook her head. "It was ... I was always in your shadow, you know? I was Plain Jane. And you—you had everybody's attention—from the time we were tiny kids. I was ... jealous. I wanted to strike out on my own. I'm sorry."

Sarah swallowed. "Jessica ... I love you ... and... you have to know ... I always felt that way about you. You were always Mom and Dad's favorite I thought. You were going to be the only one to follow Dad into the Foreign Service."

"I think I'll skip that now," Jessica said.

"True," Sarah said. She felt bleak.

"What are you going to do about school?"

Sarah shrugged. "I didn't finish. I was thinking about registering at BCC this year. They'll still let me go back and finish my senior year. I checked."

Jessica swallowed. Her eyes looked huge. Sarah thought Jessica was about to cry. She said, "Do you think ... I could come with you? Back to school? That we could finish together? We'd be class of 2015, I guess."

Sarah whispered, "I'd love that."

The Washington Post. September 20, 2015.

### Ambassador Richard Thompson Convicted of Murder Under the 1996 War Crimes Act

By Bill Leiby

Former Defense Secretary nominee and Ambassador Richard Thompson was convicted Friday of 223 counts of murder under the provisions of the 1996 War Crimes Act. Thompson was sentenced to 223 consecutive life sentences. Thompson was acquitted of multiple charges of assault and rape.

The murder charges and life sentences were the result of a grand jury investigation last year which concluded that Thompson and Leslie Collins were primarily responsible for the acquisition of chemical weapons which were used in a village in remote Badakhshan province in the winter of 1982, resulting in the death of more than 200 civilians. Until last year, it was believed that the Soviets were responsible for the massacre.

The accusations of rape, along with the murder charges, were revealed in detail in the Pulitzer Prize winning series by Post reporter Anthony Walker last May. Collins was murdered the same day. His murder remains unsolved.

The rape charges were brought by Thompson's former wife, Adelina Ramos, who recently relocated to London with her youngest daughter, Andrea, who will be attending the exclusive Chelsea Independent College in preparation for University studies.

Family spokesperson Julia Wilson said in an official statement, "Our father is a complicated and disturbed man. The family will not be commenting on his conviction or imprisonment, except to extend our heartfelt and abject remorse and apologies to the victims of his actions."

## Andrea. London.

"Mom!" Andrea called out as loud as she could when she entered the townhouse. Adelina had bought a stupidly expensive townhome in Chelsea—big enough that all of her daughters could visit when they wanted to. At one time or another they all had.

Now the size worked against her. Andrea shouted again. "Mom! Mom!"

She heard steps upstairs. Running. Adelina appeared at the top of the stairs, concern on her face. "Andrea, what is it?"

"I got accepted!"

Adelina screamed. "Oh my God!"

Andrea met her halfway up the stairs and threw her arms around her mother.

For the last nine months Andrea had been completing a final year of senior school to make up the deficiencies in her education. She didn't realize she *had* any deficiencies until she'd applied for college at King's College in London. The college had provisionally accepted her, but required her to take a year of preparatory school.

Now she was in.

Adelina followed her downstairs to the dining room and looked over the acceptance letter. She looked up at Andrea. "I'm so proud of you."

"I have to call Jessica and Sarah. And Julia. And … everyone. They'll scream!"

Jessica and Sarah had both decided to stay in Washington, DC after they graduated high school, both attending Georgetown University and living with Carrie and Rachel. Andrea didn't think that would last too much longer. Carrie seemed to be ready for them to move into their own place.

Of course, she'd see them all soon enough, when they arrived in London next week.

She took her mother's hand.

Adelina said, "You know … three years ago, I never could have imagined … this. All of it. Us being together like this. I'm so happy."

Andrea smiled. "I am too, Mom. You have no idea. Okay. I've got to call."

She picked up the phone, trying to decide which sister to talk to first.

## Adelina. Calella, Spain.

When Adelina Ramos stepped out of the taxicab she took a deep, cleansing breath and closed her eyes and counted to twenty. Then, for good measure, she counted a little more before opening her eyes. It had been more than twenty years since she'd stood on this sidewalk, next to this building, and the last time she'd had a panic attack that resulted in a months' long hospitalization.

There would be no panic attack this time. She clutched her bag under her shoulder and walked through the crowd that spilled out of the bar at the base of the apartment building.

She knew the way.

Up three flights of stairs, then down a long hall. It was brighter in here than she remembered, and cleaner. But then, the few months she'd lived here with her mother, she'd been in a deep depression. Grief at the loss of her father and of her innocence.

Finally she reached the door. Number 32. She took a deep breath, bracing herself, then knocked on the door.

Inside, she heard shouts. Luis, she supposed. "Mamá. Someone's here!"

Seconds later, the door opened.

It was Luis. Older, *much* older than the last time she'd seen him. His face blanched, and he choked out a half strangled word she couldn't quite make out.

"Hola, Luis," she said.

He took her hand. "I ... I didn't think you would come. Ever."

"Luis!" The shout came from the living room. "Who is it?"

Luis swallowed. "Come in," he said.

Adelina walked forward. She could feel her chest tightening; the beginnings of what could become a panic attack. She hadn't had one in a long time. But she'd never be wholly healed.

But she hadn't come here to be healed. She'd come here to see her mother. She followed Luis into the living room.

The apartment was different. Brighter, yet somehow smaller. The breeze blew the light cotton fabric of the drapes, and a television blared laughter in the corner. An old woman leaned on a recliner watching the television.

Adelina stared at her mother.

The years had not been kind to her. Her mother was at least seventy now. Her eyes seemed hollow, and deep trenches furrowed her skin. A cigarette burned in an ashtray next to her, the smoke lazily floating toward the window.

Then she turned her face toward Adelina. Her face seemed slack, her eyes unfocused, as if she were blind and couldn't quite make out what she was seeing.

"Who are you? What do you want?"

The words were knives in her stomach, and Adelina actually took a step back, gasping.

Luis moved to their mother's side and kneeled. He whispered, "Mother, it's your daughter. It's Adelina."

Her mother's eyes widened and she seemed to search the room. "Adelina?" Tears began to run down the old woman's face.

"Hello, Mother," Adelina said. She sighed, letting out a long breath, as her little brother, now in his forties, looked at her with worry in his eyes. Adelina had come to Calella daydreaming of confronting her mother. She'd imagined the scene, imagined telling her mother exactly how she felt about all those years of hurt.

She'd imagined herself saying, *You destroyed my life. You broke my heart.*

But now, tears were streaming down her mother's face. She was shaking, looking up at Adelina with fear in her eyes. She expected it. She expected the explosion, the accusations, the tirade. It was clear enough that so did Luis.

Adelina couldn't do it. Her daughters had once thought the same things of her.

Instead, Adelina slowly dropped to her knees beside her mother, and whispered, "Te extrañé, Mamá."

*I missed you, Mommy.*


## Julia. London.

"This is insane," Alexandra said. "I thought *my* wedding was too complicated."

Julia laughed a little under her breath, then said, "Royal weddings are something else entirely, aren't they? I'm glad I didn't have to organize this one."

The crowds in London had been enormous. *Enormous.* Julia had never imagined anything quite on this scale. But they were away from the crowds now. Unlike the larger royal weddings, which were as much affairs of state as they were personal unions, this wedding was taking place at St. George's Chapel at Windsor Castle.

In *Windsor Castle.* Julia had been in a lot of places, including meals at the White House. But this was something else. From the room where they waited, she could see from the castle to the chapel itself. At any moment, Julia and her sisters would be summoned to the cathedral.

Meeting the Queen had been terrifying. George-Phillip had seemed as nervous as any of them when Adelina presented all six of her daughters, along with the spouses of those who were married. The wedding itself had only a few hundred guests. Or maybe a *thousand*. Most of the titled nobility of Europe were here, along with many of the senior members of the House of Commons, the Prime Minister, the US Ambassador, and the Archbishop of Canterbury, who was presiding over the ceremony itself.

In short—for one of the first times in her life, Julia found herself overwhelmed.

Julia, Carrie and Alexandra had walked through the cathedral yesterday afternoon, while their younger siblings had decided to go to an amusement park instead. The chapel was incredible. Vaulted ceilings with dozens of banners and flags above arched windows of stained glass. The walls, erected of stone hundreds of years ago, appeared so light that they could blow away, with tendrils of stone arches supporting the ceiling above them. The cathedral could seat hundreds, easily.

In this church were buried kings from hundreds of years ago: Edward IV, Henry VI and Henry VIII along with one of his wives, Jane Seymour. Later kings were buried in the Royal vault and the Memorial Chapel—including George-Phillip's grandfather. History Julia had only read about had taken place over hundreds of years in this room, and now her mother would be joining part of that history.

Julia, though, thought that did not account for her odd, maudlin mood. She was happy for her mother—incredibly so. Prince George-Phillip had been the man Adelina had lived and loved, even as she was a virtual prisoner, all those years. Julia had long since made her peace with her mother, and even her father, though it had taken more years of therapy to do so.

But there was one thing she'd never made peace with, and her encounter with Harry Easton had brought that screaming back to her mind.

Harry had been at an official reception in London two days before, which the sisters were invited to. She hadn't expected to see him, but in retrospect, there was no reason to be surprised. After all, he moved in these circles. They were polite—not quite friendly, but not unfriendly either.

Running into him, however, reminded Julia of the one thing in her life that *no* amount of money could buy. Now that she was in her mid-thirties, she'd accomplished everything she'd ever wanted in life. Except, in moments like this ... moments when she watched Rachel laughing as she ran down the hallway chasing Jane, or watched Alexandra protectively curling her arms around her belly, when she watched Dylan and his joy at the prospect of being a father—Julia wished she could have that joy. She wished she could share that joy with her husband.

But it wasn't to be. Even the adoption agency they'd worked with had told her it might take a long time.

*People will be reluctant to place a baby with a family in your situation.*

By her situation, they meant, rock stars. Musicians. People who moved around too much. Never mind that Julia was chief executive officer of a major corporation.

She closed her eyes. The longing grew worse every year, but today wasn't hers, it was her mother's. She reached out and took Alexandra's hand. "Are you going to be okay?"

"Of course," Alexandra replied.

She was glowing. *Of course.* At six months pregnant, Alexandra was clearly showing, and was vividly happy. In a few months she'd begin her final year of law school. Dylan had graduated and was working in a social work internship at a Vet Center in the Bronx. His primary job there was counseling of war veterans with PTSD, and he'd never looked happier.

One of the protocol officers who worked for the Queen appeared in the doorway. "Ladies, please come join the bride."

Julia took a deep breath. She reached out and took Carrie and Alexandra's hands. They in turn, reached out to Jessica and Sarah. Andrea closed the circle. Julia said, "Let's go." She smiled, and broke the circle. The six women went down the stairs to meet their mother. They wore matching blue dresses with long flowing skirts. Julia thought that some of her sisters were more comfortable in these outfits than others. Sarah looked like she wished she'd been able to sneak in combat boots. She *was* probably the only woman in the cathedral with visible tattoos.

Adelina was ready when they arrived. She had dyed her hair back to its normal black—she'd been greying more and more in recent years. She wore a beautiful white gown, which glistened with tens of thousands of hand-sewn pearls. Julia knew exactly how much the dress, with its pearls, had cost. She'd commissioned it in China and had it flown to London for her mother.

Adelina reached out and took Julia's hand. She wore white gloves, and her skin was flushed. Her eyes were brimming with water.

"Please tell me that's waterproof mascara," Julia said.

Adelina blushed. She *blushed*. Julia swallowed. She'd often thought of her mother as a harridan, as old, as vicious. She'd never once thought of her as a *bride*.

"Oh, Mother, I'm so happy for you," Julia said.

Adelina leaned forward and gently kissed her eldest daughter's cheek. "I'm so grateful to have you here with me," she whispered.

The ceremony was planned to be informal. The state royal weddings were much more lavish, including, normally, the arrival of the bride in a horse-drawn glass carriage. George-Phillip and Adelina had made it clear early on they wanted a much smaller and more private ceremony, with family and friends only. Windsor Castle and Saint George's Chapel was selected as the site primarily due to its privacy.

The procession began with the pounding of drums outside, probably heard for miles around, followed by the sound of the band. Julia and her sisters slipped to the window to look out toward the chapel, but at the insistence of the protocol officer, Adelina stayed put.

Outside, the procession had begun. Julia watched as a team of horsemen crossed the courtyard, followed by Prince George-Phillip, and his cousin, the Prince of Wales, who walked on foot. George-Phillip wore the black uniform and white belt of the Royal Marines, with his medals from the Falklands War and his reserve service. Although he no longer served, he was an honorary Colonel and still wore his uniform on state occasions.

Behind the two Princes were the guests of honor. Adelina had insisted on breaking with tradition, and had six bridesmaids, all adults—her daughters. In order to balance out the wedding party, George-Phillip was accompanied by six other men, including a visibly uncomfortable Dylan Paris and Bear Wyden, both of whom seemed to squirm in their tuxedos.

Bear had almost violently resisted attending the wedding, but after Dylan personally went to his apartment and argued with him, he finally agreed. Now Director of the Joint Terrorism Task Force, Bear was based out of New York City, with frequent visits to Washington to see the kids. His ex-wife, Leah, had long since recovered from her injuries.

Julia turned back and walked to her mother. Adelina was breathing slowly and deeply, and wore a dreamy smile on her face.

Julia said, "I think it's almost time. They just went in."

A moment later, the protocol officer opened the door. Just outside the small chamber stood Crank's father, Jack Wilson, who had agreed to act in lieu of her father who had passed away many years before. Jack was a former Boston cop, sentimental and demonstrative, and when he saw Adelina in her dress his eyes watered. He held an arm out and she took it. He glanced back at Julia and she smiled at him. Of course. He had a tiny orange, white and green flag on his lapel—the national flag of Ireland. Julia suppressed a laugh. The papers in London would get play out of that for years.

The chamber orchestra just inside the entrance of the cathedral began playing. The walkway between the castle at the chapel was two hundred yards, guarded on both sides by a phalanx of Royal guards in bright red uniforms. On the grass on either side were hundreds—possible thousands—of spectators. Royal weddings in general got a lot of attention, Julia knew, but George-Phillip was so far removed from the throne it normally wouldn't have attracted much interest. But the media attention around the events following Andrea's kidnapping—and George-Phillip and Adelina's decades long love—had captured the attention of both countries. For days, news media on both sides of the Atlantic had replayed the video captured on the front steps of the federal courthouse in Washington, DC, when George-Phillip had saved Adelina's life.

Jack and Adelina began their slow walk across the courtyard. Adelina's daughters followed in pairs—Julia and Alexandra first, then Carrie and Andrea, followed by the twins. They were organized by height, rather than age. Behind them in the procession, Adriana Poole walked. She wore a blue dress, and held the hands of Jane and Rachel as she walked. Jane and Rachel were far apart in age, but wore matching green dresses. Rachel's face was rosy and chubby. Since the bone marrow transplant, she'd needed no further transfusions, and was as healthy and happy as any little girl on earth. She didn't listen very well though. She tugged on Adriana's hand, trying to pull away, then twisted in circles. Jane came around the other side and picked her up and the two girls giggled.

Julia took a deep breath as she stepped forward with Alexandra at her side. Julia hated that she was envious of her sisters. She didn't want to feel that way. But when she watched the beauty of Rachel's laughter, and the swell of Alexandra's belly, she ached inside to be a mother.

The music got louder as they approached the entrance to the cathedral. Though she'd been in there the day before, this was different, she realized, as they walked up the steps and entered.

The crowd hushed, hundreds of people standing on both sides of the aisle facing inward. Julia heard as Andrea, behind her, sucked in a breath as she saw the crowd inside the cathedral.

It was hard to really get a sense of the scale of a cathedral like this. But with hundreds of people in the cathedral, with *trees* extending down both sides of the church, overhanging the aisle and still not reaching the ceiling which was *way, way* up. The detailing on the ceiling was incredible; the windows were huge, making the entire structure feel light and tenuous.

The procession continued down the aisle. Enormously tall but slender columns stretched into the sky far above the people on each side, who wore colorful outfits, dresses of green and red and blue, the men in suits with far more variety of style and color than would happen in the United States, and the *hats*. So many hats, some of them crazy, some of them beautiful, some ... better not mentioned at all.

As they moved further down the length of the cathedral, she saw Crank, sitting in the third row, not far from the Queen. Julia flashed him a smile, and he returned it, then winked at her. They'd been married for considerably more than a decade, but she still felt a flush down her face and body at his wink.

At the front of the cathedral, George-Phillip stood nervously, hands at his side. His eyebrows seemed to move of their own accord as he gazed on his approaching bride. He tried to look serious and royal, but he couldn't keep the tremendous smile off his face.

Finally, they reached the crossing. Jack, who had obvious tears on his face, passed Adelina's hand to George-Phillip. Then he bowed to the Prince and stepped to the side.

George-Phillip and Adelina joined hands.

As the ceremony continued, Julia's eyes moved from her mother to each of her sisters, standing in a line at the front of the cathedral. Carrie, who had lost a husband, but gained a beautiful little girl and a father. Rachel stood with Adriana Poole and Jane to the side of the cathedral, waving at the audience, a toothy smile on her face. Carrie stood straight and tall, a smile on her face as she watched their mother finally reaching for her own happiness.

Alexandra's face was flushed. The night before, Julia had felt her stomach, and felt the baby move. She'd visited Alexandra and Dylan several times during their pregnancy—all of the sisters were closer now than they had once been. Dylan and Alexandra were incredibly happy. When asked where she planned to work, she'd announced she was going to try for the American Civil Liberties Union. "Abuses like Dad's and Leslie Collins' shouldn't be allowed. I want to work for someone who can provide a counterbalance."

Sarah looked radiant. College agreed with her—as did her now long-term boyfriend. Her twin Jessica had a warm smile on her face. Jessica's recovery had been a long and difficult struggle. She and Dylan had become close as they occasionally attended 12-step meetings together, both in New York and Washington. He'd acted as a mentor to his younger sister-in-law.

And Andrea. The youngest sister, and arguably the one who had suffered the most because of Richard Thompson.

Julia had been to London half a dozen times since Andrea moved here with their mother. And every time she felt staggered by the joy she saw on her sister's face.

Julia looked back at her mother and the Prince, who were now facing each other as the Archbishop blessed their marriage. George-Phillip took her hands and bent down as Adelina lifted up on her toes and the newly married couple slowly and lovingly kissed.

Tears ran down her face as the Archbishop called in a loud voice, "I give you their Royal Highnesses, the Duke and Duchess of Kent."

## Julia. Boston.

Like every other celebration, the wedding of Prince George-Phillip and his wife Adelina faded from memory. The couple now lived with Andrea at his townhouse in Belgrave Square, and after a few days of celebration each of Adelina's daughters had returned to their own lives.

That meant Julia returned to Boston and her offices on Broadway in South Boston. She was there, preparing to convene a staff meeting, when her phone rang.

She stared dumbly at it for several seconds. The phone call was from United Methodist Family Services—the organization where she and Crank had applied to adopt. Fourteen months had passed since their home study with no word.

She scrambled. "Hello?"

"Julia? It's Renee Hunt."

"Yes?" Apprehension shot through Julia. She stood up, scanning the open work area and its fifteen employees. Crank was nowhere in sight. "What is it?"

She waved at her administrative assistant, then mouthed, *Find Crank!*

"Is Crank available?"

"Hold on, I'm not sure—wait, there he is. Hold on." She waved at him. Crank's eyes widened at her urgency, and he half jogged across the floor.

"What is it?" he whispered.

She put the phone on speaker, and said, "Renee, Crank is here. Now—what is it?"

On the other end of the line, Renee Hunt took a deep breath. Julia reached out and grabbed Crank's hand and squeezed, probably too hard. Then she heard the words.

"Are you guys busy tomorrow? I have good news. We have a baby for you."

Tears began to pour down Julia's face. Happy, joyous tears. "No. We'll cancel our plans, whatever they are."

She threw her arms around her husband.

## Rachel. Bethesda, Maryland.

Mommy told me Daddy lives inside the rock at the big green park. I met him a bunch, at least three times. But he's dead inside the rock and can't play. I get sad for Daddy locked in the rock. Did you know that dead means you can't come out and play anymore? But Mommy says Daddy is with God and happy.

Maybe God plays with him. I'd be sad if I couldn't come out and play.

Mommy said we only go see Daddy on Memory Day. That's when everybody members their daddies and mommies if they don't have one. We have a picture of Daddy at home. Sometimes the picture makes Mommy sad, except when it makes her smile. I'm glad Daddy's happy with God. I wish I could meet him some day, and he could take me to the playground.

But now Mommy says I get to have another daddy for my birthday. When she kisses him she smiles. His beard is ticklish. That's why it makes me giggle.

When I giggle and my second daddy laughs, it makes Mommy smile. I like when she smiles. She says having a second daddy is like having two scoops of ice cream.

My birthday is tomorrow, and I get my second daddy.

I love him.

So does Mommy.

END

# Author's Note

**W**hen writing a work of political fiction, sometimes the parallels to real life are inescapable.

Ronald Reagan, Eugene Jackson, Henry Kissenger and Margaret Thatcher and Queen Elizabeth II are all known historical personages. However, their roles in this story are completely fictional.

The Wakhan Corridor largely missed the violence of the Soviet invasion of Afghanistan, just as it has missed most of the violence of the current war in Afghanistan. However, the fighting has lasted 35 years, more than a generation--first with the Soviets, then the Taliban, and finally the United States. Much of the violence I described was typical, including massacres of civilians. There was no use of chemical weapons as described in this book.

Events in the Falkland Islands and the bombing of the Marine barracks in Beirut, Lebanon took place pretty much as I described them here. But virtually all of the details are left out.

Prince George-Phillip obviously does not exist. Some other members of the Royal family mentioned in this story, such as Princess Alexandra, do. However, everything described about the royal family is fiction.

I know little about the operations of the State Department's Diplomatic Security Service. Where I couldn't find the information on Google I just made it up.

www.ingramcontent.com/pod-product-compliance
Lightning Source LLC
Chambersburg PA
CBHW030541260626
47157CB00006B/2131